PRAISE FOR ERIC SCOTT FISCHL

"Eric Scott Fischl offers up a powerful alchemical elixir concocted of post Civil War historical fiction, dark fantasy, Felliniesque flavoring, all in a ruby goblet of lapidary prose. Take the goblet, and drink deeply."
  John Shirley, author of the A Song Called Youth trilogy

"*Dr Potter's Medicine Show* is a brilliant study of characters struggling against the monstrous to retain their own humanity. Fischl's talent for voice and knack for characterization finds humor and beauty amidst horror and depravity. It's heartbreaking, elegiac, and an absolute pleasure to read."
  Carrie Patel, author of the Recoletta series

"A word of advice: whatever you do, don't drink the Sagwa. One part history, two parts fantasy, and three parts toe-curling horror. Drink it down. A grotesque elixir of history, fantasy, and toe-curling horror. Warning: may cause nausea, sleep disturbances, and compulsive page-turning. Not to be taken orally."
  Arianne "Tex" Thompson, author of the Children of the Drought trilogy

"Fischl has infused his tale of the Old West with one part of alchemy and one part of gangster movie. The resultant brew is deliciously dark and entirely compelling."
  Rod Duncan, Philip K Dick Award-nominated author of The Bullet-Catcher's Daughter

"Dirty, dank, and dangerous. *Dr Potter's Medicine Show* is the missing season of Carnivàle you didn't know you needed until now."
  Adam Rakunas, Philip K Dick Award-nominated author of Windswept

ERIC SCOTT FISCHL

DR POTTER'S MEDICINE SHOW

ANGRY
ROBOT

ANGRY ROBOT
An imprint of Watkins Media Ltd

20 Fletcher Gate,
Nottingham,
NG1 2FZ
UK

angryrobotbooks.com
twitter.com/angryrobotbooks
Quack

An Angry Robot paperback original 2017

Cover by Steven Meyer-Rassow
Set in Meridien by Epub Services

Distributed in the United States by Penguin Random House, Inc.,
New York.

ISBN 978 0 85766 638 3
Ebook ISBN 978 0 85766 639 0

Printed in the United States of America

9 8 7 6 5 4 3 2 1

This book is dedicated to Tata
and
In memoriam, Betty

— DRAMATIS PERSONAE —

Dr Potter's Medicine Show

DR ALEXANDER POTTER	...	A Seller of Patent Medicines
HERCULES (OLIVER) WILSON		A Strongman
LYMAN RHOADES	...	An Illusionist
MERCY RHOADES	...	A Chanteuse
PASCAL LEVESQUE	...	A Scientist
RIDLEY MATTHEWS	...	A Shill
AH FAN	...	A Fortune-teller

Various and Sundry Freaks, Terrors, and Wonders of Nature

The Hedwith Apothecary Emporium: Dr M Hedwith, Proprietor

DR MORRISON HEDWITH	...	A Chemist
ANNABELLE HEDWITH	...	A Wife
JOSEPH CASTLE	...	A Valet
BENJAMIN WOOD	...	A Clerk
JOHNATHAN WOOD	...	A Clerk
MR TWIST	...	A Laborer

Unaffiliated

D SOLOMON PARKER	...	A Murderer
A. AGAMEMNON RIDEOUT		A Gambler
JOSIAH McDANIEL	...	A Husband
ELIZADETH McDANIEL	...	A Sister

"I will therefore nowe deliver unto you a great and hidden secret. One part is to bee mixed with a thousand of the next body, and let all this be surely put into a fit vessell, and sette it in a furnace of fixation, first with a lent fire, and afterwardes encreasing the fire for three dayes, till they be inseperably joyned together, and this is a worke of three dayes: then againe and finally every part heereof by it selfe, must be projected upon another thousand parts of any neere body: and this is a worke of one day, or one houre, or a moment, for which our wonderfull God is eternally to be praised."

from THE MIRROR OF ALCHIMY, COMPOSED BY THE THRICE-FAMOUS AND LEARNED FRYER, ROGER BACHON, SOMETIMES FELLOW OF MARTIN COLLEDGE: AND AFTERWARDS OF BRASEN-NOSE COLLEDGE IN OXENFORDE. ALSO A MOST EXCELLENT AND LEARNED DISCOURSE OF THE ADMIRABLE FORCE AND EFFICACIE OF ART AND NATURE, WRITTEN BY THE SAME AUTHOR. WITH CERTAIN OTHER WORTHIE TREATISES OF THE LIKE ARGUMENT. *London. Printed for Richard Olive, 1597*

PART ONE
THE MEDICINE SHOW

"And because corporeall things in this regiment are made incorporeall, and contrariwise things incorporeall corporeall, and in the shutting up of the worke, the whole body is made a spirituall fixt thing: and because also that spirituall Elixir evidently, whether white or red, is so greatly prepared and decocted beyonde his nature, it is no marvaile that it cannot bee mixed with a body, on which it is projected, beeing onely melted."

1.
[OREGON, 1878]

"FEAR!"

"Nameless dread!"

"Sleepless nights!"

Dr Alexander Potter sweeps his arm out dramatically, muffling a cough with the back of his other hand. "My friends, these are merely a few of the sundry maladies that plague the human condition. I, too – I, myself! – before discovering the healing powers of this amazing elixir, which I now hold in my hand, was afflicted with these very same troubles. Yes, the very same. Many was the night that I lay sleepless, restless, friendless even, such was the severity of my illness. Yes, friendless, I say because, like many a man, I turned to liquor – corn and mash – to ease my sorrows."

He looks over the listless crowd below him, tucks another cough down into his shoulder in the guise of rubbing rain off his beard. The miserable, wet weather has settled into his lungs again. There are maybe thirty people standing in front of his garishly painted wagon, the sides of which proclaim in bold, colorful lettering:

DR POTTER'S MEDICINE SHOW
Wonders of Nature
Illusions & Musical Delights
Medical Miracles
THE CHOCK-A-SAW SAGWA TONIC
Cures Complaints of Mind & Body
Low Price
VITAL FOR HEALTH

The small crowd has drizzle running off their hats and bonnets, the steady rain pooling in puddles underfoot. To a person, they look poor, dirty, and wrung out, or at least give a convincing imitation thereof. A bent-backed farmer grimly digs inside his hairy ear with a finger, while his bug-eyed, nervous children clutch at his scrawny wife's skirts. Two dispirited prostitutes huddle together under a ratty parasol; one has a worse cough than Alexander, even, a viscous tubercular rattle that he can hear from forty feet away. To Alexander's eyes, this pitiful excuse for a town looks as if a stronger rain than this one would wash it apart and sweep it away, all the way down to the Columbia. Perhaps for the best, he thinks. It's like many of the towns they pass through, really. But, still, even with the rain coming down, there the people stand, wet and shivering, to see the entertainment. However shabby it may be.

"Now," he continues, "now, I don't begrudge any man a sip of liquor, should he feel the need. I, my friends, though, *I* was not a sipper, but a *gulper*. When at my whiskey I was a *fighting man*, quarrelsome and quick to fists – you know the type, I'm sure – and this rascality of mine *drove* those friends of which I speak right from me, like the Gadarene spirits, though I myself was the swine, if you understand my meaning."

He continues his patter, tossing the words out to fall on uninterested ears. "But *fear*, I say: fear and sleepless nights, fighting and ill spirits brought on by whiskey. *Why*, you may ask? Why? Friends, I will tell you, so hear me well, I beg of you. These crippling maladies of the mind and spirit are *mere artifacts* of the maladies of the *body*! Artifacts! It is God's own truth." Alexander holds in another cough as he continues troweling on the bullshit that comprises his pitch.

"Complaints of the bowels! Headaches! Catarrh! Agues and fevers! Rheumatism, bleeding gums, lassitude and the jaundice! Good people, these are maladies of the *body* that, once cured, will perk the *spirit* of a man or a woman, a child or a grandfather. The healthy man sleeps like a baby at night, worn out from honest labors."

Honest labors! he thinks.

"A woman, rosy cheeked in wellness, suffers not from *black moods*, but gathers her family unto her loving arms, of an evening."

The molly rattles another wet cough, raises a stained handkerchief to her lips to spit.

"Friends," Alexander continues, raising his arms as if in benediction, "I, myself, I was once a wretched, sickly man, racked by pains and fevers, sodden with drink, sleepless and pitiful. And now, look at me: I will not see sixty again and yet I am the *very picture of health*." He chokes down another cough. "I have the vitality and strength of a man half my age, I tell you. Why, I would wrestle any young buck among you, right this moment, as Greek Herakles did Antaeus, if I did not fear for the cleanliness of my fine suit." He pauses for laughter that is stillborn.

"Hurry it up, old man," a voice shouts from the crowd.

Alexander knows that the townies are merely biding

their time until the other acts start. He'll be lucky if he sells two bottles of the elixir to these poor fools. He smiles as best he can, though, raises the bottle of Dr Hedwith's Chock-a-saw Sagwa Tonic like a monstrance.

"My friends, I hold in my hand the *secret* of my robust health, the very elixir that healed me body and spirit, a mere tablespoon at a time. Such was my *amazement* at its efficacy that I closed up my own medical practice so that I might go out and *share* its powers with the citizens of this fair country, one town at a time. Now, as a medical doctor, I had some small talent; I say that with no false modesty. But Dr Morrison Hedwith, the creator of this amazing product, is a man of genius, a true visionary." Alexander grits his teeth around his smile, swallowing something sour. "The good doctor is a man of science and learning, a master of the chemical arts after long study in the most prestigious universities of Europe. Taking that peerless knowledge, he spent years with the Red Savages of the Wyoming territories – and points eastward – learning the secrets of their medicine men, their shamans, knowledge *forbidden* to any white man before."

He pauses dramatically. One man in the crowd is determinedly picking his nose and the molly continues to cough. "The Chock-a-saw Sagwa Tonic I hold in my hand contains a *secret mixture* of natural roots, herbs, and berries, a mysterious and powerful preparation of the Red Indians, which the good doctor has *fortified* and *potentiated* using a patented electro-chemical induction process, which binds these natural ingredients to a variety of rare minerals, creating a *vital tonic* that contains everything needed for robust good health." In reality, the stuff is mostly cheap grain alcohol, laudanum, dandelion shoots, and tobacco for color.

Alexander opens the bottle and pours a generous measure into a large spoon, which he then ladles into his mouth. Swallowing, trying to ignore the taste, he works to keep his gorge down and his smile up. Behind the small crowd he can see fat Lyman Rhoades watching him, arms crossed, tapping his fingers along one elbow. Lyman cocks an eyebrow at him and smiles a sharp smile that makes Alexander's stomach tighten further.

"You there, son," Alexander calls out, pointing at a thin, spotty boy in the crowd, gangling and red-haired, with a wisp of gingery moustache that seems more the idea of a moustache than the thing itself.

"Me?"

"Yes, you. Come on up here, lad." When Ridley mounts the step to the wagon box, Alexander puts an arm around him. "You seem a strong young man."

"Yes, sir?"

Alexander reaches down, picks up a heavy iron bar from the wagon bed. Leaning forward, he hands it to a large, surly man in the front row of the crowd. "Sir, feel that bar there, if you would. It's heavy iron, is it not? Could you bend that bar, sir?"

The man narrows his eyes, gives the bar a halfhearted push. "Nah," he mutters, handing it back, wiping his hands on his stained overalls.

Alexander gives the iron to Ridley. "You, son, how about you? Go on, give it a try." Ridley hunkers down and squeezes, gritting his teeth and groaning elaborately.

"*Not too much,*" Alexander murmurs under his breath.

With a gasp, Ridley lets up. "Gosh, sir, no way could I bend that." He hands the bar back to Alexander, at the same time stepping off the open end of the wagon with one foot, almost falling. As he flails his arms, kicking at the step and drawing the crowd's eye, Alexander quickly switches the bar with the soft lead fake hidden behind him. Ridley regains his balance with help and then takes the new bar while Alexander pours a shot of the tonic into his spoon, cautioning him about the step as he hands it over. Trying not to wince, Ridley gulps it down. "Why, it tastes good!"

"Now, just wait a moment, son. Do you feel it? Can you feel the revitalizing electro-medicinal atoms spreading through your system, after mere seconds? Tell me that you don't."

All Ridley feels is incipient nausea. "Gosh, sir, I think I do!"

"Now son, you are too young to know the perils of whiskey, but instead of ener*vating* you as does liquor, this tonic is ener*gizing* you, as we speak, binding to your blood and organs and infusing them with a boost of health. Try that bar, now. Go on, try it! See if you can't bend it."

"I don't know, sir." Ridley hefts the bar doubtfully. "It's awful thick."

"Go on, son! You have the Chock-a-saw Sagwa in you now!"

Furrowing his brow, leaning over, Ridley goes through the motions of bending the soft lead bar, overdoing the dramatics per usual, to Alexander's eye. As a shill, the boy leaves much to be desired, but he's learning. Alexander doesn't kid himself that any but the dimmest in the crowd will be convinced by their foolery. Some random stranger that no one knows, picked from the tip to demonstrate the healing powers of the patent medicine? Of course it's a plant. It's an expected part of the act, though; routine theatrics, nothing more. Alexander is required to be a showman as much as a salesman. Most who choose to spend their two dollars on the tonic would be buying it for the alcohol and opium it contains anyway, although some hopefuls would be curious to see if it's any more effective than Killmer's Swamp Root or Brandreth's Vegetable Universal, both as useless – but less dangerous – than the Sagwa.

Ridley has the bar bent into a U. Red-faced and gasping, he cries, "I did it! This tonic is a miracle!"

Biting off another cough behind his teeth, Alexander smiles at the crowd, opening the cash box.

Later, near sunset, Alexander walks around the tents of the show. The rain has let up only slightly and the sky is darkening, the clouds heavy and sullen overhead. From the main tent he can hear Mercy singing *L'amour est un Oiseau Rebelle* to the wheezing of her battered, tuneless accordion, the chords gasping out around bent reeds, staggering in and out of time because the old Pancotti is too big for her to easily play. Lyman will no doubt find some takers for Mercy, after the show, in the small tent he pompously styles *Le Palais de Eros*: she's pretty, French, and sings like a nightingale, representing quite an upgrade from the haggard, consumptive girls already working the horizontal trade in this town.

Lyman, in his robed guise as Lymandostro the Magnificent, Master of Illusions, is sitting on a stump behind a wagon, listening to his wife sing. He gives Alexander that knife of a smile again, rubbing a meaty thumb and forefinger together. Alexander ignores him, passing on to the other side of the main tent, thinking, as he always does, that a magician shouldn't be fat.

A few feet away, Oliver is standing outside Ah Fan's fortunetelling tent, cupping a cigarette in his palm. A leopardskin robe is pulled around his broad shoulders; under the robe he wears very little, even in the wet chill. Oliver squints at the townies milling about, on the lookout for trouble. The Black Hercules is big enough that he doesn't fear much danger directed at himself, but feeling against the Chinese still runs hot at times, particularly when the yokels get bored and restless and have some liquor in them. Ah Fan's tent glows with lamplight and smells of the incense he burns to seem more mysterious. Their last fortuneteller, the ill-fated, blind Colonel Batts, had read from a similar script to Ah Fan but, because Fan is a Celestial, he somehow seems more legitimate to the rubes. Or at least he's more successful, judging from the amount of money he brings in. Mystery and legitimacy don't preclude trouble when a drunken townie looks to raise some hell, though, so Oliver has taken to standing guard near Ah Fan's tent after his own strongman show is done.

Alexander stands beside the Black Hercules, rolling a cigarette of his own and accepting a light. Drawing the smoke into his lungs makes him start coughing again, so he opens a bottle of the Sagwa that he keeps in his pocket, grimacing as he swallows. The opium in it will help his cough at least.

"You using that stuff too much," Oliver says, nodding at the bottle. "You'll wind up like Fan."

Alexander looks up at the big man, shaking his head while trying to scrape the taste of the stuff from his tongue with his front teeth.

"You think it can't get worse?" Oliver asks.

Alexander just shrugs, drawing on his cigarette again. "How was the show?"

"Same shit, man. Same shit. Shoulder's still a bit sore."

"You should take some Sagwa for that."

"Shit, old man."

Alexander smiles, and then becomes serious. "Lyman

say anything to you?" It will happen two nights from now, one way or another. Lyman's work. Their own, if they're lucky. He wishes Pascal were here, although he's not sure what else the Frenchman could do that he hasn't already. It's on me, now, Alexander thinks. This is the best chance they're likely to get. Unconsciously, he touches his pocket.

"Naw." Oliver closes his eyes, sighing. "Not yet." There's a pause. Oliver looks around, lowers his voice to the barest of whispers. "Are you sure about this, Alex?"

"Of course I'm not fucking sure. But..." He trails off, shaking his head. "Listen, you want to back out? I can do it all myself, you know. Really. You don't have to get involved." He doesn't mean it like that, it's just the truth, but Oliver glares at him for a moment, anyway, before looking away to scan the crowd for trouble again.

They're quiet for a time, smoking and watching the drizzle run down the tents. A woman comes out of Ah Fan's tent, pulling her shawl closer around her head. It's the coughing molly. She starts, caught off-guard, before regaining her composure. "Now that's a big buck," she says, running her eyes over Oliver appraisingly. She turns to Alexander. "You come see me, medicine man, you won't be sorry." Her insincere smile turns into another cough and she turns away, walking off through the rain, handkerchief to her mouth.

"Be sure to try the Chock-a-saw Sagwa Tonic for that cough, madam!" Alexander calls after her. The tent flap opens and Ah Fan leans out, fiddling with his queue. His eyes are rheumy and his nose is running. Alexander can tell that he needs a pipe. "Go on, then, Fan. There's no one waiting." The flap closes again.

Alexander pulls out his pocket watch and checks the time. Mercy is done singing and Lyman's show will be starting soon. He wants to check on the others before he has to go to the main tent and hawk the Sagwa again. He'd only unloaded a few bottles the first time around but, later in the evening, the festive atmosphere will hopefully contribute to better sales. There are also the other bottles that needed selling – or giving – but he just hadn't had the heart to do that yet.

"Be seeing you, son," he says to Oliver. "Watch yourself."

"Always do."

The special tent is set away from the others, the flap chained shut. Unlike the rest, with their bright, brassy colors, this one is simple black oiled canvas. Even in daylight it somehow seems ominous but, now, the sun failing, it draws the gloom even more. This tent won't be opened until well after nightfall. Lyman will be pitching the rubes on its delights, wonders and horrors to be seen only after dark. *Some things shouldn't see the light of day*, Alexander thinks, not for the first time. He fishes the key out of his pocket and opens the lock, pulling the flap aside enough to step through. There's a movement at the back.

"It's just me," Alexander says, lighting the candle that he knows will be on the barrel to the side of the door. He breathes in the oily, dusty smell, overlaid with something organic and foul. "How are they?"

"Quiet." Ridley steps into the candlelight. "Pretty much just sleeping, although Rula was doing some moaning earlier. She quieted back down a while ago." He pauses. "So how'd I do? Today I mean, with the act."

Alexander checks a sigh. "Kid, you're getting better but you're still overdoing it. You need to dial it down some. It's too obvious." He can see the boy deflate. Really, Alexander doesn't even want Ridley with them, at all, but he keeps making excuses to be shucked of him. Having the boy around as a general dogsbody and part-time shill is fine, but he wants him gone before Lyman takes an interest. "You're getting better, though," he adds. He knows he shouldn't encourage him, but he hates seeing him mope.

Ridley brightens. "I'll keep working on it, Dr Potter. You bet."

Alexander claps him on the shoulder as he walks past, raising the candle to the first cage. Bascom the Halfhead is sleeping, curled around the ragged doll he keeps with him at all times. Every so often he twitches with some dream. In the next cage is Holly Long-Eye, her stalks drawn in and closed. She's rocking back and forth on the stumps of her legs, humming to herself.

Rula is in the last cage, her eyes open and empty. She has no real mouth to speak of but can make a range of noises in her throat and, from the sound, Alexander can tell she's crying again. He opens the cage door and puts his hand inside, patting her shapeless mass, resting his palm gently on her, trying to convey something with simple human contact. Her crying stops for a moment and one blue eye briefly regains focus, staring at him helplessly before fading out again.

"I'm sorry," he whispers.

Alexander closes his eyes and breathes out, gathering himself, and then shuts and locks the cage again. He turns to Ridley. "Now, you get the gaffs all set up and those bottles wiped and clean. Doesn't do any good if no one can see inside, does it? But not too clean, of course. Keep some mystery. Then make sure that those three get fed and don't you tease them any. Just feed them and get them ready. I'll be back here a bit later and you be gone by then, all right? Check in with Oliver and see if he needs help with anything. And stay away from the townies. Got it?" He knows that it isn't necessary to tell Ridley all this, that the boy knows his job by now, but it helps him to focus his own mind on something other than Rula and the others and what will happen, two nights from now. What *could* happen.

"Yes, sir."

He claps him on the shoulder again. "All right, then." Alexander leaves the tent, looping the chain, and walks back through the rain. He reaches into his jacket for the bottle of Sagwa and takes another sip. When he replaces it, Alexander feels the bony press of the thing in his pocket. A finger, wrapped in a handkerchief that's stiff with dried blood. The message, hidden in a lesson.

He looks up. It's almost full dark now.

2.

IN THE DINGY, mold stinking room over the livery, Pascal Levesque looks up, peering out of his one skewed and splintery window. It's almost full dark. The rain is coming down, as it's been for weeks, a thin mizzling sop that permeates everything. He feels damp all the time, even when he's technically dry. Pascal is always cold, always hungry these days, not only from the meager rations he's kept on but perhaps because he's burning so much of his energy merely by shivering. He's never been a large man, but he's alarmingly thin now. On top of the hunger, the ache in his hand has become a hot burn, and he fears that it's not only the wet and the cold that are making him shiver now.

He fights the urge to pick at the soiled bandage, which covers the place where he'd once had an index finger. Only a stump remains now, extending to just under the second knuckle; Pascal is thankful that Lyman has left him that much, this time. The little finger on his right hand was taken entirely, down to the palm, two months ago.

He looks out the window again, but can see nothing, just the dark and the steady drip of water from the eave. There's a gassy, grassy stink from the horses below him, the smell of wet hay and damp shit but, aside from that, he could be anywhere, trapped in yet another of the cold, dingy rooms Lyman finds for him in one town or the next, since Pascal had lost the finger on the right hand for his own recalcitrance and been separated from Mercy and the others. Whether to keep his disobedience from inflaming the rest or only as another punishment, he's not sure. Likely for both reasons, really.

The rooms are always the same. The doors, which lock from the outside. The poor food: thin soups and stale bread, stringy meat when he's lucky. Water that is none too clean, a compensatory bottle of cheap liquor from time to time. No company but his own, or Lyman's, which is worse than being alone. When they're on the road, he's kept in a locked coach, which has been kitted out as a sort of mobile prison. Like he is some beast in a traveling circus. Which, in some ways, he supposes he is. A clever ape called upon to dance to his master's tune. *Comme il est devenu tellement ridicule.*

Sometimes Pascal fantasizes that the rooms are all in fact the same one, that he's not moving at all, just stepping back out of the coach after bouncing around in a long circle, returning whence he came. Over and over and over.

He doesn't know where Mercy is, exactly, where the others are, but he knows they're close. Pascal knows he's kept nearby, near enough for Lyman's convenience, far enough for Lyman to keep him on this leash. Keep him cowed, still this new disobedience before it becomes a tasteless habit. Two fingers gone. *Perhaps this is enough, yes? Please, Pascal. It pains me to have to do this. It pains me,* Lyman had said, each time. *Don't make me do this.* But still, the shears had closed and Pascal tried, unsuccessfully, to bite back the screams. *And now we must show the others,*

Lyman had said with a sigh, his plummy, affected accent so mournful. *We must show them.*

Pascal picks at his bandage again, smiling to himself. It had been a gamble, this second finger, but he'd guessed correctly. Hadn't he? To Lyman, what is a punishment, but a teaching moment? It was laughable, really: only a self-absorbed fool like Lyman could have ever believed that he, Pascal Levesque, would actually try to escape, in earnest. Leave Mercy, for whom he'd already lost one finger? Of course not. *Jamais.* But, perhaps, such things are simply unfathomable to a man like Lyman Rhoades.

And so, Pascal had transgressed again and a demonstration had been required. A lesson. A message sent to Alexander and Mercy and the rest, reiterating, once more, just who is in charge of the medicine show, and all in it.

And, of course, another message, unknown to Lyman. Along with it, one small bottle on which his hopes now rest.

Pascal smiles again, riding the swelling burn of his growing fever. He thinks it will be enough. If not, well, he has more fingers, after all.

He wakes from the dream, the one of home. The same one, always. He wakes and, in the dream-dark night, wishes again, only the one simple thing: that he'd never gone north to Paris, those years long ago. Full of himself, ready to make his name. Lavoisier, Gay-Lussac, Laurent, *Levesque*. The hot, swollen pride of youth, the dreams of imminent glory. Now, though, in this stinking, shivery room, Pascal dreams only of his childhood home: the touch of the hot, dusty mistral on sweating skin, the warm dry perfume of lavender, the humming of the bees. If there is a more perfect place in this world, he has not found it but, like all perfect things, he'd recognized its perfection only when it had passed from him. The quiet south should have been enough. He should have found a plump, pretty wife with a comfortable competence to add to his own, should have settled on becoming just another provincial doctor who dabbled in chemistry. A gentleman scientist from the long French tradition thereof. Had he never gone to Paris, he would not be here in this wretched room, now, mooning about the lost past, wrapped up in the same useless, bitter dream.

Never this, never that, he thinks. *Never, never, never.* Putain de merde, always *never.* These are stupid thoughts from a stupid old man. Thoughts will get him nowhere, and crying about it is so much wasted time.

Angrily, he swipes the back of his wrist across his watering eyes, sits up, cradling his wounded hand. It will all be paid back soon enough. Pascal lights the lantern, looks at the bottles and jars on the cockeyed little table in the corner of the room, the small retort and gas burner he's been given. The notebook, open to a page of figures and symbols. His work, such as it is, that to which he has been put. What does Rhoades think he can accomplish here? In a wretched succession of rooms, with a few basic chemicals, some battered instruments. A book or two. Pascal knows that he is no Lavoisier, regardless of the dreams he had in his youth. And Lavoisier himself wasn't working from a chipped and wobbling table above horse stalls, with no more equipment than that of a small-town apothecary.

Soon enough, though, there will be no more need to curse Rhoades, curse this place, the wet and the cold and the rest of it. No need for ludicrous experiments that make no sense. No more missing fingers, no more worries about Mercy's safety. Two nights more, he hopes, and they will be free. Pascal will take Mercy and disappear, then; it is all in motion now. It must be. They'll ride to San Francisco and a ship and, after a few months, will be back to where they belong, back to that perfect place. There's a spacious house in Vaison-la-Romaine waiting for them, the very one in which he had been born, all those years ago. They'll have picnics at the little bastide near Séguret that was built by his grandfather; they'll eat fresh bread and heavy, creamy cheese, dry salami and wine that tastes like summer. Sitting by the stream, listening to the bees, hot southern sun on their faces. He'll find Mercy a husband, a kind and gentle man, a good provider; soon enough he, Pascal, will be bouncing grandchildren on his knees. He has plenty of money salted away, enough for a simple life. If Mercy wants to sing, she can sing to her children, lift her voice at Mass. It will be a good life, for all of them. It will be enough.

Pascal moves to the rickety wooden chair. Shivering, he wraps a thin, scratchy woolen blanket around his shoulders. It smells like mold and horse sweat; he's sure he doesn't smell much better. Two days more, though, that's all. Two nights.

He scratches his fingers through his greasy hair, hissing as he inadvertently rubs the end of his stump, sending a hot knife of pain up to his elbow. For a moment he's nauseated; he takes a swig from the almost-empty bottle of whiskey on the table, trying to keep his guts down. Look at him, drinking this filth. In France, he drank good wine and better brandy. He wouldn't have used the contents of this bottle to clean paintbrushes, much less washed his belly with it. Look at him. How has his life come to this? He takes another drink.

But soon, soon, soon. Soon they will be free.

Pascal thinks of Alexander.

He, himself, has done his own part, and now Alexander must do his. There is no guarantee, but Pascal has faith in Dr Potter. Alexander is afraid, of course, and for good reason, but sometimes all a man needs is a push. Sometimes a man needs that. Pascal looks down at his hand, fussing at the bandage again, and then reaches over and carefully picks up the little sprig of flower that he'd saved, left over from the bundle he'd managed to collect on one of the very rare, supervised, constitutionals that Lyman has allowed him since taking him away from the others. A sign from God, perhaps, stumbling over them like that, on the path outside whatever little town that had been. *Just flowers, Monsieur Rhoades,* he'd said when Lyman, walking beside him, had asked. *Only flowers. A bit of color for my room.* Lyman had merely grunted, continuing on with his blather about essential spirits.

Only flowers, nothing more. Just lovely blue blossoms. *Aconitum columbianum*, common western monkshood, among other names. Wolf's bane, devil's helmet. But they are *les fleurs du mal,* the *aconitums.* The Queen of Poisons, another of their vulgar names.

Lyman Rhoades, the supposed man of science, the learned, is no naturalist, or he would realize that he had signed his own death warrant the moment he'd let Pascal botanize, that day.

If all went as planned with Alexander, of course. There are so many, many things that can go wrong, still, and neither of them is foolish enough to underestimate Lyman. It's a fair chance Pascal has fashioned, a good one, maybe, nothing more than that. Pascal tells himself this, tells himself again that he shouldn't raise false hopes. But still, but still.

Better to fail in this attempt than make no attempt at all.

3.

MERCY EASES, with a hiss, into the small copper tub. She's sore and the water is scalding; it takes a moment of adding cold water from the basin beside her until the temperature is tolerable. Not much cooler, though: she likes the water as hot as she can make it. The barely endurable heat makes her feel clean, or as clean as she ever feels any more, although the water quickly becomes tepid and the illusion is fleeting. She's a small woman but still the tub is barely big enough for her to sit in; her shoulders chill regardless of how often she ladles warm water over them. In this weather, the tub isn't relaxing, not even particularly pleasant. It's almost more effort than it's worth, really, but she will not give it up. A whore's bath – face, crotch, and underarms, a splash from a basin – is not enough for her to feel clean.

Whore. It's such an ugly word although, truly, it merely describes her profession, not her person. No, it isn't even ugly, per se, not really: it's just a word, no different than *blacksmith* or *clerk*. But, still, it's not a word that, in her prior life, she'd thought could have ever become attached to her. She's a singer, an artist. That's how she thinks of herself. That is what she is. Not this, never this; never that word. *Mais oui, il est là.*

31

Really, when she's honest with herself, she's almost stopped caring about it all. It's just a thing, only one thing among the many things that make Mercy Yvette Levesque Rhoades. It isn't her, not at the heart of it. The shame that was once there has gone; to where, she's not sure. She isn't proud any more, and caring has simply become too challenging, most days. One must pick one's battles in this life, after all.

She only hopes that Papa does not truly know the depths to which she's sunk, has been sunk, that he's unaware of the things her husband makes her do, night after night. It's a fiction, perhaps, Papa's innocence, but she clings to the idea that he thinks her only a failed singer in a shabby traveling company, doing her best to make something beautiful, to make art, with nothing but her voice and a winded, reed-sprung accordion. Nothing more than that; certainly not that other word, that word that describes what it is she does, once the music has stopped for the night. It's only when thinking of her father that the shame comes back.

Il est là.

Of course, she's lying to herself, about Papa. Mercy understands that, really, regardless of the stories she tries to make herself believe. Pascal is no fool and he knows Lyman as well as anyone, better than most. Would he really be all that surprised, seeing her now, seeing the marks on her skin, the bruises and scrapes and scratches? Knowing, just by looking at her, what she is? It's no mystery what kind of a man her husband is. That's why her father is here, after all, why he'd come after her, after she'd left Paris with Lyman. When she'd called for him, the panicked telegram sent from Boston. *Je veux que vous, Papa. I need you.* He thinks he's protecting her, that he's come to save her. But her father doesn't understand that she was only a tool to bind him here, to Lyman, and whatever it is Lyman has set him to doing. He doesn't know that the telegram had come from Lyman himself, in her name. She never would have brought her father to this place, knowing what she knew by then.

Mercy reaches up, touches her necklace. Lyman has ordered her never to take it off, even in the bath. Her father's fingerbone, the small one from his right hand, dipped in some kind of clear sealant to preserve it; a twist of copper, which blackens the skin at her throat's hollow, attaches the bone to the leather cord around her neck. A reliquary, of sorts. A reminder from her husband.

She'd watched, that day, as her father had come limping into camp, wincing at every step. One hand in the other, held huddled into his belly. *Mercy,* he'd said, when he'd stopped, *Lyman would like me to give you this.* Reaching out, a bloody handkerchief in his good hand.

Friends, her father said then, woodenly, looking at Dr Potter, Oliver, and Mercy, who Lyman had ordered to the clearing by the black tent. *We all have our parts to play in this endeavor. We all have our own work. I have failed you all, and I have failed our employer, as I have failed myself.* It sounded as if he was reading from a script, a prepared statement, which likely he was. Lyman was fastidious about detail. With a stiff bow, Pascal had turned and, without another word, limped back to the waiting wagon, which drove off with a creaking of springs on the rutted road.

By the next afternoon, Mercy had a new necklace.

Now, poor Alexander has a reminder of his own although, so far, his only lives in a pocket. Perhaps Lyman is still searching for the proper setting for it. A watch fob, perhaps. Such elegance that would be. Another gift from her father, by way of Lyman. Another point made, a lesson. *We travel together* was all Pascal had said to them, this time, stepping forward to hand the handkerchief to Dr Potter, looking sharply at him, nodding. *We travel together*. He repeated it once more, folding Alexander's hands around the bloody cloth. *We travel together*. Saying what he couldn't say, the implication of what he'd tried to do.

Mercy hadn't believed it then. She doesn't believe it now. Her father would never leave her to Lyman. He will never abandon her and, so, neither will ever get away.

After a time, she realizes that the bathwater has gone icy cold.

After the bath, she walks the outskirts of the show, a shawl wrapped over her head and around her shoulders. It feels good to walk, to stretch her muscles, breathe the night air and get away from the smells of camp: sawdust, wet canvas, damp cigarette butts, the musty fug of the black tent. She'd taken care of Holly and Rula and Bascom earlier, fed them all again and cleaned up the girls as best she could. Ridley would do for Bascom. Now, she has some precious time to herself, which is in short supply, always. The rain has even died off, mostly, and she relishes just being away, from everything. There's the persistent fantasy, from step to step, that she can just walk off into the woods and keep walking, forever, get as far away as any person can ever be from another.

But that's all it is, of course, a fantasy. Soon enough, she turns around and walks back to the edge of camp. She has one last stop to make before returning to the tent she shares with Lyman. Mercy makes her way to the dry clearing she'd seen earlier, under the overhanging branches of a large fir. It's almost like a room, really, once you duck under the drooping limbs. She sits on the soft, spongy ground, leans back against the trunk. Breathes in the sharp green smell of the tree, of life.

She shouldn't be here. It's dangerous, most likely; she doesn't think for a moment that she's fooled her husband. He'll know where she is, who she's with, like he seems to know everything. But she's been at this, most nights, for weeks now and, so far, Lyman has done nothing. Perhaps it's just one small something he allows her, for herself. A minuscule little bit of reward to offset the rest of it. It could be that he just doesn't care but, more likely, he gives her this time of night so that, one day, he can take it from her. Best not to think about that, best to just enjoy it while it lasts. What will happen, will happen.

There's a rustle of fir branches and Ridley pushes his way into the little space. Even though it's dark, she can tell that he's smiling. She pats the ground next to her, lifts an arm.

The first time they'd met, away from the others, it had happened by accident. Or so she'd thought, and then soon enough realized that Ridley had sought her out deliberately. She'd sighed, knowing what was coming. He was only a boy, after all; he was alone and at that age and well, this was something she could give to him. It meant little enough to her and, if it would bring him pleasure, some happiness, then let this be a gift. But she'd been wrong. At first, still, she thought he was only shy, as any boy of that age would have been in the situation. He was not yet a man: spotty, gangly, elbows and knees, but not entirely a boy still, either. Liminal. She herself was a woman; if she was anything, she was that. A mystery, to a boy of that age, an exciting, terrifying possibility. There was a charm to it, she thought, smiling to herself and, so, she'd reached out to him, tried to pull him into a gentle embrace, bring his face to her own, but he'd pushed away. *No*, he'd said, *no, not that. Can't we just talk for a while? Maybe just talk?*

So they had; they'd spent an hour talking, hesitantly at first and then with greater ease. The next night it was the same, only talking, of small things at first. The state of the weather, the routine of their working day. Interesting faces in the crowds, the shape of the passing country. Sitting close enough for their shoulders to touch, sometimes, but chaste, like an older sister with a callow younger brother. Motherly, really, not far from it, Mercy realized. It was a strange feeling, but natural in its way. She still expected the inevitable to happen, eventually, once Ridley had become more comfortable with her, with himself. The awkward, shaky embrace. A kiss that was ill-aimed and clumsy. But no, night after night there was only this, this warm, mothering companionship. She'd reach out without thought and brush down the cowlicks in his thick, dirty hair; often, she'd realize they were holding hands while they talked. Mercy had never had siblings; her own mother had passed when she was very young. But, again, it felt natural. Maybe it was only some maternal atavism that all women possessed. Even a woman such as she.

Over time, she – and only she, among Dr Potter's company – began to learn something of Ridley's own past. Why he'd run off to escape it, what had brought him here and, knowing what she did, perhaps it was only natural, then, that this was the thing he craved, this quiet talk and gentle touch. Someone to listen to him, understand him. Not that other thing. A boy could find a whore anywhere, after all.

"How has your evening passed?" she says now,

leaning over to fuss with his collar. She sniffs. "You've been smoking, haven't you?"

"Aw, just a butt, Mercy."

"It's a filthy habit, smoking."

"But everyone smokes."

In some ways, their relationship has something of sweet-natured caricature to it, like two children playing house. Mercy, unfamiliar with the role, perhaps overacts her part, exaggerating the years between them although, in truth, they've no more than fifteen or so years separating them.

She huffs, although really she couldn't care less whether he smokes or not. "It is a filthy habit," she repeats. "*Une sale habitude.*"

They talk of nothing much for a while; by now they're comfortable enough with each other that silence can be pleasant, warm. Sitting, their shoulders touching, Mercy fiddling idly with the cuff of Ridley's sleeve, just smelling the fir and listening to the quiet sounds of the night. The drip of water, the click of bats, the faint grassy mumble of the grazing stock.

"What's going on here, Mercy? I mean, you know. With the show. What's going on?"

Mercy feels a cold jab in her belly; she's been waiting for Ridley to ask this sort of question for weeks now. They all have, she and Oliver and Alexander, anyway. Ridley is young, but he isn't stupid. It has to be obvious that there is something wrong about Dr Potter's Medicine Show, after extended association with it. That there's something else to it, that they do more than sell bunk medicine, while staggering and wheezing through their acts. Ridley's been with them for a few months now, after all. It isn't surprising that he's asking, it's only surprising that it's taken this long. He's already been caught, once, trying to look into something he shouldn't. It was only a matter of time.

Mercy knows that Alexander wants the boy gone. She does too but, at the same time, she's selfish enough to want these warm, mothering nights to continue. Just a bit longer, just a bit. She has little else, after all, only Alexander and Oliver. Let her have this. Her feelings for Alexander and Oliver are complicated by circumstance, but what she feels for Ridley is simple, good. Pure and clean, unlike so much else in her life. "What do you mean, what's going on?" she says. "This is the life, *cherie*. The life of the road. *La vie artistique*."

"No, it's not that. Something is wrong. Don't tell me it isn't."

"And what would you know of wrong?" She squeezes his arm, pinches him playfully. "You are an expert now?"

"Come on, Mercy, don't be like that. Something isn't right. Just tell me. I deserve to know, don't I? I work here too."

Mercy is glad that it's dark, so Ridley can't see the bleak look on her face. *Not right? Oh, my sweet, if only you knew. Yes, yes, cherie, there is something wrong here. Something very wrong.*

"I must go, *mon petit*," she says, instead, forcing brightness into her voice, though it tastes flat and metallic in her mouth. Mercy rises, brushing fir needles off the back of her skirt. She leans down and grabs Ridley by the hair at his temples, giving him a quick kiss on each cheek. "My husband will be looking for me."

Something is wrong, yes. If only you knew, Ridley. But you must never.

4.

SOMETHING IS WRONG.

Dr Morrison Hedwith hurls the flask against his workshop wall in disgust. It's an action out of keeping with his usually calm demeanor but, yet again, the preparation has eluded him. Something is wrong with it. Yet again. Something is missing. This time, the liquid has thickened down to a viscous, rubbery fluid, not at all suitable for the experiment. Not at all. He's spent days waiting for a suitable result – days of precise, fastidious labor – and for nothing. Instead of a dry, metallic powder, ready for mixing with the other elements, he has nothing but a sludgy mess. Another wretched failure. More wasted time that he can little spare.

As if on cue, he feels a twisting in his guts, a cramp that makes him lean over, holding his belly. His forehead breaks out in sweat even in the cool basement laboratory where he works. He rests his head on the rough wood of his workbench, tries to concentrate on the muted sounds of the footsteps moving quietly above him. One of the Wood twins is ringing up a last customer, from the muffled ding of the big brass register that looms over the shop's counter. A shout brings what can only be Mr Twist, judging from the low scrape of a dragging leg on the floorboards overhead, called to assist with loading a purchase as the shop readies to close.

The basement feels hot and close with the pain in his guts; the sweat beads on his forehead and runs down his ribs, held tight with his elbows. The stink of chemicals in the alembic and the warm, sulfurous smell of the furnace on which it sits rises sharp in his nostrils. For a hot moment he thinks he's going to lose his guts; he presses his skull tighter to the rough surface of the table, feels a throbbing behind his eyes.

"Is it bad, sweetheart?" he hears from somewhere behind him. "Are you in difficulties?"

He can only groan and make the semblance of a nod, pivoting his head slightly on the table. Dr Hedwith feels long, bony hands stroking his shoulders, slowly following the path of his upper arms down towards his pinched elbows.

"Oh, my dear," Annabelle says, "my poor dear."

Morrison says nothing, just concentrates on keeping his gorge down. The cramp in his belly is loosening slightly, but he still feels fevered and sick. The point of his wife's sharp chin presses into the crease of his neck and shoulder.

"Is there anything I can do, dear?" Annabelle asks in a soft voice. "A cool cloth, perhaps?" When Morrison doesn't respond, she says, "Some of the Sagwa, then?"

Morrison twists away from her, straightening up slowly, feeling the knots in his guts unwinding somewhat. He concentrates on the movement of his fists clenching and then relaxing, willing his twisting muscles to loosen from the neck down. Taking a cloth from his workbench, he sniffs it and then, judging it safe, wipes his sweaty brow and face. Exhaling slowly, he turns back to his wife, fashioning the juddery semblance of a smile.

"Thank you, my dear," he says, "I'm fine now. Truly. A small episode, nothing more. Something I ate, I'm sure." He wipes his brow again. As he does, Annabelle steps towards him, folding her long, narrow form around him, her skinny arms clamping around his ribs, hugging him tightly. Even through the crinkling, heavy folds of her stiff dark dress he can feel her skeleton pressing against him, unnerving him.

Despite the fact that she is no beauty, and that they are childless, Annabelle is a good wife to him, as these things are measured. Her family money has built this laboratory and largely funds his researches, of course, after his earlier financial setbacks in London. The Hedwith Apothecary Emporium covers its costs and provides a bit of profit but, given his substantial research expenses, he needs the extra Alberton income. Morrison has no interest in children or fatherhood, per se, but he vaguely wishes that they were blessed with a baby or two, he and Annabelle, if only to give his wife something else to do with her time. Afford a bit more privacy to his own. She has her work with the Temperance Union, of course, and the other charitable and social endeavors with which women of her class and station pass their time but, still, sometimes, it must not be enough to fill her days, given her regular appearances in his laboratory. He doesn't like her down here, interrupting his research.

Morrison gives his wife a vague pat along the small of her back, imagining that he can feel her bones rattling around under her skin, her ribs clacking like marimba bars. "Thank you, my dear," he murmurs, trying to get her off him, as he hates being touched, as a general rule. His wife's incessant grasping is something of a trial to him. "Do you have a meeting today, then?"

Annabelle slowly unwinds herself from her husband,

straightening and nodding severely. "Yes, Morrison, I do," she says. "We have a gathering of the Calvary Committee later this evening. That is the reason why I am down here: there is an upcoming auction to raise funds for the new church building and I was hoping we could commit some cases of the Sagwa and some of the other products to the cause. Yes?"

"Certainly, my love, certainly," Hedwith says, simply wanting to get his wife out of his laboratory so he can resume work and study what had gone wrong with this latest preparation. "As much as you like, just tell one of the Woods and have the man set it all aside in the storeroom. As much as you need." Morrison could care less about stock and inventory and such things. That is a matter for clerks; let them sort it out. Really, Annabelle should have just gone to the Wood brothers directly and not bothered him with these trivial matters.

"Thank you, dear." She leans forward. For a moment Morrison is concerned that she means to wrap herself around him again, but she merely gives him a dry kiss on the cheek. "Back to work then, doctor," she says, smiling. When she smiles, Annabelle is almost pretty.

"Yes, dear," Dr Hedwith says, returning the smile as best he can. "Back to work."

Later, sitting by the fire in the parlor, Morrison broods. Annabelle will be gone for an hour or more yet, so he enjoys the brandy that Castle, his valet, had brought earlier. It's an irritant, having to enjoy his liquor of an evening in secret, but that was just one of the things that came with his married life and, so, must be endured.

Dr Hedwith sips the brandy, relishing the hot sweetness on his tongue. He holds the glass to the light of the fire, swirling the warm amber liquid inside it, watching it catch and reflect the phlogisticated spirit of the aether. Nonsense, of course, he knows; the theory of the phlogiston, the elemental substance that existed inside all combustible bodies, had been proven obsolete for a hundred years, but it's hard to let go of the terminology at times. And, truly, while the science has changed, the underlying feeling has not. Sipping the brandy, it's easy to imagine the tiny particles dancing on his tongue, infusing his blood with burning potential. Brandy in firelight seems phlogisticated matter made incarnate.

"Will there be anything else, sir?" Castle asks, interrupting his reverie. The man looms to the side of his chair; his broad shoulders, beady eyes, and pugilist's twisted nose bely the surprising dexterity of the large, heavy-knuckled hands, hands that can pour a brandy, draft a schematic, or bludgeon a man with equal skill, as called upon by circumstance. Castle has been with him for many years, in several cities, as a majordomo of sorts, protector, and de facto body servant. Hedwith keeps him as close as he distances Lyman, though Rhoades has been with him much longer and is not without his own talents. It is a question of personality, of temperament. Castle's scarred visage hides a keen mind and an aesthetic spirit, in many ways like Hedwith's own. Castle is rarely far from his master's side; he occupies a small set of rooms under the stairs, where he spends his free time in study.

"No, Mr Castle, that will be all, thank you. Enjoy your evening, my friend." As the man turns to go, Morrison changes his mind. "A moment, Castle, if you would, though." He holds the brandy to the light again, twists the glass in front of his eyes.

"Sir?" Castle, impassive as always, turns, the serving tray and brandy bottle in his hands.

Morrison pauses and is forming his thoughts, about fire and brandy and the elemental spirits, when the spasm strikes. The glass drops from his hand, spilling the expensive liquor on the rug. As he clutches his belly, his vision greying, he hopes that the stain will not be too apparent to Annabelle.

Castle moves quickly but without hurry, setting down the bottle and tray, and picking up Dr Hedwith in his arms, carrying him to the sofa with no more effort than would be required to lift a small child. Dr Hedwith's body shivers and twitches; blood is dripping out of his nose and left ear. His eyes move rapidly from side to side, as if in a dream. Castle sits back and waits, wiping the blood from his employer with a clean handkerchief.

Several minutes later, Hedwith comes to. "Long?" he asks, weakly, looking up.

Castle shakes his head. "Not very long, sir, no. A few minutes." He presses a hand to the doctor's chest, preventing him from rising. "You'd better wait a few more minutes before you get up, sir."

"No, no, I'm fine, Castle. Really. Thank you." Hedwith tries to sit up but his vision swims and his head begins pounding, so he sits back. "Perhaps you're right, then. Just a moment more."

"Very good, sir. I'll just clean up the brandy." Castle goes down to the kitchen for a wet cloth. He knows it wouldn't do for Mrs Hedwith or the maid to find the spill. He comes back with the rag, kneels, and begins dabbing at the spot, soaking up the liquor as best he can. There will be some smell, but perhaps it will go unnoticed. He glances over at his employer. "The episodes have been coming more frequently, sir."

Morrison doesn't answer. He knows that he is running out of time, that, as Castle said, the fits are coming more often and with greater intensity. He will have to act soon, with all the trouble and danger that entails, if his current experiments continue to prove flawed and fruitless. He sits quietly, holding his belly, gathering his strength as he watches Castle at his work.

"There," Castle says, standing upright. "I think that will be fine." He looks over. "Do you feel able to get up, sir? Mrs Hedwith will be home soon. Best she didn't see you in this state."

"Yes, Castle, I'll be fine. Just give me a moment."

Dr Hedwith lies there, going through the latest course of experiments in his pounding head, doing his best to concentrate through the pain and lingering nausea. Something is still wrong with the process, with the vital elements. Something is missing, but he's confident that he can find the errors, fix them, if he only has more time. Just a bit more time.

5.

"IT'S BECAUSE you're a terrible fucking gambler, is why," Sol Parker is saying. "I don't even know why you try to *call* yourself a gambler."

"That's a load of crap, Solomon, and you know it. Anyone can have an off night." Agamemnon Rideout is in a huff. He and Sol have been having this same argument for the last hundred miles, since they'd had to leave Twin Falls in a hurry yesterday. The sun is just on the edge of setting and they still need to put as many miles between them and their latest mistake as they can. He leans over his horse's neck to spit. "I'm surprised you ain't killed no one in the last five minutes."

"*I'm surprised you ain't killed no one,*" Sol mimics in a high-pitched, mincing voice. "I wouldn't have *had* to kill no one if you were a better gambler, Ag. I mean, really, you can't deal right sober, much less drunk as you were. Even *I* could see you were palming, or fucking trying to, and I was otherwise occupied, as it were."

"Bullshit, Sol, bull and shit. No one saw what I was up to." Ag holds out his hands, palms down. "Look at these. Just look: steady as rocks. Even with a dram of liquor in me, they're steady and you know it."

Sol rolls his eyes, making a rude motion with his free hand.

"Listen, *you* were one that started the whole fracas, brother," Ag continues, "getting all cozy with that young lady. *That's* what made that gentleman take exception."

"Well, then, I don't know what I was thinking, trying to do the right thing, Rideout," Sol replies. "I should have *let* him knife you. Hell, I should be riding with *that* fucking gentleman now, instead of you, fool. The company would certainly be better."

"Then maybe you shouldn't of killed him, Sol. Study on that, idiot. He wasn't *going* to knife me. I keep telling you: you just got all worked up and panicked and shot the poor bastard. And now we're in this godforsaken mess."

Actually, the murdered gentleman in question was in rude health, his haberdashery requiring a mend being the full extent of his injuries. It was anyone's guess what had actually started the excitement; the only things truly known were that no knives had been drawn and that both Sol Parker and Ag Rideout had been so profoundly drunk that it was a mercy no lasting harm had been done in the affray. Once Sol had started shooting and Ag had commenced to hollering, dropping his own gun when he'd fallen over a chair, it was only divine providence and Sol's poor aim that had prevented actual injury to anyone. A quick-thinking barkeep had shouted that the boys had killed the man – who'd merely hit the deck in self-protection – encouraging them in no uncertain terms that they needed to get out of his tavern, and Twin Falls in general, sharpish, before the law arrived. The saloon patrons were still laughing about it.

Sol and Ag had been pushing their horses ever since, bickering all the while, one eye over their shoulders for the posse they were sure followed. Even as they griped at one another, they were both somewhat stunned at the turn their lives had taken in the few short weeks since they'd left their mother's ranch. They were the kind of brothers – half-brothers to be precise – that, when together, sounded more like an old married couple than siblings. Their arguments, as a general rule, were overtired and stretched thin from long use. This new squabble had been worn to a nub in a matter of hours.

"And what will the girls say, knowing that now they have a murderer and a outlaw for brothers?" Ag continues. Both boys were fiercely protective of their two younger sisters, the product of their mother's third and, so far, final marriage. Their mother was apt to say, privately, that she'd had little luck keeping husbands alive and even less luck getting anything good out of them while they'd been around, her daughters notwithstanding.

"Oh, you're a *outlaw* now, are you, Ag? Is that what you're saying?" Sol snorts out a puff of air. "Far as I can tell, you never did anything *outside the law* to begin with. Unless there's a law against being a shitty fucking card player or dropping your goddamn gun with those *steady hands* of yours. *I'm* the one who is in all the trouble now, just for saving *your* narrow ass. A deed which, let me tell you, I'm regretting more and more. You, Mr Outlaw, are just tagging along behind me like a goddamn duckling, quacking your damn gums."

"That's a load of crap, Small-a-man."

"Goddamn it, Ag, what did I fucking tell you about that?"

"What's that, Small-a-man?" Ag replies innocently.

"Just don't, boy. *Don't.*" Like many short men, Sol is touchy about his height.

They lapse into sullen silence for upwards of five minutes before reverting to carping at one another again, trying to make the dry miles pass until they reach San Francisco. They're broke and neither has much in the way of ideas on how they're going to make any money, being both wanted men, as far as they know, and lacking much in the way of skills. As boys, they'd fantasized vaguely about card sharping or robbing banks but, in practice, neither one has much desire now to continue a life of crime, after their brief introduction to it. However, both young men are deeply and secretly convinced that they have profound and hidden skills at, well, *something*, which has not yet made itself known to them. But even Ag will admit to himself, privately, that perhaps he isn't a natural talent at the gamblers' art. Sol still feels guilty and sick that he's shot and killed a man, tough as he likes to think himself. Each hopes that something, somewhere between here and the Pacific coast, will steer them towards some kind of money-making revelation before the law catches up and hangs them. They just need to keep moving.

On the other hand, Josiah McDaniel is motionless, drunk, and lying in the dust. Not a little drunk, but the kind of inebriation that requires the closing of one eye to bring the world back into focus. Just then, though, his left eye was already swollen shut, courtesy of a rancher's heavy fist, but the other allows him to make out his wife's features in the silver locket that he holds close to his face in the fading daylight. A tiny, admittedly poorly done, portrait of Mary looks back at him from the left oval of the locket; from the right a sharp-dressed, eager-eyed version of himself keeps watch. He looks little like his portrait now: his clothes are torn and stained, his bruised eye is puffed shut, and his smile lacks the component part of two of his incisors, knocked out by the same rancher that did for the eyeball.

A dentist with missing teeth wasn't right, Josiah thinks, muzzily. Like a shaky-handed barber or a banker in shabby clothes. It isn't reputable. It doesn't inspire confidence. No one likes a dentist, anyway.

"No one likes a dentist," he hollers sloppily at his horse, after swigging from his whiskey bottle. "No one likes a dentist, anyway." The repetition seems important. The horse ignores him, placidly nosing around for forage amongst the sagebrush. It's only the creature's inherent laziness that keeps it around, still saddled, with the reins hanging loose. A smarter horse, unhobbled as it was, would have wandered off to find better grass or, at least, a better owner, after Josiah had fallen off this last time. Maybe the horse is simply used to him dropping from the saddle by now, the way it's used to the pungent fumes of whiskey, vomit, and long-unwashed clothes. Perhaps, to the horse, falling off is simply an idiosyncratic behavior of this particular rider.

Josiah scratches a hand through his dirty, unwashed hair, prods his tongue across the holes in his gums where once he'd had teeth. Mary had liked his strong white teeth. She'd liked the fact that he was a dentist, a professional man, a good provider with clean hands and a sober disposition. He knows that she'd shudder to see him now, drunk, lying in the dirt with filth caked under his broken nails, vomit down the front of his shirt. She wouldn't see him, though, not ever.

"Mary liked a dentist," he mutters.

With the hand not holding the whiskey he scrabbles at his jacket, trying to dig the small bottle out of his pocket. The pocket seems to be moving on him but, eventually, he gets his fingers inside it and pulls the bottle out. *Dr Hedwith's Chock-a-saw Sagwa Tonic*, he reads, for the thousandth time, once he gets the label in focus. *Vital For Health. A Cure for Ills, Agues, Fevers, and Low Spirits. Pat Pending.* With his dirty fingers, he squeezes the thick glass so hard he hopes to break it, to feel the shards cut into his flesh, but again is defeated. Instead, he lifts the whiskey bottle in his other hand and drinks.

He has to lean over and weakly puke again, then, dribbling liquor and bile out of his split lips. "*Vital for health!*" he yells to the horse once the gagging subsides. His vision swims a bit and he has to lie down on his back. He closes his eyes, trying to concentrate on the smell of sage in the dry air, the sound of the wind murmuring through the canyon.

He'd left Boise for good on the back of this latest beating; he won't be returning, he thinks. He won't go back. To hell with all of them. He just wants to lie here; he's far enough outside of town that, when he finally dries up and dies, no one will try to bring him home and shake life back into him again. When the last bottle of whiskey runs out he'll just curl up under the sagebrush and wait until he can open his eyes and see Mary again. The damn horse is smart enough to find its own way back.

"*No one likes a dentist!*" He yells it again, feeling satisfaction in the drunken leitmotif, as some men get when at their liquor. To Josiah, it sums up what his life has been drawn down to: the fact that he can't even sit in a tavern, quietly mourning his wife, a husband's right, without some dentist-hating yokel taking exception and beating on him.

He's already forgotten how he'd worn out his welcome in most of Boise's saloons, with his drunken carrying-on and belligerence during the last weeks. People went to taverns to enjoy a drink and cheerful company, not listen to a crazed toothpuller hollering about a dead wife and a patentmedicine conspiracy. The rancher that had blacked his eye and knocked out his teeth had finally simply lost patience with Josiah and let his temper get the best of him although, not two nights before, the man had carried him to his own home and put him to bed, not for the first time, making sure Josiah didn't get himself into any mischief.

"They took her from me," Josiah mutters, "they took her." For some reason he can't help, he starts to laugh, rolling over on his side, spilling most of the remainder of his whiskey. He curls up into a ball, laughing and then crying into the dirt and then laughing some more, before flopping over roughly onto his back again. *"No one likes a dentist!"* he drunkenly screams again at the darkening sky.

"Now, what the hell is this?" a voice says from above and behind him.

"Someone who hates dentists, I reckon," a second voice says.

Josiah scrabbles and scrambles towards upright, making it about halfway before overbalancing and falling over some sagebrush. "You get back," he yells, waving an arm as he tries to reach his feet. "Just stay right there."

"I reckon he's got a right to beef, Sol," the first voice says. "Look at his mouth."

"That right, sir?" the man called Sol asks. "Some fucking dentist do you poorly? Looks like he must have beat on you some, too. You look like you been used hard."

"I'm a dentist," Josiah mutters.

"That seem strange to you, brother?" the first voice says.

"It sure does, Ag. Seems like a dentist should have his teeth. *Physician, heal thyself*, as Mama would say, out the Good Book."

"You're right, Sol." Ag looks down at the filthy little drunkard weaving around his horse, still loosely waving an arm around. "Sir? You OK, sir?"

"Luke," Josiah says blearily.

"OK, Luke, you OK? You need some help?"

Josiah shakes his head, tries to swig from the empty bottle he somehow still has hold of. "Gospel of Luke. *Physician heal thyself*. Matthew, Mark, Luke. I'm a dentist."

The brothers look at one another.

"So you said, sir," Sol says. "Do you…"

"Josiah McDaniel."

"That the dentist who whaled on you?" Ag asks.

"I'm Josiah McDaniel! That's my name. *I'm* a dentist and they killed her. They killed my Mary. Don't you…" Whatever else it is that Josiah has to say is thrust out of his lungs in a huff when he hits the ground, dead to the world.

"Well, we can't just leave him here, Sol," Ag says. "I mean, look at him. He's a mess. We need to at least wait until he wakes up and then we can get him back on his horse."

"Goddamn it, Ag, listen to yourself. Remember how you're the big fucking outlaw? Well, sometimes us *outlaws* have to do some things that ain't necessarily what you'd call neighborly. I'm not saying we kill him or bother him: let's just take what he has of value and be on our way. He's not but a day's walk from Boise. He'll be fine." Sol shakes his head at his soft-hearted brother.

In truth, Sol's vestigial, but deep-seated, morality is struggling with the idea of robbing a pitiful, unconscious drunk, but sometimes life is hard and you have to just button your pants and get on with it. So he tells himself, trying to work up to the chore.

Ag looks at his brother, knowing that the hard stance is more than half bluster. Probably it's all bluster, when it comes right down to it. You didn't just leave a sick man to die out here in the middle of nowhere. You might cheat a little at cards and you might shoot off your gun in a moment of excitement, but cold-heartedly robbing a little man who is obviously doing poorly was just not right. He knows that they're in a tight spot and need money, but this is too much, and he wants no part of it. He tries to back out with some logic. "The law will hang us for horse thieves, Sol. It ain't worth the risk."

"Goddamn it, Ag, the law's *already* going to fucking hang us for Twin Falls, or maybe you don't remember that. Or maybe it's because *I'm* the one who's going to get hung, not you, Mr Outlaw. Now that there's some fucking skin on the table, the game's too rich for your blood, that it?" Sol points a thick finger at his brother. "It's all fine and good, long as I'm the only one who's in real trouble… that right, Mr Lawless?"

"Bullshit, Sol! Don't you play that on me!" Ag yells back. "What would Mama think, if she found out that we'd robbed – and probably killed, by un-Christian neglect – some fellow traveler, lost in the hills?" At times, Ag tends toward the poetic.

"What would Mama say? *What would Mama say*? She'd say that we're in a tight fucking spot and he had it coming, dipshit." Sol slips off his horse, reaches into his saddle bag for his canteen, takes a long swig of tepid, tinny water. "He ain't *lost*, Ag, he's drunk. Maybe you remember drunk: it's when you can't cheat at cards without almost getting fucking killed, you remember that?" He points at the man on the ground. "Also when you get beat up and your teeth knocked out, and then pass out drunk in the goddamn dirt." He starts to walk over to the man's horse, which is still placidly nibbling at the brush.

Ag is off his own horse and at his brother before Sol is able to grab for the reins. Soon enough, they're both rolling in the dust, hollering at one another and wrestling, slap-fighting in the manner that boys who have grown up together will do. Josiah's horse calmly moves out of the way as they fight and curse, ignoring the two while finding a patch of scraggly grass to nibble. Even given their varying sizes, the brothers are evenly matched: Sol has the weight and low center of gravity but Ag knows how to use his long body for leverage and, more importantly, knows his brother's style. He knows that Sol is impatient and easy to drive into a fury, where Ag himself is better at biding his time until he finds some advantage.

They grunt and roll and curse on the ground. Sol gets atop his brother but, before he can pin him into immobility and commence to slapping in earnest, Ag hooks a long leg around Sol's neck and flips him over onto his side, trying to ride the momentum to get onto his brother's back and choke him in the crook of an arm. Sol flings an elbow back as they turn, catching Ag in the ribs, driving his breath out in a gasp. Had they spent more energy actually fighting and less on cursing at one another there may have been an advantage to either party but, as prior scuffles would indicate, they'd simply keep slapping and twisting and grunting profanities until they tired each other out.

They're nearing this point, hot and sweaty and exhausted, full of righteous indignation, when the whiskey bottle comes sailing weakly over, bouncing off Ag's head. Sol immediately leaps off his brother, one fist raised in a fury, storming over to where the little drunk lies half-sitting on the ground. "You don't throw fucking bottles at my fucking brother, dentist!" he hollers.

"You two stop that," Josiah mumbles. "You quit fighting." He tries to sit a bit more upright. When he'd hit the ground earlier, the impact had been enough to slightly wake him from his stupor, although he could only lie there for a long time, with his eyes closed, breathing in the dry smell of dirt and sage, listening. In his whiskey-fogged mind, though, he's latched onto a single thing: these men are outlaws. They're killers.

"Perhaps you should mind your own business," Ag says, bitterly, rubbing the back of his head, where the whiskey bottle had landed. "If I want to put this black-hearted rascal in his place, it ain't no concern of yours."

"But it is my concern, young man," Josiah says, looking at them owlishly. "It *is* my concern. I'll show you." He fumbles around in his coat, pulling out a thick wallet, tossing it on the ground between them. The brothers can see that it bulges with bills. "I want to hire you boys," he continues. "I want to hire you two to kill a man."

Sol and Ag look at the wallet, then at each other and, for once, neither has much to say.

6.

ALEXANDER SITS on the tailgate of his wagon, a bottle of whiskey by his side, sipping from a tin cup and looking up at the night sky. Another day has passed; his throat is sore from salesmanship and too many cigarettes, and the lousy whiskey is doing it no favors. His pipes feel dry and narrow in his neck, gristly, but he takes another sip, grimacing as he swallows, rumbling a cough in his chest. The cup is empty, so he takes the bottle at his side and refills it. Drinks, refills it again.

The second days of the show are usually slower than the first, the troupe's novelty having faded a bit, but they'd done all right today. There's fuck-all to do in this town, by the looks of it, so most people from yesterday had just come back to see the acts all over again. To watch Oliver heave his weights and Lyman pull doves from thin air, listen to Mercy sing over her warbling accordion and Potter himself wheeze on about the benefits of the Sagwa. Another day done.

A slight wind is up now, but the rain had finally stopped around midnight and the clouds have loosened their crowding overhead somewhat; black gaps open and close now between them, lit by the sullen moon low on the horizon. The weather won't hold, not with this wind that promises another dreary, indolent rainstorm, but, for now, Alexander can see patches of stars, for a change. He misses real weather, thunder and lightning and truly angry wind, snow and sleet and ice-caked trees. The constant, drizzling rain here in Oregon saps his spirit; the dour, cheerless soak for nine months of the year further drains what feeble enjoyment of life he feels he still possesses.

He takes another swallow of whiskey, looking at Orion's shoulder, or perhaps it's part of Ursa. Astronomy has never been a particular skill of his. Leave that shit to Lyman. The whiskey is foul, rough, but drinking it is better than remaining entirely sober. He douses the stuff with Sagwa from time to time – for his cough, he tells himself – but really in an effort to kill the taste of each with the other. Really, all he does is enhance the sickening flavors of both but, after enough of the stuff, his tastebuds have stopped working anyway, in protest.

Alexander swings his legs from the tailgate, back and forth, as he tries to light one of his damp cigarettes. After the third match gives out he tosses the unlit tobacco to the ground in disgust and has more whiskey. The yokels are long gone, the last straggler having left Mercy's tent an hour or more ago. This is Alexander's favorite time of night, when the show has wound down and most of its occupants are busy with other things, their own private rituals before trying to sleep. Ah Fan dreaming at his pipe. Mercy soaking herself in the small copper tub. Ridley will be nosing around the tents, looking for dropped cigarettes, Oliver taking one of his nighttime strolls, which he did in all weathers for reasons of his own. Alexander doesn't want to know what Lyman does when left to his own devices.

He puts a hand in his pocket and feels Pascal's finger, still wrapped in the handkerchief. The bottle, Alexander has hidden in his trunk. The scrap of note, bloodstained and nearly illegible, the handwriting tiny and crabbed, he'd destroyed, its contents memorized.

A–

This is our moment. We will not get a better chance. I have done what I can. Aconite, as strong as I can make it. You know what you must do, now. To the eyes, the face, it is quick. When he is distracted, at the conjunction. As we have discussed. Remember the Elements.

We travel together, my friend, but in this I can do no more.

You know what you must do, now.
   – PL

We travel together, Pascal had said, handing Alexander the handkerchief, that intense look in his eyes. Alexander is in awe of Pascal. What he'd done to himself, merely to pass on this bottle and message. There can be no doubt as to the depths of the man's conviction.

Now, Alexander has to swallow his fear and do his own part. It's such a simple thing. A second, and then it's done. Such a simple thing, he tells himself again.

Our torments also may in length of time / Become our Elements. Pascal had quoted him that, once, when still he traveled with them, before Lyman took him away. Back then, the little Frenchman and Alexander used to share a drink after the show's work was done, during this same quiet time of night Dr Potter now sits through alone.

Eventually, they began speaking, so quietly, of things best not heard by others.

Treason.

Milton, apparently, the quote. Or was it Donne?

Alexander can't remember but, whoever the poet was, they'd summed up, in a line, the life he leads, this life he's led for so long. The life he allows to continue because of his own inaction. Because of his own cowardice. *Our torments become our elements.*

But no longer, now that eight-fingered Pascal Levesque has put that bottle in his hand. *Aconite.* Made from a flower. Henbane? No, wolf's bane. Medea and Theseus and all that. He tries to remember what he knows about it from his medical training, and can recall precious little except that it's nasty stuff, not to be touched. Gardeners' poisoning, through the skin, something like that. And, if Pascal the chemist has somehow made it stronger, Alexander isn't inclined to doubt its efficacy.

Sitting on the wagon, now, Alexander thinks ahead, plotting out how he will make it work. His plans get more elaborate and involved, twisting around in his head but really going nowhere until he wonders if he's maybe overthinking it all because he's so fucking scared. Just take a step forward when Lyman is focused on his work, toss the stuff in his face, and run like hell. Hopefully it acts as quickly as Pascal says. If not, Oliver will be there and, well, they'd just have to figure it out.

He and Oliver have discussed it, but so far they've come up with not much in the way of ideas, should things not go as planned. One thing is true, though: this is the best chance they'll likely have for a long time. Yes, they're cowards but, if they wanted to finally get out from under this life, even with the inevitable consequences that will follow, this is the time to act.

Alexander touches the handkerchief in his pocket again, trying to take some strength from Pascal.

This is the time to act.

•••

The rain is drizzling down again. Alexander isn't sure if he's drunkenly dozed off or simply been lost in thought. Perhaps a bit of both. The clouds have closed in again and, with no moon, it's tough to tell the hour; he has no idea how long he's been sitting here on the wagon, but he's cold and damp, his bones achy.

The cup is still in his hand, so he chokes down another sip of Sagwa-laced whiskey, feeling it seep into his tired body. Rather than energizing him as advertised, he feels himself getting heavy, dense, sinking down into himself again. His spirits aren't lifted so much as removed, lurking morosely a small black distance away. When he feels them looming closer, he takes another sip, which helps push to the back of his mind the thoughts of Pascal and his own worry about what is coming. He knows that he's using the tonic too much, the normal stuff, that is, that if he isn't careful he'll wind up like Fan, as Oliver has warned, chained to the opium in it. During the war he'd fallen into that trap; getting extricated from it had been a painful process, the very thing that led him to the state in which he now finds himself, bound to his fate even tighter than Fan to his pipe.

He drinks again. Refills his cup. Drinks, huddling into his coat. He should really go to his tent, get out of this weather, which is doing his lungs no good. Instead, he fills the cup once more, raises it to his lips. It clacks against his front teeth, spilling most of its contents down his front. Evidence of his increasing drunkenness, as is the fact that the cup is now empty again. He should probably stop, call it a night. Instead, squinting, he sloppily pours in another measure from the bottle, spilling it over his hand and wrist. He sucks the liquor from his skin and douses in a shot of the Sagwa. *Fuck it*, Alexander thinks. After a hefty, foul swallow from his cup, he busies himself trying to roll and light another soggy cigarette, wasting another few matches before giving up and tossing it down with its fellow.

There's a scratch behind him and the smell of hot tobacco; a red ember passes close to his shoulder, a paper pinched between two large fingers. Without looking over, he takes the proffered cigarette and draws the smoke greedily into his lungs, which starts him coughing, even over the copious amounts of the Sagwa he's had that day.

"Thanks," he mutters, when his breath comes back. Inhaling deeply again, he asks, "How was the walk?"

"Damp, old man," Oliver says, sinking down on the tailgate beside Dr Potter, causing the wagon to lean alarmingly to one side. "Damp and dark. I hate this damn country." The Black Hercules is from a part of Texas where it's flat, dry, and hot, brown and sere, not like this wet, green crumple of a place. It's better to the east, from what he's seen, past the gorge of the Columbia to the high desert; these rainy forests of the Cascades that they're in now, though, seem too close and full, high but not high enough, unlike the sharp Rockies they'd passed through last summer. Oliver is a man of specific tastes: if he has to be in mountain country, he wants them tall and spiky; he wants his plains flat and his forests thin, his rivers shallow and his deserts dry and brushy. This combination here of short mountains and busy forests unnerves him, puts him off his stride.

Alexander is coughing again. "You need to see to that cough, old man," Oliver says. "Something wrong there. You're the doctor, you should know that." He accepts the tin cup from Dr Potter, grimaces around the taste. "Merciful Jesus, man, that Sagwa is doing nothing good for the flavor of this whiskey. You'd do better to just hit the pipe like Fan than drink this foul shit." Oliver only touches what Sagwa he needs, the special preparation, not the stuff they sell to the general public.

"Sorry. Forgot that it was in there. Here." He hands the whiskey bottle over.

Oliver takes a healthy sip. "Sweet mother Mary, that ain't much better, now, is it?" Oliver shakes his head, grimacing again. For a while they're quiet, from time to time taking a drag on their smokes or wincing down a drink. Eventually, Oliver asks, "So how'd we do?"

Alexander shrugs. "About the usual. Not great. Enough to buy more food and some shitty whiskey, pay us the starvation wage we earn from this glorious endeavor. What you'd expect."

"And...?"

"And what?" Alexander knows what Oliver is asking, but doesn't want to have to say it.

"You know what I mean. You get all six out? It's tomorrow, old man."

There's a long pause. Alexander takes a heavy drag on his cigarette, blows smoke out with a sigh. "I know it's fucking tomorrow, Oliver. I know, all right?" He sighs again, shaking his head. "But not exactly. Besides." The rest left unsaid.

"Not exactly what, Dr Potter?" Lyman steps out of the darkness, stopping in front of them with his hands on his meaty hips, rocking slightly back and forth on his heels. For a fat man, Lyman Rhoades has an unnerving way of just appearing, soundless as a ghost, usually when he is least wanted. Maybe he actually *is* a magician, Alexander thinks, trying to still the roil in his belly.

Instead, he just shrugs, drawing on the stub of his cigarette, holding the tin cup out, hoping his hand isn't shaking more than is normal. "Whiskey?"

Lyman looks at the cup as if it contained a fresh turd. "No, I don't think I will, thank you, Dr Potter. That garbage you drink will rot your insides. Rot it." Lyman always has a supply of high-dollar brandy: fine, expensive liquor he never shares. "You were saying, though?" He cocks an eyebrow, his heavy round face tilting to one side like an inquisitive dog.

Even Lyman's eyebrows are fat, Alexander thinks; they're like bloated caterpillars crawling across the man's suety face. He looks overripe, corrupt, although perhaps his own fear is just running away from him or, maybe, he's just way too fucking drunk just now. He knows what Lyman wants, so there's no more use in putting it off. "Three bottles short," he says.

"Come again?" Lyman asks, smiling broadly.

"We're three bottles short, Lyman. Half. As you fucking no doubt know. There just weren't enough likely candidates. There weren't. There's no reason to waste the stuff, after all." He raises his whiskey again, trying not to think of the finger in his pocket.

Lyman's smile is fixed in place. "No likely candidates, Dr Potter? Well, of course."

The slap knocks Alexander's tin cup painfully against his lips, snapping his head back and nearly sending him off the wagon. Before he has a chance to draw breath, another catches him on the other side, knocking him into Oliver, who has started to leap up, saying, "Now, wait…"

Lyman is unnervingly quick, given his size: a short, hooked knife is at Oliver's belly before he's barely raised himself from the tailgate. "Sit down, now," Rhoades says, flatly, without emotion, still smiling the hard, sharp smile that stops well short of his eyes. "Just sit down."

Oliver sits, then, turning his head away from

Alexander. Even without the knife, it had been stupid for him to stand. He knows that, big man that he is, he's outmatched by Lyman. They all are.

"Now," Lyman says, leaning over Alexander, who's rubbing blood off his lips. "Now, Dr Potter, now. What was that about likely candidates? Yes? Do I need to remind you what it is we do here, and what are the consequences of failure? Do I now?" He slaps Alexander again, lightly, contemptuously, just to get his attention, the way one would slap a recalcitrant child. The smile is gone.

"No," Alexander mutters. It's useless to argue. He'd known when they'd closed the show for the night that he'd done a foolish thing. Stupid, really. If he couldn't sell the three final bottles, he should have simply given them away. Who got them didn't matter. The idea of a "proper candidate" is a fiction, and he knows it. The whole purpose of their endeavor is to disperse bottles of the Sagwa, the *special* Sagwa – *Vital for Health* – and then see what comes of it. Tomorrow night, at Lyman's conjunction, however he calculated it and whatever it really was, they'd know what, if anything, they'd accomplished in this particular little town. Tomorrow night they'd know a lot of things, but it was stupid, useless, and dangerous for him to balk Rhoades now. Just now, Alexander knows he needs to be more careful than ever.

Lyman Rhoades takes a step back, grinning as widely as a cherub again. "There now, gentlemen. I knew that we were of a single mind. I knew it. Excellent. Yes, excellent." He claps his fat, damp hands together. "Now, I myself am going to retire to my quarters and get some rest. I'd recommend you do the same." He looks up at the sky. "Yes, get some sleep, gentlemen. We have another early morning and likely a long, long night tomorrow. Sleep well." Tipping an imaginary hat, he vanishes into the darkness, disappearing in an instant in that strange way he has.

Without saying anything, Alexander fills his cup again and hands the bottle to Oliver.

The next morning, Alexander wakes with a staggeringly impressive headache and his cough has burrowed even deeper into his lungs. He rolls off his cot and limps out of his tent, hacking, spitting a thick mess of mucous between his feet and, then, painfully stands up straight, knees creaking and back aching. He examines the spit with a professional eye, noting the color and consistency; the absence of blood encourages him somewhat although, considering how he feels, he isn't sure if wouldn't be better just to die right now.

It's raining again, of course. He puts on his shapeless hat and shrugs into his oiled canvas coat, pulling it around him with a shiver, scratching his belly. As he walks over to the trees to piss, he hears the rest of the troupe going through the business of getting up and ready to pack, to start another long, bumpy day on the road. Oliver and Mercy, always early risers, are already up; Mercy is cooking bacon and heating water for coffee, Oliver tending to the stock. Alexander unbuttons, holding himself and waiting. Finally, after a few fitful dribs and drabs, one of the gifts of age, his stream starts and he sighs with relief. He reaches over and strips rainwater from the fronds of a nearby fern, which he wipes on his face and lips, then tilts his head upwards, letting rain fall into his open mouth. One of the few benefits of this wretched weather is that it's at least wet, he thinks, considering how thirsty he is.

He staggers stiff-legged to the fire, sits on the old blanket next to Mercy, who wordlessly hands him a dipper of cold water which he gratefully drinks down, returning it to her to refill. After the second cup, he feels almost human again, albeit like a human somewhat near death. He hunkers down, drawing his coat closer around himself and letting the seemingly excessive weight of his head sag against his chest, coughing from time to time. From the corner of his eye, Alexander sees Mercy look over with a little smile. She rarely speaks during the morning, Mercy, simply goes about her business solemnly and with a kind of quiet dignity at odds with her profession and personal situation. When the coffee is ready she hands him a mug, touching him lightly on the back of the hand and giving him another encouraging smile.

As he sips, he thinks, not for the first time, that Mercy would have made a wonderful wife: she is quiet, pretty, an excellent cook, plus she sings and, as he knows from one, perhaps ill-advised, professional experience, is certainly not lacking skill in the boudoir. Plus, she's somehow, still, gentle and kind, even given what she's been through, what she goes through every day. Lyman and everything else, it's enough to harden and embitter anyone, but Mercy remains herself. Maybe it's that, over the years, we just become more like who we really are deep down, Alexander thinks. Which is certainly no compliment to himself.

Alexander had never married, and he regrets that in an abstracted, wistful sort of way. There had just never really been the right time. As a young man, he'd come close, once, but it hadn't worked out, and then there were some troubles he'd had, and then the war and what followed after and, now, here he was, years later, an old man with no wife, no family to call his own. But such is life. In some ways, though, he's glad that he *is* old now, even with the aches and pains and problems pissing, the nights awake, tossing and turning in his bedroll. In many ways, it's easier. Simpler, more than being young ever was. Being old is pleasant in that he can sit by a pretty girl of a morning, drinking coffee and feeling comfortable with her, lacking the need to flirt or otherwise try to get under her skirts. It can be melancholy, maybe, but it's a sweet sadness that only hurts a bit, remembering those other days. From time to time, he still gets the randy urge, of course, but, by and large, the needs he has for women now are these moments of quiet companionship, content simply to be near them, enjoying their presence in the world.

His reverie is interrupted by Ridley throwing himself down by the fire, chattering about the mules and the weather and whatever else comes into his head, in a voice that's overloud for a morning, particularly for those given to whiskey headaches. Oliver sits down as well, and Alexander doesn't need to look at him to know that the man feels fine; the Black Hercules seems to have an immunity from hangovers, no matter how much he drinks. Alexander supposes it's something to do with his size. It's irksome, is what it is, he thinks but, fortunately, Oliver isn't the type to gloat about this fact, merely murmurs, "How you feel, old man?" Already knowing the answer but simply being polite.

Before Alexander can respond, Ridley says, "Are you sick, Dr Potter? Is it your cough? Can I get you anything?" He's already halfway to his feet before Alexander is able to wave him down, explaining yet again that he needs nothing but this coffee and a bit of quiet, thank you. It isn't that Ridley is dim, per se, he simply suffers from the self-absorbed oblivion of youth. Most mornings Potter is hungover to one degree or another and, most mornings, Ridley is blithely unaware that the malady from which the doctor suffers is brought on by liquor and will cure itself in time. For his own part, Alexander is again tempted, hearing that abrasive voice cutting into his headache every morning, to spend an evening getting Ridley so fearfully drunk that, the next morning, the boy would have some new perspective on the merits of a quiet breakfast after a night of drinking. By the time Alexander's hangover has worn itself out, though, he knows the desire would pass. Ridley is what, fourteen? Fifteen? He'll discover the wages of drink soon enough on his own, particularly given his current company.

By the time the bacon is ready, Alexander feels back to halfway normal again by virtue of coffee and the smell of cooking pork. Mercy scoops up a plate for him, with several slices and a portion of eggs, well seasoned with the herbs and wild onions she seems to be able to find wherever they go. They're all quiet as they eat, hunkered down under the tarp spread between two trees. Fan wanders over and takes a small piece of bacon before heading back to his tent. The Chinaman seems to live on nothing but opium smoke and the occasional bite or two of breakfast. Lyman is nowhere to be seen; for a fat man, he lives on nothing at all, unless it's the expensive brandy he drinks.

"How far we going today, chief?" Oliver asks, finally, as they sit back, nursing a last cup of coffee. Ridley is helping Mercy clean the dishes, chattering on as he bangs pans around. *Was I ever so young?* Alexander thinks, watching him.

He shrugs. "Not far," he says. "Down the river a ways and south, would be my guess. I expect Lyman has a spot already picked out." They need to get away from the town they're camped outside, but not too far, before they receive whoever may visit. Lyman has the distance down to something of a science: they'll set up near enough to encourage their guests, if they have them, but not so close that the citizens of the town would decide to come find them, on the off-chance they realized just what it was that Dr Potter and the medicine show had brought into their little town.

"How far, you think?" Oliver trails off. He lowers his voice. "And what about…"

"Hell, I don't know, Oliver. Lyman hasn't told me exactly so I won't guess, all right?" Alexander stands up, cutting him off and knocking back the last of his coffee, suddenly angry, which happened more and more these days. "What I do know is that I need to evacuate my fucking bowels, so perhaps you'll excuse me." He stomps off, aggravated at himself for snapping at Oliver. He knows Oliver is just nervous, same as him, even as he tries not to think about what they're planning to do.

Finding a likely spot tucked back in the bushes, he drops his pants and squats, after checking for the three-lobed leaves of the poison ivy he's rubbed his bare ass against more than once in this wretched Oregon country, this soggy overgrown fucking place where you can't even shit safely. After a time spent heaving and grunting, his anger at himself, then the land, has worked its way to his stoppered bowels. It had been days since he'd had a good movement; no amount of coffee seemed to help, which he knows is a side effect of all the Sagwa he's drinking for his cough and to flavor his whiskey, to help him stop thinking and remembering. Opium dries the bowels like nothing else; soon enough he'll be so bound up that he'll have shit coming out of his mouth, he thinks. Actual shit, not just the sales patter he spewed during the show. Pulling his trousers back up, he resolves to lay off the Sagwa at least until he is able to defecate again. He wonders how Ah Fan does it; the man is thin as a rail, but perhaps there is some Oriental secret to keeping regular when on the pipe. Or perhaps that is why the man never eats more than a bite or two: he simply has no room. Alexander himself feels taut and bloated, his belly sticking out hard and tight in front of him.

He stomps back to the camp, irritable and out of sorts, full of days-old shit, angry thoughts, and foreboding about what's ahead of them. He realizes that his hands are shaking again. *We travel together.* He yells at the others with more venom than is necessary, hollering at them to get packed up so that they can get on the fucking road. As he goes over to break his own camp, he sees that Lyman is back, standing in front of the special black tent, smiling that unctuous smile and holding out a pocket watch. Rhoades nods at him and then unlocks the chain that secures the front of the tent, winking as he ducks inside. Alexander quickens his pace but, before he gets far enough away, he hears Rula start up.

7.

"NO, LISTEN, SOL, *we can't do this*," Ag is saying. "We just can't. I can't even believe you're considering it."

They're sitting next to one another by the fire, heads together, whispering furiously even though the dentist, if he's still awake, is yards away. It's bitterly cold for May. Their breath smokes and a wind is up that cuts through their clothes and pulls the fire over sideways. The moon is tucked behind one of the hills and the stars are hard and icy sharp above them. So far, Ag Rideout is mightily unimpressed with life outside the ranch, particularly this outlaw's life he's somehow fallen into. To date, it has been nothing but wearisome and scary, running as they are, his only company being his fool of a brother and the constant bickering and, now, this frigid wind that gets up under his clothes and bites at his skin. Every shadow likely hides some fearsome creature, a cougar or a bear or the like, or, worse, the law finally come to hang them, should they be able to find a tree high enough in and around all this scrub and sagebrush. More likely the posse will just beat on them a while before taking them back to Boise or Twin Falls to make a spectacle of their deaths, to shame their mother's good name with the evidence of their own black deeds. And now his idiot brother is convinced that they should *stay* outlaw, that they take up this drunken dentist's offer of a job to kill some man in Portland.

Sol brushes aside his brother's complaints with a raised hand. "Shut up, Ag. It's not like we got much choice. Perhaps you recall: *I* suggested that we just fucking rob this fellow, but no, *no*, that was too cruel for poor, sensitive Ajax Agamemnon Rideout. You remember that? And now, here we are, offered gainful employment, a fair wage for a difficult task, and *that* don't sit right with you, either. What the fuck *are* we going to do then, Ag? We're flat fucking broke, and I for one am not going to go crying home to Mama for help. I will not do that. So, you holding out on a mess of money? Maybe you got gold nuggets up your asshole? That it? Well, shit some out, son, and we can go to San Francisco like you wanted, get work in a saloon or livery stable or a cathouse or something. I know: maybe we can *buy* a cathouse with that butthole gold of yours, and live the rest of our days in the company of beautiful young ladies, drinking whiskey and making love like a couple of fucking pashas. That work better for you?" He snorts in disgust.

In reality, Sol is far less sanguine about the idea of becoming a gun for hire than he lets on. Even though this opportunity has landed right in their laps, which is perhaps a sign of divine providence, it feels wrong. In a fight and, to be fair, drunk, he knows now that he could kill a man, if called upon, as much as it keeps him up at night. But, as he sees it, it had been a matter of that man's life or his little brother's. Ag is a fucking fool, but he's family and that counts for something. The idea of just up and shooting some stranger he doesn't know, though, some respectable city doctor, in cold blood, just because another man had paid him to do so, that doesn't sit quite square in his mind. If a man has a grudge against another, one that was so severe as to require violence, fine, fair enough: that man should just deal with it himself. Paying someone to do your own dirty work doesn't seem right although, Sol supposes, that's the way of the world more often than not, if one has money.

What Sol hopes is that they can just travel along with this dentist fellow towards Portland and that, during the trip, Sol can convince his brother to go along with his original goddamn plan, to rob the dentist and go their own way. Really, it's the only sensible thing to do and it's only right for them to take advantage of the opportunity they've been given. They'll never have an easier chance for fast, safe money like this. Robbing the man is a bit cold, Sol knows, but far less of a black fucking mark on their souls than murder for hire. Ag is simple and easily led; Sol is sure that, given enough time, he'll be able to sway his brother to the task at hand. Then, once they had some money, they could go to San Francisco or wherever, maybe open up a dry goods store or something along those lines. Although, now that he'd said it, running a string of girls sounds like a fine line of business for a young gentleman such as himself.

From where Josiah is lying, trying to stay warm and sipping at another bottle of whiskey to kill the ache in his head, he can hear the two men murmuring to each other, arguing with some heat in low voices. From time to time they glance his way. He expects that they are debating when and how to rob or kill him, maybe both, but finds that he doesn't care. He wants it, death, but he knows that he is too big of a coward to take the requisite steps himself. His plan, such as it had been, had simply been to go out to the desert, drink all his whiskey, and then hope that he'd somehow expire, of starvation, exposure, maybe eaten by some wild thing. It's all the same to him. It would have been far easier to put a pistol to his head but he lacks the strength, perhaps due to some tattered remnant of his Christian faith, perhaps simply out of that cowardice. It doesn't much matter. He'll wind up dead one way or another, soon enough.

But he wants to take the Chock-a-Saw's Dr Hedwith with him, drag him down to Hell to pay for what he'd done. For what he'd taken from Josiah. His hate wars with his apathy, though, this lack of caring about whether these criminals with whom he finds himself will kill him, Josiah, or just rob him and leave him to die afoot in the desert. Perhaps he remains more of a Christian than he realizes, as he feels it a question best left to the Almighty. If God wants Hedwith dead, as seems right and proper to Josiah, the Lord will deliver His servant from the clutches of desert criminals and bring all of them to Hedwith as the instruments of his, Josiah's – or His, God's – wrath. If Josiah presumes on the territory of the Almighty, he will die in these wild lands to the west of Boise. It's really that simple. Although, perhaps his desire to put the decision in the hand of God is less a result of his threadbare faith than that apathy, this bleak heaviness that's laid upon him since losing Mary.

Really, the only thing that retains his interest any more is liquor, and that only as a vehicle of forgetfulness. When he drank until he passed out, dropping over a saloon table or in the street somewhere, he rarely dreamt of his wife, of her sickness, of what came after, the mad things he'd seen. He just passed from one moment to the next, dropping off sick and waking up sicker, with a splitting head, like as not covered in filth. The pain and disgust were distractions in and of themselves, keeping his mind from thoughts of Mary and Hedwith and the impotent rage he felt. No one in town had cared, not really, no one listened to the things he said; they thought him merely a grief-stricken drunk. They were kind and solicitous until they weren't, until their patience ran out. But they hadn't been there, hadn't seen the things he'd seen.

Josiah levers himself upright on an elbow, the better to get at the lowered level of liquor in the current bottle. The two men across the fire cease their whispering, looking at him with the wind-whipped flames glinting in their eyes. Looking more closely at them now, he realizes that they aren't much more than boys. The tall one looks wild-eyed and scared, the squat one sullen, but both are young, callow and nervous. He wonders just how much experience they've had at the job for which he's hired them. But these are the men that providence, or mere chance, has put before him. The Lord truly does work in mysterious ways.

"Don't suppose you'd let us have a little of that whiskey, partner?" Sol asks, hopefully. The dentist doesn't say anything, just shakes his head as he drains the last couple of swallows, gasping as he tosses the bottle into the brush. *Really? The nerve of some fucking people*, Sol thinks. It's fucking cold out tonight, with that wind up; the least the dentist could do was share a little bit of his goddamn whiskey. They'd saved his fucking life, nearabouts anyway, and it looks like he's already had plenty to drink, after all. Sol's temper is coming up and he has half a mind to cross the fire and give the man a kicking, on general fucking principle, when the dentist says, "Saddlebag," wiping his mouth with the back of his hand. "More in my saddlebag. Go ahead and bring a bottle over, young man."

Sol's temper dampens as quickly as it had raised. He's a hothead, for certain, but is generally unable to hold a grudge for long, aside from the myriad and long-lived grievances he has against his brother. "Thank you, Josiah," he says. "That's right neighborly of you." He tosses his chin at Ag. "Go on then, Rideout, grab that whiskey that Mr McDaniel here has been kind enough to offer."

"Why do I have to get it?"

"Jesus, Ag, because you're fucking closer, all right? Just get the goddamn whiskey and stop moaning for once." Sol shakes his head, looking mournfully at Josiah. "Do you have brothers, Mr McDaniel? I wouldn't recommend the practice, as a general rule."

Ag unwinds his long body in a huff and stomps over to where the bags lie, bending down and rooting around until he finds a bottle. He stands back up, opening the whiskey and taking a long swallow, gagging a bit.

"Well, come on now, Ag, bring it over," Sol hollers.

Agamemnon just glares at his brother, the steely effect of which is spoiled by a greasy belch as the whiskey repeats on him. He forces himself to take another swig, to make a point, and then slowly saunters back to the fire, ignoring his brother's outstretched hand, passing the bottle to the dentist. "Much obliged," he says, muffling another belch. He can feel Sol's angry stare boring into the side of his head when he sits back down, but chooses to ignore it, concentrating instead on keeping his stomach from flipping around as the whiskey takes hold. Aside from some youthful forays around the ranch and the time in Twin Falls, he's new to drinking with intent, and finds that he lacks some skill at the endeavor.

Sol himself is a natural; when Josiah has taken several

long swallows and the bottle at last makes its way to him, he upends it without delay. Blowing out a hot rush of liquor-fired breath, he whoops a bit and smacks his lips. "Now, that does hit the spot, Mr McDaniel, and I again thank you." He pauses to quietly belch, and then to think, wanting to broach a touchy subject but unsure of how to proceed. "We're going to Portland, then, you say, sir?"

Ag looks at his brother. "Well, obviously we are, Sol. The man already told us that, if you'll recall." He rolls his eyes, shaking his head and sending Josiah a conspiratorial look.

Sol gives his brother a narrow stare. "Yes, I *recall* that, Agamemnon; thank you for your input. Perhaps if *you'd* not flapped your generous gums in interruption, I could carry on with my interlocution of our employer here." He holds a placating palm out to Josiah as he takes another long sip of the whiskey before passing it to his left. "You'll excuse my brother, sir; I'm afraid to say that he is in fact a bit of a simpleton, inclined to chatter when his betters are conversing. Now, hush yourself, Ag, and let the adults speak."

Josiah says nothing, eyes on the bottle as Ag raises it to his lips, accepting it as it comes around his way again. He drinks deeply, feeling the hot sweet burning all the way down into his chest.

"Now, sir," Sol continues, "earlier, when we spoke about the job to hand and your desirousness to hire two rough rascals like Mr Rideout and myself, well, I'll just say that you seemed to be doing a bit poorly – at the time – and perhaps some details germane to the task were lost in the telling, per se. What I would like to know now, though, is if there are a few more notions about our employ that you would be able to give us, to enlighten us, if you will, about our present employment and your particular desires, thereof, per se." Sol has little experience speaking to educated men but understands that, in such cases, the accepted practice is to use the maximum number of words to convey a given concept, the mark of a heavy thinker.

"Now," he says, "we don't necessarily *require* a whole barrel-full of details and particulars to *do* our job, forthwith, but, I'm thinking that, perhaps, the *more* information we have about the labors for which you have engaged us, the better our chance of ultimate success in said endeavor, per se." He also doesn't quite fathom the exact meaning of *per se*, reckoning it merely a Latin phrase that learned men use to indicate a verbal pause, something that drew attention to the fact that the previous sentence had contained a generous fucking helping of information, and that more of the same followed. Sol puts his hands out, invitingly, as if suggesting that his employer contribute the next phase of the conversation, a discourse between two erudite gentlemen of the world.

Josiah just stares at Sol, wondering why the boy's verbiage has quite suddenly grown thorny and syllabic, to the detriment of clarity. He's having difficulty following. Particularly given the amount of whiskey he's imbibed over the last few hours, which affects his powers of concentration.

Sol misunderstands his employer's confusion for reticence, and worries that he's committed some callow faux pas.

"Mr McDaniel," he continues, hurriedly, "if you don't feel comfortable enlightening us about further details and ramifications of the particulars of our employment, at this temporal moment, that's just fine. We can still do our job and understand and comprehend fully and completely your fucking parameters for our employ, don't we, Ag? If you'll excuse my rough language, sir," he adds.

Ag looks at him, a baffled expression on his face. He'd been focused on his stomach for most of his brother's monologue and, when he began paying attention, couldn't quite pick up the thread of just what Sol was on about.

Josiah, for his part, finally makes the connection that Sol is asking to know more about just what he, Josiah, has hired them to do. "What is it you want to know, Mr Parker?" he says. "I told you, I simply want you to kill one man on my behalf: Dr Morrison Hedwith, currently of Portland, Oregon. Is that not enough for you? It seems fairly straightforward to me."

Sol raises his hands, palms out, making pushing motions away from himself. "Now, now, sir, that *is* true: you did indeed impart to us that very important tidbit of information, yes. I suppose, what I'm asking, per se, is, well, why?"

"Why what, Mr Parker?"

"Well, why do you *want* us to shoot this gentleman, Mr McDaniel? Is it because of your teeth? Is he the one that did you poorly, dentally speaking? Now, my brother and I are not the type to judge, of course, and that's your own business, sir, but maybe just a firm beating for this scoundrel is more in line with what the Good Book would say on the subject, that *tooth for a tooth* line, if I remember it rightly?" He shrugs. "We're happy to shoot the man, but maybe you want to think this through a mite? I do reckon that your teeth are your livelihood, kind of an advertisement for your services and all, but–"

"Are you gentlemen married men, Mr Parker, Mr

Rideout?" Josiah interrupts. "Have sweethearts, maybe?
No? Well, I was married. I was married to a lovely girl,
my Mary. Mary O'Brian, maybe you know the family?
No? Prominent in our state, prominent. Her father is a
respected rancher to the south." Josiah pauses, taking
another drink of whiskey from the near-empty bottle
when it comes his way. His head feels hot and loose now,
even in the freezing, biting wind. The more he speaks,
the looser it gets, as if it's expanding on the stem of his
neck, swelling as he talks.

"I would have sparked my Mary had she been the
daughter of the poorest sod farmer, though, gentlemen.
The poorest. If you'd seen her..." he pauses, trailing off,
looking into the darkness with unfocused eyes, "... if
you'd *seen* her, you would have too. She was so small,
barely this high." He raises a hand above his head.
"Well, maybe taller than that, but just a little thing.
Probably ninety pounds soaking wet, with the tiniest
wristbones you ever saw. I could put my thumb and little
finger all the way around them." He holds up a hand,
demonstrating. "I'm not a big man, but when I was with
her she fit right into my arm. Like we were made for one
another, from the very start. It's tiresome, having to look
up at a woman all the time. You wouldn't understand,
Mr Rideout, tall as you are, but you know what I mean,
I'm sure, Mr Parker." Sol bristles, but Josiah continues,
oblivious, lost in the telling.

"Mary had the thickest, softest hair, straight as long
grass. It came almost down to her waist when she let it
down. She'd never had it cut, never. I loved watching
her brush it at night, over and over and over, long,
slow strokes. Sometimes I'd take the brush and do it
myself. So thick, and shiny too, dark as a crow's wing.
Dark as a crow's wing." He pauses, the whiskey bottle

resting in his lap, abandoned.

"But she got sick, not a year after we married. She started to cough, a horrible deep cough that was too big for such a small girl. Too deep. She coughed so much and her ribs would ache so fiercely she could hardly breathe. I'd heat up little sacks of cornmeal for her, hold them to her sides at night because she'd get so sore from all the coughing. And when the blood started coming up, well, we both knew what it was, even before she saw the doctors. Oh, we knew…" He trails off again, shrugging, remembering the whiskey in his lap and taking another long swallow, finishing the bottle.

Josiah is quiet for so long that Sol thinks he's finished. He's getting ready to speak when the dentist starts again, in a voice so low that both he and Ag have to lean forward to hear.

"Then they came," Josiah says. "With wagons and tents and a miracle cure. I knew it was nonsense, of course, that there's only one cure for consumption: a warm, dry climate, rest, a helping of luck or God's mercy, but Mary had heard wonders about a new tonic, one that cured everything from barrenness to the plague and anything in between. At heart she was a simple girl. Innocent. She simply wouldn't rest until she tried it. And what could it hurt, I thought? Really, what could it hurt?" He clenches his fists, rubbing his knuckles on his temples, scratching through his dusty hair. "It wouldn't do any good, but what could it hurt?" He looks up, a gleam in his eye.

"So we bought a bottle, right there at the show. A little bottle, just a few ounces. And you know what? The stuff really *did* seem to work, for a time. Mary coughed a little less and felt a little better. But, then again, why wouldn't she? The tonic was just alcohol and opium, with some weedy rubbish thrown in for effect. Why, *I* felt better when I tried a couple spoonsful." He smiles, wanly.

"Well, that first bottle didn't last long but, if she wasn't getting cured, she also wasn't getting worse and her coughing wasn't so rough of an evening. I went to the medicine show's camp to buy more, but they'd left by then, though I was told they'd be passing back through Boise as their circuit continued. Mary's improved health over the last few days was more of a reprieve than I'd hoped for, really, but I was still making plans for us to go to Los Angeles or Santa Fe or somewhere else dry and warm, somewhere that might help her." The weak, wan smile fades.

"By the time the medicine show came back to Boise, Mary's health was declining again, so I returned to their camp to buy another few bottles. *A new formula*, I was told. *Something special. Something stronger, different, even more efficacious*. That's what the man told me. *Efficacious*. I returned home, then, and Mary started this new bottle of the Chock-a-saw Sagwa Tonic. But something went wrong. Something went very wrong. That bottle *was* different, somehow." He spits the last words out. "It was different, and it took my Mary from me, from one night to the next. Just like that."

He flicks his fingers out as if blowing away a puff of dander.

Josiah hangs his head. When he lifts it back up, long moments later, trying to drink from the empty bottle, he has tears in his eyes. After a long, fumbling second he realizes the bottle is empty and hurls it away, hearing it break on a rock in the darkness.

Sol and Ag look at each other, embarrassed at the man's outward show of emotion. There is an awkward, uncomfortable silence, until Ag breaks it. "It killed her, did it, Mr McDaniel? Poisoned?" he asks in a soft voice.

"That's a terrible thing, sir, and I sure am sorry that you had to go through that. I can't even imagine." Ag is a kindhearted boy; in his mind's eye he sees an image of one of his little sisters, wrapped in a shroud for burial, a bloodstained cloth and empty medicine bottle by the bedside. He feels his own eyes tearing up a bit.

Josiah looks up at the brothers, the firelight gleaming in his eye and an odd smile on his face. He wipes the back of his hand across his lips. "Killed her? No, sirs, no: I never said it *killed* her. No, gentlemen. Not my Mary. Not exactly." He shakes his head, still smiling that twisted, strange smile. "It didn't kill her, no." He wipes his lips again, then slaps his hands on his knees and rises unsteadily, making his way over to the saddlebags for one of the last bottles of whiskey that remains. The wind howls overhead, pulling at the fire, and the moon has just peeked above the hills.

"No," he says, looking back. "It was much, much worse than that."

8.

AT LYMAN'S SHOUT, Oliver pulls the mules to a stop. Lazy Bucephalus halts immediately, nosing for grass. Incitatus, as always, tries to keep going for several steps, as if making a personal statement, succeeding only in twisting the harness between them. Driving the animals is a constant struggle between their two opposing ideals, although each is as stubborn as their species suggests and both are free and canny with their flashing hooves. Bucephalus had once, in his wilder youth, stomped a prowling catamount to death, returning to his graze moments later in a state of complete unconcern, calmly stepping over the corpse of his adversary. As Oliver steps down to unhitch the mules, he makes a wary circle around the ungrateful creatures.

As he's loosing them, Lyman comes trotting up on his thin bay mare. There are few things more foolish-looking than a fat man on a skinny horse, Oliver thinks. Man looks like a pumpkin on a fence rail. "Where's Potter?" Lyman calls over, turning the horse in a showy circle. He fancies himself an equestrian.

Oliver jerks his head toward the wagon. "Inside, suh."

Over the years he's spent with Dr Potter, since the war, Oliver has mostly broken himself – at Alexander's urging

– of the habit of calling all white men *sir*, at least those whites he works with in the show, or comes in regular contact with. Strangers are a different matter, but that is just the way of the world, even after Emancipation; being a free man didn't make you an equal. But the white folk in the show he just calls by their Christian names, and they call him Oliver. It's a strange thing, but one that he likes. Oliver is a big man, but it's still easy to get to feeling small, when everyone called you *boy* or *nigger* all the time.

Lyman he always calls *Mr Rhoades*, or *sir*. At least to the man's face; behind his back, speaking with Alexander out of earshot, they might use other words, harsher words. Whisper them, but even that is a risky proposition. Mr Rhoades has ways of knowing things, and he damn sure isn't a man to rile, fence-rail pumpkin that he might be.

"Well, what is he doing, boy? Is he passed out drunk again?" Lyman looks up at the sky. "It'll be night before too long and we have preparations to make."

Oliver nods. Yes, they have preparations. He tries to keep his voice steady. "Yes, suh. I expect he's tending to Rula and the others, Mr Rhoades. I expect so, suh, yes I do." With Lyman, Oliver can't help but lapse back into the marble-mouthed, ignorant-sounding *yah-suh, no-suh* bobbing and shuffling bullshit he'd grown up with in Texas. *Acting like a field nigger again*, he thinks, disgusted with himself, nothing but a big dumb nigger, even as he hunkers and casts down his eyes. Trying to look small and inoffensive, someone less than who he is, really, and that's a man who can read a book and holds a paying job and who has learned something about this world. "You want I should get him, suh?" He feels that he should be twisting a ratty old hat in his hands.

"I'm right here, Oliver," Potter says, crawling out of

the back of the wagon, tying the canvas loops tightly back together behind him. "Did you want something, Lyman?" He's casual, calm, or at least sounds that way to Oliver.

"How are they, Doctor?" Lyman asks, smiling his rubber-lipped smile, nodding towards the wagon in which Rula and the others travel.

"About what you'd expect. This the place, then?" Alexander looks around. They're in a little clearing, a soggy, low, grassy spot wedged in between the looming Douglas firs that make up these Cascadian forests. Around the clearing are clumps of ferns and some twining vine, wrapped around the trees, that looks like poison oak. When he steps down from the wagon, the ground is spongy underfoot. "Bit open, isn't it?"

Lyman shakes his head. "*Our* spot is just up that path, there," he points, "where that deer trail goes past those big rocks. Just there." He pulls his ornate gold pocket watch out from his coat, ostentatiously, checking the time and giving it a judicious wind. "Get everyone settled in, then. We're going to be busy later. And you might try to get some rest after dinner, Dr Potter: you look like shit, and we have a long night ahead of us." Lyman turns his skinny horse, Llamrei – Lyman had insisted on naming the stock – with a flourish, and rides off into the trees, following the narrow path.

"Would you look at that fat fool," Alexander says.

"Like a damn tick on a shinbone, back of that horse," Oliver mutters.

Alexander gives a cheerless laugh, slapping Oliver on a meaty shoulder. He sighs. "I guess we should get to it, then." Best if they just get on with their usual work; there's little else they can do, now, aside from waiting and hoping that they are as ready as they can be. Best to stay busy, try not to think. Alexander touches the bottle in his pocket, trying to steady his trembling hand.

"How are they?" Oliver asks, nodding towards the wagon. "Really?"

"About what you'd expect, Oliver. About what you'd expect." He has a bleak look on his face, remembering other nights.

"What do you think's gonna happen tonight, Alex?"

"I don't know," he says, shaking his head. "Maybe something. Maybe nothing. I don't know."

"Maybe something bad."

"Maybe. But what do you want to do? You want to just fucking give up? I don't." He feels old, just now, more so than usual, even. Tired. He prods at a tooth with his tongue. "How are you feeling? I mean lately. You know it will be bad tonight, regardless of what else happens. You sure you're up for it?" They've deliberately not talked of what the consequences of success will be, skirted around the issue entirely.

Oliver shrugs. "It's always bad, old man. You know that. I expect we'll just have to do what we can."

Later, when the mules and horses are fed and hobbled, the tents up, and Mercy is cooking dinner over the fire that Ridley, after several aborted wet starts, had made, Alexander sits in the back of the hooped wagon, sipping Sagwa-laced whiskey and listening to Rula and the others as they fuss and fret. Tonight they'd stay in the wagon, not their tent. It was safer. All three have been restless since he'd fed them earlier. They always knew, somehow, when Lyman was working. Alexander can feel it, too, feel his blood shifting in his veins, even though the business is still hours off yet. He doesn't much believe in Lyman's conjunctions; he reckons the way he feels, now, is only some kind of sickness picked up from Lyman himself. Contact insanity, something like that. Whatever the cause, the symptoms themselves are real. Real enough to Rula and the rest, to be certain, listening to them now. Perhaps there truly is something to Lyman's astrological tables, then. His mystical bullshit.

Alexander knocks back a shot of whiskey and then takes a sip from his flask: the other Sagwa, the special mixture. The one that keeps him alive. He feels his blood shift even more, resonating with whatever is in the stuff, threatening to pull him out; he grits his teeth and focuses on remaining inside himself, keeping it all in check as he's done for so many years now. He'd never tell Oliver, but these last months he's been feeling worse, much worse, more out of control than usual. His persistent cough is only a symptom of a greater malaise, so he's been using the special Sagwa more and more, trying to keep it all under wraps. He worries that tonight will put him over the edge, one way or another. He tries to push any thoughts of what's coming from his mind, tries to just focus on the present, but he's less than successful and it looms up in front of him. You only have one simple thing to do, he tells himself. Lyman's guard will be down, for once. Don't overthink it.

The Halfhead gives a laughing bark like a hyena, clutching his doll closer. He rocks from side to side, shaking his malformed skull. Holly's stalks are waving wildly back and forth; her face is pressed against the bars of her cage and the red eyes at the ends of her stalks seem to seek Alexander out. Rula just sounds her low, weeping moan, deep in her throat, a sound that rends the ears. Holly and the Halfhead have been with Alexander for years now, so long that he's forgotten how they'd once been. Rula, though, Rula is new enough that every time Alexander sees her, he doesn't see the shapeless, mouthless, weeping mass of flesh with the cloudy blue eyes. He still sees her as she'd been, that first night. Every one of her moans feels like another indictment of his weakness, his complicity. His cowardice.

He reaches into his pocket yet again, touching the bottle and the handkerchief.

Dr Potter knows that, if there is any road back, any way to save himself, tonight is his chance. His life has been a long, black dream, and yet he's clung to it, done all that he could to keep it. He's not sure why, even now. Maybe the war changed him, before Hedwith had. The stink of smoke and blood and shit. The screams and prayers. The piles of limbs outside the tent wall, built up hour after hour as he sawed away the minié balls' work, day after day. At first it had been a horror, and then became just a labor, the severed arms and legs evoking no more emotional response than a pile of cordwood. Particularly when he'd started drinking too much whiskey and using the laudanum in earnest to cope with what he saw. He'd watched so many boys and men die, calling for their mothers or their sweethearts, begging him for help as if he, a mere doctor, had some power to save them. The only ones that went peacefully were the ones who were unconscious. Is that what waits for him, then, something dark and horrible that only the dying see? Is that why he's so afraid, why he's grabbed tight to life, however he can? Even a life like this?

"Oliver said you wanted to see me, Dr Potter?" Ridley's spotty face comes through the canvas flaps and draws Alexander back to the present. For a long moment he doesn't know who the boy is. He's drunker than he should be, he realizes. With a deliberate effort, he caps the bottle of whiskey. He'll need his head about him tonight.

"Yes, that's right, Ridley. Come in, have a seat, son." He pats a folded tarp on a barrel beside him. "I need you to do something for me tonight, all right?"

"Sure, Doctor, anything." Ridley is as eager as usual.

"Now, it's not a big thing, but it needs to be done right. I need you to watch these three with particular attention tonight, son. Particular."

Ridley deflates a bit. Watching the Halfhead and the rest is a normal part of his job, most nights. He'd hoped that the doctor was going to ask him to go with them, with him and Oliver and Mr Rhoades. He knew they did *something*, these kinds of nights, and he wants to find out what it is. He deserves to know; he's a part of the show too. Maybe he'll be less uneasy if he just knows what it is. One night, weeks ago, he'd tried to sneak off and go after them but Mercy had caught him and kept him in the camp. She wouldn't tell him why, and she hadn't answered his questions since.

"This is serious, Ridley. I've had Mercy keep watch of them, before, these kinds of nights, but you're a responsible young man and I think you can be trusted with this." Really, he just wants Ridley kept in camp for sure tonight. Mercy had told him about the last time: it had only been blind luck that she'd gone off to make water and came across the boy trying to follow Oliver to where Lyman had set up; she'd caught him and kept him from trouble. It isn't ideal, Ridley watching the cages, but it's better than him stumbling into what they're up to. Particularly tonight, of all nights, it's even less safe than usual. There will be time for explanations later. Maybe.

"Sure, Dr Potter. You bet."

Alexander takes a deep breath. "Listen, it's going to be different tonight. You can probably already see that they're worked up, and I can tell you right now that it's going to get worse. I'll explain later. Tonight, though, I need you to just stay here with them, calm them down as best you can. They know you by now, they like you. Sing to them, maybe. Hell, I don't know. Just try to keep them occupied."

"Why are they worked up?"

"Never mind that. Now, this is important, Ridley, so pay attention. You need to just try to not listen to them, if they start talking. Well, not Rula, but the other two. Just ignore what they say. It will only be nonsense anyway and if you try to talk back to them, it's just going to make them more antsy and maybe hurt them. You wouldn't want to hurt them, would you, son? Their lives are hard enough as it is."

"No, sir."

Alexander can tell that the boy is confused, but there's nothing to be done about it. He just hopes that Ridley won't overhear anything that will get him in a state. The Halfhead rarely speaks any more, and of course Rula can't but, from time to time, Holly will start screaming things that no one should hear. Again, he knows that he needs to be rid of Ridley, for the boy's own good, if tonight doesn't work out. Although, *if* tonight doesn't work out, Alexander isn't sure that he himself will still be around, or at least capable of making any decisions: he'll most likely be in a hole in the ground, like Colonel Batts, if not suffering some worse fate. Best not think about any of that, though.

"All right, then," he says, slapping Ridley on a knee. "Let's get some dinner and some rest. It will likely be a long night tonight." He sees that the boy wants to ask questions, so he puts his hands on Ridley's shoulders and gently lifts him up, turning him towards the wagon flap. "Let's get some dinner, son."

•••

Lyman skips dinner, as he does most nights. He rarely needs to eat much more than one small afternoon meal that he makes himself, and some sips of Dr Hedwith's special Sagwa, these days. Brandy, a gentleman's pleasure, of an evening, like the doctor himself. It irks him, therefore, that he remains plump. He is a short man, and short men look particularly foolish when plump, he thinks. He has a sneaking suspicion that the doctor did this to him on purpose, those years ago, another small humiliation to enforce the master-servant relationship. Which he supposes is the prerogative of the man and, really, he can't complain overmuch: with all that the doctor has given him, to complain about a few extra pounds would be churlish.

He takes a sip of Sagwa as he walks the circle, checking for any errors. After all this time, he can draw the forms in his sleep, but he's a meticulous person and the doctor will not tolerate failure. They are close, he knows. Perhaps tonight will provide the key they seek. He looks up at the sky, checking his estimate of the hour against his watch – a gift from Dr Hedwith – pleased to see that his guess is within a few minutes of clock time. Looking back up, he notes the spot where Jupiter will breast the horizon, then looks across to where Venus, the active rising, will transit, though it will be hidden behind the hills to the east for much of the night. Perhaps tonight the great work would finally reach apogee. Then, finally, he can be free of this odious show and the fools that comprise it, no longer the performing monkey and nursemaid that he is now.

Pausing to adjust one tiny outline, he steps back, finally satisfied in his preparations. Lyman knows that he should rest, but he's too keyed up. He looks at the sky again; it's not yet fully dark. When it is, he will

begin the calling. He pulls out his watch again, shielding
it with a palm from the drizzle. They are only a few
short hours from the little town where they'd left the
latest protean Sagwa. If he starts the calling in another
hour, any respondent will arrive well before dawn. It
gets more tricky, as the days grow longer, to time the
work appropriately; the calling needs to finish before
dawn, before the queen, the moon, the incarnation of
becoming, received her king, the ruler of being, for that
brief and magical moment. He knows that if, tonight, he
finishes too early, the becoming will stagnate; too late,
and the being will overwhelm it. It's a difficult task, but
Lyman has had long practice over these many years. He
knows Dr Hedwith tends to scorn the classical forms,
thinking them largely a superstitious remnant of an
ignorant time but, to Lyman, they still hold power. He
sees it firsthand, night after night; he feels it.

Pascal doesn't believe, either, but Pascal is another
problem. Lyman wishes that he could have brought
them together earlier, Dr Hedwith and Dr Levesque,
with himself as the glue to bind them. Hedwith, with
the old knowledge, Levesque on the leading edge of the
new. He'd seen the Frenchman's genius, much as he'd
recognized Dr Hedwith's own, years ago. The fusion,
then, of their two minds making something greater than
their constituent parts, not unlike the joining of the
red and the white itself. Lyman's own contribution to
the great work. But no, no, no, Pascal's presence must
be kept hidden; Dr Hedwith has always insisted on the
strictest secrecy in their labors, the strictest. He mustn't
know how Lyman had summoned Levesque from
France and set him to important experiments. No matter
Lyman's motives, Dr Hedwith mustn't know. It's a mess,
really, the whole situation; convoluted where it could

have advanced the work that much more quickly. Dr Hedwith has always underestimated him. But perhaps he's right, the doctor, as he's been so many times. He's a brilliant man, after all, and they will see an end to the work together. Things must pass as they must.

Lyman takes a step back, surveying the circle one last time, assuring himself that the signs and symbols are in order. For a moment, thinking of the doctor, he second-guesses himself, wonders just how many of the arcane and complicated preparations *are* necessary, in this scientific age, whether the doctor is correct and that he, Lyman Rhoades, is merely hidebound with the traditions and strictures of earlier days. He supposes it doesn't matter: if opaque, mystical trappings are required to accomplish their goal, he'd scribe Solomonic proportions into his own flesh, if that's what it took.

But now, he must focus, become ready. Taking a deep breath, calming himself, he removes the brazier from his saddlebag, unwrapping the thick flannel that protects it and attaching its three small legs. As always, it seems heavier than it should be, given its size. No metal should weigh as much as the small, dull bowl, deeply inscribed with the Hermetic symbols, does; it's too heavy to lift in one hand, even as strong as Lyman is. It's as if the brazier has absorbed something vital, some arcane matter that has thickened and condensed the material far more than other earthly elements. The doctor had simply said, when asked, that the thing was as it was for the reasons it was, an atypically obscure pronouncement from the man.

Remembering, Lyman returns to Llamrei and unties the box he'd secured to the saddle. Looking around, he finds a large, flattish rock nearby and carries the box to it, giving it a fond pat before walking away.

Carefully stepping over the circle now, Lyman places

the brazier in the very center, the location of which he had divined earlier with his geomantic tools, building the signed shape out from around that locus. From one pocket of his coat he removes several large chunks of carbon, simple charred oakwood. Arranging the pieces just so, he draws another small bag from his coat, along with the knife he carries next to his heart. He looks at his watch, glances at the heavens, and waits.

Two hours later, the signs are right and he lights the brazier with a phosphorous match, saying the first words. When the coals are sufficiently glowing, he again consults his watch and then, with a decisive movement, draws the knife over his palm. The blade needs a sharpening and, grimacing, he saws back and forth across his seamed and scarred flesh until the blood flows. Holding his bleeding hand over the brazier, he says the second words, sprinkling the lesser elemental salts from the small bag, chanting as the blood steams and hisses. Lyman's aesthetic sense feels that, at this point, there should really be some flash of light, eerie colors or strange noises but, as always, his blood just sullenly smokes with a coppery smell, faintly augmented by the salts. After the blood stops flowing from his palm, he sits back on his heels, chanting the final words, over and over. He waits, knowing that it won't be long now.

The chanting and the hot scent of the coals lull his thoughts, and he almost misses the first arrivals. A large shape, followed by a smaller, hunched one. Lyman's eyes are almost shut but he can see that the others are rocking slightly, back and forth, in time with his chants. He feels his own blood swelling, drawing upward inside him, pushing at his flesh. Without quieting the words, he draws his small flask from inside his coat and takes a sip.

•••

Oliver had taken some of the special Sagwa earlier in the evening, after he'd left camp for his post-dinner walk. He used the bare minimum, as always, though he was edgy and tense, a feeling he knew would intensify as the evening progressed. Now, at Lyman's fire, he forces himself to keep his hands away from the flask in his pocket, though he feels the need rising hot and fast, calling to him.

Alexander has already succumbed, adding another hefty swig of the Sagwa to that which he'd imbibed earlier, after leaving Ridley. Sitting with Oliver now, he feels that he's just barely holding on, already, though the night is young. He tries to concentrate, but the chanting dulls his mind, the brazier pulls at his thoughts; he can feel something inside himself beginning to separate, to attenuate, leaking away until he begins to panic at his incipient loss of control. Trying to focus himself, he looks upwards into the rain, at the cloudy, looming sky. Even with the thick covering of clouds, his eyes are drawn to where Jupiter is rising, invisible but inexorable. He doesn't know if he's going to make it through the evening, if he'll be able to do what he has to do. Maybe it's already too late: he can feel himself sweating and shaking, his guts flipping around inside him, and it's barely begun. He touches the bottle in his pocket, trying to calm himself, still the jittering of his fingers.

A heavy, strong hand grasps him around the upper arm, squeezing so hard it hurts. Looking over, he sees Oliver, wide-eyed and scared, trying to nod encouragingly at him. He tries on a smile of his own, a sick, lopsided thing, wavering on his lips as he looks up at the big man.

"I think I'm OK," he says in a thin, papery voice. "I'll make it. I'll make it."

Oliver nods, a few times too many before reining

his head back in. "You'll make it, old man. Damn it, that's right. Be over before we know it." He squeezes Alexander's arm again, too tightly. "Be over soon." It's the same, every calling, this pain and sense of dissolution. Whatever the reason, magic or science or whatever it is, it's always the same. They've held it together before and, tonight, they'll damn well hold it together again. They have to. Whenever Alexander is ready, Oliver will do what he can.

"I'll make it," Alexander says again, to himself or Oliver, he's not sure.

Lyman Rhoades smiles to himself, one small part of himself aware, the rest lost in the singsong of the words of calling.

It's hours later, not long before dawn, when the answer comes. Alexander barely has hold of himself. His flask of Sagwa is long empty; he feels so drawn and tight inside that he's sure he will break apart. There's no room in his thoughts for the other thing. No matter how he screams at himself to act, the sickness in his blood has taken over, and he'll have to wait it out. If it doesn't overtake him entirely, that is, as he can feel it threatening to do. The poison inside him is growing stronger as he weakens, Lyman's droning voice calling to it. Oliver has ceased being able to help Alexander keep himself together; he's lost in his own misery, fighting for control. An increasingly large part of Alexander's mind tells himself to just let go, to give in, give up, let the poison free. It wouldn't be that bad. He's seen the others, after all. He should just let go and be done with it.

But no, no, Pascal is counting on him. *This is his chance*. He reaches into his pocket, but his hands are shaking; his eyes are wet and blurry. Alexander feels older than

his years, and what if he misses? What then? Is Lyman's
guard truly down, or is he merely waiting? Alexander
only has this one little bottle. He needs to act, but his
thoughts are scattered, driven away by the need inside
and Lyman's incessant chant; he retains just enough of
himself to listen to his own mantra: *let go, let go, let go.*
Alexander is trying to will the shaking from his hand, to
gather some semblance of courage, when someone steps
into the dim circle of light.

For a moment he doesn't recognize her, and then
her face catches the moon's light. It's the prostitute, the
consumptive girl who'd been working the town, the
name of which he's already forgotten. The girl who'd
once called him medicine man and promised weary
delights back at her room. Her face is so flushed that
it almost looks healthy, if it wasn't for the shine in her
eyes. She doesn't cough. Alexander doesn't remember
giving her some of the special Sagwa, but perhaps he
had. He'd been drinking hard that night, after all. Maybe
she'd taken it from a client or a friend, not knowing what
was in it, and how could she? Whatever the reason, she's
here now, panting, responding to Lyman's summons.
She takes a few quick, short steps towards the brazier,
her eyes focusing hungrily on the smoking coals. She's
breathless, sweaty from the long journey from town.

Alexander looks around, peering into the dark as best
he can, but the girl is alone.

"Hello, my dear," Lyman says, smiling, placing his fat
body between girl and brazier. She ignores him, trying to
edge around and get closer to the coals. "Now, now," he
says, placing his stubby fingers on her arms. "Not quite
yet. No, not quite."

"What is it?" the girl asks. "What's in there?"

"Just wait, love." Lyman strokes her arm, rests his

hands on her shoulders. There's something different about the girl, more than the flushed face and lack of cough. She seems fuller, somehow, she radiates something hot and ruttish. Alexander himself feels a rising in his trousers, taking his mind for a moment away from the need in his blood, the shaking of his hands. He can't tell which arouses him more, the girl or the fire.

"I'll suck your cock," the girl says, wiping her lips, looking up at Lyman beseechingly. She fumbles at his pants. "Please, I want it."

He pushes her hands away. "Now, now," he says again, chidingly, and then slaps her, rocking her head back and starting a slow drip of blood from one of her nostrils. "I said wait." He grabs her chin, tilts her head up so he can look closer into her eyes, shifts her face from side to side, like a man evaluating a horse, eventually pulling away. He seems disappointed. "Maybe," he mutters. He puts a hand on her head, pointing at the ground with his other. "Sit," he tells her, like a dog. "Sit and you'll get what you want."

The girl drops as if her body has gone boneless, flopping to the ground, staring at the brazier, her nose lifted as if trying to catch the faintest scent of smoke. Oliver and Alexander look at one another, knowing what's coming. They step closer to the girl.

"Hold her," Lyman calls, over his shoulder.

They move in, each taking one of her arms. She puts off a furious heat, even in the chill drizzle. Oliver hears her whimper, and tightens his hand around her. Alexander does his best to ignore her heat and her sex, her need that's amplifying his own.

Lyman goes to his bags and removes a battered tin cup, thinly scribed with figures. For such an important part of the work, it's a poor-looking thing, the kind of cup a pauper would have, but it's old and full of power. He can feel it, even empty. Opening the latest flask of the protean Sagwa preparation, he pours in a generous shot, and then lifts a small coal from the brazier with a pair of tongs. He drops it into the cup.

As the contents inside hiss, the girl gives a gasp, her eyes rolling back in her head as if she's in the grip of orgasm. Alexander feels her body begin to shake; he himself feels hotter, tighter, and even in his distraction he can see that Oliver is gritting his teeth.

Lyman looks over and smiles. Clenching his cut hand into a fist, he lifts the steaming cup with the other. "Open," he murmurs to the girl; her mouth gapes hungrily and he pours the liquid down her gullet.

For a second, she goes limp, her eyelids fluttering. There's a long pause and then her body arches upward, her spine bowing. It's all that Oliver and Alexander can do to keep her still; her arms feel as if they'll separate from her shoulders. She fights them, twisting and straining for release, tendons taut on the sides of her neck, the eyes showing nothing but white. A bloody froth is on her lips and then, suddenly, she goes limp again. With a faint moan, she sags, body bent forward on the pivot of her shoulders, her head hanging, fluid dripping from her slack lips.

Lyman watches objectively, hopefully. "Set her down now," he orders. "Lay her back." When Oliver and Alexander lay her on the ground, near the brazier, Lyman squats beside her, running his hand down her arm. "Now we wait."

Alexander walks heavily over to the edge of the little clearing, sitting down and leaning his back against a fir. He's sweating, even in the cold wet air, and feels wrung out, exhausted, too tired to even be afraid any more. His own need has dried up with the girl's struggles – why, he is never sure, but it always passes this way – and he begins to cough. Taking a bottle of the normal Sagwa, he takes a long sip, hoping to loosen the tightness in his lungs. Oliver sits next to him, feeling almost as wretched, and sips from a flask of whiskey, which he passes to Potter. Alexander tries to gather his will; if he's going to act, he needs to do it soon. But he's just so tired. He looks up at the sky, trying to guess the hour. With the clouds and his exhaustion, it's nearly impossible to judge. They have a wait, whether long or short, and the waiting is the worst part of this endeavor.

Get up, old man, he tells himself. *Just get the fuck up. Lyman is as distracted as he'll ever be. You need to move, Potter.*

"What do you think, Alex?" Oliver asks, quietly, looking at the woman. Lyman is sitting near her, a hungry look in his eyes.

Move, Potter. He puts his hand in his pocket yet again, feels the little bottle. *Go, now.*

With the girl, what would come would come. It didn't matter what happened to her, not now. It was done. Best not to overthink it, really. Alexander knows that the mortgage on his own soul is long overdue; what happens to the woman is immaterial. She's merely another in the long series of black marks on the ledger of his life. He finds it difficult to care any more, or so he tells himself, and he'd damned her when he'd given her the Sagwa, if she was here now. He couldn't take it back and there's nothing he can do to stop the resulting train of effect now. He'd do what he could for her, afterward.

But he could make it all end here. Make sure she's the last.

Get up. Move.

Alexander had dispersed the special bottles of the tonic, and only the girl had felt the summons. The others had either not taken the stuff or proven immune to its powers. There's something in the girl that the substance had called to, some weakness or strength in her that resonated with whatever arcane ingredients the Sagwa is comprised of. Alexander knows this from experience, as does Oliver: the Sagwa, in its special form, only affects the damned. Maybe God is judging her.

Lyman watches the girl, trying to judge every nuance as she fitfully sleeps. Something about her tells him that she isn't right, but it's impossible to know. Perhaps his natural cynicism merely keeps him from hoping that, in this pitiful, consumptive wreck of a woman, lies the key to what Dr Hedwith searches for. The thing that will free him, and by extension Lyman himself. The girl's eyes move from side to side, as if in a dream and, from time to time, she gives a little whimper. Her color is off – was it? – and Lyman thinks that he can discern a subtle change in her skin, even in the faint, damp moonlight. It's impossible to tell: the Sagwa affects everyone differently. He wonders if he should have Potter's pet blackamoor build up the fire, to give a bit more light, when the girl suddenly sits up, all at once.

"What?" she says, her eyes blank.

Alexander and Oliver stand, take a step closer. Lyman leans forward, watching, hoping. She looks normal, sitting upright. What he'd seen in her skin had perhaps been just a trick of the light. The woman looks flushed, healthy even with her eyes darting around fearfully. He realizes he'd never asked her name.

"Dear? My dear?" He snaps a finger in front of her rolling eyes. Her gaze slowly comes around to his own. She seems normal, better than normal, really. He remembers her from town, her drawn, sallow face, that racking cough. Now she's the picture of health. Could it be?

"What?" she says again, a bit more intensely. "What?"

Alexander steps forward, looking at the questioning woman, whose face for a moment seems almost beautiful, even given her large nose and spotty skin. On a sudden, time feels slow, lengthened; this is a liminal moment, where anything can happen. The woman could stand up and walk away, she could take Alexander in her arms and kiss him, heal him, she could simply lay down and die, as he's seen too many times. In that long moment, Alexander can see the spittle shining on Lyman's lips, the flat gleam in his eye.

Now.

Alexander reaches into his jacket, wedging his cracked fingernails into the little cork that stoppers the bottle of aconite. He mustn't get any on his skin. One splash into Lyman's face, his eyes. It will only take a second.

He takes another step.

The girl says, "What?" one last time, and then she begins to change.

Her head arches back, too far, and she gives a long, rattling inhale. At that moment, her skin starts to tighten and harden, twisting into dry whorls of flesh, the very beginnings of which Lyman had seen in the dim light. As her flesh shrinks, cracks begin to open, weeping a thin, yellow fluid. Her eyes sink into her face and her arms twist against her chest. She's pulled into a fetal position, gasping a thin whine. One of her shins breaks with a loud crack, like kindling snapped over a knee.

Alexander is moving, pulling the bottle from his pocket, when Lyman turns his way.

It only takes a look, calm and expressionless and yet

knowing, and whatever revolt Alexander had thought he had in him is gone. Just like that. Gone. Emptied. Lyman glances over at Oliver and then returns his attention to the girl.

Alexander's hands are shaking so badly he can barely re-cork the bottle.

Lyman stands and watches the change which, after the initial violence, subsides into a slow, steady drying over the course of a few minutes. After his first disappointment, he looks on dispassionately, wondering idly where it will stop. Alexander can't turn away as the girl dries and twists into something that only vaguely recalls the woman she was; she's become a thing desiccated and contorted, loose in her clothes, barely recognizable as human. Oliver can't watch at all and walks away to the edge of the clearing, wiping his mouth over and over with the back of his hand.

Eventually, after several minutes, Lyman turns to Dr Potter again. "She appears to be done, then, eh?" His voice is dry, flat, hiding his displeasure with the experiment's result. "Alive?"

Alexander shakes his head, looking at the thing that, before he'd given her the Sagwa, had been a woman. "I'm not sure." His voice not much more than a whisper.

"Perhaps you should check, Doctor." His voice invites no dissent.

Alexander squats down on his aching knees, then, putting his trembling fingers to the woman's neck, searching for a pulse. Her skin feels like old, dry leather, bereft of moisture, scaly to the touch. Her body has been so twisted up that it hardly reflects the female form any more; she looks like one of those gnarled, stained things pulled from the bogs of Ireland. He takes her hand. Her fingers have no warmth, no movement, no life. Alexander is gratefully about to pronounce her dead when she gives a quiet whimper, in defiance of her dried throat.

"Well, there you go, then," Lyman says, dusting off his hands. "Can you use her?"

"As what, Lyman? She's barely alive and will be dead soon enough. I don't even know how we'd feed her."

"As what?" Lyman scoffs. "That's your job, Potter. You're the showman. Call her *The Mummy Queen* or the like. Who cares? We might as well make use of her, like the others."

"*The Mummy Queen*?"

"What's wrong with that? Make up some rubbish about Egyptian curses or such. Call her *Gristle Woman*, for all I care. It's not my problem. Not mine." He walks over to his horse, who placidly grazes amongst the dawn-wet ferns.

"How are we even going to feed her, Lyman?" Alexander murmurs. "Look at her."

"Perhaps you didn't hear me the first time, Potter: *it's not my problem*. Just take care of it." Lyman removes the hobbles and mounts his horse, stroking her smooth neck. "I'm tired, and I must prepare my notes, so we'll rest here for a day. No one will be looking for the girl; she was only a whore, after all. A day's rest, yes, then tomorrow we're off west. We're close to home and the doctor will want my report on this circuit. So get to your work, gentlemen." He gives them a long look. Alexander is expecting more, the inevitable but, instead, fat Lyman Rhoades turns his skinny mare with his customary flourish and trots off down the path, back to the tents.

Alexander is still staring at the poor girl when Oliver comes back over. He knows what they need to do.

"What do you think, Alex?" Oliver says. Dreading the

answer, either way. Not mentioning the other thing at all, or maybe that's what he really had meant.

"I don't know how we'd feed her," Alexander says again. "Look at her, Oliver."

"I expect you're right," Oliver says. He reaches into his coat, feeling the straight razor he keeps in an inner pocket. "You want me to…?" He stops, looking at Dr Potter, the razor still in his jacket.

Alexander sighs, passing a shaking hand over his eyes. He'd gratefully pass this to Oliver, but it's something he has to take on himself. One last thing, maybe, if Lyman decides to take his due. It's his responsibility. He's a coward and this is what has come of it. Alexander can't hide from that fact, regardless of what he'd like to tell himself. The truth is that he's nothing but a fucking coward, and this is the result. This is the only thing left that he can do. Lyman will be angry, but none of that matters now, does it?

"I'll do it," he says, reaching out a hand, still looking at the girl. "Hand it to me." Silently, Oliver passes the razor over. Alexander keeps his gaze on the sunken white eyes of the girl, eyes that show no iris or pupil, only blank, bloodshot orbs that twitch from time to time. Taking a deep breath, Dr Potter places the blade on the girl's scaly throat, breathing a silent prayer. He feels Oliver's big hand on his shoulder.

"I'm sorry," he whispers to her. He wonders how many times he's said that phrase, to the Halfhead, to Holly, to Rula, all the rest. He wishes he knew this girl's name. "Trust me, this is for the best."

As he presses down on the razor, the girl's drowned eyes roll forward the slightest bit, focusing on Alexander for a moment. He pauses, wondering if she is still inside herself, hoping and not hoping. The eyes roll back to whites, then, and a ragged breath rattles in her dry throat. Dr Potter waits another long second, and then pulls the blade across her neck, as gently as he can.

They're beginning to dig the nameless girl's grave when there's the sound of a horse and Lyman comes back up the path. He stops Llamrei at the edge of the clearing and points to the box that's sitting on the flat stone by the circle. He ignores the dead girl, the digging, as if he'd expected nothing less.

"Gentlemen," Lyman says, smiling. "I almost forgot. I have another gaff for you, for the black tent. Sometime to amuse the rubes. Yes. I picked it up in town. Go see if it will work for you, and then you can jar it up, later."

"I'm sure it will be fine, Lyman," Alexander says, when he can. Knowing somehow. He can feel the blood draining out of his face, his belly cramping tight.

"No, you must see it," Lyman says again. "Go, go." He flaps his hand towards the box, as if shooing them there. When they don't move, the smile drops away. "*I said go.*"

Alexander stands upright, swaying for a moment. Oliver has to hold his arm until he's steady. They walk over to the box, then, each step heavy and leaden. Alexander fumbles at the latch, with clumsy hands, until the lid is opened.

Pascal Levesque's head stares up at them, eyes half closed. His severed hands are tucked neatly at the sides of his cheeks, his remaining eight fingers cradling them, as if holding his head for a kiss. Oliver takes a step back, gagging, but Alexander just stares. He feels empty now, no longer even frightened about what will be coming, or anything else, really. Simply empty, hollow. Dead. He knows, now, that there is no end to this life, none that he will ever be able to make. He belongs to Lyman.

Now, more than ever.

Lyman chuckles, turns his mare. "We'll speak later, gentlemen. I'll expect to see the new gaff labeled and in the tent by the next show. *Le Rêveur Français,* I think. Yes, that will be an admirable name for the jar. *The French Dreamer.* Poetic, no? Make up a suitable backstory for the placard. Something with a bit of panache, yes? And Potter," he says, over his shoulder, as he taps his heels to Llamrei, "you'll leave what's in your pocket outside my tent."

He rides off, leaving Alexander and Oliver to wonder just who will be the one to tell Mercy.

9.

DR HEDWITH thrashes in his sleep, deep in the dream, sweating, the blankets twisting tightly around him like a burial shroud. He whimpers and moans, pleading through his clenched teeth, asking for more time. It's behind him as it ever is, the same dream, always. A nameless, formless thing, stalking him. Death; it didn't take an alienist to realize that. He begins to shout, which wakes him from the dream into a nighttime terror as he struggles to get out of the tangled bedding, feeling trapped and terrified in his confusion until reason sinks in a few rapid heartbeats later. His chest pounds and, for a moment, he thinks he's pissed the bed, but it's only the sweat of his body, soaked through the sheets.

Hedwith sits up, breathing shakily. With trembling fingers he tries to light the candle by the bed, snapping two matches before managing to get the thing going. His ribs ache and there is a cramp building in his calf; he leans forward to massage his leg and a spot of blood drips down onto the sheet, in the candlelight looking almost black against the sweaty linen. Morrison rubs his fingers against his upper lip, smearing the blood leaking from his nose. Stupidly, he looks at his bloodied fingers, having to squint one eye; the other he can barely see out of. There is a faint tap at the door, startling him.

"Come in," he whispers, repeating it after a moment in a stronger voice. "Yes, come in," expecting Annabelle.

The door opens and Castle peers in. "Are you all right, Doctor? I thought I heard shouting."

Of course it's Castle, Hedwith realizes. Of course. The man always seems to know when these things happen. It's one of the many talents he has, one of the many reasons he is such an excellent servant and companion, even if he looks like a dockside thug. Castle's presence is soothing, almost fatherly in a way, even though Morrison is of course the much older man. Is Castle getting more grey, though, he thinks, the hair thinner? Are the seams and wrinkles in his face more pronounced, among the various lumps and scars? He realizes, with mild shock, that Castle is getting old.

"It was just a dream, my friend," he says now, trying to smile. "A nightmare, you know. I'm fine, thank you. I'm fine. I didn't wake Annabelle, did I? Her door is shut?"

"Yes, sir. I don't believe Mrs Hedwith is awake, no. Her room was quiet when I passed." Castle looks at his employer, lying there disheveled and sweaty in the twisted-apart bedding, the back of a finger pressed to his nose to stop the bleeding. Hedwith looks pitiful: old, small, and weak, trembling in the dark like a frightened child. "I'll bring you a damp towel, sir, and something for your nose. Would you like anything else?"

For a hot, scared second, Hedwith doesn't want Castle to leave the room, doesn't want to be alone in the dim light again, with the memories of the dream. Just having him there seems to push the dark and the fear and the memories away. With an effort of will, he gets himself under control. "Thank you, Castle. That would be lovely. Perhaps a bit of warm milk."

Castle leaves, returning several minutes later with a towel, some gauze pads, and a small basin of warm water. While Hedwith busies himself with wiping the sweat and blood off of himself, Castle fetches the milk from the kitchen stove. "I'm sorry, sir," he says, when he returns, "the milk is only lukewarm. The coals were almost dead. If you like I can stoke the stove up and get it warmer, but it may take some time. I'll speak to Mrs Connor about leaving the firebox better prepared at night."

Morrison waves his hand. "No, no, that's fine, Mr Castle. There's no need to go to the extra trouble. The milk will be fine." He takes a sip of the stuff, fighting down a grimace. He hates warm milk, milk in general, really; he doesn't know why he'd asked for it, aside from some vague memory that the stuff is supposed to be soothing. He looks down at the thin china cup, squinting his bad eye to see better. "Are these laurel leaves?" he asks.

"Pardon me, sir?" Castle looks up from gathering the towel and basin.

"The pattern. Here on the rim of the mug. Are those laurel leaves, do you think?"

Castle leans closer. "I'm not rightly sure, sir. They very well could be." He returns to tidying up.

Dr Hedwith has a sudden image of Price. It's the laurel that brought the memory, he assumes, although he also recalls that James had been overly fond of warm milk. "Do you know what happens when you distill the leaves of the cherry laurel, Castle?" he says, "What you can create? Prussic acid, sir. A deadly poison, although not without its medicinal qualities, used in moderation. Fearful stuff to gauge, though. Dreadfully difficult."

"Laurel water was used by the Romans to poison the

wells of their enemies," Castle says. He is a student of history, enjoying nothing more than to sit down at night with a heavy book, in his little rooms under the stairs.

"That's right, Mr Castle. Suetonius?"

"I don't rightly recall, offhand, sir. Tacitus, perhaps." He stands up to go, wanting to return to his bed and salvage some of the night's sleep. "Will there be anything else, Doctor?"

Again Morrison feels the fear, not wanting to be alone. "Did I ever tell you about my friend Price, Castle? James Price? He drank laurel water, you know. Please, please, sit for a moment." He points to the chair near the bed, hoping he doesn't seem too eager. Leaning over the nightstand, he reaches back into a drawer and removes a small silver flask from behind the Bible.

Castle checks a sigh, placing the tray on the dresser by the door, seating himself in the spindly wooden chair, which creaks under his weight. "Thank you, sir," he says, accepting the flask from Hedwith, taking the smallest sip. It's fine, expensive brandy, but Castle isn't a drinking man. He hands the flask back to his employer, watching Hedwith's Adam's apple bob in his bony neck as he drinks greedily.

Morrison can feel the liquor spreading warm in his chest, strengthening him, the excellent brandy and Castle's reassuring presence combining to further drive away the dark. He takes another sip from the flask, nodding at his valet. "Yes, Mr Castle, laurel water is what my poor friend drank, just swallowed it down as we looked on, fell over dead right in front of us. It was quite the shock." James had been a good man, but a fool. He had lacked the internal substance and fortitude for the great work, the strength of character to see it through, and it had finally killed him.

"Why did he do that, sir?" Castle asks.

"Well, he thought himself ruined. Not financially, you understand, James was disgustingly wealthy right up until the end. His reputation, rather. You see, James, like myself, was a scientist and, somewhat earlier in his career, had made some quite astounding discoveries." Astounding indeed, Morrison remembers. For a time Price had been the toast of Oxford and London, the man who had successfully transmuted baser metals into silver and gold. He'd been feted and garlanded at Oriel and lauded by the king himself, even though his process to change the metals was four times as expensive as simply buying gold on the market would have been. But, for months, James Price had been the darling of the chemical world, inducted into the Royal Society and regarded as one of the most distinguished young men of the sciences.

"But there was a problem, you see," Morrison continues, shrugging. "He was a fake. His results were uncertain. Oh, it wasn't deliberate fakery, or even self-deception, really, but poor James couldn't replicate his earlier results when called on to do so."

"I can't do it again, Morrison," Price says to him. "There has to be a way to do it without that." They are in James's lavish Guildford laboratory, poring over the latest results. The experiment has been a failure, as Morrison had known it would be. The earlier success had been predicated on an ingredient that is now lacking.

"I'm telling you, James," he says, "it's not going to work without the vital spirit. You know that."

"Maybe a dog…"

"Don't fool yourself, man. How much time are you going to waste with this nonsense?" Morrison waves a hand at the

retorts and burners, at the sludgy mess of metal in the bottom of the glass, the latest failed attempt at the Stone. "It was only one poor wretch, before."

"It was a child."

"An unwanted orphan. Oxford is swimming with them. She is far better off with the Lord in Heaven than she would have been here in the gutter, lifting her skirts for bread in a few years, if she hadn't already." He raises a hand, forestalling his friend's objection. "Yes, James, I know it's distasteful, but it is in the name of science. If we can finally perfect the Salt, think of the things we can do to better this world." It's an old argument, but Morrison feels himself getting worked up again, as always. "No more sickness, no more death. Metal into gold? Simply a curious and venal side-effect of the great work." He has to pause to cough, long and hard, hacking bloody phlegm into his handkerchief, sagging into a chair.

James waits until the coughing subsides. "The cough sounds worse, my friend. You need to get out of England, leave this damp. Go to the colonies, somewhere warm, dry your lungs. Maybe by then we can divine another way."

Morrison shakes his head. "There is no other way." He looks up. "I'm running out of time, James."

They argue again, parting that evening in foul tempers. Morrison will only see James a few more times in the coming months, as Price removes himself to his laboratory, rarely leaving, admitting no visitors, not even his friends and colleagues. Not even Morrison Hedwith, his co-conspirator in the great work. Morrison knows, now, that James lacks the discipline to push the process forward. The child had been regrettable, but the great work is not for the squeamish, the weak in spirit. James is convinced that the new chemical sciences will divine an alternate way to produce the Stone, but Morrison knows differently. Perhaps if James had only accepted that, things would have gone other than they had.

Without access to Price's well-stocked laboratory, Morrison's own experiments are put on hold. His own income is small, too small to afford him what he requires. He studies and ponders as best he can but, lacking the tools and chemicals for his research, he is forced to wait, trying again and again to gain access to Price, to make him see reason. He resigns himself to reconciling with Price's ineffective approaches, biding the time it will require before James sees reason and returns to the proper path, time he could little spare. But, alas, things passed as they had. Poor man.

"It was pride, then, sir? Being thought a fraud?" Castle is asking now. "That's why he took the poison?"

Morrison nods, smiling sadly. "Pride, yes; I suppose. He'd gone from a lauded scientist to scoundrel, in the eyes of some. Some merely thought him a fool, a man who had prematurely released results that he didn't yet understand."

"And you, sir?"

"I, what?"

"What did you think of him, your friend?"

Morrison pauses, taking another sip from the almost-empty flask. He'd thought James was a fool, yes, of course, but not for the same reasons as everyone else. He'd thought him weak, selfish, lacking the true vision. But it was more than that. At the end, he'd understood poor James. It had become a lesson to him. "I thought him sad, Castle. That is it. Sad. He had been a great man, James, for a time, and could have become so again, but he lost hope." He shakes his head. "Hope is the most precious thing in this world, Castle. Don't let anyone tell you otherwise. Wealth, love, good health: they are all less than worthless if hope is taken from you. You must never let go of that precious thing. You must hold hope tight to yourself, Mr Castle. You must hold it tight."

Both men are quiet for a minute, listening to the rain pattering on the roof.

"When was all this, sir? Your friend dying?" Castle asks, looking at his hands.

Not for the first time, Morrison wonders if Castle has any inkling of his, Morrison's, true age. The man is something of a historian, a student of the past, after all; it's entirely possible that, over the years, Morrison has dropped one piece of information too many. There's something in Castle's tone now that makes him wary.

For now, though, he can't explain that his friend James Price took his fateful draught in 1783, almost a hundred years ago now. That Morrison himself had been nearly seventy at that time, nearing the end of his first body.

He is on his third, now, one that is rapidly wearing out as he seeks the Salt of Life, the Stone, the substance that will bring him health and immortality, fixing him in one perfect body for all of eternity, or for as long as he cares to stay alive. Near the end of his first life, he'd learned the secret of transferring the vital spirit, the *anima*, from one vessel to another, but it is a dangerous and imprecise process. Twice he's been successful, but he knows that he'd teetered on the edge of luck each time.

Even with his prior failures isolating the Stone, Dr Hedwith feels now that he is close, that the substances hidden in the Sagwa will finally bear fruit, after so many years, and that this vessel will be his last. Perhaps the latest variant of the elixir has already succeeded. Yes, perhaps Lyman will have that very news for him upon his return from the latest circuit, where he tests the formulae and gathers data on behalf of his employer.

Without hope, a man has nothing, just as he'd told Castle.

"Oh, it was a long time ago, Mr Castle." Morrison smiles. "Now, you must forgive an old man's rambling. I think I'll try to get some sleep. Why don't you do the same?"

Castle looks at Dr Hedwith for a long moment, his questions hidden behind an impassive face. "Very good, sir. Sleep well."

He leaves the room, closing the door softly behind him.

PART TWO
THE GREAT WORK

"Alchimy therefore is a science teaching how to make and compound a certaine medicine, which is called Elixir, the which when it is cast upon mettals or imperfect bodies, doth fully perfect them in the verie projection."

1.
[VIRGINIA, 1864]

"DR MORRISON HEDWITH," the man says, sitting, hazily looming into Alexander's vision, across the small table. "I'm pleased to make your acquaintance, Captain."

Alexander blinks slowly, lifting his glass to his lips with some effort. The glass has grown very heavy and some of the liquid inside splashes over the rim, down his open uniform jacket. Waste of good fucking whiskey. The man's face swims into clarity for a moment. Older fellow, lavish side whiskers, a crooked smile. Talks funny, though. And why he talking to him in the first place? Can't he see that Alexander has fucking drinking to do? Why is his hand sticking out across the table like that? It's fucking rude, is what it is. Alexander raises his glass and tries to drink, but there is no more whiskey in the thing, somehow. Closing one eye partway, he studies on it, trying to make sense of the situation.

Morrison lowers his unshaken hand, putting it to better use raising the bottle and refilling the captain's glass, although he certainly doesn't seem to have lacked for drink so far tonight, and would probably benefit from a pause in the proceedings. He looks terrible: the wavering light of the tent's lantern casts twisting shadows over his haggard features, the deep lines in his face and heavy bags under his eyes. Even in lamplight his skin looks sallow and unhealthy, his eyes red and rheumy, the pupils miotic pinpoints. Laudanum, Morrison thinks. By the look of the man he's no stranger to it. The shaking hands and the burst capillaries on his nose and cheeks show that the captain is a lover of the grape as well, or at least a lover of the rotgut liquor here on the table. A fairly pathetic-looking specimen overall, this gentleman.

Morrison looks around the large tent, smiling amiably at the other doctors, trim military men and prosperous-looking civilians like himself, sitting in groups of threes and fours, and who seem to be shunning the man with whom he now sits. He turns his attention back across the table. The captain's uniform is disheveled, the jacket open; myriad stains cover both it and the formerly white shirt underneath. The man's thick grey hair is lank, greasy, and stands on end at one side, as if he'd just woken up. His shaking hands are scabbed and dirty, the nails rimed with dark crescents of what looks to be blood.

"Much obliged," the captain mutters, downing the glass of whiskey in one, reaching it out beseechingly towards Hedwith again. "You say your name was? Got an accent, don't you?"

Morrison gives his warmest smile. "Dr Morrison Hedwith, sir. Lately of London, hence the accent, I suppose, most recently resident in your great city of Boston."

"Alexander," the captain says, sticking out a grubby hand to shake, which Morrison takes with some distaste, now that he's seen the state of it. "Potter. Alexander Potter. Surgeon. Pleased to meet you, I guess." He takes another drink, belches. "The fuck are you doing here, Morris? We're in the middle of a war. Don't you know that? Go back to fucking London, is what you should do." He blinks heavily at the Englishman, nodding. "Go right the fuck on back. Drink?" He laughs, at what, neither man is sure, and then fumbles at the bottle, almost knocking it over, before slopping more into his glass and over the table.

"Thank you, no, Dr Potter. I'm afraid spirits don't agree with me." Morrison wipes his hand on his pant leg under the table.

"No need to be afraid of spirits." Alexander's head feels too heavy, unbalanced on his neck. "What?" The Englishman is saying something again, in that pompous accent. It grates on his ears, the way this bastard talks. Why won't he go away?

"I said, sir, that it appears that we're going to be working together. You see, I've recently taken a surgeon's contract with the Union. I felt that this war, regrettable as it may be, is an opportunity that can't be missed, for medical men such as ourselves. Wars may be terrible things, yes, but you must admit that they advance the course of surgery and medicine." He shrugs, ruefully. "When else do we find so many wounded men, so many fascinating cases, to study as we try to heal them, as best we're able?"

Dr Potter jerks his head up from where it threatens to loll against his chest. "Heal them? The fuck are you talking about, Morris? Cut off their goddamn arms and legs all day: that's what we do. You ever seen what a fucking minié ball does to a body?" Who is this prick, Alexander thinks, blearily. If he doesn't leave, Alexander might have to show him the goddamn door himself. Wouldn't be the first fucking time he'd done it, either, and fuck the major and his threats. The rest of the medical staff know by now to leave him well enough alone at night. They know it, and this prick would learn it, too. Alexander just wants to be left alone. That isn't too much to ask. And sure, fine, so there have been a few fights with his colleagues, but that wasn't his fault, was it? Still, if there were more available surgeons, the major would have put him in the stockade long ago. But fuck him, there aren't. So, if he had to take this limey asshole to task, he'll merely be given another sound ass-chewing by the major and told to sober up, and that's it. Alexander knows that the others think him an angry, most likely crazy, drunken old man, anyway. Fuck them, that keeps them away from him, a state of affairs that suits him perfectly, and one which this limey prick would do well to emulate. If Alexander wanted company, he'd go find a working girl. Not some English nancy with stupid ideas.

During the day, reasonably sober, he's a competent surgeon, one of the most experienced in the company, actually. They all know it. Yes, OK, he's been having some difficulties lately, but the laudanum helps steady his hands in the mornings, and a little whiskey straightens the rest of his system out, of course. He has his holistic fucking method all worked out. It's fortunate that there's no shortage of opium because he knows that, by now, he is well and truly hooked on that shit, like a fucking Chinaman to the pipe. Fortunately, he has an arrangement with an enterprising quartermaster who keeps him in bricks of the stuff. Getting off the opium will likely prove difficult, someday, after the war is over, but he needs it just now to steady his hands and calm his head. He needs it. One thing at a time, after all. He's got an opiated whiskey preparation of his own devising, and it keeps him serene and effective in his work, his senses sharp but distant. It helps him do his fucking job, and it's the only way he *can* do it, day after day, to deal with the terrible things he has to see. Smell. Hear.

He's not sure just when it all became too much; at the beginning of the war it was only terrible, not intolerable. He doesn't know just what has changed inside him. He's not even sure if he's the same person any more.

And to hell with the rest of them, because listen, he has a fucking talent: he can take off an arm or a leg faster than any of the other surgeons, by quite a stretch. Quick sharp, the scalpel and then the saw and it's done, like magic. Just toss the severed appendage in the heap with the others. The pile that they keep under constant guard lest one of the camp dogs make off with a limb before the mess can be burned in the evening. He's a deft hand with his tools, more a carpenter than a doctor by now, he thinks. Maybe it's that skill, or maybe it's just his personality – this inexplicable anger he can't control, that's rising on him now, the instability that doesn't lend itself to a bedside manner – but he's kept at a nearly endless string of amputations, it often seems like. Other doctors might primarily be called upon to treat the fluxes and fevers, broken bones and burns, but he, Dr Alexander Potter, MD, has been reduced to a fucking tradesman, little better than a barber or dentist, the man you saw when you had a limb too many.

"Where'd you do your medical training, then?" he asks now, vaguely. Swallowing more whiskey, wondering why he's encouraging conversation. He can feel the anger already bleeding back into weariness. It comes and goes like that. He can't fucking understand it. He can't understand a lot of things, really, particularly right now. He should really call it a night.

Hedwith smiles modestly. "Oriel. Oxford, you know. But I've been practicing in Boston for some years now."

"And now you want to saw off fucking legs. Well, suit yourself." Alexander shakes his heavy head. He leans over, resting his forehead in his palm, elbow on the table. He's very tired now and it's getting harder to stay awake. He decides that, after he finishes this bottle, he'll go back to his tent. He will. If he passes out here, though, someone will get him back. Or not; it doesn't fucking matter.

After what seems like a long time, he lifts his head again, which wobbles too far back on his neck before he bounces it somewhere close to straight. The Englishman is still there, smiling at him. It makes him uncomfortable, having someone just sitting there looking at him, not even drinking. It's fucking unnerving. "What do you want?" he says, suddenly closer to belligerence again. "Have a drink or leave me the fuck alone."

Alexander feels his head drooping as he reaches for the bottle, electing to just forgo the glass this time and drink straight from the source. The rim of the bottle clacks heavily against his teeth as he lifts it, and then he wraps his lips around it like a teat. He still has hold of the bottle when he slumps to the floor.

Old fool, Morrison thinks, lugging the limp form of Dr Potter into his own small tent and dropping him onto the cot. He doesn't know if he means Potter or himself. When the drunken captain had fallen off his chair, rolling over onto his back, Hedwith had looked around helplessly. Military customs are not something he, as a civilian, is familiar with, particularly here in America. Should he just pick the man up? Or was there some kind of batman or orderly for this sort of thing? The rest of the

medical staff had ignored him entirely; apparently the
sight of Dr Potter passing out in the officers' tent was not
uncommon of an evening. Finally, one of the other men
had taken pity on him.

"Just roll him over," the man called out.

"So he don't puke down his throat," another doctor
added.

"Aspirate, you know," the first man said, not to be
outdone. "Choke and die."

"Thank you, gentlemen," Hedwith had answered,
relieved, squatting down and levering Potter onto his
side. A thin line of drool was running down Potter's wet
lips; he still held the empty bottle in one hand. "Will
someone see him safely to his tent?" he asked.

"He'll be fine," the first doctor responded.

"Won't be the first time he slept here," his colleague
said.

"Nor the last," said the first man. "Come morning he'll
be right as rain. Or as close as he ever gets, poor bastard."

"Fastest man in the Hospital Corps with a bonesaw,
though, Potter."

"Regular artist."

"Drinks, though," the first man concluded, somewhat
pointlessly, given the situation.

"Regular artist," the second repeated, turning back to
his drink.

Hedwith had been a bit nonplussed by their rapid
back-and-forth. American speech still baffled him at
times. "Thank you, sirs," he repeated. "Dr Morrison
Hedwith, late of London, currently of Boston."

"Sure you are," the first man replied, turning his back.

Not entirely sure what to do in the awkward situation,
Morrison had gathered up his bag from the table and
prepared to leave. Just then, Potter gave a low, puling

sigh from the floor, making Morrison stop. He looked down at the pitiful man, lying there whimpering. There was blood mixed with the drool running down his lip. For a moment Morrison had a vision of himself, in the bad days before his first breakthrough, curled up in his musty bed, coughing bloody spume into a rag, so weak that, more than once, he'd soiled himself before the man he'd engaged to check in and bring food could help him to the chamber pot. It had been a close-run thing, but here he was now, looking at another tired old man, not long for the world by the look of him.

Before he could think further, he'd squatted down again and pulled one of Potter's arms around his shoulders, pushing himself back upright, balancing the heavy, loose-limbed man. Hedwith was not large, himself, but strong; even so, he nearly dropped Potter trying to maneuver him out of the tent door. "Thank you for your help, gentlemen," he called over a shoulder at the two doctors, who completely ignored him.

Now, standing over the man snoring on his own cot, Hedwith wonders just why he'd tried to help. A moment of weakness, perhaps. But now, here the man is, in Morrison's own bed, which he'd probably piss during the night. Well, it's done, he thinks. Nothing more to do but make the best of it, you soft old fool.

It's late, but he isn't tired. Kneeling on a scrap of canvas, Morrison opens his steamer trunk, cataloging his instruments and chemicals yet again. Perhaps a bit obsessively, but it's a worry. He'd only been able to bring so much here with him, and he hopes that his supplies will be adequate for the time being. The war looks to be slowly wrapping up, the Confederates beleaguered and lacking supplies, but if all goes well, what he's brought will last long enough for his experiments to gain some traction. He wishes, yet again, that he'd been able to get here sooner, but his new marriage and setting up the household had taken so much of his time, time that could have been better spent gathering data for the work. A war on this scale might not ever come again, one that would provide so much raw material for his researches. He is so close, he can feel it.

It was only the debacle in Boston, and his subsequent need to leave town, that had finally allowed him to come south and join the Hospital Corps. Surgeons were in demand and it took him no time to secure a contract position. He hopes that Lyman and Castle can get things in Boston settled quickly enough and then bring him the rest of what he needs for his work, before he runs out of materials. He wishes Castle was here now; Morrison simply feels safer with the big man at his side. He's in a war zone now, or at least on the outskirts of one. He's lived too long and made too much progress in the work to leave himself open to chance and ill fortune.

From his trunk, he removes the small wooden case of bottles, tightly packed in straw. Before he'd left Boston, Morrison had drained the contents of several bottles of Dalby's Carminative and refilled them with his own solutions, numbering each as he went. Opening a leather notebook, he checks each bottle against its inscription again, noting the precise mixture of ingredients and methods of preparation. He has two dozen such bottles that he will test, one at a time. He's sure that, by the war's end, he will finally have enough experimental data to complete his long search for the Stone.

Dr Hedwith turns the notebook to a blank page and loses himself in thought. Pondering the work, while a labor, has its own kind of satisfaction. Hunting for the beauty of pure truths is a sublime pursuit, one which is nearly as energizing as it is wearying. It's easy to drop down into it and forget all the mundanities of this flawed world. When he at last looks up from his page, then, he is only mildly surprised to see that the sky is lightening. He requires little sleep, generally, and more often than not will work through the night like this, a small nap during the warm hours of midday resting him sufficiently. Working at night is far preferable to enduring the nightmares, after all, the dreams that come more often than he likes. Closing his notebook, he packs away his materials and, stretching as he stands, decides to go find some breakfast. On his way out, he glances down at Dr Potter, still snoring open-mouthed. He's pleased to see that the crotch of the man's trousers is still dry.

There are demons in Alexander's head when he wakes; they're pounding on the inside of his skull and digging behind his eyes. One of them has shit in his mouth, by the taste of it. He levers one eye open with some effort, squinting in the dim morning light, which makes his head pound still further. He's in a tent, not his own, on a cot. A shiver ripples through his body and his guts cramp; he feels an almost overwhelming need to defecate, but manages to clamp his sphincter tightly shut until the spasm passes. When he sits upright, his vision swims and his head shrieks with pain. The small of his back is in a knot and he can feel sweat streaming down his ribs. He stinks of old sweat and the liquor that's seeping from his pores. His head, cramping guts, and his own smell fight to bring his stomach up, but Alexander just grits his teeth, fighting back the need to puke, a skill he's honed after long practice. Just the beginning of another normal day, then.

Mornings are the worst times. In some ways, it's a

blessing, getting the most terrible pain out of the way early, going from needing to die to only wanting to, over the course of another long day spent with the stink of blood and shit and sweat in his nose, the moans and screams of the wounded hot in his ears. Not every day's work is as bad, of course; it fluctuates with the fortunes of the war. Lately, it's been bad but, some days, he's merely looking after the patients whose limbs he's hacked off at some other time, those that still lived, watching the progress of fevers and infections. The irony is that the standard of care has gotten much better: at the beginning of the war most of the medical tents were not much more than places for men to die in some shade. Now, with all the advances the Hospital Corps has made, oftentimes patients actually live, merely missing arms, legs, feet, and the like. They are even well-stocked with ether for the amputations now, instead of merely providing hard sticks for the patients to bite while the saws cut bone. They have bedpans and water basins, trained surgeons, laudanum for the pain, well-made crutches for the maimed. What a wonderful world it is.

The thought of laudanum makes his sweat increase and the knot in his back tighten. He needs it, now; his body cries out for it. The combination of a hangover and the lack of opium is one that he is well familiar with, but it doesn't make it any better. He pats his pockets, frantically, hoping he has something with him. Nothing. He staggers to his feet, weaving as he readies to go find his own tent, when he notices a doctor's bag on the lid of a large travel trunk. Alexander has a vague, hazy memory of some new doctor bothering him last night, an Englishman with an irritating accent. Martin? Michael? It doesn't matter. Potter opens the bag, rifling through it for some form of opium, anything. Surely the man has some. But, again: nothing.

He tosses the bag on the cot, kneeling down in front of the trunk. He has to hold onto it for a moment, closing his eyes once more against the need to vomit but, after some effort, his shaking hands get the lid opened. He roots around through the clothes and books and personal things. The man has a veritable laboratory of flasks, burners, beakers, and bottles of chemicals, none of which are laudanum or anything like it. What does this fool think he's going to be doing here, with this mobile apothecary shop? He'll be sawing limbs and sewing flesh all day like the rest of them, trying to stop fevers and fluxes and infections, not playing chemist. Fucking Englishmen, Alexander thinks, wanting to shake his pounding head. He's becoming frantic as he notes the labels on all the various bottles and boxes and has almost given up when he opens a small wooden case. Taking out a bottle, he reads the label: Dalby's Carminative. He doesn't recognize the brand but knows what it is, immediately. In a frenzy, he works the cork free and raises the bottle to his lips, drinking greedily.

"What are you doing?!" A shadow passes in front of him and a hand slaps at the bottle, just as he downs the last swallow. Alexander closes his eyes, fancying that he can feel his dried-out, pain-racked body expanding with relief, cell by cell, as the weak tincture spreads through him. It's hopefully enough to take the edge off; when he gets back to his own tent he can fortify himself with his own supplies.

"What are you doing?!" the voice says again, pitched higher now, screaming at him.

Alexander opens his eyes, looking up with a sigh. "Ah," he says, "Martin. Good morning. I was feeling a bit poorly and borrowed some of your laudanum here.

Hope you don't mind. There's plenty in the supply tent, if this was for your personal use. Bowel complaints, is it?" He smiles. His own guts have ceased churning. It's been a while since he's had a good shit, come to think of it. Maybe he should have waited a bit longer this morning and let the diarrhea clean him out some. Well, no matter.

Morrison looks down at Dr Potter, aghast. That bottle in his hand would have served for three subjects, maybe four. And this fool has swallowed it all, just like that. What was he even doing in his trunk in the first place? He wants to strike Potter, to slap that greasy smile off his face, to raise a foot and kick his head in. He feels his hands clenching into fists; for a moment he thinks he actually might attack the man, but then reason regains hold of him.

"Give me that." He snatches the bottle out of Potter's hand, turning it over to note the number penciled on the back of the label. Pushing Potter aside, he reaches down into the trunk, whose contents have been scattered everywhere – if the man has broken anything, he will flay him – finding his notebook. Morrison flips through the pages until he finds the corresponding entry. It's even worse than he'd feared: the idiot has taken a bottle from the middle of the course, one that is specifically meant to be used after some similar, earlier formulations, to compare the effects. Potter has put a gaping hole right in the middle of his experimental methodology. A gaping hole. Again he wants to hit the man, who now sits on Morrison's cot, regarding him with that same stupid smile. Best make what he can of it, Morrison tells himself, gritting his teeth. He calms himself with severe effort. What's done is done but, perhaps, something can be salvaged here.

He looks closer at Potter, searching for changes, even though he knows it's far too soon, if they are even coming. He still looks terrible: wild, greasy hair, sagging sallow flesh, red-rimmed, bloodshot eyes. A thin white stubble covers his cheeks and jaw and his breath would gag a vulture. Are his eyes slightly less red, though? The skin of his jowls a bit more taut? Morrison leans over, pulling down one of Potter's lower eyelids with his thumb.

"Hey now, what are you doing?" Alexander says, trying to get away. The man has hold of the top of his head with one hand now and is pulling at his cheek with two fingers. "Stop that."

"I am a doctor, sir. Perhaps you recall what that is. Now, hold still: I am trying to examine you. Tell me, how do you feel?"

Alexander is baffled. "What? I feel fine. Leave off, now." He tries to get up, only for the Englishman, who is surprisingly strong, to push him back down to the cot.

"I said hold still." Morrison grasps Potter's chin, turns his head from side to side. "You feel fine, you say? Just fine? Anything else? Aches, pains? A burning sensation anywhere? No? How about your innards? Anything?"

What the fuck is this man on about? Alexander wonders. Is this how it is in England, where full medical attention is indicated after a bit of a whiskey night? No wonder they'd lost the American colonies, then, the delicate nancies. Now that he thinks about it, though, he in fact feels pretty fair. Better than usual, of a morning. Maybe that Dalby's isn't so weak after all.

"Actually, I feel fairly good, Martin," he says. "Rejuvenated a bit. That Dalby's you have, that's an English product? Do you happen to know the formula?"

Yes, I know the formula, you cretin, Morrison thinks. He

stands back, looking down at Potter. Maybe the man does look a small bit better, but it's too early to tell.

"You seem well, Dr Potter. I am sorry I shouted at you. You must understand, though, that seeing you in my personal possessions was something of a shock. Perhaps it's how you do things here in America but, where I am from, we are a bit more respectful of a man's privacy."

"I'm truly sorry for that, Martin. Really, you're right: that was uncalled for, and I apologize. I only found myself in a bit of a bind, you see." Alexander tries to look contrite. Really, he does feel good, surprisingly good. It's hard to keep from smiling.

"It's *Morrison*, Dr Potter. Morrison Hedwith." He extends a hand and they shake. Potter's grip seems a bit firmer, perhaps. "Now, as you're here, I wonder if I could ask you to assist me, though, later tonight, with something I'm working on. Just a minor thing, you understand. An experiment I've been conducting. Won't take but a moment. I'm afraid you are, so far, the only man I know in camp." He looks over at the open trunk significantly, suggesting with his eyes that it's the least that Potter can do, given the circumstances.

Alexander himself isn't sure that he wants to agree to the suggestion. Nights he reserves for getting so blind drunk as to forget these bloody wartime days. That said, he doesn't want to commit to anything, but figures that he probably does owe the man for what has transpired. He can play laboratory assistant and then go drink afterwards. And maybe, if he works it right, he could talk the man out of some more of that Dalby's. It's really wonderful stuff, he thinks.

"Absolutely, Dr Hedwith. Again, please accept my apologies. I'd be happy to assist you tonight. The least I can do, given this misunderstanding." Particularly if there is more Dalby's to be had. "Now, if you'll excuse me, I think I need to clean up a bit and get a bite of food before my shift."

"Of course. Until later, then." They shake hands again.

"Until later."

Alexander ducks out of the tent, facing the risen sun, feeling positively spry.

"Screaming won't help, sir," Morrison says, holding down Dr Potter as he writhes on the cot. He presses the rag over the man's mouth and nose, glancing over his shoulder to the door of his tent. In a few moments, the ether takes effect and he's able to release his hand. Moving quickly to the door, he pulls the flaps closed and ties them. It's unfortunate, having to do this right in the middle of camp, but inevitable. Besides, he supposes, this is a field hospital, a place certainly not unfamiliar with screaming men. Before the ether wears off he makes sure that Potter's arms and legs are securely tied to the cot, another rope running across his chest. He hopes it will be enough: Potter is a thick, fleshy man and more than one other subject has contrived a way to break limbs while in the grip of the experimental Salts.

It hadn't looked good when Potter burst into his tent earlier, the sun barely down. Morrison had not even thought to go look for the man for at least another hour, but there he was, blood running from his nose and a look of agony on his face.

"What's happening?" Potter gasped. "Something isn't right. Am I poisoned?"

Fortunately the man had come to him rather than going to one of the medical tents. Like called to like, he supposes. The great work holds many mysteries; this is one of them, as are the varying levels of the Salt's efficacy, during certain conjunctions of the heavens. Much of the work is shrouded in obscure Hermetic claptrap, things long proven nonsense by men of science like himself. But still, empirical evidence has shown that the work requires at least some attention to the positions of the stars and planets, whatever the reason for it, and certainly there is ample indication that there is something in the Salt itself that can be sensed by unknown, arcane means, to those so attuned. He doesn't doubt that it was the power of the Salt, unrefined as it yet was, that has brought Potter here tonight.

"I don't know what is happening to you, Dr Potter," he'd replied, when Potter had first come stumbling in. "This is what we are to ascertain." The look in the man's eyes had been confused, frantic, until a spasm took him, bending him over to vomit blood on the ground at Hedwith's feet. "Dear, dear," Morrison clucked. "Let's get you onto the cot, Doctor."

Now he leans over, jotting quick impressions in his notebook as Potter starts to wake from the ether. Later, he'll take the time to flesh out the details but, just now, he needs a focused, observant mind as he records the symptoms of Potter's struggle with the protean Salt. Again, he thinks how unfortunate it is that the man has taken one of the formulae from the middle of the course, which will make precise quantification of effect that much more difficult. He sees that Potter has come fully awake again, now; he's gasping and struggling with his bonds. Morrison checks his pocket watch, noting the time in his book.

"What are you doing to me?" Potter thrashes in the ropes, pulling his head back to scream.

Hedwith puts a hand firmly over the man's mouth. "Do not scream, Dr Potter, or I will need to gag you, which I would rather not do. You are a man of science, and this is an opportunity for you to expand mankind's knowledge, if you can report your symptoms before you lose the ability to speak. Yes?" He looks down at the man, nodding encouragingly. "This is your own fault, after all, for getting into my things. Now, may I lift my hand? You will be silent?" He raises an eyebrow inquisitively, removing a small amount of pressure from his palm, feeling a jerky nod under his hand.

Alexander's eyes are wide and scared, his teeth clenched so hard against the pain that he feels he might crack them. An hour or so ago he'd been in his tent, enjoying a sundown whiskey after another day trying to repair mangled flesh, still feeling surprisingly fine, full of energy and barely needing any laudanum, when the first cramp had hit, a burning wave of pain that started in his bowels, tearing upward through his chest. When the pain reached his head, he'd fallen over, curled up on the floor of his tent, flopping and gasping like a landed fish. He'd never felt anything like this agony. For a long while, he couldn't even sit up and then, from one moment to the next, the pain left him in a rush of blood that poured out of his nose and dripped from his ears. He waited for his life to dim, sure that he was suffering a massive stroke but, after another moment, felt almost fine again. He'd shakily made it to his cot and was reaching for his cup again when the next attack hit, less severe but burning through him nonetheless. Alexander had managed to lever himself upright and stagger out of the tent, stumbling through the camp, ignoring the main hospital tents until he came to Hedwith's, pushing himself inside. He didn't know why he'd come, he'd just felt that this was the place he needed to be. Morrison would help him.

"What's happening?" he whimpers again, now, as Hedwith's hand comes off his mouth. Alexander has the unwholesome feeling that his skin is loosening over his bones, that it's going to sag and tear right off of his skeleton. Dr Hedwith sits on the trunk across from him, calmly writing notes in a small book, staring impassively at him.

"Well, Doctor, I'm afraid that you had the fortune, or misfortune, rather, to drink a vital elixir of my own devising, experimental only, of course. A substance that, one day, though, will provide the key to eternal health and eternal life. I am quite serious, sir. But misfortune, I say, because the formula is, as yet, incomplete. The bottle you so greedily consumed in your morning distress was merely one preparation in a series, each designed to isolate and determine some important aspect of the elixir's composition." He shakes his head sadly. "Now, there is nothing to do but determine just what course it will take in your body. How are you feeling, then?"

"I feel like my bones are splitting apart," Potter gasps against another wave of pain, feeling blood dripping from his nose again. He arches upward against the ropes.

"Careful, Doctor: it's entirely possible that you *will* split your bones, if you keep thrashing like that. Try to remain calm. Tell me everything that you are feeling. Everything."

"You have to save me, Morrison. Please, I'll do anything–" Alexander's words are cut off in a low, weeping groan.

"I'm afraid there is nothing to be done, sir. Tell me your symptoms, Dr Potter; at least make your passing add to the annals of science." Although, as Hedwith says the words, he realizes that perhaps it *is* possible to save Potter, if he gives him an amount of the fixative preparation that he uses himself to keep the protean Salt, the variant he had ingested so long ago, during his own time of distress, stable in his body. Morrison needs to take the preparation daily, to keep his system from rebelling against the imperfect vital spirits which had, eventually, allowed him to move from one failing body to another, younger, stronger form, to transfer his own anima and thoughts into a different vessel. The process had been difficult and, perhaps due to some residual spark of the body's original owner, came with this painful, chronic need for the stabilizing preparation. Once he is able to isolate the pure, stable form of the vital Salt, the Stone, there will be no more need for transference or for reliance on daily fixative; his own body will remain in a state of perfect, ageless health.

He wonders, though: perhaps that same fixative Salt, given to a man whose body suffers from the impure, experimental formula, could return that man to health, at least for a time, in his *original* body. It was maybe because Morrison's own need for the fixative had begun *after* he'd left his first form that he'd assumed it an artifact of the transference but, is it even simpler than that? The idea is worthy of further inquiry and here, perhaps, is his subject.

Ah, but maybe not, he thinks, returning from his reverie, looking at Potter. It may already be too late; it doesn't look like the man is in fact going to survive much longer. Morrison notes the blood streaming down Potter's arms, where the skin has begun to tear. This loosening of the skin is a strange phenomenon that is often present in the subjects, for unknown reasons. Sometimes the effects are more dramatic, the body reacting to the formula in surprising, often horrifying, ways. Some simply die, quickly and quietly, without any outward signs of distress. It was all very puzzling, which is why he is here at this field hospital, to gather his data as quietly as he could.

Morrison has a sudden thought, looking down at Potter. One more mundane but perhaps as important to the research as any one subject's struggles. Potter can be an asset here, in another way. Morrison knows that, here in America, even in a war zone, he will have to be very circumspect in his researches. Boston has taught him that, if nothing else. If, suddenly, the soldiers under his care begin dying in horrible, unnatural ways, someone will notice, eventually, no matter how careful he is. Many subjects will no doubt just perish under the Salt, without overt drama, but there is always a chance that one too many will draw attention. But, if Potter lives, and returns to treating patients of his own, Morrison can insulate himself from the risk of discovery. Spread the load out, as it were. It's an intriguing idea.

"Help me," Potter gasps. The tears in his skin are becoming more profound but, alas, there is nothing in his symptoms that Morrison has not seen before in other subjects. It is disappointing, given that perhaps a medically trained man could have described his passing more clinically than the orphans, streetwalkers, and low-class refuse that have comprised his subject pool up until now. He has little hope that soldiers will prove to be much more observant, but he is required to work with what resources he is given. And now, he has been given this man Potter.

Time is of the essence.

"Potter," he calls, lightly slapping the man's face. "Wake up!" Both Potter's eyes have hemorrhaged, the sclera red and bloody. "Listen to me, sir. There is a chance that I can save you, I realize that now, but it is a slight one at best. Do you understand?"

"Save me," Potter whispers. His teeth are loose in bleeding gums.

"If I try this, Dr Potter, it will mean you are *beholden to me*. Do you understand? There is a treatment I can attempt but, if it works, you will always require a substance that only I can give you. Only I. If you don't have it, you will return to this state. Or perhaps something worse. I really don't know. Do you want to proceed, knowing this?" He knows the answer, of course.

"Save me," Potter murmurs again. "The pain…"

Hedwith opens his trunk, shielding the contents from Potter's sight, removing a large bottle, upon which is a label with a drawing of a skull and bones. *PRUSSIC ACID: POISON!* is written in a large font across the front, a little joke to himself at poor Price's expense. Really the bottle contains the fixative he's devised, the thing that keeps him alive and well enough to pursue his researches. Making a guess, he measures a few ounces into a flask, and then doubles it, swirling it over the lantern until it has slightly warmed. When he turns back to the bound doctor, he leans forward, holding the flask in Potter's sight.

"Now, Dr Potter," he says, severely. "This liquid may save you or it may kill you. I honestly do not know. If it *does* save you, though, sir, I repeat: *you are beholden to me*. Do you understand? From this day forward, if you want to live, if you want to remain free of the state in which you now find yourself, *you will require this*. Let me say, too, that it is not unknown for the suffering you are enduring to last many days, weeks even, before death." This is a lie, of course: no subject has ever lasted more than a few hours before expiring. But, now that he's had this idea of making use of Potter, he is excited about the prospect, and wants to make sure the man is bound to him, much as Lyman has been bound. Dr Potter will be one more tool to move the great work forward.

For a moment he feels a hint of shame, regret, even, that he's forced to treat Potter in this way. The man is an opium eater, a drunk, a wreck of a man, but he is a man likely no better or worse in his heart than Morrison himself. Perhaps it's the war that has brought him to this state, perhaps the death of a lover, a friend. Who knew? This world is a cold, hard place for mortal men, a place that can drive even the best to unfortunate depths as they seek to survive and flourish. This Morrison knows well. He isn't a religious man, but he is a moral one; it is difficult sometimes to reconcile what he has to do to advance the work with what any normal, moral man would feel is right. That had broken James, of course, but Morrison is made of sterner stuff. One day the sacrifices he's made will be repaid in full.

"Dr Potter, I want you to understand that I do this to save you," he says. "It was you who put yourself in this conundrum, not I, but I perhaps can save you. If – *if* – I am to do so, you will in return do whatever I ask of you, yes? *Whatever*. If that is not in your power than you must steel yourself, sir, and prepare to meet your Maker. If I give you this formula, *you will do anything I ask, for as long as I ask*. Is that clear?" He fixes the man with his eyes.

"Anything," Alexander whispers. He'll do anything to stop this pain.

Anything at all.

2.
[OREGON, 1878]

MERCY IS SITTING in the black tent, a piece of board across her knee, when Alexander enters. He starts, not having realized that she was there, and mutters an apology for disturbing her; he backs away as quickly as he can, his hands held behind his back. Trying to hide what it is he carries.

"Lyman told me, Alexander," she says, before he can leave. "He told me about Papa."

Dr Potter lets out a huff of air that's something between a sigh and the aftermath of a punched belly, and steps back through the tent flap, dropping it shut behind him. The wash of afternoon sunlight is covered by the canvas, leaving the interior dim, dust motes dancing on the air. Rula, Holly, and Bascom are quiet, most likely sleeping. For several moments, Alexander can't speak, just swallows around the knot in his throat. "I'm so sorry, Mercy," he finally says, thickly.

She looks up from the board, upon which is a piece of heavy white paper that she's been illustrating. Beside her is a book. "It wasn't your fault, Alexander." Her voice sounds falsely bright, unconcerned. She looks down again, making a few small crosshatches with her pen.

"No. Yes," he says, stumbling over whatever he's trying to get out. "I don't know. Mercy…"

"Look," she says, lifting the paper, holding it to the light of the lantern that's burning low beside her. "What do you think?"

Alexander leans closer. Mercy has done a very credible sketch of a dismal-looking room, the perspective shown from the outside facing in; it looks much like a prison cell, with bars on the one window and cobwebs in the corners. Several bottles and flasks and a candle sit atop a splintery table, a clock with hands pointed upward looms overlarge on the wall. Outside the barred window, off in the distance, is a hill and, on the hill, is a tent that looks much like this one does, from the outside. Below the sketch of the room, in a fine, ornate hand, she's written, in large script, "Le Rêveur Français". Underneath it, in smaller letters, is what looks like a poem:

> En rouvrant mes yeux pleins de flamme
> J'ai vu l'horreur de mon taudis,
> Et senti, rentrant dans mon âme,
> La pointe des soucis maudits;
>
> "La pendule aux accents funèbres
> Sonnait brutalement midi,
> Et le ciel versait des ténèbres
> Sur le triste monde engourdi.

"It's very well done, Mercy." He can't say that it's beautiful, because the overwhelming feeling of the drawing is one of despair. But perhaps dark things have their own beauty. "My French is rusty at best," he finally says, not able to come up with anything better. "What does it say, then, the poem?"

Mercy closes her eyes, smiling faintly as she recites, in a soft voice:

"Opening my eyes full of flames
I saw my miserable room
And felt the cursed blade of care
Sink deep into my heart again;

"The clock with its death-like accent
Was brutally striking noon;
The sky was pouring down its gloom
Upon the dismal, torpid world."

It's horrible, is all Alexander can think, when she finishes. Who would write such a thing? Moreover, why is Mercy doing this? Is this the way she shows her grief? He doesn't understand any of it, not at all. But perhaps he isn't meant to understand; Mercy's grief is a personal thing. He has no right to intrude on it. "Mercy," he says again, swallowing once more. "I…"

"It's Baudelaire, Alexander; do you know him?"

"What?"

"The poet. Charles Baudelaire? This is from *Les Fleurs du Mal*. I don't profess to understand it all, but it sets a tone, no? I think it is perfect."

"Mercy, I'm not much for poetry."

"But listen, Alexander, listen. This you will like." She flips the book open, paging until she finds what she's looking for. "*Écoute*. Listen:

"Sur l'oreiller du mal c'est Satan Trismégiste
Qui berce longuement notre esprit enchanté,
Et le riche métal de notre volonté
Est tout vaporisé par ce savant chimiste.

"C'est le Diable qui tient les fils qui nous remuent!
Aux objets répugnants nous trouvons des appas;
Chaque jour vers l'Enfer nous descendons d'un pas,
Sans horreur, à travers des ténèbres qui puent.

"On the pillow of evil Satan, Trismegist,
Incessantly lulls our enchanted minds,
And the noble metal of our will
Is wholly vaporized by this wise alchemist.

"The Devil holds the strings which move us!
In repugnant things we discover charms;
Every day we descend a step further toward Hell.
Without horror, through gloom that stinks."

Dr Potter just stares at Mercy, who's smiling absently again as she closes the book. Her eyes look too wide, emptier than they once were. *Oh, Mercy, what has Lyman done to you?* She returns her gaze to her illustration, making a few minute changes to the leafy outline she's drawn around the text of that awful poem. She looks back up, tapping two fingers on the book of poems.

"It is appropriate, no? *C'est le Diable qui tient les fils qui nous remuent!* They say that every sentiment in this world can be found in poetry, Alexander. Did you know that? Every one. Although I have never been sure quite who *they* are." She sets the board aside, holds out her arms. "*Alors,* now let us see this French Dreamer you have made. Come, Alexander, I know what you have behind you. Let me see my papa in his new home."

Later, after Alexander leaves, Mercy spends time with her father, polishing his jar so that he can be seen by the rubes, using paste to mount her illustration on the board. Getting everything just so. Pascal Levesque was a precise man, attentive to detail. He was a scientist, after all. Destined for greatness at one time, the youngest man in his class at university. He would want to look respectable in this, his new role.

"Oh, Papa," she murmurs as she works, "why didn't you tell me? I would have stopped you." In the pit of her belly she knows that she herself is the cause of all of his misfortune. She always has been, from the time of her birth onward. She accepts that now. Perhaps too late, but she accepts it. It is only true: her premature, difficult birth and the irony, then, of the odd name her father had given her, upon her early entry into the world, after such struggle. Before her mother had died, of course. *Merci-à-Dieu*, which Lyman had later insisted she Anglicize. Merci-à-Dieu Yvette Levesque, who became Mercy Rhoades. Had her mother lived, Pascal could have remained attentive to his studies, instead of wasting his time raising a daughter. Even now he could be a famous lecturer, a man who was advancing the knowledge of the world.

Instead of what he has become, because of her.

Had her path not crossed with Lyman's, her father would still be alive. That is the bare truth of it. She's often suspected, truly, that Lyman only wooed her to pull Pascal into his orbit. Surely she hadn't bewitched the man with her voice, as he'd claimed during their brief, strange courtship, before she'd known better who he was, what he was. By then, of course, it was too late to get away. But Lyman had seemed besotted with her father, from the first time they'd met. Much like the way he worshiped Morrison Hedwith, if perhaps not quite so strongly.

"He would never have let you go, Papa," she says now, rubbing a smudge off the glass. One of her father's eyes has rolled back up in his head; she wishes she could reach in and straighten it somehow. He wouldn't want to look like that. "He would never have let you go," she says again. "He won't let any of us go. Silly Papa." And Papa *was* silly, foolish really, to think that he, or any of them, could have prevailed over Lyman, who had this morning explained Pascal's whole ridiculous plot to her. How Lyman had known of it, she didn't ask. He just did, he always did. That was his power, the ability to know what a person would do before they knew it themselves.

"Oh, Papa," she says again, trying to keep herself in that empty place in her mind, the place she went to when it all became too much. The place where she didn't have to think or feel, just exist, far away from herself. That place she went to so often.

"Mercy?"

"Go away, Ridley." The voice brings her out of reverie; her legs are numb. She doesn't know how long she's been sitting here, staring at the Dreamer. It doesn't matter, really. At some point, the man in the jar stopped being the man she knew, Pascal Levesque, her father. The warm, kind man she had loved, the one who had raised her, who had given her that silly name. No, the man in the jar is only the Dreamer. She doesn't know this man. He is only a prop, a gaff. She doesn't know him. Better for him that she doesn't. The people she knows are cursed. She is a poison.

"Mercy…"

"Ridley, go away."

"But…"

"*I said go away!*" She stands and turns, hurling the book of poems at him. "*Get out!*"

•••

"Mercy?"

Later, still. Her chin lolls on her chest; the voice brings her head wobbling upright. She'd been asleep, dreaming of a locked room. She dreamt of fire and there was a burning pain in her chest, her eyes. She sits upright, wiping her fingers across her lips. They taste like blood.

Lyman sits down on the bench next to her, takes her hand, pats the back of it absently. With his free hand he lights the lantern that's gone out, on the barrel next to the seat. To one side of them, Bascom and Holly begin moving in their cages, huffing. After a few moments Holly starts muttering incoherently, shouting, banging her hands on the bars; Bascom clutches his doll to his chest, hunkering in the corner of his crate, shivering. On the other side of the tent, Rula weeps.

Ignoring the commotion, Lyman merely sits quietly, squeezing Mercy's hand. At first, he simply holds it, but the pressure increases until it's all she can do to keep from gasping as her knuckles grind against each other. Lyman stares ahead of him, at the shelves that house the gaffs. There's the requisite conjoined cow fetus, a lamb with an extra set of legs, a fish with what look like hands. This and that, some natural, some not, guaranteed to scare, amuse, and delight their customers. In pride of center is the most recent arrival: the French Dreamer, his hands caressing his cheeks, a look of surprise on his face, aside from his newly lazy eye.

Releasing her hand, Lyman stands and steps closer to the placard, which he'd ordered Mercy to make. *Follow your own dreams* was all he'd said when she'd asked him what he wanted on it, aside from Papa's new name. *Follow your own dreams, my dear.* Now, he reads the poem, his lips moving as he scans the lines. When he finishes, he's still for a long time, his face expressionless.

Mercy wonders if she's gone too far, if Lyman feels that he's being mocked. *Nos péchés sont têtus, nos repentirs sont lâches / Nous nous faisons payer grassement nos aveux. Our sins are obstinate, our repentance is faint / We exact a high price for our confessions.* Baudelaire again. Every sentiment in the world is in a poem, yes, it must be true. But she *isn't* mocking, though, surely Lyman knows this. She had only followed her dreams, like she'd been told. She had only followed them. It was natural that her dreams brought her closer to her father. How he'd been, before the end. Surely Lyman would understand that.

Lyman is motionless, merely stares at the Dreamer. Eventually, a sad smile creeps onto his lips. "Oh, Pascal, my friend," Mercy hears him murmur, "this was an unfortunate thing. Yes, unfortunate." He turns toward her. "You should have stopped him, Mercy."

"I know, Lyman," she replies automatically. Even though she'd had no idea of her father's plans, she should have stopped him, yes. You didn't argue with Lyman. "I'm sorry."

"Yes. Yes, you're sorry. Everyone is sorry. Yes." He puffs out an exasperated breath of air, reaches up to pat the glass near the Dreamer's cheek. "An unfortunate thing," he says again, shrugging, appearing to put it behind him. He clasps his fat hands together. "But you have done lovely work, Mercy. The poem, the drawing. All of it. Quite lovely. You have a real talent, my love. You are a sensitive soul." He extends one hand which, rising, Mercy takes.

"Thank you, Lyman." When he squeezes, her knuckles grind against themselves again and she can't help but let out a thin sound, while she tries to keep her face expressionless. There is a way these things must go.

"Now, my love," Lyman says, "it's time for bed."

As Lyman holds the flap of the tent open, courteously gesturing her through first, Mercy can hear Rula's low grief, the undertone to Holly's screaming.

3.

SOL MOVES HIS fist just in time, missing the girl's face and punching a flat rock instead which, however more chivalrous, hurts like a fucking bastard. He rolls off her, holding his hand to his chest, cursing and hollering. Ag is running around the campfire, wide-eyed with fear, holding his gun to the darkness and threatening to shoot in all directions, yelling "Who's there? Who is it, Sol? Who's there?" Sol regains a semblance of composure just in time to avoid being shot by his own terrified brother.

"Don't shoot, Ag! Goddamn it, don't fucking shoot!" He grits his teeth around the pain in his hand, lying on his back, gingerly flexing his fingers and sucking at a bloody knuckle. "It's just a girl."

The girl in question has regained her feet, not pausing to dust herself off before striding over and kicking Sol in the ribs. "What on earth are you doing?" she yells, kicking again over Sol's howls at her to stop.

Sol has never been kicked by a woman, certainly not with the intent that this one is displaying, trying to stave his ribs in with her boot. He's never fought a woman, either, until a minute or so ago, and vows to eschew the practice in the future. "Stop it, goddamn it!" he yells. "Just stop it! Ag, get her the fuck off me!"

Ag stays where he is, still terrified, gun in hand in case he needs it. He has no idea what's happened: one minute they were all sitting around the fire, blearily putting the finishing touches on another bottle of whiskey, and the next all hell was breaking loose. A horse had come trotting up, someone called out, and then his brother was up and running, pulling the rider off and hollering about the law. Things got even hazier then, Sol and the lawman wrestling and fighting just outside the glow of the campfire, and then his brother started screaming and cursing loud enough to wake the dead. Ag had been ready to shoot, he had been; at what, he didn't quite know, but he felt that he should be doing something, anything, and then Sol yelled at him to put up his gun.

Now his brother is back to hollering again, yelling for help, even though Ag is reasonably sure Sol had said it was a girl come to get them. Ag does the only thing he can, at that point, which is to lean over and vomit from too much whiskey and excitement.

Josiah had sat through the whole debacle, boozy and confused. The rider had come up and, for a second, he heard a voice like Elizabeth's, and then Parker was up and attacking. He shrugs, now, figuring the man knows best, and goes back to drinking. Things will work themselves out.

Elizabeth McDaniel steps away from the man on the ground, giving him another kick for good measure as she does so. "What on earth were you thinking?" she yells at him again, dusting herself off as best she can. She strides into the firelight. "And what on earth were *you* thinking?" she yells at her brother. "Who is this fool?"

Josiah blinks up at his sister, not understanding just why she's here and why she has been wrestling his hired gun. He shrugs once more, raising the bottle to his lips again. It's all a bit too confusing. Mr Parker is over on the ground yelling, Mr Rideout vomiting nearby, and now Elizabeth is here in his camp, instead of in Baker City where she belongs. It is all very strange, he thinks. Very strange indeed.

"Josiah!"

He nods to himself, looking up at his sister, who appears to be in a towering rage. No doubt it will all start to make sense at some point. "Hello, Lizzie," he says, mildly. "Whiskey?"

Elizabeth has to restrain herself, to keep from kicking her brother, now that her leg is limbered. This has been a very, very long day, and to end it by being pulled off her horse and almost punched out by some foul-mouthed lout is almost too much to bear. And now – now! – her brother is offering her a drink, as if he'd just seen her that morning, as if she hadn't spent the last several – extremely uncomfortable – days in a bumpy wagon, and then the long trip riding out alone from Boise after she'd found out that she'd missed Josiah in town. She grabs the bottle out of his hand then, and takes a long swig. Who cares if it isn't ladylike behavior? Gagging at the taste, she gasps out a hot breath.

"What are you *doing* out here?" she yells, then tries to calm herself some. "What are you doing out here?" she repeats in a quieter voice. "Why aren't you in Boise? Everyone is worried about you, Josiah. What are you doing?"

"Why, drinking, Lizzie," Josiah explains, nodding. "And then I'm going to Portland with these gentlemen." It seemed clear enough, to him.

Elizabeth feels her hand clenching so hard around the bottle that for a moment she's worried she'll break it. Out of the corner of her eye, she sees the man who'd tackled her skulking back to the fire, sucking on the back of his finger. The other man is still on his knees, weakly gagging, and then mostly just collapses where he is.

"Ag, you all right?" Sol calls, seeing his brother keel over.

"I'm just resting, Sol," comes the slurred reply back. "Just resting."

It's embarrassing how his brother handles his drink, Sol thinks, watching the woman, wishing she would hand over that fucking whiskey she's ungraciously monopolizing. How was he to have known that she was a girl, that she somehow knew McDaniel? She'd just sneaked up on them like a thief, so it was entirely natural that he'd moved, catlike, to defend himself and Ag. They're wanted men, after all, and it's entirely likely that a posse from Twin Falls could have caught them up by now. And it wasn't like he'd actually hit the girl, anyway. His fucking hand was probably broke from hitting that rock.

"You," the woman says, swinging a finger his way. "Sol, is it?"

"Yes, ma'am," he says, sullenly. "Sol Parker. That's my brother Ag, yonder."

"I couldn't care less, Sol Parker. Why did you pull me off my horse? That his doing?" she points back to her brother, who has a hand held out for the whiskey. She takes a step back.

"No, ma'am," Sol says. "You fucking startled me, is all. If you'll excuse my mouth." Saying that, though, he starts to feel a bit indignant. Why the fuck is he apologizing? Granted, his mother had frowned on strong language, but she isn't here, is she? Sol, himself, has always been of the belief that some saltiness lends gravitas to a man's speech, so he'll be goddamned if he is going to start apologizing for it now. "Why were you sneaking up on us, anyway? You don't sneak up on a man's fire, girl. You're lucky that I didn't shoot you."

"He's right, you're lucky." Ag's voice drifts over from where he lies.

"Goddamn it, shut your hole, Ag."

Elizabeth rolls her eyes, turning back to her brother. "You say you're going to Portland with *these* two, Joe? Why on earth would you do that?"

Josiah nods, several times, over and over, his head sinking lower and lower on his chest. When he finally lifts his face, Elizabeth sees that he's crying. "Going to kill a man, Lizzie," he says. "Going to kill the man that took Mary."

Elizabeth's anger evaporates and she hunkers down next to Josiah, putting her arms around him and letting him sob into her shoulder. He looks – and smells – terrible, she thinks, absolutely terrible. She's lucky that she caught him before something even worse happened to him, before he'd fallen off his horse drunk and broken his fool neck. After she'd gotten the letter from their cousin Esther in Boise, there was only one thing that Lizzie could do, and that was to go fetch Josiah back. It was inconvenient, but Elizabeth couldn't just stand by and let Josiah drink himself to death.

Elizabeth McDaniel wasn't a woman who let overthinking a problem get in the way of solving it. She'd done little in the way of travel before this, certainly not on her own, but getting in the wagon with a stranger, and then renting a horse and tackle a few days later, setting out alone to track down Josiah, was simply something she'd set her mind to, a chore that needed to be done. Nothing more than that. She lived her life on those simple terms, taking each of life's difficulties in stride, one at a time.

Upon arriving in Boise, dusty and tired, she'd spent an evening asking around town after discovering that she'd missed her brother; the general consensus was that he'd headed off northwest. That was fine, as that was back in the direction of home; she'd just find him, then, and bring him to Baker City. The man in Boise who'd rented her the mare had been aghast that she was just riding out into the desert, alone, with poor supplies and only a vague idea where her brother might have gone. He was convinced that she'd wander off lost and die of thirst or get eaten by a wild animal. His unspoken fear was that lawless men would take her and use her in terrible ways, a pretty young girl like that on her own in the wilds. She refused all offers of help, though, having little money and not wanting to be beholden to strangers, but did accept the use of a small tent, a pair of heavy, too-long trousers, a hat, and some camping supplies, on the condition that she could return them, along with a bit of money for the loan, when she had finished her errand.

Even with her staunch self-belief, Elizabeth couldn't help but have some fear as that first afternoon out of Boise, on her own, had settled into evening and she'd had no sign of Josiah. She realized that she had no idea how one went about tracking a man in the first place: she watched for signs and marks but the dirt and brush just looked like dirt and brush. Once, she got excited, thinking she saw a hoofprint, and then discovered that it was her own mare's, that she'd somehow made a looping circle around a low set of hills while lost in thought. When the sun had started to go down, she just kept riding, as she didn't quite know how to put up her tent and had also forgotten to bring matches. So, when she saw the fire at the base of a small rise, she put her heels to her horse. If it wasn't Josiah, at least maybe someone there would let her borrow a few burning sticks for a fire of her own. She was confident that she'd figure out the rest, given time. Not for the first time she wished she'd brought a gun of some kind, though. Upon setting out from Baker City, she'd simply assumed that she'd ride the wagon to Boise and fetch Josiah back; after finding him gone, then, she'd just ridden that momentum into her present predicament. She understands, now, that the matter likely had deserved a bit more thought and planning before she'd set out.

She glances over her brother's shoulder at the man who had dragged her from her horse. He's watching her sullenly, still rubbing one hand. He's young, she realizes, close to her own age. His youth, combined with his expression, makes him look like a pouty boy, almost like one of her students back in Baker City. Wordlessly, not knowing exactly why, she extends her arm, holding out the bottle his way. His sullen expression evaporates almost instantly and, while he doesn't smile exactly, he lightens up considerably.

Sol takes the bottle from the girl, putting it to his lips and taking a long drink to knock the dust out of his throat. He watches her over the bottle; she's rocking Josiah, who is blubbering uncontrollably. Is that his wife, he wonders, the one who is supposed to be dead? On closer inspection he reckons not; this girl is bigger than Josiah, just by a hair, but certainly not the tiny thing the man had described earlier. They have a similar look, he notices now, same brown hair and sharp cheekbones. Sister, maybe a cousin. The girl, whoever she is, is pretty enough, even in the odd getup of a dress worn over old men's pants, rolled up around big boots. Her hair is a little crazy under a wide hat and she is as dirty as he is, from rolling in the dust.

Sol feels somewhat guilty and foolish, now, having wrestled the girl. Also a bit distracted: the image of rolling around on the ground with her has a way of catching in the mind, he realizes. In retrospect, he wishes he'd paid a bit more attention to the matter, although he has to admit that, at the time, he'd been too intent on his own fucking terror before things had gotten straightened out. The girl glances over at him then and he looks guiltily away, understanding that he's been staring. He tries to smooth his hair a bit, brush some of the dust from his clothes. It's disconcerting to have a girl right there at their fire. Of an evening, lately, he's used to cursing and bullshitting around the fire with Ag, farting when he needs to and pissing close by their camp. He has a moment of panic now when he realizes that he'll have to piss far away from the fire, out in the dark. It is one of Sol's most closely guarded secrets that he still has a fear of the dark, that he worries a bear or bandit or the like is lurking out there, waiting for him.

Josiah seems to have cried himself out, and Elizabeth can feel his heavy, sloppy liquor breath on her neck. She shakes him a little, but he appears to be out cold. She lays him down as gently as she can, then, rolling him on his side in case he's sick – not the first time, by the smell of it – and cushioning his head with his battered hat. She pulls a nearby saddle blanket over his body. *Josiah*, she thinks, *what am I going to do with you?*

She hears her horse whicker and realizes that she needs to take the saddle off and perhaps hobble her for the night, rub her down, maybe. She isn't entirely sure of the process, relying on a livery stable at home for such things the few times she goes riding. When she looks over, the saddle is already coming off, though, and the stocky man who'd tackled her is carrying it near the fire, her bedroll and bags in his other hand.

"I've got it, miss," he says, sounding embarrassed. "I was just over throwing a fucking blanket on Ag there and seen that your horse was still cinched up."

"Thank you. I was just going to hobble her." The man is standing there looking at her. "You can put down that saddle if you like."

"Oh," Sol says, feeling foolish, kneeling down and setting the gear near Josiah. "Right. You don't probably need to hobble her, the horse I mean. She ain't going to go nowhere. Horses like to stay together." He stands up. "Are you Mr McDaniel's cousin, then, miss?"

"I'll just put up my tent," Elizabeth says, ignoring him. She doesn't need any further help, just wants to get some sleep and, in the morning, get Josiah on the road back to Boise, where she can put them both on a train to Baker City, whenever one comes through. She's too tired for idle conversation with some ruffian. Elizabeth takes the tent over to a flattish spot on the edge of the firelight and spends several minutes wrestling with the poles and ropes. She'd get two propped up and then the others would fall over, or she'd have it mostly erect and the whole thing would collapse when she pulled the ropes. Her frustration is getting the better of her and she is considering just taking out the poles and crawling under the flat canvas as-is when Sol Parker comes over and, in a short minute, has the tent up, just like that. He shrugs at her, looking embarrassed again.

"One of those things, miss. Takes a time or two to get the hang of it." He smiles at her. "I guess we got off on the wrong foot. My name is Sol, again, Sol Parker. Ag over there is my brother."

"Well, you should go sleep near him then, Mr Parker,"

Elizabeth says crisply, crawling into her tent with her bedroll and drawing the flap. "Family should stay together, after all," she calls from the inside.

Sol stares foolishly at the tent for a moment and then walks back to the fire, pausing to pick up the orphaned bottle of whiskey, which still has a couple inches at the bottom. Women are a thirsty proposition, he thinks. He stares at the moonlight on the girl's tent, not feeling a bit sleepy.

"Oh no you're not, Josiah!" The effect of Elizabeth stamping her foot is somewhat lost in the fact that it tangles with her rolled pant-leg, making her stumble. "You are *not* going all the way to Portland, not in the state you're in. You need to come home, take some time to mourn. Properly mourn, I mean, not drink yourself to death. Why do you think I'm here? You're coming back with me." She storms over to where her brother is queasily trying to mount his horse, looking green.

"Hush with the yelling, Lizzie," Josiah mutters. "I have a headache. And you're my little sister, not my mother." He feels awful, as he does nearly every morning, and there is only one cure, he knows, more whiskey and time. Well, two cures, then. He scrabbles at his saddlebag, fishing out another bottle, lifting it to his lips and turning his back on his sister as she tries to take it.

"Give me that, Josiah! Give it!" She slaps at his back, trying to get around him as he drinks.

The whiskey – or perhaps the desire to keep it from his sister – gives Josiah the boost of energy needed to finally get on his horse, although he nearly falls from the off side; he clutches at the saddle horn with his free hand, feeling his rubbery stomach flip over inside him, trying not to vomit as his vision spins.

Sol is watching the whole episode bemusedly, standing there holding the girl's horse like a simpleton. He feels grim himself, dry-mouthed and achy, and her carrying-on isn't helping the pounding between his eyes. Last night Elizabeth had seemed soft and feminine, lovely in the firelight, even in her ridiculous get-up. A girl he wanted to know more about but, this morning, he would gladly turn his back on her, for all time, if she would only stop yelling. He wishes he had the whiskey that Josiah is keeping away from the girl, just a bit to moisten up his dry skull again. He contents himself with a canteen of stale-tasting water.

"You ever try to take whiskey away from me of a morning like that, Ag, when I need it, and I'll fucking shoot you," he says to his brother. "Mark my words, boy: I will fucking shoot you." He hands up the canteen instead.

Ag just groans, leaning over the side of his horse, a thin line of vomit dripping from his mouth. He rests his head on the roan's soft neck. "Puked on my horse," he gasps. "I puked on my horse," which turns into another gag of vomiting. Sol just shakes his head at the folly of youth, stepping away a bit lest he get splashed.

Feeling slightly better, Josiah has turned his own horse and heads off in a direction he hopes is northwest. His emotions are twisted up at having Lizzie there with them. On one hand, it's tempting to just give in to some sisterly mothering and let her lead him back to Boise or to Baker City or wherever. She's come all this way, just how he doesn't quite understand, but she has done it for love of him. It's a hard thing to ignore, but he can't let his resolve waver. He'd made the decision to avenge Mary and, by God, he would do it, even if he knows it won't bring her back, even if, at some level, he knows it is a stupid and pointless thing to try to do.

He has nothing else. His wife is gone, along with his hopes for a family, and his business is in ruins. He's a laughingstock in Boise, now, his reputation destroyed. The last of his money is gone, sitting in the pocket of these off-brand outlaws he's hired. What else *did* he have but this self-appointed mission, however ill-advised it might be? Yesterday, he'd put the decision in the hand of God but, now, he doesn't like to consider that maybe Lizzie's arrival was in fact the work of the Almighty. More than likely it's just a product of his sister's bossy nature, he thinks. She'd always been that way, even when they were children: she was the baby of the McDaniel clan but, from an early age, she'd taken on the idea that she ran their family, particularly after their parents had died. Elizabeth is headstrong and brassy but, this time, he won't let her order him around like a wayward child. And, after all, Josiah thinks, if he's wrong about God sending Lizzie to find him and bring him back, the Lord can smite him and he will accept that.

Elizabeth stares at the back of her brother's horse, dumbfounded that Josiah is just riding away from her like that. This isn't the way things were supposed to work. She'd dropped her life and come all this way, through assorted dangers and inconveniences, to bring her brother back home. He didn't just turn around and walk away from her. No, he did not. For several long seconds, she isn't quite sure what to do; her script reads: *Go to Boise, fetch Josiah home.* She supposes that it had been in the realm of possibility that she wouldn't be able to find him, at least for a time, but the idea that, once found, he'd balk her, simply doesn't register at all. Even drunk and sick as he is, though, there's a look in his eyes that she doesn't recognize. Something she doesn't like.

"I expect he's not quite ready to go home yet, then," Sol says. He'd sidled up nearer to Elizabeth while she stared off at his retreating employer. "Man's got the bit between his teeth, I reckon." He tries to ignore the silent, venomous look she gives him. "I'll just pack up that tent for you right quick, then," he says instead.

Elizabeth stares at Sol's wide back as he kneels to take down her tent. "We're not going to Portland, Mr Parker. I'll tell you that right now." He doesn't answer, busying himself with rolling up the canvas. "I said, *I'll tell you that right now.*"

Sol isn't quite sure why he's bothering with the tent, trying to be helpful. This girl is getting nothing but worse on closer acquaintance, shouting and carrying on as she's been, and her bossy tone isn't doing wonders for his headache. He stands up, fed up all of a sudden.

"I reckon you can *tell* me what you like, little girl, and I'll *do* what I see fit. You didn't fucking hire me, Mr McDaniel did; if you have a problem, then, take it up with him. I'm done here." He drops the rolled tent at her feet, walking off. "Portland is that way," he calls over his shoulder, waving vaguely towards Josiah. Ag's horse has headed off at a tangent, his brother still slumped over its neck, gagging weakly from time to time. "Once I round up my brother, that's where we're headed. If you're coming with us, you'd best hurry it up. If not, well, you know the way back to Boise." He mounts his own horse, turning a bit to give her a sarcastic tip of the hat. Turns out there's nothing like righteousness for a hangover, he realizes, feeling noticeably more spry as he trots off after Ag.

Elizabeth can feel her mouth hanging open in shock; she snaps it shut as her fury rises. She wants to run after the man and pull him off his horse, as he'd done to her

the night before. Then she wants to take his gun and
shoot him in the ass, followed by shooting her brother.
Sol's own brother would be spared, as he hasn't yet vexed
her and already appears to be suffering enough, from the
look of it. Her violent fantasies war with the desire to
just turn east and go back to Boise, washing her hands
of Josiah and his idiotic life. It's tempting, so tempting,
for a hot moment, but Elizabeth is a woman that, when
challenged, gets her dander up. She'll be damned if she'll
let Josiah go against her like this.

Gathering up her tent, bedroll, and baggage, she
secures them to her horse as best she can, given her lack
of skill with ropes. Fortunately Sol Parker had already
saddled her horse for her, as she has only a vague idea
how to do that on her own. After a try or two, then, she
gets her things tied tightly enough to the horse, using
an unorthodox array of square knots, so she can mount
and be on her way. Josiah by then is a small speck on the
horizon, his hired morons further back. The rising sun
at her back, Elizabeth points her horse west and trots off
after them, letting her anger lead the way.

4.

THE SUN IS barely up and Alexander can already tell Lyman is angry, that he's woken in a mood, the way he's stomping around camp, muttering. As he sips his coffee, thinking, Dr Potter watches Mercy move gingerly about the campfire, cleaning up the breakfast dishes. Lyman never marks his wife, nowhere visible, anyway, but Alexander can tell from her movements that she's hurting. He knows that, if asked, she will just drop her eyes and tell him it's nothing; if he presses too much, and Lyman overhears, well, it isn't a thing to contemplate. The fate of Colonel Batts had been an object lesson in the virtues of caution around the man, the need to guard one's tongue. Alexander is already due, after all, and Lyman is only holding back so that he can savor the dread he'll know Alexander and Oliver are feeling as they wait for whatever will be coming. All the same, regardless of his own worries, it's hard for Alexander to watch Mercy hide the wincos. But, he realizes, sadly, that he's of course seen much worse over the years.

For once it isn't raining; the morning is actually pleasant. Not sunny, as such, but the kind of hazy day that can become beautiful by afternoon. The air smells like spring for a change, fresh and clean, instead of just smelling damp, as it usually does. It's a lovely morning, but Lyman's news, when he comes over to give it, threatens to spoil the day. Before he can stop himself, Alexander speaks up.

"But we just *came* that way, Lyman. Why go back? We're only two or three days out from Portland."

Lyman's heavy-lidded eyes, the skin bagged dark and bruised-looking underneath, swings his way. "Excuse me, Dr Potter?" he says in a deceptively mild voice.

There's nothing for it but to just push ahead. It's not like Alexander has much more to lose. "You heard me, Lyman. Why turn around *now*?" Alexander doesn't like Portland much, as a town, but he yearns for an actual bed to sleep in again, a wooden roof over his head and some good whiskey to drink, not the rotgut garbage they pick up on the road. They've been traveling for weeks now, had started as soon as the mucky spring roads had become remotely passable again. "Everyone needs a break, Lyman: we're going to be gone all summer and we need at least a few days out of this wet weather. Besides, we're low on supplies and I'm sure the doctor will want your report." He knows he's already said too much but, when he starts, it's hard to stop. What will happen will fucking happen. It's not boldness or bravery he feels, it's apathy. He has nothing left inside himself, so why not just say what comes to mind. Lyman will do what he wants.

"Just give us a few days in Portland," he continues. "You can report to the doctor, the others can get a break, we'll stock up, and then we'll be ready to go for summer. Turning around now just doesn't make sense."

Lyman is silent, staring at Potter with his dead eyes, knuckles slowly clenching. He can't believe what he's hearing, really. Potter, growing a spine, after what's happened? Not bloody likely, and yet he can't remember

the last time the man has shown the slightest ounce of
dissent when given an order. Perhaps he was too lenient,
the other night. Potter knows what Lyman can do to
him, after all, but maybe merely knowing isn't enough
right now. He is in arrears, Potter, and Lyman is owed his
recompense. Lyman glances over at Mercy. It is always
unsatisfying, with her, not being able to indulge himself
properly. When they finally isolate the Stone he will
have a bit more freedom.

Lyman had only slept a few minutes after his time
with Mercy, last night. A few minutes had been enough
though because, this morning, he'd been woken with
the knowledge that they needed to head back east again,
that there was something left incomplete. From time
to time Lyman is given these sudden flashes of insight,
whether due to some residual effect of the work, the
incomplete Salt that infuses his blood or, perhaps, simply
some synthesis of unconscious ideas. Almost never do
these flashes prove incorrect; the few times they had,
he'd chalked it up to his own misunderstanding of the
message rather than the message itself. Now, he's been
told to go back east for a time, and so they will. He's tired
and irritable from the lack of sleep, this latest failure and
that, now, they have to retrace their steps, but there's
nothing to be done about it. He has a job to do, after all;
the great work must always come first.

Potter is right, of course: they're low on supplies
and probably could do with a break from travel. Lyman
knows that he himself would enjoy sleeping under a
real roof again. The supplies are the concerning thing.
The few employees of the show are just that: employees,
who will do what they are told. He does a quick mental
inventory in his head, counting up the few remaining
bottles of the special Sagwa and, more importantly, the

fixative version that keeps him, Potter, and big, black Wilson alive. There should be enough to sustain them for a few more weeks; if not, there is enough to sustain *him*, which is what matters.

"Everyone needs a break?" he asks now, feigning confusion. His voice goes quiet. "Now, what is it that it says on the side of the wagon? Just there. What does it say?"

Alexander is silent.

"What does it say on that wagon, *Doctor*?" Lyman repeats, slowly, leaning forward and pointing.

"Dr Potter's Medicine Show," Alexander mumbles, wondering if, now, he's finally pushed Lyman too far. Particularly given what had happened before. Maybe now he'll wind up like poor Batts, buried in a shallow hole and forgotten. He almost hopes so. They'd found another fortune-teller; Lyman could always find another Dr Potter. He realizes that his hands are shaking again; perhaps this new apathy hasn't quite entirely overwhelmed his native cowardice.

"Whose show?"

There is no right answer here, Alexander knows. "Dr Potter's Medicine Show," he repeats, waiting. The urge to close his eyes is intense. He can feel Mercy's gaze. Just look away, he thinks.

But Lyman merely reaches over and presses one thick, stubby finger hard into Alexander's breastbone, pushing so that he almost falls back. Rhoades leans even closer, putting his fleshy lips so near to Alexander's ear that hot breath ruffles his hair.

"My show, Potter," Lyman whispers. "*My show*." He sits back again, his eyes never leaving Alexander's. "Now get *my fucking show* packed up and ready to go. We're headed east."

•••

That night, after they've camped, Mercy lays in the tent she shares with Lyman, as far away from her husband as the space allows. It's been two nights running, this, which means that Lyman must have something on his mind. Normally his attentions are less frequent. The skin of her stomach is raw and abraded; her shoulders and elbows ache from the way Lyman had stretched and twisted them, earlier. Her husband has any number of tricks like that, ways to punish and hurt her to maximum effect, without causing lasting harm. Physical harm, that is; as she huddles on her side against the wall of the tent, her mind draws into itself, to her away place. Lyman makes her go so far from herself that sometimes she feels she might never find her way back.

"I wish you could have seen how I looked, before," he's saying. "*Beautiful* was really the only word for it." It's her husband's same old theme, particularly after the time he spends with his wife. He's flushed and sweaty, now, the rolls of his fat belly slick and wet. His teats are bigger than Mercy's own. "Now, *beautiful* isn't really a word that you would normally associate with a man, but that's what I was. Like…"

"Adonis," Mercy murmurs, on cue. She knows her part in the charade by now, her prompts in the stage show.

"Adonis, exactly. Thank you, my love." Lyman runs a hand slowly down his chest and belly, pushing off the sweat, wiping his hand on the tent's canvas. "But look at me now," he says, disgusted. "I'm a veritable whale. Cetacean is the word. A whale, yes. I was never like this, before. My stomach was flat and my shoulders broad. I was tall; I had long, strong legs." He rolls over on an elbow, running his hand down his wife's naked side. Mercy tries not to flinch. "I don't like to say it, Mercy, but

I think the doctor gave me this form *on purpose,* when I had to leave that beautiful body of mine." He pauses.

"He's always been jealous of you, dear." She feels him nodding.

"Yes, he has, hasn't he? Yes. He's a great man, after all, but he's always been jealous of my skill with the work." Mercy wonders just how much of the story Lyman himself believes, whether the endless repetition of his grievances has changed the actual facts of the matter, in his mind. Lyman goes on, talking more to himself than anyone else, reliving whatever he sees of the past. "Of course, I *had* to leave that vessel. It was dying; I had a knife in my guts."

Mercy wishes that the knife had done its work. "But the doctor saved you, Lyman."

"He did, Mercy. The doctor saved me. That he did. And he's told me, more than once, that this vessel of mine wouldn't have been the one he would have *chosen* for me, had he the time, but that it was a necessity of the situation. It wasn't his fault, really. The urgency of it, you understand." *But why won't he let me move again, now, to a younger, slimmer body?* Lyman thinks. *Now that there is no urgency. I'm willing to accept the pain, the risk. After everything I've done for him, for us, for the work, those things that Dr Hedwith is incapable of doing for himself. I deserve it.*

"He's always been jealous of you, dear," Mercy repeats, knowing the pattern of his thoughts. "He's always felt you were the better man." She wills her body to be still as her husband caresses her side again, murmuring to himself. She hopes his needs are sated, for now.

Lyman doesn't have sex with Mercy, not sex in the normal manner, anyway. There is nudity, but no intercourse, simply pain. His member grows hard and he eventually reaches his climax, but only through his wife's suffering, or that of whoever he's with, she supposes. Tonight, he'd pinned her face-first to the hard floor of the tent, which is merely canvas over the ground; naked, he'd straddled her, pulling her arms up and behind her, straining at them until her shoulders were on the edge of dislocation. With his knees, he'd pushed into her ribs, driving her naked belly and breasts against the rough canvas. She'd wanted to scream, but knew that she had to play her part; if she screamed too early Lyman would get angry and perhaps hurt her even worse. Instead, he twisted and pulled her arms, working the pain into her elbow and shoulder joints while pressing her belly into the ground so that she could barely breathe. When she was just on the very edge of passing out he would let up, allowing relief to flow back into her. And then he would start again. Finally, after a few repetitions, she couldn't keep herself from screaming and, soon after, she felt him shudder and the hot splat of his semen on her naked back, mixing with the sweat from his body that dripped down onto her.

Now, face against the tent, she tries to pull further away from herself, away from her husband and this life she leads. In her head she sings: *L'amour est un oiseau rebelle / Que nul ne peut apprivoiser. Love is a rebellious bird / that none can tame.* It's her favorite aria from the show, one that she'd learned at the behest of Dr Hedwith, who is a music lover and always enjoyed listening to her sing when she was in town. Even though the Bizet opera is barely three years old, Dr Hedwith had gotten a copy of the score, which she'd reduced to a semblance of playability on her accordion, lacking an accompanist as she did. Once, many years ago, she might have had a career on the stage; she'd been good enough to sing at some of the smaller theaters in Paris at a young age and, with the right patronage, might have gone on to greater things.

Instead, she'd found Lyman, or he'd found her, while passing through Paris with the doctor. He'd found her father. Mercy still isn't entirely sure how Lyman had courted her so successfully, perhaps through means she doesn't entirely understand. *Love is a gypsy's child / it has never, never known the law.* Mercy wonders if Lyman had ever desired her, as a woman, even at first, or if she was always only the lure for poor Papa. He was certainly solicitous for a time, Lyman, those first weeks and months and, though their marital intimacies were not of a normal nature, they weren't the wanton cruelties he soon turned to. Likely, any allure she'd once had has now faded; over the last months his brutalities have gotten harder and more painful. She knows that, eventually, he will kill her. Now that Papa is gone it won't be much longer. She's wanted to run away so often but, when he'd caught her that first time, the things that he'd done had been so horrible as to serve as a deterrent for future efforts.

If Papa only had asked her, he could have learned from her mistakes.

At first, it had been almost enjoyable when the doctor had sent them out on the road with the show. She got to sing once more, dress in fine clothes and try to recapture some of her lost youth: on a stage again, admired for her voice, bringing people the beauty of music. She'd loved it, the show, until she'd learned what it was that they did. Until Lyman decided that her talents also extended to being a traveling whore, selling her to eager men in each town they visited. They don't need the extra money; it's just another of Lyman's cruelties. It excites him.

At least she's still herself, as awful as that is at times;

she isn't yet trapped as the others are, Alexander, Oliver, Lyman himself. Her slavery is of the normal sort. She's certainly better off than the Halfhead, or Holly, or Rula; at least she is still a woman, broken though she might be. She knows that Lyman visits the cages from time to time, visits of a sexual nature, or what passes for it for him. She wonders if he's able to perform as a real man with them, jaded as he is and given their own limitations. Maybe it's something else. Perhaps the bruises and abrasions she finds in what remains of Holly and Rula's intimate regions, when she cleans them, are simply little reminders of what her husband is capable of.

Lyman is murmuring about the work again, about how close they are to finding the Stone, after so long, which will fix his fat, ugly body and make him beautiful once more. He keeps licking his lips, talking of his body and how the doctor had betrayed him, great man though he is.

"He's always been jealous of you, dear," she whispers, turning her head further away, pushing against the tent wall. *But if I love you / if I love you / Take guard yourself.*

5.

CASTLE STANDS BACK in a doorway in one of the Theatre's galleries, listening to this poor excuse for *O Patria Mia*, sung by a warbling soprano with only a passing acquaintance with key. The New Market Theatre had opened with great fanfare several years ago, a brick and iron monolith that's the pride of Portland's uppercrust set, a place to be seen with their fellows: those bankers, and wheat, timber, and shipping princes that hadn't been made back into relative paupers after Cooke's collapse and the Panic of '73. In the New Market they can listen to operas and symphonies and pretend that they live in anything but a muddy, provincial little town. Quite a number of Portland's elite had held on through the Panic, though; looking down, Castle sees Ladds, Corbetts, Dekums, Reeds and, of course, his own employer, rubbing elbows in a second-tier sort of way thanks to his wife's Alberton family connections. There's plenty of money and influence in the room but, for a man like Castle, watching these Portland peacocks strut and gabble is laughable; the town has a mere twenty thousand or so people in it, after all. Napoli has over half a million, and has certainly seen better opera than this.

Oh my homeland, I will never see you again! / No more,

never see you again! the soprano quavers in Italian. Castle wonders himself if he'll ever see Napoli, or even Brooklyn, again, if he'll ever hear Italian spoken – or sung – in an accent that sounds right. Giuseppe Castello yearns for home, sometimes, but the time isn't yet ripe to return. There's something about Dr Hedwith, something to discover, which Castle has sensed from the very beginning. Hedwith is both more and less than he seems, and Castle is not a man who easily lets go of a mystery; he stays in this silly little town, therefore, content to wait, to be nothing more than a trusted servant, assistant, and bodyguard. Biding his time.

Lyman Rhoades had originally hired Castle for muscle, many years and several cities ago, for the kinds of jobs that the fat man couldn't take on himself. Castle's own varied competences had brought him to the attention of the doctor himself, though, which had gradually evolved into his present role, much to Lyman's dismay. Castle despises Rhoades, a feeling that's mutual; it's fortunate that the medicine show keeps Rhoades away so often, as Castle knows that, someday, there will eventually come a reckoning between them. It's inevitable. Lyman may think him just another semi-illiterate immigrant, but he'd learn how wrong he was.

No one knows the real Castle. He is a man who keeps himself close, and his reasons for emigrating to America are his own. America is a place where a smart man can reinvent himself.

He's learned much during his years with Hedwith, in one city or another. He's been required to do some distasteful things, yes, but earns a generous salary and is allowed free use of the bulk of his employer's substantial library. To better himself, to learn and to further his education. Over the years Castle has lost almost all of his accent and, while he will never pass as a gentleman, he is much more than a simple thug and a criminal. He isn't a man who craves wealth, power, or fine things: what he has is an almost obsessive need for knowledge, for understanding, which makes the world seem bigger, both more mysterious and more comprehensible at once. These are the things that keep him with Dr Hedwith, at least for now; the future will bring what it brings, so best not worry about that, overmuch. Best to make use of the advantages he currently enjoys.

What he *doesn't* understand, though, is how this wretched production of *Aida* has managed to stay together and fill theaters, even in third-rate towns like this one. In '73, in New York, he'd seen Ostava Torriani and Campanini; now, watching this woman butcher Verdi is like having teeth pulled, and he doesn't even want to think about the man playing Radamès. He tries to concentrate on something else, anything to distract himself from the noise at hand. Finally, after what feels like a thousand years, the last act ends, with enthusiastic applause from the clueless audience. Castle leaves before he has to witness someone giving the soprano a bouquet.

Downstairs, in the dance hall, he stands against one of the walls, with the other servants, waiting for Dr and Mrs Hedwith to come down from the theatre proper. With the opera finally over, there's to be an auction to raise funds for the new Presbyterian church, put on by the women in Mrs Hedwith's Temperance chapter. A collection of dour old bats, to his mind, even though he himself is not a drinker.

Eventually, the genteel press of the elegant makes its way into the hall; they accept flutes of champagne from tuxedoed waiters, mill about under the gaslit chandeliers, chatting, ignoring those servants, like Castle, whose services are not presently required. He sees Mrs Hedwith separate herself from the doctor's arm, joining the women of her WCTU claque to discuss some final logistics of the coming auction. Rearranging, yet again, the various donations which are stacked on a long table near a rostrum.

With Annabelle off his arm, Dr Hedwith looks to be at something of a loss. His wife is the social force of the marriage; the doctor himself is used to working largely in solitude. Castle knows Hedwith to be an awkward man; the glad-hand and hail-fellow-well-met is not one of his natural skills and the accumulation and growth of money for its own sake holds little interest for him. As such, he seems to have little to say to the likes of the Dekums and Corbetts and Failings, whose men focus on commerce and whose women occupy their time with society occasions such as these, uplifting social pursuits like the Temperance and women's rights movements, spiritualism, nonsense of that nature.

Castle watches his employer, standing in the midst of the throng like a lost boy, nodding occasionally at passers-by, a vague smile on his face. He's like a dull, innocuous rock in the middle of this stream of society. At one point, a large man with dramatic side-whiskers accosts Dr Hedwith, leaning forward and talking loudly, pausing from time to time to slap him on the shoulder with a meaty hand. Castle can't tell if the doctor is actually able to hold up a conversational end, or is simply occupied with nodding and smiling and trying to lean back out of the man's face. After a time, Dr Hedwith disengages himself, making his way to a doorway and exiting the hall. Castle follows.

"Are you all right, sir?" he asks, catching up with the doctor, whose face is both pale and flushed, splotchy, with a sheen of sweat on his forehead.

Morrison turns with a start, not realizing that Castle had come up behind him. "Oh, it's you, Castle. What was that you said? Ah. Yes, I feel fine. Just a bit warm, you know."

Castle nods. "Can I get you anything, Doctor? Water, brandy?"

Morrison gives a wan smile. "A spot of brandy would be excellent but, I fear, given this crowd, the smell of it on my breath would win me no friends." He waves an arm vaguely back towards the hall, sighing. "I'm no good at these kinds of things, Castle. So many people close in makes me uncomfortable. And I don't understand these people, not really. I'd rather be back in the lab, working." Suddenly he feels very lightheaded; when he tries to take another step his legs go loose and it's only Castle's quick motion that keeps him from stumbling.

"Are you sure you're all right, sir?" Castle asks, holding Dr Hedwith upright by the arm. "Perhaps you should sit down." He leads his employer to a velvet-cushioned chair, settling him onto it, looking down with concern. "I'll get you some water, Doctor."

Morrison doesn't notice when Castle leaves; his head is spinning now, feeling heavy on his neck, and he's having trouble focusing his eyes again. There's a burning in his guts and his joints feel as if they have broken glass inside. He fights for control, knowing that he might pass out or have one of his fits, here, of all places, with Annabelle and the cream of Portland society looking on. Gritting his teeth, he tries to focus; to take his mind off his body he sings in his head a song his mother used to sing when he was a boy, a grim song with a catchy tune:

"Abroad I was walking
One morning in the Spring,
I heard a maid in Bedlam
So sweetly she did sing;
Her chains she rattled in her hands,
And always so sang she."

The song had been one of her favorites, ironically as it turned out: his mother had lost her mind after the deaths of her young children, one after another, leaving only Morrison; eventually she'd been carted away to Bedlam herself, screaming and singing all the while. She'd died of a fever shortly thereafter, joining Morrison's father, so Morrison himself had been sent to live with an aged aunt and uncle in Sussex. They were distant and cold, regarding him as nothing but a noisy imposition on quiet lives in their large, dusty, empty house. But, as fate would have it, the uncle was a secret – if talentless – practitioner of the great work. Eventually, his uncle took him on as a dogsbody and general assistant, simply to save the expense of hiring someone. He'd never warmed to Morrison but had given him a start in what would become a life's quest. In moments of introspection, Morrison has often wondered if his early obsession with the great work was merely a result of the need to fill a family-shaped hole in his life. Perhaps, if the uncle had been a gardener, a painter, a sportsman, Morrison's life would have turned out far differently, and ended far sooner.

He doesn't know why he's thinking of all this now, why his mother's song had even come into his head. He hasn't thought of his family for years. Perhaps it's the recent thoughts of Price, of the past.

When Castle comes back with the water, Dr Hedwith

is feeling more in control of himself. His vision is back and, though he still has a pain in his head and aching joints, he feels up to rejoining his wife's event. The auction is starting and it will look ill if he isn't there to show support. With Castle's help he regains his feet and, after a few wavering steps, is able to walk by himself with some degree of confidence. He enters the hall, quietly slipping into a vacant seat near the front, smiling at Annabelle, who is just finishing her opening speech, by the sounds of it. Dr Hedwith nods encouragingly at her.

Annabelle, however, almost loses her train of thought when she sees Morrison come in. He looks terrible: sweaty, flushed, and with an uncertain stride. Is he sick? Did he eat something that didn't agree with him? She can see Castle at the back of the hall, watching the doctor make his way to his seat, his expression grave and concerned. Forcibly pushing thoughts of Morrison's health from her mind, for now, Annabelle concludes her welcoming speech.

"... and on behalf of the Friends of Calvary Church and the Women's Christian Temperance Union, I thank you all for attending tonight. We have a number of fine items, generously donated by members of the community, that I hope you find of interest and, dare I say, bid vast amounts of money for!" She chuckles along with the other women in the audience, while the men smile indulgently. "After all, ladies and gentlemen, this is for a very good cause: our new church, which will be a centerpiece of our fine city. As a relative newcomer, I am both honored and proud to be able to contribute to this noble effort. I would like to thank you all again, and especially the fine ladies of the union, who have taken so much time out of their busy schedules to make our auction happen. Please, everyone, let's all give ourselves a round of applause!" She pauses for the self-satisfied claps, patting her own hands together vigorously. "And now... to the bidding!"

The first few items go quickly and for goodly amounts. There's a fine humidor, a session with a well-regarded local dressmaker, an ornate fowling gun. The selection of items they'd amassed holds a little bit of interest for everyone, she hopes, although, really, the items themselves don't much matter: these people will give money simply to give it, for their own satisfaction and, perhaps more importantly, the recognition of their peers. She and the women had at first considered a silent auction, but then realized, though they didn't say it in as many words, that they were far likelier to raise more money if the giver could be publicly acknowledged for his philanthropy. Nothing drives charity like vanity. This thought is in Annabelle's mind as she works her way through several more items, the prices rising encouragingly as she goes.

"And now, the next item, ladies and gentlemen." One of her assistants moves a wooden box to the front. "Oh! This next item was donated by my own husband, Dr Morrison Hedwith, whom you all know, of course." She waves. "Hello, dear – oh, he's shy," she giggles, raising a few more indulgent laughs. "Well, at the risk of a self-serving advertisement, let me just say, ladies and gentlemen, that a supply of Dr Hedwith's Chock-a-saw Sagwa Tonic is the very thing to have around the home. Agues, fevers, catarrhs – how does it go, sweetheart? I'm afraid I'm not much of a saleswoman." She looks towards her husband with an exaggerated shrug, bringing more laughter. "But, as it says right on the bottle: *Vital for Health!* I use it myself, as do many of our ladies here tonight, and I'm sure all will vouch for its efficacy." She turns to her assistant. "Go on, Barbara, if you would, tilt up the box there so the good people can see it. Thank you, dear. Now, who will start the bidding?"

When Annabelle's helper lifts the box, Morrison starts, nearly falling out of his chair. He rubs an eye, hoping that his vision is simply wavering again. *Oh, dear Lord*, he thinks, looking closer. *That's not the right Sagwa.* He looks around for a moment, almost frantic. How can this have happened? That idiot Wood must have grabbed the wrong box. But how would the stores have gotten mixed up? He keeps the experimental mixture far from the normal product. Would Castle have moved it? No, no, certainly not. And neither of the Woods even has a key to that particular storeroom, now that he thinks of it. The only thing that Morrison can figure is that he must have accidentally moved it himself, perhaps after one of his attacks, which often leave him foggy-headed.

"One hundred dollars," a voice calls out.

Morrison looks over. It's that fool Ladd, the banker with more money than sense. Word from Annabelle is that the man is already donating the land for the new church. Hasn't he done enough? "One hundred fifty," Morrison shouts. Several people look his way in surprise.

"Why, Doctor," Annabelle says, "that's very generous, but don't we have enough of the Sagwa at home? It's wonderful stuff, of course, but perhaps we should let these other fine people have some of their own." There is general laughter.

"It's just such a good cause, Mrs Hedwith." Pausing. "Really good," Morrison finishes, somewhat lamely.

"It is, sir," William Ladd says from across the aisle, smiling and looking around. "So I will myself bid five hundred!" There are some cheers at the outrageous price.

Damn it, Morrison thinks, panicking. *Five hundred dollars*? He has a terrible suspicion that Ladd's stiff-necked pride will prevent him from being outbid, and there's no way that Morrison can match the man dollar for dollar. He has to keep that Sagwa from getting into Ladd's hands, though; who knew what could happen? That's the whole reason for the medicine show, after all: getting the stuff out to subjects, small-town peasants that no one will miss, far away from Dr Hedwith. He can't very well have the great and good of Portland society dying – or something far worse – right under his nose. It would be another Boston mess all over again.

Perhaps it will be fine; the preparation, in its current forms, affects everyone differently, sometimes not at all. It's only a certain type of person whose blood truly resonates with the Salt, after all, in its present versions. Eventually, Morrison will find the person for whom the vital Salt, once prepared correctly, reacts perfectly, stably, melding Salt and anima, the red and the white elixirs. That person will serve as a catalyst for the rest. It's too risky, now, though, to merely hope that the experimental substance will have no effect on Ladd or his household; the danger is simply too great.

"Six hundred!" he calls, grimacing inwardly. The pain in his head is increasing again and one eye is watering.

"Seven hundred fifty, sir!"

Damn it, Ladd, you idiot: I'm trying to save your life, man. "Eight fifty!"

"One thousand, Doctor! My, you are a staunch proponent of your own product." Ladd smiles at the laughter, although inwardly he wills Hedwith to back down.

Annabelle has no idea what her husband is doing. *Eight hundred and fifty dollars?* Is Morrison drunk? She knows he's partial to a secretive tipple of an evening, which she chooses to ignore for the sake of marital harmony. But *here?* Is that why he looks so bad? The sickly grin on her face wavers a bit at the next bid from her husband.

"Eleven hundred!"

"Fifteen hundred!" The audience is rapt now, watching the bidding war escalate, wondering if Dr Hedwith has secret reserves of cash, the way he keeps going. The Ladds are one of the wealthiest families in Portland.

"Sixteen!" Morrison's head is pounding. He feels wetness on his lip; raising a finger, he realizes his nose is bleeding. As casually as he can, he stoppers a nostril, pretending to fuss with his moustache. He looks around for Castle, not seeing him. He has to tell Castle to get that box of Sagwa, any way he can.

"Three thousand dollars, Doctor!" Ladd exclaims with a grim look in his eye. At some point this has moved beyond a game for him. There is no way some upstart medic with a bony wife is going to make him, the Honorable William Ladd, look a fool. He doesn't even want the blasted tonic but, by God, he'll have it.

There's a gasp from the crowd at Ladd's bid. Three thousand dollars for a dozen bottles of cheap medicine? Several women of the Temperance Union clap their hands, cheering. Annabelle is at a loss, still smiling that greasy smile, needing to continue with the auction. *Don't bid again, Morrison!* she wills silently. *Don't!*

"Dr Hedwith," she says, as steadily as she can. "Do you have another bid?"

At Ladd's last bid, Dr Hedwith's head has started to swim and his vision is greying. He presses his finger tighter to his nose, trying to keep the blood from spilling out. *I heard a maid in Bedlam / so sweetly did she sing* is again going through his head, unbidden. For one flashing instant he remembers his mother, the last time he'd seen her, mad-eyed, fingernails tearing her own breasts.

"I bid," he says, gasping, trying to focus. *Her chains she rattled in her hand / So sweetly did she sing.* "I bid…" *Her chains she rattled in her hands…*

Vaguely, he hears Annabelle screaming as he slumps off his chair, the blood pouring down his chin. He can't see anything but hazy black forms and his head is splitting. It's hard to draw breath and he feels as if he's drowning in the thick air. *I heard a maid in Bedlam. I heard a maid in Bedlam. Her chains she rattled in her hands.* He feels a crowd around him and hears more screaming and then feels a sensation of being lifted in strong arms. He tries to tell Castle to get the Sagwa, get the Sagwa

– *Her chains she rattled in her hands* –

– *So sweetly did she*

6.

AG WANTS A PIE. A hot, flaky, buttery apple pie, the kind his mother makes. A big, thick slice of pie, with whipped cream on top. He's wanted one for miles. It's the only thing he can think of, mile after dreary, sore-assed mile, even over the sounds of his brother's constant griping. It's taken Ag an entire day and night to get over his hangover, his queasy guts and headache; when he finally had, he just wanted that pie. Even though, at first, while puking all over his horse's neck, he'd been sure he'd never want to eat again – certainly never drink – now he wants a pie. Maybe when or if they get to Portland, he can find one at a café. Probably not as good as Mama's, but he wants a pie.

"I tell you, Ag, I don't like her," Sol is saying, for the hundredth time. "She's uppity."

Ag knows now that he isn't cut out for the outlaw's life. He'd suspected it before, but now he's certain, one hundred percent. When Elizabeth McDaniel had ridden into their camp and Sol had tackled her, Ag had never been so scared. He'd been too terrified to shoot and had a sneaking suspicion that he'd crapped his pants the tiniest amount. That night had been even scarier than when Sol had killed the man in Twin Falls; that saloon hadn't been some dark campsite in the middle of nowhere, and there hadn't been a posse after them, then, come to hang or shoot them.

"Do you see the way she squints at me, when she'll deign to even fucking talk to me? Like I smell funny to her. I smell like a man, goddamn it, and that's the way I'm going to smell."

It's easy to ignore Sol; Ag has long practice at it. His brother has been griping and bitching about Elizabeth McDaniel for the last two days, but Ag notices that Sol rarely takes his eyes off her for long, that he looks at her when he thinks no one else is watching. He knows his brother and it's easy to tell that Sol is sweet on her. Or maybe it's just that Sol's pride is wounded because she won't give him the time of day. She *is* a bit uppity, maybe, but, after all, Sol *had* tackled her off her horse and damn near punched her in the face.

Ag could never have just jumped up on a stranger and tackled them like that, girl or not. He simply isn't a fighter, not in the same way Sol is. Or, maybe, how Sol is trying to convince himself he is, with the cursing and the whiskey and the rest of it. Trying on something he isn't. Oh, Ag will wrestle and slap at Sol but, when it comes to fighting for real, he just doesn't have it in him. Maybe, once, he'd thought he had, like most boys, particularly those with brothers; no one likes to admit that they aren't tough. Men are *supposed* to be tough, after all. In a way, it's almost a relief to realize now that, when it comes right down to it, he isn't. He just isn't, so he doesn't have to worry about it any more. Sol may think he's a fighter but, really, it's only because he's always acted first and thought about it later. Ag is different. Some people might think him slow, but he's just cautious. He likes to think things through. He doesn't think that outlaws are, as a general rule, supposed to be cautious.

"And don't even start me on the liquor, Rideout," Sol says, bitterly. Once again. "What kind of fucking woman smashes three perfectly good bottles of whiskey – *the last goddamn whiskey for miles, I might add* – just to make a point? It wasn't even hers!" He shakes his head, angrily, looking up the trail at Miss McDaniel's back. Once again.

Really, it had been a relief when Elizabeth had broken those last bottles, Ag thinks. He'd been so whiskey-sick at the time, though, that even the smell of the bottles leaking their contents out into the rocks had set him to puking again. That was another thing: outlaws are supposed to be able to drink, and he just has no skill at it. If he never saw another bottle, it would be too soon. Sol had raised a ruction, though, carrying on and hollering; Mr McDaniel had kind of just deflated, looking miserable. Had Ag himself been less sick, at the time, he might have thought that Miss McDaniel had looked her prettiest then, all fired up with anger. It had given her a high color that Ag would normally have found quite fetching. She's pretty enough, in general, although he doesn't quite see whatever it is that Sol sees in her. It's nice to have a pretty girl to rest one's eyes on from time to time, though, he thinks, something to break the monotony of the horses' asses, visually speaking.

"Are you even fucking listening to me, Ag?"

And now there's this pie he can't get his mind off. Outlaws must like pie, he supposes, but probably they weren't obsessed about it like he seems to be. A posse could ride right up to them, this very minute, hanging ropes in hand, and he'd quietly go with them if they had that pie. Really he just wants to go home, even though he's terribly embarrassed at the utter wreck he and Sol have made of things since they'd left the ranch. At this point, he's willing to go crawling right back, though. Or, if not back to the ranch, maybe just to a town where they could get quiet jobs and not have to shoot people or tackle girls or get so drunk, where they could stay put and not have to feel the wind and the dust and stare at the backsides of horses all day. He realizes that the pie is maybe just one of those what-are-they-called, metaphors, for something else, for safety and security and family and not having to live an outlaw's life any more. Although he'd eat a whole damn pie if he had one right now.

Sol spurs his horse forward, away from his brother. Ag isn't even listening to him; his brother has been quiet and subdued for a couple days now. Surely he can't still be sick. The boy cannot hold his liquor – that is a fact – but even he can't still be sick two days later, can he? Lately Ag just won't talk much, won't hold up his end of a conversation. Sol had needled him with some of the usual subjects that are generally guaranteed to kick up a lively argument, but Ag just muttered and grunted and moped along. It made for boring travel.

He closes a bit of the distance between Ag and Elizabeth McDaniel, looking at her back. The sun has a way of catching her hair where it sticks out of her wide, man's hat, making a kind of sparkle around her shoulders. He's tried to engage her in conversation on a few occasions, but she always just gives him that pinched look, the one that says that David Solomon Parker isn't a fit fucking conversationist for the likes of Her Majesty Elizabeth McGoddamnDaniel. It chafes him powerfully, that look. He enjoys a woman with some vinegar, but this girl is entirely too full of herself. Even if she does have that sparkly hair and those green eyes. It seems like the dirtier and dustier her face gets from travel, the greener those eyes are. He'd apologized for the misunderstanding of that first night, after all, but all he ever gets from the girl is that narrow stare. Which is irksome as all hell.

Sol needs someone to talk to, some way of passing the miles, but Ag is useless, Elizabeth is icy, and Josiah McDaniel is sunk into some private misery, even worse than Ag. The man has had some sad misfortunes, true, and is likely now feeling the lack of liquor, but sometimes a man just needs to button up his pants and move on, as his mother would have said, to just fucking get over it. Perhaps some conversation would take Josiah's mind off his troubles; does no one ever think about that?

Sol knows his own mind needs distraction as, mile after mile, he's still fretting, more and more, about this job they've taken on, whether they shoot that man in Portland or just rob Josiah McDaniel and get on their goddamn way, as he wants to do. Sol hasn't even bothered to try to convince Ag yet that it's the right plan of action, robbing Josiah, for the seed money to get them settled and away from the Idaho law, get them started in a respectable career running girls or selling liquor or the like; deep down, Sol himself isn't entirely convinced. He doesn't want to do either thing, murder or robbery, when it comes right to it. It had been hard enough when it was just the fucking dentist but, now that the sister is along, both plans look to have large and unsavory holes in them. He doesn't think that Elizabeth McDaniel is the type to take kindly to killing or robbing and, given that she'd up and ridden halfway across two states just to round up her brother, Sol worries that she'd hare off after him and Ag if they did something she didn't fancy. He wouldn't be surprised if she rode up and fucking shot them herself, from the looks she gives him. It was one thing to tackle a young lady – inadvertently and completely understandably, given the situation – but Sol knows that he doesn't have it in him, getting in a gunfight with a girl.

He mopes along, trying to think his way out of this mess they've got themselves in, to come up with something that doesn't involve just giving the money back to the dentist and leaving. They need that money. Without it, what are they going to do, then? Go slinking back home, prove to their mama that they're indeed nothing but a couple of fools? Sit around the ranch and wait for a posse to come from Twin Falls and string them up? Hell no, but it's a conundrum, what they should do, and one that Sol is having difficulty cracking open. He watches Elizabeth's back and that sun-sparkly hair, wishing that someone would just talk to him.

Elizabeth's rage has mostly burned itself out by now, but she's plagued with low-level vexation at the situation in general. Josiah hasn't spoken to her since she broke the whiskey bottles – an act that was for his own good, after all – and the Parker boy speaks to her too much. A few times a day he comes near her and tries to engage in some idiotic pleasantry, clearly not understanding that she has much on her mind and no desire for chitchat with the likes of him. She doesn't like to be rude, as a general rule, but she needs time to think, to figure out the best way to get her brother off of this stupid quest of his and back home where he can start to heal.

At least they're heading in the direction of Baker City; surely something would happen between now and then to persuade Josiah that he has to quit this lunacy. If nothing else, Elizabeth wonders if she can simply have some of her students and their burly

brothers stop him by main force. It might technically be
kidnapping but, after some time, Josiah would thank
her. He's making her nervous, now that he's sober; this
black, wordless depression he's in seems far worse than
his alcoholic excess. Perhaps she should have left the
bottles. She didn't think it was possible for someone
to just give up on living, to stop breathing and will his
heart to stop but, seeing Josiah, she worries. He won't
talk, won't eat, just sits slumped on his horse all day
and then curls up under a blanket immediately after
they stop at night.

She hears Mr Parker's horse ambling up behind her
again, and spurs her own horse forward, clenching
her shoulders. Damn the man. He isn't quite what she
expected a hired gunman would be like, though, even
given her first introduction, when he'd yanked her off
her horse. He doesn't seem overtly hard or cruel, stupid
or mean. He's ignorant, certainly, to hear his flowery,
grammatically-tortured speech – when he isn't simply
cursing – but, more often than not, he smiles when
he speaks to her and seems to be genuinely protective
of his brother, even as he gripes at him all day. Both
of them seem callow, a bit innocent even, not the
hardened killers she'd expected or that Mr Parker had
intimated they were. Maybe – likely, even – they're
charlatans, just common swindlers looking for an
opportunity to rob Josiah and herself. They might
have Josiah's money now but they certainly won't be
keeping it or getting a cent more, not while she is with
them.

They can't be terribly far away from Baker City by
now. She'll think of something before then and get
this whole vexing situation straightened out. She has
her students to return to, after all. Josiah is family, but

she can't spend the rest of her life taking care of him. In Baker City she'll get him back on track and they can both return to their own lives. A dentist can always find work.

Josiah doesn't even notice the wagon that's slowly coming their way, even though he's far out ahead of the others. He doesn't seem to see much at all these days; the world is just an endless procession of sage and dust and then hills and trees. Much of the time he doesn't even have his eyes open, just ambles his horse along, half-asleep. He isn't much of a rider and his buttocks are sore and chafed but even that doesn't hold his attention. In a distant way he realizes he's uncomfortable, but it doesn't really matter. Now that the whiskey is gone there's no good way to remove himself from his constant thoughts of Mary and all that's happened.

He's just so tired. In the morning he wakes up more exhausted than when he'd gone to bed, even though as soon as they camp he falls asleep immediately. The dreams are just too bad, too close and hot, without the liquor to keep them at bay. Riding tires him out even further; sometimes he feels that he doesn't even have the energy to stay on his horse and he just wants to slump off into the dust. If he didn't know that Elizabeth or one of the others would pick him up, he might just do that, lie there in the brush and sleep forever.

Josiah doesn't even care about killing Dr Hedwith any more. It's pointless. Maybe the man had had nothing to do with Mary's death, maybe it had just been a terrible accident. Even if it wasn't, he supposes that it was the men who sold the stuff at the traveling show that are really to blame, even if they didn't actually make the medicine. His memories of that night are so twisted and strange; even now he doesn't know what happened. There might not even *be* a Dr Hedwith; maybe that was just a name that the other doctor, Potter, uses for his product. Josiah doesn't really know where his obsession with Hedwith came from. He supposes it was because he has the bottle with the man's name and business address on it, that it's merely something concrete he can fix his mind on. Rather than just the memory of some vagabonding collection of peddlers, who had been long gone again by the time he regained something of his sanity, after losing Mary. But it doesn't matter: Mary is gone and revenge has no savor any more. Perhaps it had just been an artifact of the whiskey. Or, maybe, it's the Almighty's way of telling him that he is on the wrong path. They're headed to Portland now, though, and they might as well just keep going; it's too much effort to come up with something else to do.

He vaguely notices Parker trotting his horse past, followed by Elizabeth. Opening his tired, gummy eyes, Josiah looks up, mildly startled to see another traveler on the road, an old man and young girl in a battered wagon. When Josiah gets closer, he hears them talking about local news with Sol and Elizabeth, the state of the road and the weather in Baker City and events of note. He moves his horse to the side and is riding past them, not wanting to talk, not caring about Baker City or the weather or any of it, when he hears something that cuts through his fogged mind.

"Show in Baker, you know," the old man is saying. "Patent medicine. Got 'em a African strongman and a Chinaman tell your fortune and a magic man."

Josiah stops his horse, looking over, startled. "What did you just say?" he asks in a whisper. "What did you just say?" He repeats it, stronger.

The old man spits a stream of tobacco off the side of the wagon. With his long, white beard he looks like a prophet. "Medicine show, son. Got 'em a pretty French girl that sings the opera too." He spits again, squinting his eyes, a ray of sun catching his face.

For the first time in many days, Josiah's heart speeds up, the muscle punching against his ribs. When he'd doubted the Lord, in this, his darkest hour, he's been given a sign. Even though he doesn't deserve it, even though he's let himself turn to drink and self-pity and thoughts of death. Even though he'd abandoned his faith, he has not been forgotten. Josiah feels tears hot in his eyes and a burning in his belly as his spirit rekindles. He spurs his horse forward into a fast trot.

"Where on earth are you going, Josiah?" Elizabeth yells.

"Change of plan, Mr Parker!" Josiah shouts over his shoulder, ignoring his sister. He calls back something else that is lost. He feels bright and hard inside, full of life again, just like that. Just like that. He is the righteous hammer of the Lord, he sees it now. In his time of need the Almighty has come to him. Josiah spurs his horse on even faster, bouncing in the saddle at the ragged gallop.

Elizabeth and Sol look at each other, baffled. Ag comes trotting up, a curious look on his face. "What's going on, Sol? Why's he riding off like that?"

"Boy really wants to see that show, I reckon," the old man in the wagon says, smiling beatifically at them, spitting again. "Sings like an angel, that girl," he adds. "Like the sound of heaven."

7.

ALEXANDER RECOGNIZES the little man skulking at the back of the crowd right away, and his heart falls. *Not again*, he thinks. *Shit, not again.* He interrupts his patter to make a quick glance around the tent, looking for Oliver. There's no sign of the Black Hercules, which means that he's likely outside Fan's. Damn it, Alexander thinks, I need him *here*; Fan's fine. They have to get that man away before Lyman sees him. The last time had been bad enough, but this time Lyman will just kill the little fellow and be done with it.

The dentist is moving furtively in the dim lamplight, ducking from person to person in a way that he no doubt thinks is stealthy but, in reality, just makes it apparent that he's trying to stay hidden. Besides, the whole effect of stealth is spoiled by the man's direct, piercing gaze, right at Alexander, those mad, too-wide eyes that never move from him. Hatred in them, and something else. The eyes of a zealot. It's enough to throw Alexander off his pitch, and he stumbles through the long recitation of maladies that the Sagwa will supposedly cure, a specious list he can normally rattle off in his sleep. Somewhere between agues and catarrhs he feels his own cough rumbling back to life, and has to duck his head in an effort to hide it. When he lifts it back up, the little man is gone. *Shit*.

Dr Potter hurries through the rest of his spiel, looking around distractedly, repeating several lines more than once until he just gives up and announces a two-for-one sale; he offloads a few bottles as quickly as he can, promising that the lovely soprano Mercy Rhoades would be onstage again soon to sing the beloved arias of European opera. Alexander locks up the crate of Sagwa while the crowd listlessly mills about and then he ducks out of the back of the stuffy tent. He's jogging through their little camp, looking for Oliver, when he quite literally bumps into Ridley.

"Go get Mercy, boy," he says, "tell her she's on."

"Ain't it a little early, Doctor?"

"Goddamn it, Ridley, just fucking go get her! You hear me?"

Ridley is slightly taken aback at Dr Potter's tone. The doctor never yells at anyone, not often anyway. He gets crabby and will snap and grumble at people from time to time, but not like this. Plus he'd about run him down, just now, and didn't even apologize. "You bet, sir," he says, as the doctor trots off again. "I'll just go find her, then," he calls after him. Ridley wonders what the hurry and fuss is all about, when Dr Potter abruptly turns around and jogs back.

"Listen, if you see Lyman, don't say anything about the change in schedule. I'll deal with it. Just go tell Mercy."

"What if he's with her?"

"Damn it, just tell her," Alexander says, realizing that the request makes little sense, but whatever, the boy can figure it out. "Say I'm not feeling well. Just say something. I said I'll deal with it."

"Yes, sir," Ridley says, confused.

Alexander starts off again and then stops a third time. "If you see a weedy little guy about this high," he raises his hand, "who looks a little scruffy and crazy, come find me. *Immediately*. Trust me, you'll know him if you see him. Just keep clear of him and come see me straightaway. Understand?"

"But what about Mercy?" Ridley is thoroughly baffled now.

"Goddamn it, Ridley, just come get me!" Alexander trots off to Fan's tent and is dismayed to find that Oliver isn't there. He stands there, outside the tent, looking around stupidly for a moment, ready to head back to the main stage in case he'd missed him there, when Oliver steps into the ring of lantern light.

"Where the fuck were you?" Alexander yells.

"Hey now, I was pissing, old man. That all right with you?"

"Listen, that little dentist is back. We need to find him before Lyman does."

"What little dentist? Who are you—"

"*From Boise!*" Dr Potter interrupts.

Oliver's eyes widen. "Oh, shit. Lyman will kill that boy."

"Which boy is that, Mr Wilson?" Lyman steps from behind Fan's tent, arm in arm with Josiah McDaniel. Josiah's wide-eyed, crazy stare is dazed now, and he walks along meekly, unseeing and absent. Beside him is a pretty young girl, wearing a similarly foggy look. Alexander doesn't know if Lyman somehow drugged them or if their state is the result of another of Lyman's talents. They seem unaware of their surroundings; the girl doesn't move when Lyman rubs a hand slowly up her arm. The dentist is breathing fast, harsh little gasps, and is weaving a bit on his feet.

"Gentlemen," Lyman says, smiling. "Allow me to introduce Miss Elizabeth McDaniel. I'm sure you recall her brother. Fortunately I found them a few moments ago – a purely serendipitous accident – because I'm afraid they're not feeling very well. Not very well at all. No doubt they need a doctor." He smiles wider, slowly, and his eyes fix on Alexander. "No doubt some of the Sagwa will fix them right up."

Josiah is in the nightmare again, even though he knows, or thinks, he's awake. A man is holding his arm. There are words he hears but doesn't understand; he can't catch a breath, can't think. Mary is calling.

– Run, love! she is saying, or had said, months ago. *Run, love!*

They're somewhere outside Boise. Josiah staggers into the little circle inside the rocks, holding a pocketknife, a pitifully small thing. He gasps for air; his eyes are wild and white and he calls to his wife, over and over, his voice hoarse from shouting.

He'd followed her, after she'd taken to her bed, after she'd died, after she'd gotten up, red-faced and staring, after she'd run out into the night, faster than a sick girl should be able to run. She hadn't been dead. *She'd been sick, that was all, sick, and whatever she'd taken in that bottle of medicine had only made her sicker. She'd fooled the doctor, she'd fooled him, her husband, a medical man of sorts himself.* She hadn't been dead.

She wasn't well, though; she shouldn't be able to run like that. She shouldn't. Josiah wishes he'd thought to grab a horse, because she'd run for miles without stopping, so fast he simply couldn't keep up. His breath is jagged in his throat, now, and his legs feel as if they will collapse. More than once he'd feared he'd lost her, only to catch some far glimpse of her slender form in her white nightdress, reflecting the light of the moon. She couldn't hear him, or she wouldn't; she was just running and running towards whatever was calling her. She was so fast. For a long time, hours maybe, he thought he'd lost her completely, but then had seen the faint glow of firelight in a little tuck in the rocks.

There are men there when he reaches it; his Mary is in the center of them. One of the men is huge and black, one is old, and the third is chanting something over and over. Calling a demon, maybe, a devil. Not his wife. Not his wife. Why is she here? They're good Christians, the both of them, not devil-worshippers. When Josiah calls to her, though, she doesn't answer. Her eyes are wide, vacant, lost in the chanting and odd-smelling smoke.

He tries to go to her, still shouting her name, when the huge black man wraps him in meaty arms. Josiah tries to struggle, but it's useless. Don't look, *the man says, strangely gentle.* You just don't look. *He turns him away from the fire, from Mary. Even when she starts screaming, a horrible, wordless scream, Josiah can't turn around; the man holds him tight. Josiah is screaming himself, weeping, struggling futilely for escape.*

– Get him out of here! *another voice says, the old man.* Just get him away!

– What about –

– Just go! Get him out! I'll deal with –

And then the huge black man is dragging Josiah away from the fire. Finally, Mary seems to hear her husband's calls, seems to know that he is there. That he's come for her, to rescue her. To save her.

– Run, love! *she screams,* Run! *Her voice sounds strangely thick, throaty, as if the words are barely escaping her lips.* Run, love!

At the last instant, before the black man drags him out of the rocks, Josiah is able to turn for just a second. He sees Mary, his slender, beautiful Mary, reaching towards him, still screaming words that twist together, a plea for him to save himself, her words slurred and blurred until Run love Run love Run love *piles up and elides into something that sounds like* Rula, Rula, Rula.

"Damn it, hurry up, Ag," Sol is saying. "We're going to fucking lose them if we lag-about much longer."

"Listen, it ain't *my* horse that come up lame, Sol," Ag says. "I can only walk so fast. And I told you to just *take* my horse and go if you're in such a fired-up hurry to get there."

"Jesus, we've been over this, Ag. I can't trust you to not get lost, dipshit. You know how you are." Really, Sol just feels like he wants Ag with him; his brother is useless, but he reckons it more prudent not to rush off into an unknown situation without at least one person he trusts at his back, useless though that person might be. When Josiah had gone galloping off, Elizabeth had followed and so had he, only for his goddamn horse to pick up a sharp rock in its hoof and pull up lame after less than a mile. At first Sol was in a fury, just wanting to get after the McDaniels as quickly as he could, but the doctoring of his horse gave him a chance to think things through a bit more thoroughly. If Josiah had gone off in such a hurry, that could very well mean that the man they're looking for might somehow be near, and Sol isn't quite yet ready to blindly run into a killing that he still has little interest in doing. Maybe something worse waits for them up there. A little caution would not be fucking remiss, just now.

Sol hasn't yet entirely thought all the way through this latest development. He's not certain just what they should do. They already have the money, after all, so maybe they should just turn around and head back the way they'd come, or go somewhere else entirely. It technically isn't even robbery, really, this situation; it's more along the lines of breach of contract, a fuzzy legal proposition if ever there fucking was one, to his mind.

Ag himself doesn't see what all the rush is about. They know where the McDaniels are going and, after all, it's getting dark. If they just sprint ahead like idiots, dragging their horses along behind them, one of them will turn an ankle or step in a hole and then where would they be? In trouble, that's where. Ag has no desire at all to limp to Baker City on one foot, or to carry his heavy, broke-legged brother over a shoulder, after the fool trips over a rock in the dark. He wishes Sol would just shut up and take his horse, already, and let Ag come along at a more reasonable pace with Sol's own, if it's so important for Sol to get there fast.

"The hell's the dang hurry, Sol?" he says, yet again.

"We been hired to do a job, brother, let me remind you of that," Sol replies, disgusted at the question, for which he has no good answer and, more so, at the situation in itself. "Where is your fucking work ethic, boy? Mama raised us to be diligent."

Ag mutters something unintelligible.

"That you said, Rideout?"

"I *said*, Mama didn't raise us to break our legs running off into the dark like fools. Pretty sure of that."

Things continue on in this vein as darkness falls. The moon is climbing by the time they reach the outskirts of Baker City, along the Powder river. Baker City is half the size of Boise, but still they wonder just how they'll find the McDaniels, now that they're here. One of the first things they see, though, after they tie up their horses, is a small collection of brightly colored, brightly lit tents, in a meadow their side of the river, just north of where they stand. When they get closer, they hear music; a high clear voice is singing in a language that isn't English, the sound climbing over the babble of the small crowd outside the largest of the tents. People mill around, waiting their turn to go inside. A tatty banner placed between two poles reads:

DR POTTER'S MEDICINE SHOW
Wonders of Nature
Illusions & Musical Delights
Medical Miracles
THE CHOCK-A-SAW SAGWA TONIC
Cures Complaints of Mind and Body
Low Price
VITAL FOR HEALTH

"I reckon this is the place, then," Ag says, reading the sign.

"Oh, you fucking reckon so, do you?" Sol says. Now that they're here, he's nervous, jittery, and irritable. He fiddles with the pistol at his side, the one he'd inherited from his father, wondering if he would have to use it to kill another man, just like he'd done in Twin Falls. "Well, go on then, fool," he says, eventually, waving a hand at his brother. "Don't just stand there. Let's go find those goddamn McDaniels."

When he follows Ag, though, something makes Sol stop before he crosses the banner's arbitrary boundary. *If I go in there*, he thinks, *I'm committed to whatever might happen*. The pause grows longer until, finally, he steps outside the poles and just goes around, which makes him feel the slightest bit better.

Ag is already moving through the crowd, working his

way to the music tent. He loves music, but what he hears now is strange; he's more used to fiddle tunes or church hymns. Whoever is in the tent, singing in that high, bright voice, isn't saying much he can understand, in the way of words, that is, but there is a longing and sadness in her song that makes him listen closer. He wonders if the meaning would become clear if he concentrated harder or, instead, if he just relaxed his ears, he'd get it, the way that when you watched rain you had to relax your eyes to see it fall, sometimes, staring past and through it. Ag tries to listen through the music, past it, but all he hears is that sadness, until his brother nudges his arm.

"You see her, Ag?"

"Of course not, Sol, she's inside the tent, genius," he says, irritated that the spell of the music has been broken. "Just shut up and listen. You ever hear a song like that?"

"Goddamn it, Rideout, not the singer gal: Elizabeth. Or Josiah. You seen them?" Sol himself is looking around, wishing, not for the first time, that he had a bit more of his brother's lank to him. He sees a lot of shoulders and hats, and that's about it. "Let's split up. Meet me back here in an hour or so."

Ag sticks out a hand. "Give me some money."

"What? I'm not your mama."

"Damn it, Sol, you got all our money." Ag pokes his brother in the chest. "Now give me some. Half of it is mine and I might see something I fancy."

Sol knows that it's useless to argue, that they have more important issues to hand, even though the lion's share of that money is by rights his and he would disperse the remaining share as he fucking saw fit. Ag will only blow it on fripperies and foolishness, the simpleton. Standing here looking at hats is making him jittery, though, not knowing if he might have to shoot the man under one of them. And then who knew what the hell would happen? Running from yet another posse, most likely, is what he expects, but it could be worse than that. Either way, he wants to be moving now, to see if he can find the McDaniels and head off whatever might happen, before it does. Besides, he thinks better while in motion. Sol slaps a wad of bills at his brother and says, "One hour. Right here, son."

8.

OLIVER IS UNEASY. This is the third time the short, stocky young man has walked past. The boy isn't looking at him, not in particular, but there's something about the expression on his face, the look in his eye, that makes Oliver uncomfortable. Plenty of people have walked by several times, but this boy isn't just walking, he's *walking*. It's a sense Oliver has, something he thinks likely just comes from being black in a white man's world, from being different. He suspects that Fan has the same skill, an ability to know that *this isn't right.* It's an instinct of self-preservation, a way to head off trouble before the trouble starts. Normally, Oliver would have simply walked off, himself, gone wherever the man wasn't, but Lyman had told him to stay here by the wagon, so here he would stay. He's already crossed Rhoades once tonight, an act for which he knows he'll have to pay, soon enough, in addition to what else he owes. In lieu of leaving, then, he tries to shrink down into himself, to look as inconspicuous as a large, nearly naked black man in a leopard cape can look. Averting his eyes from the stocky boy, he looks down at his feet.

Sol strolls by one more time, feigning innocence. Just another sightseer, here at the show. It's been almost an hour of slow circuits, looking for Elizabeth and Josiah, working through the crowd, which is thinning out now with the late hour. They have to be here, but he just can't seem to find them. Maybe he misunderstood what the old man in the wagon had said, misread Josiah's intent as he galloped off. Maybe they've already come and gone. None of that seems right, though: it just feels like they're here. He doesn't even know where Ag is, now; he'd seen him a time or two, earlier but, for the last while, his brother is nowhere to be found. The little camp just seems to have swallowed everyone up. He'd give it another circuit and, if he can't find the McDaniels, he'll track Ag down somehow and they'll go into town to check the hotels. He doesn't like the way that huge black man is looking at him, as if he knows Sol is up to no good. Unconsciously, Sol touches the butt of his gun, for security, like a baby with a blanket, even as he tries to hunker down a bit and look inconspicuous.

Oliver sees the boy put his hand to his gun and tenses, nervous, flexing the muscles in his broad shoulders, tightening his legs in preparation for action. Just in case. That boy is definitely not just a sightseer. Best be on guard. From time to time the show has trouble with thieves or with white folk looking to hassle a nigger or a Chinaman; usually, between his own size and Alexander's wits, nothing much comes of it. Sometimes a stupid drunk will be left minus a few teeth and plus a few bruises but, all in all, there was usually no real danger from the normal type of drinker, thief, or man looking for a fight. Something about this boy seems different, though.

After Sol walks past the big man again, he ducks behind the large tent to take stock of things. He's anxious and sweating even more; something about this place sets him on edge, and he has no idea why. Maybe it's the way that black strongman, who looks like an African savage in that catskin cape, is watching him. The man is damn near twice as wide as Sol and half again as tall and Sol has no desire to tangle with him. A bullet would be of no more nuisance to him than a chigger bite, by the looks of it. Where the fuck is Ag, damn it? It's time for them to get out of here, take a minute to think over the situation, and then go into town and see if the McDaniels are there. Sol has a bad fucking feeling about all of this. He peeks around the edge of the tent, trying to be subtle, just in time to lock eyes with the old man that appears to run the show, presumably the one with his name on the sign. The quack has sidled up to the huge African and they're both staring at him now. Hurriedly he ducks back around the corner of the tent.

"That him?" Alexander says, muffling a cough. The stress of the night is making his lungs tighten again, rattling thick and heavy in his chest.

"Yeah. Fourth or fifth time that boy's been around," Oliver says, rubbing a hand along the side of the wagon.

"Thief?"

"I don't know, Alex. Something about that boy ain't right." He looks down at Dr Potter. "You think…?" He cocks his chin towards the wagon's covered tent.

Alexander starts to shrug, until another cough takes him. Maybe the boy really is just a thief, just a punk. He hopes so. Not knowing why the kid is here makes Alexander worry, though, which he doesn't need, tonight of all nights. It seems too coincidental, given what's happened earlier in the evening. He figures that he and Oliver can take care of themselves, if it comes down to it, maybe not against Lyman but certainly against some kid with a pistol. He worries about Mercy and Ridley and

Fan, though. Even if the boy is nothing but the normal kind of punk, any minor ruckus tonight could turn into something much worse, for everyone, that boy included. Alexander knows Lyman has something planned, and Lyman likes his work to proceed in a certain manner.

"Well, just keep an eye on him and don't let him start into any mischief, if you can," he says. "I need to close us down and get these fools out of here. I want to check on the others, while I'm at it."

"You gonna be all right, old man?"

Alexander looks up. "Shit, I hope we all will."

When Alexander passes the big tent again, the boy is gone. He makes his rounds through the little camp, then, telling the few stragglers that they're closing, in as jovial a voice as he can summon, reminding them that they'll open again tomorrow afternoon. To a couple of the most truculent patrons, he gives a bottle of the Sagwa, the normal kind, assuring them that it cures insomnia and will rid them of the need to walk about during the night, hoping they'll take the hint. From a distance, he sees what he thinks is the stocky boy, walking south along the river with a lanky young man. Maybe that's it, then; maybe he and Oliver are simply too keyed up and the boy had been nothing but a bored townie out with a friend, on the hunt for girls. Unsuccessfully, by the looks of it.

When he sees Ridley, carrying a pail of river water to Mercy's tent, he takes him aside. "I need you to just stay in the big tent tonight, Ridley." He holds up a hand, forestalling objection. "Just do it. I'll tell you why tomorrow." Alexander knows that he won't. It's getting harder and harder to keep the boy in the dark. He takes the bucket from Ridley, clapping him on the shoulder and squeezing hard. "I need you to do this for me, son."

Ridley nods, moving off toward the big tent, looking back over his shoulder. Dr Potter smiles at him. He's a good boy. Alexander decides then and there that it's time to cut him loose, for real this time, for his own safety. Ridley has to leave the show, as much as it will hurt both of them. The kid will never know why, and he'll be bitter, but Alexander knows that it's for the best, that Ridley deserves a chance at a normal life. Maybe, if taken away from the show, the good boy that Ridley is can become a good man someday. It's small enough consolation, a tiny bit of light in the darkness of Alexander's life, but it will have to be enough. First thing tomorrow, he'll fire the kid.

Alexander calls softly into Mercy's tent, ducking under the flap when she answers. Mercy is wrapped in a dingy shawl, washing her face with a wet cloth. She looks tired, worn, used up, but, when she smiles at him, some of her beauty is allowed to peek through. "Brought you some more water," Alexander says. "It's cold, though." He shrugs.

"Is it going to be bad?" she asks, the smile fading. Unbidden, she thinks of Papa, thinks of the Dreamer in the black tent.

At first he thinks she means the water, and then realizes she's talking about Lyman. He shrugs again, wondering how she knows but then understanding that, of course, Lyman will have shared the news of the McDaniels, for no other reason than for her to suffer along with the rest of them. "Isn't it always?" They stare at each other for a long second. "I should go," Alexander finally says. "Stay inside tonight."

"Don't I always?" she says, giving a weak smile. As he starts to duck under the tent flap, Mercy feels a

sudden need to say something more, to tell Dr Potter
that he'll survive, that it isn't his fault, even the things
that are. That he's always done his best, for them all,
tried his hardest. She wishes they could have known one
another under different circumstances, in a different life.
"Alex…"

Dr Potter looks back. Mercy never calls him *Alex;* he's
always been *Alexander* to her. Once again he can see how
beautiful she really is, there in the lamplight, wrapped
in a dirty shawl, with a half-washed face, bruises on her
bared arms.

"Never mind," she says, the words not coming.

Alexander smiles sadly at her. "We'll talk tomorrow."

Sol and Ag are hidden in a little clump of trees at the
edge of the river, whispering furiously. When they'd
finally found one another, they'd left the camp and
gone through town, checking all the hotels and rooming
houses, even the ones in Baker City's small Chinatown.
Eventually, a helpful woman who knew Elizabeth had
directed them to the McDaniel house; they'd somehow
missed the fact that Baker City was her home. Sol and
Ag had hurried to the place and pounded on the door,
though the house was dark. The McDaniels weren't
there, and now Sol and Ag are back outside the medicine
show.

"Maybe they just moved on," Ag says, once again.
"They had a healthy start on us."

"I'm telling you, Rideout, *they're in that fucking camp.*
I can feel it." Sol is keyed up, not quite understanding
himself why he's so sure that the McDaniels are there,
but he knows it on some deep level nonetheless.

"Hogwash, Sol. Besides, if they are, why're they
hiding from us, then? Maybe they don't want us around

any more. We should just go." Ag is entirely less than enthusiastic about Sol's plan to sneak through the tents in the dead of night, looking for their erstwhile employer and his sister. As he sees it, if the McDaniels don't want to be found, so much the better, as it means that he and his brother won't have to do any killing or robbing and can just move on to San Francisco and make a start at something different.

Sol couldn't have said himself why he's so adamant about finding the McDaniels. Maybe it's just the sense that something isn't right. Maybe it's an artifact of the guilt he has for killing that man in Twin Falls, an act that weighs heavier and heavier on him, instead of getting lighter with time; perhaps on some level he just wants to do something to start balancing out that black mark on his ledger. It's nothing to do with Elizabeth, he tells himself. It's just that, if the McDaniels are in that camp, they aren't there by choice. Maybe. Sol doesn't know it for a certain, but he has that feeling. Sol figures there's a good chance that the man Josiah had run off after has done those two some mischief. He can't simply shrug and leave, even though the thought of skulking through a camp full of magicians and African savages and whatnot, in the dark of night, has not much in the way of appeal. Not much at all. But he's not a coward like that, regardless of how he feels. He's not, so best just button up and get on with it.

"Goddamn it, Ag, we're fucking going." Before he can let his mind out-think himself, Sol stands up and starts jogging, hunched over, moving as best he can from shadow to shadow towards the camp. He figures that Ag will follow, if for no other reason than not wanting to be left alone in the dark. Sol's fingers are clenched so hard around the handle of his Colt that he can feel five individual starbursts of pain in his knuckles.

"So, here we are, then," Lyman says, rubbing his hands together briskly. He and Alexander stand outside the black tent, watching as Oliver brings the two McDaniels over from the wagon. The man looks a little dazed, still, but the girl is struggling in Oliver's big hand. Lyman had insisted that they be gagged when he'd had Oliver tie them up in the wagon, and the girl's muffled voice doesn't hide the fact that she's now cursing in a very unladylike manner. "Now, now," Lyman says, leaning forward and pushing the gag a little tighter into her mouth. "Language."

Alexander looks up at Oliver, seeing the same bleak expression that he no doubt wears himself. From the way Lyman is acting, his warm cheer, tonight is going to be bad, very bad. They'd crossed him, twice now, and they will be punished. Lyman is not a man to carry a debt like that for long.

"Now, sir," Lyman says, smiling at Josiah. "Now. It's passing strange to see you again, I must say. You interrupted me once before, back in, where was it, Boise?" He looks over at Alexander for confirmation, and then points at him and Oliver. "But *these* two sent you on your way, that night, didn't they? They did. Yes. Oh, it's no great thing, but I don't *like* interruptions, and, you see, I don't like my privacy invaded in such a way. But you weren't to know that, were you? How could you know that?" He shakes his head mournfully.

"Really, the fault lies with my colleagues here," Lyman continues, turning a new smile their way. "*They know the parameters of my work, the delicacy, my need* for privacy and yet – *yet!* – they just sent you on your way. They did. Just like that. In deliberate defiance of my wishes, and of those of our patron, Dr Hedwith. That I will not have. No, I will not have it." He shakes his head. "But, I must say, it seems that, perhaps, you've had some tough times since then, by the look of you, sir. Some very, very tough times. For that, I do apologize. Again, you were not to know what it was you did, not exactly. A victim of circumstance. So, by way of recompense, then, I'm going to give you the thing you most want. The very thing." He claps his fat hands together, beaming.

Alexander's heart sinks. He'd had an idea what Lyman had had in mind, when he'd first seen him walking up with the McDaniels, and now he knows. Just kill the dentist and be done with it, Lyman, but no: but that would have been too easy, too gentle. Besides, this punishment is for Alexander and Oliver; poor Josiah McDaniel and his sister are simply the instruments that Lyman has chosen.

"Now, first things first," Lyman says, turning to Oliver. "Hold him tight." Lyman steps over, pulling out the gag and forcing the fingers of one hand into Josiah's mouth, widening it.

With the other hand, he reaches in with his hooked knife, cuts out the man's tongue and tosses the red, meaty thing at Alexander's feet.

"There we go, now," Lyman says, smiling, stepping back to admire his handiwork.

Josiah is too stunned to scream, at first. The pain seems to take an eternity to hit; time stretches and his mouth simply feels hollow at first and then coppery full. The pain comes then, and he gags on the blood in his mouth. Distantly, through the agony, he watches the fat man open the black tent, and then strong hands grab his arms and he's dragged inside, thrown to the floor. A lantern is lit. The fat man leans down, then, and says, "Well here she is, sir: go to your wife."

From his knees, Josiah looks up into the cage, into vacant blue eyes. He knows her from those eyes, even if he doesn't know the rest of her. She's crying a noise deep in her throat and howls are coming from the cages across from her own, the things inside thrashing and rattling the bars. What had been his wife, once, looks at him, seeming to know him now, and then his screams finally come.

Ag feels his brother's hand clamp down over his mouth as he and Sol watch the fat man cut Josiah's tongue out. He's never seen anything so horrible, the way the man just reached in there and then tossed the thing on the ground. Ag can feel his eyes growing too wide and he's having difficulty catching his breath. He knows that he'll never forget what he's just seen, that he'll still dream about it if he lives a hundred years. It isn't so much the act itself, even, it's the casual competence the man displayed, as if chopping out another man's tongue is of no more note than slapping a mosquito. Ag feels his mouth filling with spit and his stomach is ready to come up.

"Shut up!" Sol whispers furiously. "Shut it!" He's almost as horrified as his brother but, along with the fear, comes anger. This has to be the man Josiah sought, the doctor who had killed Mrs McDaniel. Right at that second, Sol feels that shooting the man would be no difficult thing, not at all. He could put a bullet into that fat fucking face without a second thought, and sleep like a fucking baby afterward. But Elizabeth is there, gagged and in the hands of that big African; there's no way that

Sol can shoot them all before the savage has a chance to snap her apart. Sol shakes Ag, trying to bring him back to himself. Ag can't shoot, or at least not well, but maybe he can at least be a distraction, give Sol time to get Elizabeth free. He'll figure something out. As a plan, it's not much, but it's all he fucking has.

Sol watches the fat man drag Josiah into the tent, returning alone. For a long few moments there's no sound, and then a horrible, ragged wail peals from the tent, a sound like a dying animal, a sound that puts the hair up on the back of Sol's neck. It's maybe the worst thing he's ever heard, and he knows, given what he's just seen, that it's a scream made with no tongue. Sol doesn't know what's in that tent, but he has to get Josiah out of there, somehow.

The fat man has come back over to Elizabeth. He raises a hand and rubs her cheek with his thick fingers, slowly. Sol creeps closer, fearing for one hot second that the man is going to cut her too, take her tongue out along with her brother's.

"You think she's looking all right, Dr Potter?" he says. "A bit peaked, maybe?"

"Lyman." The old man from earlier is looking at the ground.

The fat man shushes him, and then places a damp palm on the girl's forehead. "I think she might have a bit of a fever. What do you think?"

The feel of the man's hand on her makes Elizabeth's skin crawl. She's still in shock at what he's done to Josiah. What is happening here? What is happening? It's hard to take her eyes from the bloody piece of meat on the ground, the thing that had once been Josiah's tongue. He'll never sing again, she realizes, stupidly. Her brother had always had a wonderful singing voice, a real talent, whereas she can only ever manage a thin, off-key wheeze. Josiah, though, he can sing just about anything, in a voice surprisingly deep and rich-toned from such a narrow chest as he has. But now he can't, not ever again. All he can do now is scream.

She realizes that the fat man is asking her something. Trying to pull herself together, she understands that he's telling her that, if she can't be quiet, she'll wind up like Josiah, separated from a part of herself. For a hysterical moment she wants to tell him that she *can't* sing, not anything you'd want to hear, but then gathers herself enough to nod, letting him pull the gag down. Once free of it, for a hot second her old self comes back and she draws breath to curse him, maybe to try to bite his face, tear his flesh with her teeth like an animal, but then she sees the thing on the ground again and the breath leaks back out of her. She feels herself slumping until it's only the big Negro's hand that's keeping her upright.

"There, you see, Dr Potter?" the fat man says. "She's obviously suffering from low spirits. There's only one cure for that, isn't there?" His voice loses its cheery tone. "Give it to her."

"Lyman," the old man says again, in a weary-sounding voice.

"Give it to her."

Alexander knows he has no choice. He fingers the bottle in his pocket, the one he'd been ordered to bring. Yet again, here he is, helpless and afraid, with a bottle in his pocket. Everything he does twists into despair, that's the sum of it. Everything. His life has been nothing but one long series of mistakes and failures. The weight of it feels crushing, so much that it's almost a struggle for him to breathe. He just wants to walk away, into the dark, forget about all of this. It's too hard to think, to move.

But he must; if he doesn't give the Sagwa to the girl, Lyman will kill her, slowly. He'll make them watch. They've pushed Lyman too far, and there is no going back from that. They can't fight him, so, better then to just give the girl the Sagwa, and hope that she's one of the lucky ones. He touches the scalpel in his other pocket, vowing that he'll end it quickly for her, if it comes down to that. So Lyman can't have her, afterward. It's the best he can do. If she begins to change, he'll kill her, no matter what.

Alexander steps forward. He's tired. The little bottle is so very heavy as he raises it to her lips, nodding at her to drink. "I'm sorry," he says, the same words he's used so many times before. "I'm so sorry."

He tips the bottle up.

"NO!"

There's a shout and Alexander sees the stocky boy from earlier, running out of the darkness into the light of the lantern that hangs nearby, pointing a pistol their way and screaming, *"No no no no! Don't drink it!"* The boy comes to a stop a few feet away, wildly waving the pistol back and forth between him and Lyman, between Lyman and Oliver. Behind him Alexander can see the other boy, the lanky one, holding another pistol and looking wild-eyed and scared.

"Don't drink it!" the stocky boy says again.

Alexander sees Lyman smile, the kind of smile you'd imagine a cat would get around a broken-winged bird. "Why, son, why ever not?" Lyman says. "The Sagwa is vital for health, you know." He shrugs. "Besides, the good doctor here has already given her the medicine. It's working in her as we speak, with its – how does it go, Potter? – electro-chemical induction? These later formulae are so much more refined, after all. So much stronger and quicker. More *efficacious*." Lyman laughs.

"Spit it out, Elizabeth! Puke it up!" The boy looks desperate. She can't hear him, the Sagwa already working, as Lyman has said. Alexander knows that she will be drawn down into herself and will eventually come back, one way or another. It's inevitable now; he only hopes it will end quickly. The Sagwa doesn't hold the key to immortality, regardless of what Hedwith and Lyman believe. It contains only sickness and death.

"I'll tell you what, my young friend," Lyman says, smiling even wider. "You give your gun to the doctor here and I will have him give your sweetheart an emetic. Yes. Something to make her vomit," he explains, solicitously, seeing the puzzled expression on the boy's face. "Maybe that will be enough although, really, I don't know why you're so concerned. I do not." He shrugs again. "But we want our customers satisfied – don't we, Dr Potter? So, if you're concerned for your paramour, it's the least we can do. What do you say? Then we can sit down like gentlemen and discuss your grievances. Yes?"

Alexander sees the look of despair in the boy's eyes, his gun dropping ever so slightly as he considers, looking for a way out. *Oh, don't do it,* he thinks, *don't be stupid, son. Just fucking shoot.* He *wants* the boy to shoot: shoot Lyman, shoot him, even Oliver, if that's what it will take to get these people away from here.

The smile leaves Lyman's face and his voice hardens. "Listen, you little shit. Give us the gun or I'll have the nigger here tear your little girl in half with his big, black cock. I'm tired of this." He looks at Alexander. "Potter, go get that wretched thing."

Alexander sees the boy sag, beaten. Lyman always wins. The boy can't know that, of course, can't have understood just what he's put himself in the middle of. *Lyman always wins.* It will go even harder on the girl now, and only God knows what will happen to these two gun-toting fools. Better that they'd stayed away in the first place. His legs feel almost too heavy to move as he steps between Lyman and the boy, reaching out a hand for the gun.

"Just give it here, son. It's over," he says, softly. But it isn't. It's just getting started. It's hard for him to meet the boy's eyes.

"Why?" the boy whispers. "Why?"

Alexander remembers Rula's husband, the little dentist, saying the same thing, as they'd pulled him away outside Boise that night. That same broken, unbelieving word. Something changes inside Dr Potter, then. Just a bit: some small spark of defiance he'd thought entirely extinguished flares into weak light. Whatever the dentist had told this boy, the story is nothing like the reality. Better the boy dies without knowing what is going to happen. Before Lyman takes him. Better to just cut the girl now, too. Save her the pain that's coming, spare her the Salt's work. With his free hand, Alexander fingers the scalpel in his pocket. It will only take a moment. If he's quick he can get to them both; the other boy is too far away and will have to take his own chances. It's the best he can do. Once, Dr Potter had been the fastest surgeon in the Hospital Corps, and cutting throats isn't entirely different than lopping off an arm, when it comes down to it. Easier even, with no bone to saw through. The work of a moment. He knows he won't be fast enough to cut his own afterward but he will take what comes.

Do it, Potter, move.

But he can feel the failure growing inside him; yet again, he knows, somehow, that all he will manage to do is to make things worse for everyone. Yet again. Another head in a jar, another freak in a tent. Bruises stippling a girl's body.

Move, Potter! Move! he tells himself, but he can already feel that spark of defiance fading. *Please, you have to move.* The scalpel is slippery with sweat in his hand.

As always, Lyman is quicker.

He takes one long stride past Alexander and, without pausing, drives his knife into the belly of the girl, yanking it upwards on the way out. He steps back, smiling, as she staggers, eyes wide, and then he starts to laugh. Before she can fall, Oliver scoops her up in his arms, holding her out helplessly, staring with horror at Lyman as the girl's blood run down to his hands, dripping off his fingers. The boy drops the gun from nerveless fingers, his mouth opening and closing, making no sound. His eyes go from the girl to Alexander.

Why?

Dr Potter's thoughts leave him.

He steps forward and, with one smooth, lateral motion, draws the scalpel across Lyman Rhoades' throat, opening it to the spine. He sees himself act, as if from a distance. He feels nothing, only a vague puzzlement as to what has occurred.

A gasping hiss of bloody air bursts from Lyman's neck, one last breath, and then the blood begins to pour out, dark in the lamplight. He draws up straight, takes a stumbling step or two, and then slumps to his knees, eyes wide and shocked, his mouth hanging open. He presses his hands to his neck, trying to keep the blood in. Alexander and the others watch silently and, after what seems like such a short amount of time, Lyman Rhoades, alchemist, body thief, and murderer, falls over on his face, dead.

9.

A WEEK AFTER the incident at the New Market, Morrison finally tells all to Castle. He has no choice, really: he knows that his body is falling free of the Salt, that the fixative is beginning to fail him, once again. Soon it will no longer be able to keep him alive as it once had, and soon, too soon, he'll need another vessel for his tired spirit, assuming he can once again make the transference. The last time, into this current body, had been so much harder, so much more painful, than previous attempts. It had been a minor miracle that he'd even survived the ordeal. He worries that he's stretched too thin now, that whatever particles or atoms inside him that make up that thing called a soul, a life, are finally breaking down. Without the Salt, the true Salt, the Stone, Dr Hedwith fears that soon he will be dead, at long last, the great work lost with him.

In his current state, there is no way he can secure an appropriate vessel on his own. Perhaps he could lure down one of the Woods, but both brothers are slight, weakly. Mr Twist has that broken body, and Castle, for whom he has a true fondness, is too old. This next vessel needs to be young and strong, given Morrison's waning powers. He knows, somehow, that this new vessel will be his last; he'll have to find the pure Salt this next time around or he will die. It is that simple.

Yet again, he wonders if death is truly that horrible a state, if he's made it a bugaboo far out of proportion to the thing itself. If, after so many years running from it, fighting the nightmares, it now casts a longer shadow for him than it really warrants. Death comes to all men, after all; even Christ Himself had died. Morrison doesn't truly believe in the religion he publicly espouses, not really but, as he comes closer to the end of life, he worries that maybe there actually is a Hell waiting for him, given the things he's done in the pursuit of the Stone. He'd done those things for selfish, fearful reasons, true, but also from a pure love of science. Out of the desire to better the lot of mankind, to shine a beacon of light that will destroy that long shadow of mortality for all men. Or so he tells himself.

Where is Lyman? He should have returned days ago. Lyman *will* be back; they are bound to the great work together. Morrison needs Lyman back *now*, though, soon: he needs another vessel and Lyman is the man to find it, as he's done before.

After many days of waiting, Morrison knows that he can tarry no longer. He must tell Castle everything. His own history, the terrible things he's done in and for his work. All of it. He must tell him of the rigor and discipline, the cruel, hard acts required to continue the search, the service of science. The things he has done willingly, and would continue to do, until the Stone is found. He must tell him, so that he might enlist Joseph Castle in the great work. His hope is that Castle, knowing the secret of the ultimate search, will embrace it as his own. Castle is, after all, practical. Morrison knows some of the things Castle has done, both in his employ and before, about the violent, criminal life he has led, from what few hints the man has let drop over the years. As a practical man, would he really turn down the chance he was being offered: immortality, eventually – hopefully – certainly a life far beyond the span of a normal man? Time to spend with his beloved histories, his study, time to *watch* history as it unfolds, year after year. Castle is getting older, after all; his temples are grey and his scalp showing more and more through his thinning hair. How long does he have, twenty years, thirty maybe? Not long at all, compared to what the Stone could give him.

I need a new body, a vessel in which to live, he tells Castle. *I need you to find it for me.* What price is the life of one man, when weighed against the prospect of life everlasting?

He tells Castle about the beginning, then, the death of his parents so long ago, living with his uncle and learning the rudiments of the great work, expanding that knowledge over the years with poor Price, with Isaac, mad Taubenschus, the others who searched for the Stone. They'd been some of the last of their kind, the mysticism of the past giving way before the new sciences of the enlightened present. Few had been clever enough to see that the way forward was to marry the two, as he had. Some had tried, like Price, but lacked the discipline to see the thing through. Others, like Isaac, had largely turned their back on the past, or treated it as an object of curiosity, focusing on pure mathematics, optics, physics, what they now thought of as the *real* great work. But all these men are long dead now; only Morrison remains, different than he once was, true, but himself nonetheless.

He tells Castle about the first transference, which came about by pure accident, at the end of his first life. How, sick and dying in that shabby, musty room, out of money, old, coughing his blood and life into a soiled handkerchief, he'd formulated one last batch of rudimentary Salt, building on what he and Price had developed years before; he'd made as much of the stuff as he could, spending every remaining bit of his coin on the necessary materials. With his last strength, he'd consumed almost a gallon of the solution, gagging down swallow after swallow of the foul-tasting mixture, hoping that by virtue of quantity it would make him well enough to continue for a time, heal his diseased body for another week, a month, perhaps even a year.

What had happened had been stranger yet. As the Salt worked in him, there came a feeling of drugged lethargy; at first, he hoped that perhaps it was working, that perhaps he'd been correct. Then the pain came, wave after wave of agonies for what felt like hours, as if every cell in his body was tearing itself apart. Maybe this was death, then, finally come, he thought, when he felt the pain begin to recede, when he felt *himself* begin to recede. There was no heavenly light to follow, no infernal staircase; as he drew away, all Morrison saw, or thought he saw, was the same tatty, filthy little room. He fancied he saw his body lying there, as if from a distance, vacant.

And then the door had opened and the young student that he'd hired to bring him food and clean water, in exchange for some lessons about the chemical arts, had come in, a basin in one hand and a small bowl in the other. Morrison could *feel* the boy somehow, feel the health and life of his body, underfed and dirty as it was, and he felt a hot, strange desire, as if there was a strong magnet in the young man, drawing him closer. Not a sexual or sensual feeling, but a hunger. What happened next was painful, confusing, but, some minutes or hours later, Morrison opened his eyes, young eyes, from where he lay on the floor. Awkwardly, feeling rough and loose in his skin, he stood up. He looked down at the bed, at the shell of the man he'd once been. The body on the bed was old, ugly, toothless, with sallow, sagging skin and a foul smell. It seemed somehow less than dead; it was merely a thing, really.

Morrison had turned to the small mirror over the bedstead, staring in wonder at his new face. It *was* him, wasn't it? He remembered who he was, or so he thought, he remembered how he'd strained to piss that morning, the rattle in his chest, how his ribs ached from the cough. He remembered shivering in the cold room, gagging down the Salt, and then the pain. He touched his face, ran his hands over his chest. He *was* here, in this boy's body, the student whose name he could never remember. Where was the boy, though? Did they share this vessel now, together? Morrison cast his senses inward, looking for some remnant of the body's original occupant. If it was there, if the boy continued to live, somehow, he was silent.

Morrison took the basin from the nightstand, then, dampened a rag, and began to wash himself.

Now, he watches Castle as he talks. He is impassive, merely nodding from time to time, encouraging Dr Hedwith to continue. If Castle thinks him mad, he doesn't show it, but simply catalogs each piece of data as it comes, like the scholar he aspires to be.

He tells Castle about the years afterward, then, about his time as a respected London doctor. Of making and losing his first fortune before going to Halle to follow in the footsteps of Taubenschus. His time with one of the man's protégées, that fool Semler, who had driven another nail into the coffin of the great work as a respected field of study. Semler had made a laughingstock of the art, of himself, with his comically fraudulent – and unfortunately well-publicized – claims of perfecting Baron Hirschen's Salt. Morrison's own reputation, by association, had been besmirched and so, disgusted, feeling that there was little reason to remain in Europe, Morrison had made his way to the colonies, working again as a doctor and chemist, secretly pursuing the great work in Virginia, New York, Massachusetts.

He tells Castle about how, in London and at the height of his fortune, he'd met Lyman. That sorry tale; he made no apologies for Rhoades but made it clear that he, Morrison, knows Castle to be a different sort of man. He knows that Castle and Lyman hate one another, so he intimates, quite honestly that, should Castle join him as a partner, there would eventually be no need for the continued services of Lyman Rhoades. Castle merely nods, calmly accepting another piece of data.

Finally, at the end of the long story, Dr Hedwith looks at his valet, searching the big man's scarred face for any sign that he believes, or that he thinks him mad, or that he will turn and leave in disgust. Castle's face is still, his eyes blank.

"So?" Morrison finally says.

"So what, sir?" Castle replies politely, as if Morrison has spent the last hour or more talking about the weather.

"So, will you help me, Mr Castle? Will you join me as a partner in the work? Knowing what you must do in the course of its pursuit. What the great work requires. What it demands."

"What I must do." For once, Castle shows a flicker of emotion, one that could have been disgust, confusion, happiness, anything: it's merely a brief movement of the musculature in his face, passing across it like a fast cloud, a tiny crack in the flatness of his eyes.

"Yes, what you must do, Mr Castle."

"And that is?" Castle knows the answer, of course, but wants to hear the doctor say it, now that there are finally no more secrets between them. He sees the doctor for who and what he is, at long last, the mystery he'd always suspected, finally solved. And now, this. If he joins the man, takes what is being offered, there must be no insinuation about what he must do. No oblique hints. He must be told, be given the clear order *do this, do that. This is what I require.* Rhoades might be content to do the things he does from a mere suggestion, because that is his nature and, if *he*, Dr Hedwith, never ordered these terrible things, in explicit terms, they weigh less heavily on the doctor's conscience, Castle suspects. If Castle is going to join him, though, they will *truly* have to be partners, sharing the full moral weight of what it is they do. He wonders if, at heart, though, following orders is simply a way for him to ease his own conscience. That, if he does what is asked, it is only because he is obeying his employer's commands.

Castle is not a man to delude himself. If he makes the choice to follow this path, he will accept the consequences with open eyes. Yes, he's getting older, his knees hurt, his hair is thinning; he lacks the strength he once did. Would he be content to merely live out the rest of his days, then, working for the doctor as a valet and bodyguard while he can, studying his books, resigned to getting ever older and more decrepit, when there is possibly the chance for something else, something greater? He's done unpleasant things before, after all, beaten men for money, stolen, threatened petty cruelties. By necessity rather than choice, but he's done them nonetheless. But this, the things he will be required to do, what the doctor has described, will be far worse, by definition. These things, whatever their greater purpose, are evil. Though he doesn't go to Mass now, he'd grown up in the Church and has a real fear of Hell.

But, still: could you go to Hell, if you never die?

"Will you do these things, Joseph?" Morrison finally says, after a long pause. "Will you kidnap, will you murder innocents, will you help me carve open the living to discern the secrets of life itself? Will you give poison to the young to see the effects on their bodies? All this and more?" Listing it like this, a calm litany of the horrors that Morrison has accepted for himself, for the work, makes his stomach tighten. "Will you do all these things, knowing that they are against the laws of both God and men? Will you do them in the search for something greater? Will you do these things, so that you can live forever?"

Castle stares at tired, broken Dr Hedwith. It's a simple choice, then: will he, Joseph Castle, do these things, all that the doctor has said, perhaps more, solely for his own benefit? He doesn't fool himself that he will be doing it for the greater good, should he accept. The rest of mankind is of no concern to him, really. This is only a matter of the staining of his own soul. Of damnation. He imagines that Lyman wouldn't have blinked, given this choice, *hadn't* blinked. If Castle accepts the doctor's offer, does it make him a better man for wrestling with the decision, or a worse one?

Can he do this?

He stands up.

There is another long, uncomfortable silence. Castle stands there, looking down at his employer, lying there in the bed, old and sick. By his own admission, at the end of another long life, trying desperately to find one more.

Castle turns his back, without a word, and walks to the door.

Morrison closes his eyes. His chest feels tight, heavy, the bedding itself weighing down on him. He has done all that he can, and now he has reached the end. There will be no last vessel for his spirit; when this body fails he must finally go to meet his judgment, whatever that might be. Will the end be as painful as the transference was, or would he finally just sink out of himself?

At the sound of the door opening, he opens his eyes again. Castle is still there, one hand on the doorknob, looking back at him.

"I will," Castle says.

10.

HE IS DREAMING AGAIN.

He'd been sixteen. No, seventeen. It didn't matter; he was young and poor, but he was beautiful. It had been so long ago. He remembers being young, he remembers the alley he'd raced into, ducking behind a trash heap, trying to catch his breath after the chase.

The bag is heavy in his hand.

He listens for the sound of footsteps and, when he's sure they don't follow, he opens the bag, pulling out a thick rectangular thing. Just a book, *he thinks, disgusted. He looks at the front of it, tracing his finger over the embossed writing on the cover. He can't read, of course, but he likes the way the leather feels under his hand, likes the picture that looks like a horned circle atop a little cross. Maybe he can sell the book to the Jew, the one that pays him to suck his cock from time to time. Jews like to read, so the book ought to be worth something. Eagerly, he roots through the bag, hoping to find coins or silver, or something that he can more easily sell. The Jew is stingy, like they all are, tight with money; every time the bastard wants his cock sucked or a piece of ass they have to bargain, even though the price is the price, unless he himself hasn't eaten in awhile. Then he takes what coin the Jew gives him.*

The man he'd robbed had looked prosperous, traveling

with a servant as he did; there ought to be something better in here. Instead, he pulls out book after book, until the bag is empty. Some of the books are as nice as the leather one; some are merely poorly bound sheaves of dirty paper. Fuck, fuck, fuck. He'd been so proud of himself, getting this bag away from the man and his big servant, diving right through the carriage when both doors happened to be open. He's always been quick like that. It keeps him alive. The expressions on their faces as he ducked between them, jumping through like a fox, in one door and out the other, bag in hand; it was hard to keep from laughing. But, now, he sees that it had been for nothing but a sack of fucking books. Ah well, he thinks, philosophically, the Jew is stingy but has money, and even a little bit of money for a bag of books is better than having to suck on that mangy old cock again for a while. If that man doesn't want the books, someone else will. There is always money to be made, if you kept your eyes open. A smart young man rarely goes hungry.

He tries to add up what the books might be worth. Enough for some food for a few days, something to drink, maybe enough for a girl, even. It would be nice to get drunk and have a fuck, one he wanted for a change. He doesn't really know anything about this type of thing, though, selling books; he'll have to wing it, judge the price by feel. People always let their greed and desire show. They're stupid that way and it's just a matter of reading it and setting the appropriate value. He'd learned long ago that it isn't a matter of keeping your face flat, emotionless, necessarily: you can look however you want, as long as it isn't the way you feel. You have to keep your heart out of your eyes. If you're able to do that, you can take what you want from the world. It's part of being clever, that.

He's counting up his impending coin, still congratulating himself on his cleverness, when he steps out from behind the trash heap, directly into the arms of the big servant. Even as he curses his own stupidity, he's moving. He's always been quick.

In a flash, his little knife is out and the man's throat is open. He ducks back away from the blood, tensing his legs to sprint.

– Stop, *a man says.*

It's the toff from the carriage, the fucking dandy. A dandy with a pistol, pointed right at him. The servant is gasping out air and blood through his neck, his life running into the dirt of the alley. He and the toff both step back out of its path, away from the dying servant, not wanting to wet their shoes.

– Why did you do that? *the man continues, looking him over.* I suppose that's a stupid question, isn't it? *The pistol hasn't moved.*

– You gonna shoot me then or what? *he says, mockingly. Better to go out with some style.* Or, I can give ya's yer books back and then suck yer cock, for your trouble, like, *he says, raising the bag.* It's all here, mate. Just a misunderstanding, all it was. I know my way around, *he adds, grabbing his own crotch and licking his lips in a way he thinks the sallies like. Well, so much for style, he thinks.*

– No, I don't think so, thank you, *the man says, with a grimace of distaste. He pauses.* That was quite a theft, though, young man. Quick as a rabbit.

– I'm quick, yeah. *He can't help but boast.* They don't never see me coming.

– Well, I certainly didn't. Toss me that bag, then. *When he tosses it over, the man picks it up with one hand, judging its contents by weight, keeping the pistol trained on him with the other.* It's all here?

– Yeah, mate, it's there. I told you it's all there. I ain't had no time. *Maybe he'll get out of this after all.*

– Seems I need a new servant, *the toff says, looking down at the dead man between them.*

– Yeah, guv, that one there was no fuckin' good. Lets you get robbed, like, and then gets himself killed. Hard to find good help, innit? *He laughs. Feeling a bit safer now, his style is coming back, the bravado that he keeps tight around himself, for protection.*

– How old are you, boy?

He shrugs.

– You looking for work? I could always use a resourceful young man.

– Always, mate. Always. Got to keep the shekels coming, got to pay the servants and the taxes on the country estate, right? *He laughs again. Maybe the day is picking up after all. If this fool is stupid enough to put him to work, he'll rob him blind, and not just fucking books this time around. He sees the man giving him a long, steady look.*

There's something in the man's eye then that makes him straighten up, makes him think that maybe this toff isn't the fool he first looked, not just some rich sally waiting to be plucked. There's something behind those eyes. The smile drops off his face. Suddenly, he really wants this work. Finally, the man uncocks the pistol, lowering it to his side.

– What's your name, boy?

– Well, me *name's* Michael, mate, but everyone *calls* me Lyman.

It hadn't taken Lyman long to realize that working for the toff, this doctor called Hedwith, just to rob him, is stupid. There's more to this man than had showed on early impression, much more. Lyman prides himself on his ability to read others, and there is something about his new employer that is different than other men. Plus, the doctor treats him well: Lyman has his own small room in the man's London townhouse, with a soft bed and a door that locks. Lyman has never had a spot that was all his own before; his life to date has been spent in a succession of cribs and shared rooms when he could get them, in doorways and alleys when he couldn't. The doctor insists that he learn to read, as well, something that Lyman at first balks, thinking it a waste of time, but he quickly comes to understand that there is a power in books, that knowledge of that kind is a thing of value, if you know how to use it.

For the next years, he lives with the doctor, learning and improving himself at the man's side. His duties are much easier than the constant struggle that came with street life: he tends the horses, cleans the carriage, runs errands, fetches things for the small household staff, easy chores that leave him plenty of time to himself. Later, the doctor has him assist in the laboratory in the basement, merely more fetching and carrying at first, stoking fires and the like but, eventually, because the doctor, being who he is, a man by nature accustomed to teach, Lyman begins to learn what Dr Hedwith calls the great work, *the Hermetic arts that were once the province of the alchemists. According to the doctor, he, Hedwith, is perhaps the last of them, the real ones, those that had the deep knowledge; the rest had passed on or simply given up by the end of the last century. The nineteenth century is the century of science, the doctor says, not of superstition and mystical claptrap. But alchemy* is *a science, unfairly scorned because it marries the chemical world with the occult one, the hidden world. There is power in the old ways, though, Dr Hedwith says, if you could only separate the rubbish from the truth, like chaff from wheat; the deep knowledge is there, ready to be combined with the new learning.*

Lyman is ordered to never, under any circumstances, talk about what they do, to anyone. If he did, his employment, and possibly he himself, would be terminated immediately.

The more Lyman learns of the great work, the more it draws him in. All his life he's been one of the weak, the powerless, only able to eke his way through the world using his quickness, his beauty, his sharpness of mind. But here, though, here is *something of* real *power, an art that will one day allow him to rise above the rest, to pay them back for the things he's been forced to do, how he's been forced to live. He knows, by now, that once the doctor himself had been poor, not on the streets like Lyman but certainly not possessing the kind of wealth and influence he has now. The doctor is no aristo, but he's rich and respected and leads an easy life. One day Lyman will do the same.*

Over time, the doctor begins trusting him with more and more tasks, things that only Lyman, of all the people in the doctor's circle, can be trusted to do, a fact which makes him proud. When the doctor asks him to take the final step, he doesn't blink, merely goes out and gathers up a young tart he knows. He doesn't mind what happens to her; once, she'd stolen from him, under the aegis of her large pimp, an act which, at the time, he'd simply had to let go. Now, there she is, on the table, screaming. She will advance the doctor's work, and Lyman's — he's started to privately think, more and more, that he and Dr Hedwith are partners — and she's paid for her thievery, at long last. She was only a whore, after all.

But life with the doctor begins to sour the day Hedwith finds Lyman in the laboratory.

Dr Hedwith had been away for a few days and Lyman had taken the opportunity to find a subject, to try an experiment of his own, of sorts. Dr Hedwith has become something of a father figure to him, the only one Lyman has ever had. He wants the doctor to be proud of him. He hadn't expected the doctor home so soon, though, and the man's rage is terrible. He calls Lyman a butcher, a savage, a child-killer; cruel, hateful words that are untrue. They are untrue. Dr Hedwith can't see that Lyman is only trying to hone his skills to better serve the doctor's own work. It had taken groveling and tears, and many months, for the doctor to forgive him, but their relationship had changed thereafter, not for the better.

Then comes the day when it almost unravels for good, all that Lyman has been trying to build over these years with Dr Hedwith, all because he, Lyman, has become callous, careless, and stupid. The doctor had sent him out to find an experimental candidate; this is a task which, before, Lyman approached with all caution and stealth. Now, though, now that he is reconciled again with the doctor, now that he is once more a part of the great work, part of something larger, he has imbued himself with a false sense of power. Afterward, he realizes how stupid he'd been, how close he'd come to losing it all, because of his own hubris.

So, instead of stalking the unwanted, the bawds and orphans, those no one will miss, this time Lyman attempts to take a fat young merchant's son, simply because he'd liked the boy's jacket. Stupidly, he lures the boy into an alley, where he'd parked the doctor's little cabriolet, a vehicle just the right size for this kind of work. When the boy gets close, Lyman clouts him behind the ear with his cosh and leans him into the cab, tucking a blanket around him, as if he's just sleeping. The boy's eyelids flutter when Lyman gets him settled in; he has very pale, doughy skin, and long eyelashes, like a girl. He is soft and round, puffing out that nice jacket like a sausage in its casing. Lyman thinks that maybe he'll fuck the boy before delivering him; it won't affect the work.

When he hears the shout and feels the hand on his shoulder, Lyman spins around without thinking, knife in hand. As a boy, they'd called him Quick Lyman, but the merchant is faster, though, fat as he is: Lyman's wrist is grabbed in mid-slash and the man bends it inward slowly, painfully, until he's pushed the blade into Lyman's own guts. The pain is incredible; he feels his knees weakening as he fights the man, smelling his beery breath, flecks of spittle landing on his lips. The man is too strong, is bearing him down so, finally, out of desperation, Lyman snaps his head forward, breaking the merchant's nose with his forehead. For an instant the grip relaxes and Lyman is able to tear the knife out of his own belly and drive it into the merchant's. When the man falls, Lyman drops onto him, stabbing over and over in a fury. Their blood meets in a widening pool, mixing together as Lyman's strength begins to fade. Somehow he summons a reserve of energy; he levers himself off the man's corpse and into the cab, whipping the horses into motion, barely making it to the townhouse before collapsing.

Later he wakes up on a table, the doctor leaning over him.

– Drink, Hedwith says.

It hurts too much to drink, the pain in his belly something fiery, coursing down through his legs and rising into his throat. He fights the doctor, fights the pain, but Hedwith clamps Lyman's jaws open and pours cup after cup of liquid into his mouth. The merchant's fat son lies next to him, eyes wide and empty.

Each swallow burns, spreading agony through his body, tearing him apart until the pain in his belly is nothing compared to the fire in his veins, the burning in his throat. He can't move: there is only pressure, only weight, only pain.

Lyman pushes his head out of the dirt, gasping for breath. The torment is so intense he can't think. He doesn't know where he is, only that he hurts and can't move and that his lungs are crying for air. Slowly, agonizingly, he pulls himself out of the shallow hole he's in, fading in and out of consciousness all the while. After a long, long time, lying there in the mud and blood and filth, he realizes he's crawled out of his own grave. And then he remembers.

Alexander Potter had killed him.

Lyman remembers the shock of the blade, how it had felt both icy cold and fiery hot at the same time, the way the breath had blown out of his neck, before the blood came. The feeling of surprise when his life started pouring out, how quickly he had faded into warmth and then cold and then nothing, his last thought the taste of the mud on his lips.

But he is alive, now. The fixative Salt, it's saved him, somehow. He isn't healed, given the burning across his throat, far from it; he wonders if he's used up the last of his energy digging himself out of the shallow, muddy grave they'd thrown him in, if, the next time he passes out, he won't wake back up, but just roll back into his hole and rot. *But the Salt has saved him.* It's given him some reserve of life to tap into, deep in his bones, and it has kept him here. Perhaps the mud packed into his wound has helped, slowing the bleeding just enough for the fixative to maintain him. He knows that he needs more of it, needs as much as he can get into his body; the way his blood cries out for it tells him so.

Lyman lies on his back, gathering his strength for a final push. He is bloody, muddy, filthy; every bone and muscle aches and the gash in his throat sucks and leaks when he tries to breathe. He has to hold a hand over his neck, making a seal with his palm, to get enough air into his lungs. He manages to tear a strip off the bottom of his shirt, which he winds around his neck, packing more mud into the wound as a crude bandage. The Salt will heal him, if he can only get to it. Willing movement into his limbs, he shakily rises to his feet, wheezing from his split neck.

It's dark, no moon is visible. Lyman doesn't know if it is the same night he'd been cut, killed, or the next. Maybe he's been lying in his grave for years, the Salt preserving him until he'd finally risen like a revenant. Turning in a slow circle, he tries to get his bearings. His mind is slow and sluggish and it takes him a long time to realize that he's still outside Baker City, along the bank of the Powder, by the look of it, not far from the medicine show camp. He pushes his way through a stand of trees, hanging onto each trunk as he passes, until he reaches the edge and sees the lights of the camp. The Salt is close; he can feel it calling to him.

He watches the camp for as long as he can, gathering his energy. If Potter or that blackamoor found him, he was done; he's too weak to fight and, this time, they will make sure that he is entirely dead. Lyman inches closer on his hands and knees, keeping out of the light. Aside from the few hanging lanterns, the camp appears empty. There are no townies, no music, nothing. When he gets near the banner that hangs between the two poles, he sees a crude *CLOSED UNTIL FURTHER NOTICE* sign tacked in front of the original lettering.

He moves as quietly and swiftly as his deteriorated condition will allow. Where is everyone? After an eternity, he reaches a point near the big tent and crawls forward on his belly. Inside he can hear low voices. He closes his eyes, listening, trying to focus. He is reasonably certain he can hear Mercy, and that's enough, he hopes. Slipping away again, silently, he works his way to his own tent, taking the time to peer inside before ducking under the flap, unseen.

With shaking fingers, he pulls the crate of Sagwa from under the cot.

He opens the first bottle and settles down to wait.

11.

MERCY LOOKS from Alexander to the girl, Elizabeth, who is sitting, blinking calmly at them in the lantern light, on the cot they'd pulled into the big tent. The short boy, Sol, is very drunk, as is Oliver. Oliver rarely drinks in earnest but, tonight, he and Sol are passing bottles of whiskey back and forth like it was water. Sol's skinny brother is standing to the side, next to Ridley, neither of them seeming to know what to do. Fan is in his tent, as always.

"It's not possible," Alexander is saying again. He has the girl's shirt raised slightly, baring her midriff. There is no scar, no wound.

"I'm telling you, Doctor, I feel fine," Elizabeth says. "I just woke up and I was fine."

"It's not possible," Alexander says.

"You keep saying, Alex," Oliver offers in a thick voice. "But look at that girl. Looks pretty damn possible to me."

"It's the Sagwa," Mercy says, glancing over at Ridley. "The Salt."

Alexander stands up, angrily. "The Salt doesn't fucking work! Look at Oliver, look at me. Hell, look at Lyman. Rula and the fucking others! *It doesn't work*. Not like this."

"Maybe it does, old man," Oliver puts in, taking another swig from the bottle he takes from Sol. "Maybe they finally done it. Shit, I'd like me some of that Sagwa."

"The hell's a Sagwa?" Sol mutters, leaning on Oliver. "Guy fucking stabbed her. Look at her." He waves vaguely at Elizabeth. "Stabbed." He's been drinking heavily since last night, since the stabbing and the fat man getting killed. Since he, Sol, had fallen apart, not being able to save Josiah, not being able to save Elizabeth. Even Ag had done better than he had: at least his brother hadn't made a fool out of himself. If this old man here hadn't been so quick with his knife, they'd all be dead, or worse. Sol had just rushed out without thinking, hollering and waving his gun like a goddamn fool; he'd made things worse and gotten Elizabeth killed but, now, there she is, right as rain, no thanks to him. He's fucking useless, is what he is. Useless. Worse that that, even. Whatever that was.

"I'm fine, Mr Parker," Elizabeth says, pushing her borrowed shirt back down. "Now, where's Josiah?"

Mercy and Alexander look at each other again. Since last night, Josiah has refused to leave Rula's tent, refused all but the most rudimentary treatment for his wound; he'd insisted, even, via sign, that they open up the cage so that he could go inside with his wife. They'd tried to coax him out of the tent, at first, even considered having Oliver bring him by force but, in the end, decided to let him stay. Mercy worries that the poor man's mind has gone, that he'll never come back to himself, but time will tell. At the very least, though, Rula seems to draw some comfort from having him near; perhaps she even recognizes him in some distant way, if there's anything of Mary left in Rula at all.

"Your brother is fine," Mercy says. "He's with Mary,

now. We need to give him some time, I think."

"What're we going to do, Alex?" Oliver says.

It's the pressing question. Since killing Lyman, they'd done not much of anything. Oliver buried the body down by the river. Dr Potter and Mercy had done their best to tend to Elizabeth's stomach, a wound which, at the time, they both had known was mortal. Ridley had finally been told something more than platitudes, and then was tasked with keeping tabs on Sol and Ag, although Sol had simply gone to town and brought back the case of whiskey he'd been steadily at since then, with Oliver's help later that day. Ag and Ridley seem to have formed a friendship and have spent their time playing cards, talking about all that's transpired and making speculations.

Alexander doesn't know what they *should* do, but he does know that, now, they can at least do something, now that the girl's wound has suddenly healed. He'd seen dozens of belly injuries during the war; no one survived such a thing as that, no one. But there she is, in the peak of health. Could Hedwith finally have done it? Really found it? If he had, that's yet another of the thousands of reasons to stay as far away from Portland as possible: the stable version of the Salt is only a catalyst, the thing that will become the true Stone. Hedwith had told him so, years ago. The Stone is a metaphor, maybe, but, whatever it *actually* is – if it's real – is coursing through this girl's veins now, wedded to her blood. Perhaps it *is* her blood. If he finds the girl, Alexander knows that Morrison Hedwith won't hesitate to drain her of every ounce of it.

Merely thinking about the Salt makes his own body ache; with all that's happened, now, it's been too long since he's had some of his own, and the fixative is having less and less effect these days, anyway. If this girl has the Stone, *is* the Stone, could reprieve be as simple as drinking some of her blood, just like that? How much would it take? An ounce? A gallon? He shakes his head. He shouldn't even think it. Instead he reaches into his pocket, pulling out his little flask of fixative and taking a drink. It's almost empty; he'll need to refill it.

"South, I think, southeast," he says. "I think we should go southeast. Work our way down to the Gulf, catch a ship somewhere. San Francisco, hell, the whole West Coast is too close for my liking, so let's go to Galveston, Corpus Cristi, maybe. I want us to be far away from Hedwith. Far. Lyman was his man, and Hedwith will find out what happened, somehow. More to the point, we have the thing he wants and there's nothing he won't do to get it." He glances significantly at Elizabeth. "He'll send someone for us, after us. I don't know what kind of resources he has, who else he has working for him these days, but he's a rich man and I'm not going to chance it." He looks at Sol and Ag. "You boys are welcome to come along. Matter of fact, I'd recommend it. At least for now. You too, miss. Most especially you."

"What about my brother?" Elizabeth asks.

"Yes, and your brother. And Rula and the others. We'll figure something out. I'll talk to Fan, too. There's a Chinatown here that he can get himself lost in, if he doesn't want to come with us." Alexander looks around.

"What about me?" Ridley asks.

Alexander remembers that today is the day he's supposed to fire Ridley. Well, things have changed on that front, and it can't be helped now. "Of course you can come with us, Ridley, if you like. We'd be glad to have you." He nods at the boy and then looks around again, trying to seem confident. "All right, let's all get some sleep. The sooner we get on the road tomorrow, the better. We've got a long way to go."

They all file out to their own tents, except for Sol and Ag, who are bunking in the big one. Sol is already asleep, passed out. Ridley's tarp is spread near the black tent in case Rula and the others got restless during the night. Mercy's offered to share quarters with Elizabeth; she looks back at Alexander again as they leave, holding his gaze for a long moment before turning away.

Outside, Oliver walks with Dr Potter. "How much you got left?" he says, after a while.

Alexander sighs. "Not much. Another bottle, maybe two. We'll take what Lyman had. What do you have?"

"Same. 'Bout a bottle. Then what?" He looks down.

"Then I guess it's the end." Alexander stops, looking up at Oliver, trying to catch his eye, holding it. "You don't have to come with us, you know. I won't think any the less of you if you went to Portland, try to patch things up with Hedwith as best you can. Not that it matters. But it's going to be bad, near the end. Not sure how well you remember that. It will be bad, believe me." He pauses, looking off into the distance for a moment. "I don't intend to let it go that long, myself. You know what I mean. Before it comes to that, though, I just want to get them away from here, Mercy and the others, as far away as I can. That's all I can do, and I owe them that. But if you want to go back to Portland, I understand. I do, Oliver, and don't fucking look at me like that. Just try to give us enough time to get away, OK? Matter of fact, come to think of it, you *should* go. No reason for us both…" He trails off.

"You think there's a Heaven, old man?"

Alexander shrugs, gives a short and humorless laugh. "If there is, I'll never see it, so no matter."

"Shit, Alex, you may have just got yourself a pass by doing what you did to Lyman. Never thought I'd see you move so fast."

Alexander looks bleak, gives that same dead laugh again. "You know what? I don't even think that was me, that did that. I was just fucking standing there and, next thing I knew, Lyman was bleeding out. I'm still not sure what even happened."

"What happened? You did what you had to do, old man. Whether you thought it through or not, don't matter. You did what you had to do."

"A fucking fluke, is what it was."

"Well, I got to thank you for that fluke, then, and I'm sure the rest of those folks do too. Trust a pompous old white fool like you to overthink this shit. You know, probably it was God who made you so quick with that scalpel of yours, and don't you be questioning the Lord." Oliver takes another deep drink from the whiskey bottle he's holding, swaying a bit.

"Fastest surgeon in the Corps."

"Fastest surgeon in the Corps, yeah." Oliver flexes his arm, remembering. "You been a good friend, Dr Potter. I'm going to miss you."

Alexander looks away. For a long moment he can't speak, the words achy and gummy in his throat. He coughs, finally, and says, "You going, then? To Portland, I mean? I don't blame you, son, when it comes right down to it. Like I said, I don't. Life, even the life we've had, it's hard to just give up. It's hard. You damn well know that, just like I do." He pauses, looking back at Oliver. Swallows hard again, blinking back something hot. "You've been a good friend, Oliver Wilson." He sticks out a hand to shake. "I'm going to miss you, too."

Oliver smiles wryly, a little blearily. "Hell no, old man, I ain't going anywhere. You really think that? Shit, man, I'm sticking with my friends. Be good to see Texas again, anyway." The smile fades. "When the time comes, if you want, I can take care of you. It'll be quick and you won't feel no pain; you know that. I know you'll do the same for me, if I'm first."

Alexander smiles back at Oliver, blinking again, overmuch maybe, taking a few breaths until he can speak normally again. "What?" he says, eventually. "The Black Hercules, first to fall apart? Hell, son, you don't even get fucking hangovers." They look at each other for a long moment; there really isn't that much more to say. All they can do is get the others away from Hedwith, on a ship or a train to somewhere else, somewhere far away. From there it'll be up to each of them to find their own way. For Oliver and Alexander, though, it will be a one-way trip, but maybe some last little bit of redemption to make up for some of the things they've done. It won't matter, not on the grand scale, but it's all they can do. Sometimes that's all you get.

"Now go to sleep, you big drunk bastard," Alexander says, punching Oliver on the arm, wiping a hand quick across his eyes when he thinks Oliver isn't looking. "We've got an early morning."

Mercy smells the danger before she sees it, a musty, muddy, bloody stink as she and Elizabeth duck into her tent. By then it's too late, though, and the last thing she thinks before it goes dark is *no*.

"Hello, dear," she hears a voice whisper, some minutes or hours or days later. Her head is pounding and there's blood dripping into one of her eyes. She can't move; looking over, she sees Elizabeth, tied and still, a lump on her temple. *No no no no*, Mercy screams, silently. *We were so close*.

Lyman Rhoades, her husband, leans forward into the lamplight. Or, rather, what's left of him: he's filthy, bloody, his skin sagging, torn in spots, as if he's been rotting in the grave for weeks rather than hours. He has one mud-caked hand pressed against his neck, where Alexander had cut him. In the other is a bottle of the Sagwa which, as he drinks, leaks from the wound in his throat.

"You don't look happy to see me," he murmurs. His eyes are shining, excited, his head shaking as if from fever. He nods at Elizabeth while drinking the rest of the bottle, tossing it on the ground and taking another. The floor of the tent is littered with empty bottles. "I thought you'd at least want to tell me about *that*, my love. The girl. She's healed. *Healed*."

Mercy just nods, searching for a way out. The blow has left her mind hazy, making the world vague and dreamlike. It's hard to think. She wants to wake up, to roll over into the sunlight and have Lyman still be dead in the ground, where they'd left him.

"It's what we've been searching for, all these years," he murmurs. "The doctor and I. He truly is a great man."

"He's always been jealous of you, Lyman," Mercy mumbles, not understanding.

"No, no, Mercy. *The doctor is a great man*." He rubs one dirty hand on her cheek, wiping away some of the blood that's dripped down from her forehead. "You were always so pretty, for a whore. Now, one last kiss for your husband."

Mercy watches the torn, bloody face coming towards her, tastes the mud and blood on his lips, breathing in his smell of rot. She tries to think of Bizet again, to draw her thoughts back away from herself, away from dead Lyman, to focus on the music, on life, but all she can hear is *no no no no*.

The fire wakes Alexander from a dream of the war. For a long, confused moment, he thinks he's back in the Corps, in the hospital tent, smelling the smoke from the cannons, hearing the screams of the dying, and then he realizes that the screams are Oliver's and the smoke is coming from outside his own tent. He staggers out on his hands and knees, stumbles upright, and starts running stiff-legged towards the blaze that's burning wildly through the black tent and has already consumed Fan's. Oliver is yelling, trying to kick dirt into the fire, but it's futile.

"No!" Alexander yells, trying to drag Oliver back by an arm. "It's too late!"

Oliver shrugs him off, trying to scoop up more dirt with his hands, uselessly. Alexander sees that he's weeping and, looking past Oliver, he sees a crumpled form on a tarp. *No*, he cries inside, his voice drying up. He just stands and stares, then, feeling empty. Half off the tarp, Ridley is lying on his back in a pool of blood, eyes wide and surprised, staring at nothing. His throat gapes open, as Lyman's had.

One of the gaff bottles inside the burning tent explodes, the alcohol preservative throwing out a gout of flame. He throws his arms around Oliver, barely able to encompass his big chest, pulling at him until they both topple over backwards. They push themselves further back from the blaze that licks hot at their faces as another jar goes up. There are no cries from inside and he hopes it had happened fast, that the smoke had overwhelmed them before the burning got too fierce. For Bascom, Holly, and

Rula, perhaps this was a better end, hard as it was. He feels the tears in his eyes drying in the heat before they can fall down his cheeks, tears for Ridley, Fan, for Rula and the others, for poor Josiah McDaniel, finally united with his wife.

Oliver hunches over, head in his hands, sobbing, as Sol and Ag come running, wild-eyed and half-dressed. "Where's Elizabeth?" Sol yells. "Where's Elizabeth?"

No.

Alexander scrambles up, tripping over his feet as he runs. When he gets to Mercy's tent, he stops for a second: if he stays here, it will be fine. He doesn't have to know, if he doesn't go inside. He pauses at the door of the tent, panting, on the edge of that final moment, and then pulls open the flap and steps inside.

The tent is dim and, at first, she looks peaceful, asleep. She's lying on her cot, covered to the chin in a blanket. There's a smell, though, of blood and pierced bowel and something else, something dark and rotten. Like the fire, it makes him think of the war, the surgery tent full of the dying. His hand moves before he can stop it, pulling back the blanket as Sol bursts into the tent, flooding the inside with light.

Mercy's eyes have been removed and placed inside an empty bottle of the Sagwa, which rests between her breasts. She has a gaping wound across her throat, the same cut to the spine that Alexander had given Lyman. The same cut that Ridley has. Her belly's been opened from crotch to sternum, the organs pulled out and the cavity stuffed with more empty bottles. Alexander hopes the cut to the throat had been the first wound, but of course it would not have been. Mercy had suffered, one last time. Dr Potter hears Sol Parker gagging behind him, spitting up the contents of his stomach. Alexander himself feels empty still, numb. He can't feel grief, not yet, although he knows it will come.

He leans over and gives Mercy one soft kiss on the lips, smoothing her eyelids down over empty orbits as he does. On her forehead, traced in blood, is the horned circle of Hermes. He rubs it off, gently. There is no sign of Elizabeth McDaniel.

Alexander looks down at the blood on his fingers, trying to think.

Lyman Rhoades is alive, and he will come for them all.

PART THREE
THE STONE

"I have largely accomplisht my promise of that great masterie, for making the most excellent Elixir, red and white. For conclusion, we are to treate of the manner of projection, which is the accomplishment of the work, the desired & expected joy."

1.
[VIRGINIA, 1865]

"HOLD HIM DOWN, goddamn it," Dr Potter yells, lifting the saw back up.

"We're trying, sir," Corporal Dennis says, "but he's too damn big and he's strong as an elephant." Dennis and two others are splayed across the big man who, even wounded as he is, can't be kept still. The man's right arm is attached at the elbow by little more than gristle and splinters of bone, from the ball that had crashed into it. It needs to come off but he won't hold still. Fast as he is, even most of the way drunk, Potter needs at least a few seconds to work.

Alexander puts one hand on the soldier's chest. "Look at me, son. Look at me!" he says, leaning down. The man's wildly rolling eyes come to rest on his. "What's your name?"

"Wilson, suh. Oliver Wilson," the man says through gritted teeth. "Don't take my arm, suh. Please."

Dr Potter shakes his head. "Private, that arm needs to come off. I'm sorry. You'll get septic and die if it doesn't. That's not worth an arm."

"I need to work, suh. I need my arm to work."

Alexander pats him on the chest. "You can't work if you're dead, Mr Wilson. Now, I need you to be quiet. Big fellow like you, tossing my orderlies around, that won't do. I promise I'll be quick and it will only hurt as much as it needs to."

"Please, suh, no."

Alexander looks up at Dennis. "Hold him down, now. Merriwether, the pad." With his hand still on the man's huge chest, he can feel the muscles straining as the orderlies lay across Private Wilson again, fighting to keep him still until the ether-soaked pad does its work. After Wilson has calmed, it only takes a minute until there is another limb for the pile.

The next day, Alexander stops by Private Wilson's cot during his rounds. He's asleep and doesn't wake as Alexander checks the bandages, leaning closer to sniff for signs of rot. He hopes that he'd been able to get all the bone fragments and debris out of the wound after taking the arm off, but sometimes these things are touch and go. It's a shame, really: with the war finally wrapping up, boys shouldn't still be losing their parts.

"Quite a specimen, eh, Doctor?" Hedwith has come up behind him while Alexander is examining Wilson's dressing. "Even without the arm."

Dr Potter just grunts. The presence of Morrison Hedwith sets him on edge. More than once, Alexander has finally decided to just finish it: put a bullet in his brain and an end to this new bondage to Hedwith, but he's too weak, too cowardly to do so. Every day, then, he takes the medicine that keeps him alive; every day he does whatever thing Hedwith might require him to do. Now that the war is ending, Hedwith has become insistent, reckless, wanting to try as many formulae as possible while subjects are still free and plentiful. One day, soon enough, Dr Potter will be caught, court-martialed, and shot; he knows it, just as he knows that Hedwith himself will remain free to pursue his studies in secret. This is the devil's bargain that Alexander has made, simply to cling to his wretched little scrap of a life for a bit longer. He knows he's damned himself, and yet he continues. Maybe, one day, he will have a bullet for them both, though.

"The Negroid races are a mystery, I confess," Hedwith says. "Physically, one can't help but notice that many of them put us to shame: strong, full of endurance, whereas we Europeans are often stunted and weak, in comparison."

"Come on, Morrison: put us 'Europeans' at hard labor in a goddamn field for fifteen hours a day, and pretty soon we'd be strong and full of endurance, too."

Hedwith nods. "True, true, there is that. And the Celestials," he says, switching tracks. "They themselves are small, lacking physical force, but clever. They've had their culture for thousands of years, invented many amazing things while our own ancestors were still scrabbling in the dirt. Perhaps they're on one end of a spectrum, weak but cunning, and the coloreds on the other, strong but simple. We Europeans are somewhere in the middle, perhaps, the best parts of each."

"Or maybe we're just fucking average, not particularly good at anything, just lucky. You don't really believe this horseshit, do you, Morrison? You'll excuse me, I've got work to do." Morrison has told him about Galton's new theories of heredity and eugenics, theories which don't strike much of a chord with Alexander. Humans are too complicated to have all their traits prescribed and explained like breeds of dogs.

"Still, it raises an interesting point," Hedwith

continues, ignoring Potter. "This man here, tall, broad, strong: how would he react to the Salt? Is there perhaps some extra component of strength that the African races have, one that will bolster the healing effects of the substance?"

Alexander looks at Hedwith. "Morrison, no. The man has lost an arm, for no good reason. This damnable war is almost over. Did you see the scars on his back? He was probably a slave before and deserves a chance at a life, now. A free one."

Hedwith locks eyes with Dr Potter. "Exactly, Alexander: *the war is almost over*. We must make haste. Who knows what might happen in these last days. I understand there are shortages of all sorts of vital things. *All* sorts."

Later that afternoon, like a whipped dog, Dr Potter returns with the latest formula, the number, date, and patient's information carefully annotated in the little book he keeps for Hedwith. Oliver is still sleeping when Alexander spoons the substance into his mouth, sitting back on a stool for a time, watching, before going off in search of a drink.

He's coming back from the commissary some hours later when the screams from the recovery tent reach his ears. Breaking into a run, Dr Potter ducks inside, pushing the orderly out of the way. He sets up a curtain around Oliver's bed and sends the attendant away on a makeshift errand. Wilson is moaning and thrashing around, his big frame threatening to collapse the cot underneath him.

"It hurts," he groans. "It hurts so bad, suh. Oh dear Lord, *it hurts*."

Alexander puts a hand on the man's chest, feeling the racing heart. Wilson's muscles are twitching uncontrollably. Dr Potter is jotting notes in his little book with his free hand when he notices something incredible. Private Wilson has two arms again: one has sprouted right through the bandage at the elbow. He reaches over to the new arm, which is hot to the touch. The skin is smooth and soft like a baby's, the muscles underneath quivering. Otherwise, it's perfectly formed, no different in appearance than the one on the left. He grabs the big hand. "Squeeze, Private, hard as you can." He gasps when the fingers close on his; the new hand certainly isn't weak. Pulling his own fingers free with difficulty, he gently slaps Wilson's cheek, trying to get his attention.

"When did the arm grow back, Private? Tell me. Wilson, tell me!"

Oliver hasn't even noticed the arm. The pain inside his body is tearing him apart; it feels like he has thousands of hooks in his flesh, each pulling a different way. His mouth is full of blood and bile burns up his throat. "Help me, suh," he pleads, looking up at the unshaven face of the doctor, the man who had taken off his arm. "Please help me."

Alexander pauses in his note-taking. *Please help me.* He'd said the same thing to Hedwith, months ago, while he had gone through what Private Wilson suffers now. Even with the new arm, it's apparent that the Salt is killing him. He well remembers the pain, himself, the feeling of his own body splitting apart under the substance. *Please help me.* How? Hedwith will never give Wilson the fixative; he's an experimental subject, nothing more. He has no use. Better, in the grand scheme of things, to let him die.

Instead, without even realizing he's done it, Alexander has his own little flask of fixative Salt out and is screwing off the top. Gently, he pushes open Oliver's mouth, pouring it in, the whole flask, returning to his tent for more. After the man has settled down, Potter sits there at his side, late into the night, watching.

Oliver flexes his right hand, now, shaking out the tired muscles, remembering. After Dr Potter had saved him, at the end of the war, and explained about the Salt and Hedwith and the rest, he'd first wanted to die, wished that the man had let the stuff finish the job. He'd lived his whole life as a slave to white men, before escaping just long enough to join the Union Army and get shot. He had no desire to continue on as a slave to yet another, bound by chains of poison and what sounded like witchcraft. But he'd done so, nonetheless; the country was changing and a new life, even one within those parameters, was better than nothing at all. Dr Potter was right: he'd suffered too hard, too long, to just throw the chance away. Maybe he could find a way out.

Now, with his left hand, he rubs the muscles of his right while he rolls his thick neck on his shoulders, loosening up. He hadn't allowed either of the boys, or Alexander, to help him with the graves. The act of digging, the pure muscle-straining labor of lifting dirt from the ground, helps him to not think about the fires, about Ridley's open throat, about how Rula and Josiah had been found fused together, black and twisted, one indistinguishable from the other. They'd been laid in one grave, then, together. He hadn't known either of them, not really, but something tells him that maybe they would have liked it, being with each other like that.

Fan's body had been taken away by his people, the Celestials in Baker City's Chinatown laying him to rest according to their own customs. Ah Fan had always been something of a cipher, but Oliver already misses him; the man's constant presence in the fortuneteller's tent had been something of an anchor. You'd known that Fan was always there inside but now he's gone, along with his tent.

Bascom and Holly had gotten full-size graves, even though they weren't much bigger than children by the end. Once they'd been different, and he felt that they deserved to be laid in the ground as they'd started, before the Sagwa had taken them.

Putting the earth over Ridley and Mercy had been hard, so hard. That boy hadn't gotten a start at life, young as he was. Whatever he'd run from, he'd found a home with the show, these last months. Oliver had come to think of him as a little brother, almost; he'd lost plenty of family when he himself was young, dead or sold off to one place or another, but it doesn't make it any easier now. He keeps listening for Ridley's loud *haw haw* of a laugh, that horse's bray that cut loose a few times a day for no good reason aside from simple cheer.

And Mercy, poor Mercy. Oliver isn't ready to think on Mercy, just yet. He isn't ready.

He pats the dirt down again over the graves. Alexander has barely spoken three words since the fire, aside from his statement to the sheriff. The only time he'd even left his tent was to walk to the little cemetery when it was time for the burying. Listening, eyes empty, as the minister said the words. Alex had ignored the questions of the townies who had shown up simply because they had nothing better to do and, because a fire, murders, and a kidnapping were a big deal in a small town. He'd just turned his back and walked away. The word is out about Lyman and a posse is forming, but Oliver knows it's useless. They won't catch him. Best he and Alexander and the boys can do, then, is run, try to get far away before Lyman comes for them. Same plan as before, when Lyman was still dead and it was Hedwith they were fleeing. First thing tomorrow, they're gone.

Even though the graves are as filled as they're going to get, Oliver doesn't want to leave the cemetery just yet. Walking away from the graves is another goodbye he doesn't want to have to make. Before the service, he'd paid the sexton the normal rate for digging the graves but then took the man's shovel and did the work himself, taking more time for the farewell and losing himself in the rhythmic stretch and pull of his muscles. He'd started digging in the morning and the sun is going down now; by the time the last hole is filled, after these long hours on the shovel, he's tired and his back is sore, but the pain feels good, in a way. Any man can dig a hole, after all, but he feels that laying Ridley, Mercy, and the others in proper, well-made graves, graves dug and filled by a friend, is the one final thing he can do for them himself.

Finally, it's too dark to see, and Oliver knows he has to stop. With a last, quick prayer for their spirits, wherever they might be, he walks back down the hill to town, gives the sexton back his shovel, and returns to the remnants of their camp. Ag is sitting by the campfire, Sol pacing back and forth in front of it. If Alexander has been silent and withdrawn since the fire, Sol Parker has been the opposite: stomping around, cursing and hollering that they need to go, need to chase after Elizabeth and get her back, to put as many bullets in Lyman Rhoades as that fat body will hold. Before the service, Oliver had to tell Sol to either go ahead and just leave or shut up. They needed time to think and make their plans. What Oliver hadn't told him, then, is that Elizabeth is as good as lost; going after her will only get them all killed. He knows it, Alexander knows it, but that young fool doesn't, not yet;

he's seen a bit of Lyman, but doesn't truly know what
that man is capable of. It appears that, while Oliver was
off digging, though, Sol has managed to work himself
back up.

"Mr Wilson," he calls, as Oliver passes by the fire,
heading towards his tent, "Mr Wilson! What's going on,
now? Why are we still sitting around here on our fucking
asses when we should be *going*? We're wasting time."

"Sol–" Ag says.

"Shut it, Rideout! You just close your jaw. Mr Wilson,
I said: *what are we waiting for?*" Sol is pacing back and
forth, passing his gun from hand to hand. "If y'all don't
get it together, I'm going. I tell you, I'm going. By myself,
if I have to. You fucking cowards can stay here if you
like, but I'm going."

One part of Oliver wants to walk over there and
slap the shit out of loudmouth Solomon Parker, but
another part of him, the larger part, knows that Sol is
right: they're cowards. That's the truth, plain and simple.
But, sometimes, cowardice is just something a man has
to accustom himself to. Going after Lyman will just get
these boys killed, or worse. He and Alexander are doing
them a favor, trying to get them away, down south to the
Gulf or wherever, but away, as far from Lyman Rhoades
as they can get. It might stick in the craw but, if it isn't
bravery, it isn't entirely cowardice, not all of it, getting
these boys gone. It doesn't matter what happens to him
and Alexander; they're lost anyway. It's only a question
of time. It would have been good to go down fighting,
for once, but they can't add these two fools' lives to all
the others on their slate, and that, in itself, isn't entirely
cowardice.

"Yes, Sol, we're cowards," Alexander says, quietly,
coming out of his tent, slowly walking up to the fire,

limping slightly, coughing. *He looks a hundred years old*, Oliver thinks, hunched-over and shaky like that, with that haunted, dead look in his eyes.

"*There* you are, Doctor!" Sol yells. "The hell you been? We need to *get going*, if we're going to catch up to this Lyman fellow. You know where he's going, don't you?"

"I know where he's going, Sol. He's going to Portland, to Dr Hedwith. We won't catch him."

"The fuck we won't catch him. We will, and when we do, I'm going to finish what got started the other night. God help me, I am. We have to get going, Doctor. *Now*."

Alexander sits down, tiredly. "You're going to finish this, are you? Like you did before, huh?"

"I wasn't–"

"It's true, though, isn't it?" Alexander looks up, interrupting. "You couldn't finish it then, and you won't finish it now. Big talk doesn't mean anything, boy. So maybe shut your mouth for a change."

"Goddamn it, don't you say that. Don't you fucking say that." Sol has a wild look in his eyes.

"Alex, come on now," Oliver says, wanting to tell him to go easy on the boy, true as his words might be.

Dr Potter looks up at him. "What? Are *you* going to finish this, Oliver? You going to tear off Lyman's head with those big hands of yours? That it?"

Oliver bristles, but fights down his emotion. This is just grief coming out, Alex's way of dealing with losing Mercy and Ridley and the others. Oliver knows what Alexander is feeling: that he was supposed to protect them, to keep them safe, and he's failed.

"And what about you, Agamemnon? You going to finish this, gunslinger?" Alexander turns to Sol's skinny brother, the brother that has just been sitting there quietly.

"Sir, I don't even know what's going on. I just want to go home."

Alexander barks a single bitter laugh. "There, you see? From the mouths of children. *I just want to go home.* Smartest fucking thing I've heard said tonight." He rubs at his eyes with hands that are trembling.

"So what about *you*, old man," Sol says. "You just going to fucking sit there and blubber and *oh poor me,* tuck your tail and skulk off like a broke-dick dog? That what you planning on?"

Oliver takes a step forward, readier now to deliver the slapping he'd considered earlier. He controls himself with some effort, knowing that Sol is grieving as well, in his own way, for everything that's happened. Some folks get strappy; some, like Alex, crumple down for a time. Some men dig holes all day. It will pass but, until it does, they all need a bit of the soft touch.

Alexander staggers upright, slowly, weaving on his feet for a long second or two. He coughs, hawking up a gob from his lungs; he spits, and then rubs his hands over his face for a moment, wiping the tears out of his eyes. When he pulls his hands away, though, the look on his face isn't one you'd think to find on a sick, shaky old man. It's certainly not one Oliver can ever recollect seeing on Alexander's face, not in all the years he's known him. Dr Potter steps close to Sol, standing straighter, and points a finger at the boy's chest. Sol's eyes widen a bit and he takes an involuntary step back.

At that moment, cold, dead-eyed Dr Potter looks more than a little like Lyman.

"What I'm planning on, Sol? I'll tell you: I'm going to fucking Portland. I'm going to Portland and I'm going to get that fucking girl back. I'm going to kill Lyman Rhoades, pull out his fucking guts and piss on his fat fucking corpse until I know he's dead, and then I'm going to set him on fire and shit in the ashes. I'm going to kill Morrison Hedwith, tear down his fucking building, and I'm going to kill *every other goddamn person who crosses me*, if I have to burn down the whole fucking city to do it. *That's* what I'm planning, boy." His voice is icy, filled with controlled rage. He looks at the three of them in turn, slowly, staring into their eyes.

"Now, which of you bastards are coming with me?"

2.

THE JOSTLING wakes her first, and then the smell. Even disoriented, half-awake, with the bag on her head, Elizabeth knows at once that she's on horseback; she feels arms around her, a body pressed to her back, some person who is presumably the source of the odor, a muddy, coppery, spoiled-meat reek that wafts into her nose, making her want to vomit around the gag in her mouth. It reminds her of the time a possum had gotten under the floorboards of the schoolhouse and died, during the heat of summer, baking the classroom with the smell of dead, rotting flesh until one of the smaller boys had been prevailed upon to wriggle under the building and pull the poor creature out. Now, confused and scared, she fights against the ropes that she can feel binding her hands to the saddle; her feet are tied together by a rope running under the horse's belly.

"Now, now," a man's thick, mumbled voice says in her ear. "Hush." Instinctively she tries to snap her head back into the voice, but a hand grips her by the hair and she feels the point of a knife slipped beneath the bag, denting the flesh of her neck, under her jaw. "Let's not push it, shall we?"

The touch of the blade at her throat brings her fully

alert, clearing her head. She remembers ducking into the tent with Mercy and then a flash of motion, something hitting her on the temple. Her legs had gone weak and rubbery and her vision had receded; as if from a long distance away she'd seen the fat face of the man called Lyman, the man who had stabbed her, leaning down. He had one hand covering his own neck and, when he'd moved it, she could see the gaping cut in his throat. *But Lyman is dead*, she thought, and then she couldn't think anything.

"How are you feeling, Miss McDaniel?" he says now. "Has the Salt healed you?"

Elizabeth has no idea what the man is talking about. What salt? She has vague memories of Mercy and Dr Potter talking about some such thing, but can't recall any details now. What is happening to her? She's tied up on a horse, pushed up against a fat man who stinks like a dead animal and, worst of all, she has to pee. The jostling is doing her no favors on that score. "I have to use the bathroom," she tries to say, around the rough gag in her mouth. All that comes out is a sloppy, gnawing mumble, which she repeats several times until eventually Lyman seems to understand.

"Oh, no, dear. I'm sorry, but we won't be stopping for quite some time. No. I expect the fools in Baker City will be trailing us, so we need to make haste. Don't worry, though: they won't find us. I'll get us both safe to the doctor. Don't fret."

"I have to use the bathroom," she mumbles more urgently. "I have to... to pee."

"Just relax your bladder then, Miss McDaniel. The horse won't mind. I won't either, for that matter."

The arms about her squeeze her tighter into the dead smell. He's humming in her ear, a song that seems vaguely familiar somehow, foreign-sounding, in a way, rhythmic and stylized. Over the next hour or more, as near as she can reckon it, she tries to focus on anything but her bladder and the rotting smell of the man behind her, his wheezing, wet breath in her ear. Eventually she can't hold it any more and, ashamed, urinates where she sits.

"There you go, my dear," Lyman says. "Just relax."

She doesn't know how long they've been riding. Her thighs are chafed raw from her wet underthings and the rub of the saddle, her shoulder and back sore from trying to hunch as far away from Lyman as she can, mile after mile after mile. The feel of the air on her skin and the hazy illumination that penetrates the bag on her head tell her that it's been at least part of a night, a day, and now it's night again. Or maybe there have been more days and nights, maybe they've been riding for weeks. They've maybe been riding forever. Her head feels strange, at once muddy and preternaturally focused. She dozes, lolling in the saddle, listening to Lyman's wet hum.

From time to time, Lyman talks to her, or maybe simply to himself. His tone is always hazy and distracted, as if he's drunk. *The doctor is a great man,* he'll say, over and over. Rather, he calls this doctor a *Great Man,* each word verbally capitalized in a way that's readily apparent. Other times he'll sing in French, in a flat, off-key voice that bubbles and sucks through his neck: *Love is a rebellious bird / that none can tame,* she translates. Her mother had been French-Canadian and Elizabeth still holds a long-unused smattering of the language herself. *The bird you hoped to catch / beat its wings and flew away.* She wants to fly away, like the bird. *You think to hold it fast / it flees you.*

Other times, Lyman murmurs in a dreamy voice about how beautiful he was, once, how beautiful he'll be again soon. *I've only lacked the Stone,* he says, over and over, *and now it is come.* She wonders what he'd say if he saw himself, now, dirty and bloody with rotten-meat skin, dripping with graveworms and corruption. At least, this is the image she has of him in her mind; she can almost see him, like a physical manifestation of his dead stink. The possum, when they'd pulled it out, had had an almost human grimace on its sharp-snouted face, its body churning and rippling with maggots under its fur. *I've always been beautiful,* Lyman says in a sing-song voice. *I've always been quick; they called me Quick Lyman.* Sometimes he calls her Mercy, and tells her he is very disappointed in her, that she is nothing but a whore, that she's tricked him. Once she'd been beautiful, like him, but now she is just a tired whore. He shouts it, shouts nonsense that she tries not to listen to.

Elizabeth knows that Lyman is insane, and she is terrified that he'll do to her whatever he's done to Mercy and the others. She is in a nightmare from which she can't wake.

Finally, after many, many years, the horse to comes to a halt and she feels her captor slide off its side. There's a tug at the ropes on her ankles and those binding her wrists to the saddle; when they loosen, Lyman pulls her down after him but, when her feet hit the ground, her legs buckle and she slumps over in a heap, falling on her side in the dirt. He walks past where she's lying on the ground, exhausted and sore, pausing to tug the bag off her head. Lyman ignores her after that, taking the saddle off the horse, giving it a quick and perfunctory rub. "The horse is tired," he says over his shoulder, eventually. "We'll let it rest awhile. We need the creature." He pauses, looking around. "Just a small fire, I think."

She watches him gather some sticks and get a blaze going with a phosphorous match. The moon hasn't yet risen and, normally, a fire would be a comforting thing but, now, it does little more than illuminate Lyman's fat, half-dead face with shadowed light. He crouches over the little fire, feeding it sticks from time to time, rubbing his hands in its feeble warmth and murmuring to himself. She's cold; the sweat and urine dried to her body has chilled her. One part of her wants to move nearer to the blaze, but another fears to get any closer to Lyman.

"Come on, now, my dear," he says, looking over at her. "Don't be shy. I won't bite." He waves her towards the fire, smiling. When she doesn't move, the smile dries up. "Get over here, bitch."

She shuffles closer, keeping the little flame between them, for all the good that it will likely do. The shadows wash across his face, the light flickering in his empty eyes. She doesn't know what's happening to her, but Elizabeth's mind feels entirely sped-up now, her senses sharpened. She imagines she can see each tiny interplay of muscles and expression in Lyman's round face. She feels her blood thrumming in her ears, her heart pulsing in her chest.

Suddenly Lyman is across the fire and on her. She scrabbles backwards, swinging her bound hands, kicking her heels at him, screaming through the gag. He calmly holds her down as he pulls the gag from her mouth. "There," he says, moving back across the fire to his previous spot. "That's better now, isn't it?" He nods over and over, smiling in a vacant sort of way. The light in his eyes seems brighter now, madder.

Elizabeth watches him warily from her back, half-expecting him to pounce on her. Eventually she sits back upright, eyes still on him. She rubs at her mouth with the heels of her bound hands, trying to soothe her raw skin and lips. Her tongue feels thick, gluey. "Water," she whispers, hoarsely, trying to work up the spit to talk. "May I have some water?" Without speaking, still staring at her, Lyman tosses over a tin canteen. She fumbles the lid off with shaking hands and takes a mouthful. When she swallows, she almost vomits from the dead-meat taste of it, as if it's been corrupted by the touch of Lyman's lips. As thirsty as she is, she can't stomach any more.

"Raise your shirt," Lyman says. "Let me see your belly." Warily, Elizabeth lifts her shirt the smallest bit. "No, higher. There." He pauses, leaning forward. "There's no wound. The Salt is working. It's working, Mercy." He starts nodding again, an eager look on his face. "It's working." He's rubbing his neck as he nods, and then starts to murmur to himself again, low words she can't hear, even as close as they are.

Elizabeth watches him, trying to discover some weakness, some slowness she can exploit to get away. She can still feel her blood pounding in her body, which she hopes implies a strength born of fear that she can use in some way. *I only need a few seconds,* she tells herself, *enough time to get up and on the horse and then I'll ride. As tired as the horse is I can get a few fast miles out of it, enough of a distance that Lyman will never catch up on foot.* She looks around, trying to find landmarks, but she has no real idea where she is. The sky is overcast so that she can't even tell direction. *No matter, as long as I ride fast and far enough, I can find my way to something, some road, some help; I just need a few seconds. I just need a few seconds,* she thinks, and then Lyman is on her.

The taste of her blood in his mouth doesn't make Lyman's body sing, as he'd hoped. He still feels the pain, the exhaustion; his throat is a burning ring of agony, dry and cracked, each breath a torment. He closes his eyes, trying to feel any change, any improvement in his condition but, if anything is happening, it's slow and subtle. He hurts so badly, so very badly; the bottles of fixative Salt he'd consumed back at the camp, before visiting his judgment upon Mercy and the others, is only keeping him alive, and that just barely. It hasn't healed him. It hasn't. If the girl has the Stone in her blood, it is useless in its present state: it needs to be concentrated, strengthened, refined in some way. The doctor will know how to do so. He must. He will know, yes.

Lyman wipes a bit of blood off the corner of his mouth, licking his fingers afterward. The girl is holding her neck, sobbing with anger. He wonders how long it will take for her wound to heal, to return that smooth pale skin to its unmarred state. She is very pretty, he thinks; not unlike Mercy had been, at first. Perhaps the doctor will allow him the girl afterward. Although Lyman realizes that, by then, she will most likely be in no fit state for company. Who knows, though, perhaps even tapped of the Stone she will thrive

He hadn't even known he would do it at first but, then, the sight of her slender neck in the firelight and his own hunger for the pure Salt made him go for her, to try to suck it out of her. Like Lord Ruthven in Polidori's story, really, the one that had been so popular in the London of his youth Alas, her neck had been extremely difficult to bite into, given his weariness and loose teeth and her firm young skin. He'd gnawed more than bitten her, finally freeing enough blood that he could suck some into his mouth. It merely tasted like blood, though; there

was no power to it. The Stone was trapped inside her
and he'd simply have to wait until they reached Portland
so that the doctor could free it.

Later that night, he figures the horse sufficiently rested
and pulls the girl back to her feet and onto the horse,
retying her ankles and wrists. Mounting up behind
her, he clucks the mare into motion again, heading
northwest. He'd laid enough of a false trail upon leaving
Baker City that he's sure any posse will be nowhere
near them. More likely there is no one following at all;
if anything, the sheriff will have merely searched a close
circuit around town and then telegraphed the other
towns in the region. Lyman will be expected to arrive on
one of the main trails or, perhaps, via train. People are
lazy now, civilized, which makes those willing to be hard
and uncivilized able to do what they need without any
great fear of reprisal.

They ride with the rising sun at their backs. Lyman
hasn't bagged the girl's head yet and, leaning forward,
notices that the ragged wound on her neck is already
beginning to heal, the marks of his teeth faint and
fading. The Stone is in the girl; it is only a matter of time.
As they ride, he sings: *Mais si je t'aime, si je t'aime; Prends
garde à toi!*

3.

AG CAN'T REMEMBER the last time he'd felt in control of his life. It had certainly been before he and Sol had left the ranch, that much is obvious. Since then, it seems like he's just been carried along in a stream of circumstances that are entirely outside his power to change. First there had been Twin Falls, just days after leaving home, then running from the posse and, then, the crazy job his brother had decided they'd take from poor Mr McDaniel, to kill that man in Portland. But they weren't killers, not really. They weren't even thieves. What was Sol thinking? And *then* the McDaniels, both of them, had just up and rode off, which seems, now, like a *clear and obvious sign* that they should have just gone their own way. Just gone. But no, no: Sol had to run off after them, and then all that horror at the medicine show had happened, first that awful night with stabbed bellies and cut-off tongues and opened throats – another sign that *it's time to leave* – and then the fire and all those poor people getting killed. How much clearer does it need to be? *This isn't for them.* On some level, Ag expects frogs and locusts and all those other things that had happened to Pharaoh to start raining down on him and Sol now. Seems like it's the logical damn progression of things.

And now Sol's hellbent on saving that girl from the fat man and whoever the fat man works for. The man they were going to kill in the first place? It's all too confusing and, really, it's not even any of their business, not any more. But Sol, when he's set on a thing, he doesn't ever back down. Ag knows this. It's both a good and a bad trait that his brother has: he's the kind of man you'd want on your side, as irritating as he can be, because he'll stick. You don't want to cross him, though, because he's bullheaded and won't ever let up, stupid as he is. He's exactly the kind of man who, unlike Ag himself, completely ignores all the many, many signs that say you should just go home. Cut your losses. Things don't always work out right and that's just the way it goes sometimes.

But I can't just leave him, Ag tells himself. Much as he wants to. Sol is his brother and he's way over his head here. He might have gotten off a lucky shot at that man in Twin Falls, but this Lyman fellow is a stone-cold killer. Hell, the man is even a killer *after he'd been killed his own damn self*. Something is *very* not right with that and Ag just doesn't want to think about a man who can drag himself out of his own grave and start cutting throats and starting fires. If he's headed west, they should be headed *anywhere* but that direction, and that is a fact.

He looks out the window at the scenery rolling by in the waning daylight. Sol's head rests against Ag's shoulder; the train's rhythmic juddering and jolting has finally sent his brother to sleep after hours nervously pacing up and down the nearly empty car. Oliver had gone to sleep almost immediately, pulling his hat down and hunkering into his jacket. Dr Potter is coughing and shivering in his own jacket, a ratty horse blanket wrapped around him. The weather had been miserable

heading north from Baker City to where they'd picked
up the train near La Grande, rainy and cold with bouts
of sleet, even this late in spring. Dr Potter had taken
sick and gotten so feverish that he'd almost fallen off
his horse once or twice. He'd refused to stop, though,
ignoring Oliver's suggestions that they hole up in the
next town, long enough for the doctor to get a little
stronger. Now, his rattling cough is hacking out over the
clack of the train's wheels and his eyes gleam with fever
under his hat. From time to time Ag can hear Dr Potter
muttering to himself, sipping at a little flask.

Ag himself is exhausted and just happy to be out of
the weather, even if he can't seem to fall asleep. When
they'd finally reached La Grande, Sol had sold the horses
and they'd had little time to do much more than grab a
quick meal, the westbound train having arrived not long
after they had. Ag's never been on a train, but the novelty
is spoiled by his tiredness and worry. He tries to close his
eyes again, let the sway of the car rock him to sleep,
but it's no good. He just wants to go home; what had
happened was awful, but this isn't his fight. He wonders
if he'd feel different had he the same infatuation with
Elizabeth that his brother seems to have, although he
also wonders how much of Sol's determination is simply
because his brother feels so poorly about his showing
back at the camp, the way that man Lyman had simply
broken him like that. If it's just out of stupid pride that
he's doing all this. Yet again, Ag has the thought *but
I'm not a fighter*, and he's fine with that. Really, he is.
His own pride doesn't hurt, not at all. But Sol either
hasn't learned that lesson yet or still somehow thinks
otherwise, dumb as he is.

We're all going to die, Ag says to himself, silently at first
and then out loud, quietly: "We are all going to die." It's

hard to believe it, even said out loud like that, like *It's raining* or *I'm thirsty*, a simple sentiment that he knows, deep down, is true. *We're all going to die.* He can't decide if he's just so afraid that it makes him calm, makes the idea too big and impossible to fathom, or if he isn't afraid *enough* yet, if he's just stupid and clueless like Sol. *We're all going to die.* Either that man Lyman will gut them or one of this Hedwith's other men will shoot them, as Oliver seems to think or, somehow, they'll actually wind up doing what they're trying to do, kill these people, and then the law will catch up and hang them all. No matter what, that's it. It's really that simple. They'll wind up like poor Mr McDaniel, like that woman with the lovely voice. Like his friend Ridley, dead and in a hole in the ground.

We're all going to die.

The worst part is not really understanding any of it, just being caught up and carried along in that stream of circumstance. Ag feels small and helpless, nothing but a bystander. Dr Potter is smart, Oliver is big; hell, even Sol at least has his fired-up nervousness and his quick, stupid temper. Ag knows that he, himself, is just taking up space, making up the numbers, but that it puts him in danger anyway. It doesn't seem fair that this all had to happen so soon after leaving home, when things were just getting started with his life. He has the sick sense of making bad choices and paying the price for them, when he hasn't done any choosing at all, not really. Yet again, he tells himself that he has to stick, that Sol is his brother and Ag can't very well just leave him, no matter how awful this all is, no matter how much Ag just wants to go home and do something quiet and good for once.

He must have fallen asleep for a while as, when he wakes up, the moon has crept up in the sky, buttery

orange and beautiful. Ag doesn't know where they are,
exactly, but the train is stopping yet again, rattling into
another small town. They have to be fairly near Portland
by now. The rain has stopped and stars are peeking out
of holes in the clouds; the moonlight over the gorge and
the Columbia is almost heartrendingly beautiful, like he's
seeing night truly for the first time. Sleep has helped,
and Ag's mind feels clear now, the decision made, his
own choice for once.

Sol is slumped away from him, lying with his head
back, snoring. Oliver hasn't moved from his spot on the
opposite seat, his big shoulders rising and falling with his
breath. Dr Potter seems to finally be sleeping himself.
Even though the car is mostly empty, the four of them
are clustered together, as if for protection.

Ag stands up and steps over his brother's legs, not
looking at him, gripping the rack over the seats as the
train finishes slowing. He twists his hips from side to side,
stretching, rolling his stiff neck, working out the kinks.
When he takes down his bag, he catches a gleam of eyes
from under Dr Potter's hat. They look at one another for
a moment and then Ag nods and works his way down
the car to the exit.

"*What?*" Sol yells. "No, he goddamn *did not!*" He's in a
fury, striding up and down the car, looking from side to
side as if Ag is just hiding somewhere. The morning sun
is bright through the windows, and Ag is nowhere to be
seen. "He *goddamn did not!*"

"Just let it go, Sol," Dr Potter whispers, coughing.
"He's gone."

"He'd better *not* be fucking gone, goddamn it, he'd
better not be." Sol's anger vies with disbelief: Ag can't
have just *left*. Not like that, slinking off into the night

with nary a word to no one. Ag is his brother. He knew that they were in a tight spot and a brother always has your back. Sol, himself, wouldn't have left his brother, fool that Ag is, even. Their mama hadn't raised them like that. Family is family. "No, he didn't," Sol repeats, a bit more weakly.

"He did, Sol, now be quiet." Alexander is shivering from his fever, sweaty cold. Everything has a slightly surreal tinge to it, as if he's still half-dreaming. He'd watched Ag walk off the train a few stations back, though; that, he knew, was real. Really, he can't blame the boy, when it comes down to it.

This boy Sol reminds Dr Potter of himself, the way he was when he was that age. Loud, stupid, always at odds with the world he was trying to make his place in. Trying on this persona and that, seeing where he fit. Afraid, really, he knows now, afraid that he wouldn't. Sol thinks he's a man, that drinking and cursing and fighting make him one, but Alexander knows he's only a boy still. Sol will have to learn the difference soon enough. Maybe, Dr Potter thinks, if and when he does, he will make better choices than one Alexander Potter ever did. Assuming Sol lives that long. His reveries are interrupted by another long, painful fit of coughing.

Oliver watches Dr Potter, worried. The sickness is accelerating, and Alexander looks to be falling apart. Just now, Oliver doesn't much care that Ag Rideout has left; his greater concern is that Alexander isn't even going to make it to Portland, much less find a way to end this thing, from the look of him. And he's the one in charge, he's the clever one. They need him. Oliver himself feels far from well, going short on the Salt, rationing their last bottles as they were, but his own illness is nowhere near what Alexander looks to be suffering. The Salt is still keeping Oliver together but it's doing little for Alexander. That's clear. He wonders just how long Alexander has been keeping the extent of his true condition a secret, these last months, whether the coughing and sore guts and aches have ever really been from booze and opium at all, from the cold and the wet weather. Death is catching up with him. *How did I not see that before?* Oliver thinks. Maybe he had, though; maybe he had and just refused to admit it to himself.

When Sol comes stomping up the aisle again, Oliver reaches out a hand and grabs his arm, pulling him down to the seat. Sol struggles for a second before giving it another thought, seeing the look in Oliver's eyes. "Just shut up for a minute, boy," Oliver suggests. "We need to let the doctor think."

Sol's fury is inwardly wilting, though outwardly he's still red-faced and tense. Ag's departure, now that he understands that that is in fact what has really happened, seems to drain him, deflate him, as if his brother had taken the larger chunk of Sol's own courage away when he'd skulked out into the night. For the first time since Baker City, Sol wonders: *what am I doing?* Just a few hours before, it had seemed so clear: they'd get to Portland, find Elizabeth, kill Lyman Rhoades and this Hedwith fellow, and be on their way. Even with Dr Potter and Oliver's concerns, it seemed, to Sol at least, a sure thing. They had the weight of righteousness on their side, after all, but Sol is now beginning to get a hint that, in the real world, maybe righteousness doesn't mean a goddamn thing, not when you're put in opposition to that which is stronger and meaner than you are. *What the fuck am I doing?*

They're only a stop or two from Portland now, and Sol wonders if he should just get off the train when next he can and work his way back eastwards, try to find his brother and either beat him or thank him, or perhaps some combination of the two. Even though Sol had slept fairly well this last night, worn out from all that has happened, he feels exhausted again at the thought of what lays before him, both the choice he now faces about what he should do and the knowledge of what it will take to accomplish it, either way. He realizes that he doesn't even know Elizabeth McDaniel, after all. Is he that much of a dunce? It doesn't make sense to go chasing after her like a moonsick calf, maybe get gutted or shot, for a girl that doesn't even seem to have the time of day for him. But he can't back out now, can he? He'd never be able to live with himself. Or could he? Forgetting can be pretty easy, if you put your mind to it. *Goddamn it, Ag*, he thinks, *I can't do this by myself. Hell, I don't even know what I'm supposed to do.*

Dr Potter waves Oliver and Sol closer. Most of the night, in between bouts of fever, he'd been planning. They'll need to get in quietly. Getting out doesn't really matter, after all, at least for him and, to a lesser degree, Oliver, who can maybe hang on a while longer. Alexander knows he himself doesn't have much more time: now that he's close to the end, his body appears to have decided to completely fucking rebel on him. But maybe they can get Sol and the girl out, though. After they do the rest of what he's come to do. Just maybe. One thing at a time.

"Now, listen," Alexander says, looking at Oliver and Sol, trying to stifle another cough. "I think I might have an idea."

4.

LYMAN COMES STUMBLING into the cellar, dragging
the girl behind him and, for the first time in many years,
Castle is so startled that he briefly loses his composure,
shouting in alarm at the dirty, bloody apparition in the
doorway to the false-walled storeroom, the passage
that connects to the secret ways under the city. For a
moment he doesn't even recognize Rhoades, who looks
more like something dragged up from a muddy hell than
the primped, fat little bastard he remembers. Lyman's
eyes are wide and shining in his filthy face and he keeps
one hand on his neck, below a wild smile. The other
arm trails behind him, pulling along a young girl Castle
doesn't know.

He and Benjamin Wood are at the back shelves near
the laboratory area, doing an inventory of the normal
sorts of things Dr Hedwith's Apothecary Emporium
carries, pills and powders and salves and the like; as
Lyman steps through the doorway, appearing as if out of
thin air, Wood ducks behind Castle with a startled shout
of his own. Castle of course knows of the tunnels that
lead from the cellars to the river, having used them in
the past on errands both prosaic and unsavory, often in
Lyman's company for the latter; having the man himself

materialize in front of him is disconcerting to say the least. "Lyman!" he says, when he's regained control of himself.

"Mr Rhoades!" Wood says, at more or less the same time.

"Castle," Lyman whispers in a thin, ragged voice. "Benjamin. Or is it Johnathan? I can never tell." He smiles wider, bobbing his head on his neck, his hand pushing his sagging jowls out to the sides. "Where is the doctor? I must see him." He strides ahead, giving the girl behind him a sharp tug on the wrist, dragging her after. The girl is nearly as dirty as he is, with cleaner runnels from what look like tears etching the dried mud on her face. A dark rag gags her mouth.

Castle steps forward, imposing his bulk between Lyman and the door to the back stairs, the ones that go up to the house. "Dr Hedwith is working and has left orders that he's not to be disturbed, Lyman."

Rhoades stops, looking up at Castle. "Mr Rhoades," he says.

"The doctor does not wish to be disturbed, *Mr Rhoades*," Castle repeats.

"Move out of my way."

Castle doesn't reply, merely settles his weight forward a bit.

"Move out of my way, Castle. I have important business with the doctor. Important business."

"Be that as it may. Dr Hedwith has left explicit instructions." Now that his role with the doctor has changed, improved, Castle feels that there is little need to remain subservient to Lyman Rhoades. He's hated the man from first acquaintance and has merely tolerated him until now as a condition of his employment. Rhoades is petty and cruel, with an inflated sense of his own importance. Plus, he's fat, and Castle doesn't like fat men as a general rule: fat men are the victims of their own appetites. They lack control and discretion.

"Move out of my way, Castle," Lyman repeats in an even quieter voice, releasing his grip on the girl. When he does, Castle picks up a nearby crowbar that they've been using to open crates for the inventory. At that, Wood runs out of the room, fearing the worst.

"I'm sorry, Mr Rhoades, you'll have to wait," Castle says, calmly, bobbing the bar loosely in his grip. He makes a point of looking Rhoades slowly up and down. "Perhaps you'd like to clean up before you see the doctor. You look a bit… tired."

Lyman isn't sure where this is going. Castle is a nothing, a nonentity, a hired thug who changes bedding and pours drinks. A monkey in man's clothing. An overgrown ape, nothing more. He, Lyman Rhoades, has apparently been away too long; the man is getting uppity, getting above himself. Lyman doesn't want to have to deal with this oaf just now, though. He needs to see the doctor, tell him the news, show him the girl. *He's found the Stone!* The doctor needs to hear the news immediately; it has already taken far too long for Lyman to make his way back. If this fool doesn't clear out of his way, he'll leave him here in the storeroom to inventory his own guts as they fall out of him.

"I won't tell you again, Castle: *move out of my way.*"

Castle tightens his grip on the crowbar and it might have ended there, one way or another, had not Benjamin Wood come rushing back down the stairs, Dr Hedwith limping along behind him.

"Lyman," Hedwith says, blandly, evincing no more surprise at the man's appearance than had he seen him for breakfast. "You're back." He looks at him with some distaste. "Perhaps you'd like to clean up. Your friend is…?"

At the doctor's entrance, Rhoades straightens up, rubbing his free hand through his filthy, matted hair. He pivots on a heel, extending his arm out as if introducing a dance partner. "Dr Hedwith, may I present Miss Elizabeth McDaniel, a young lady of Baker City, Oregon. Miss McDaniel, Dr Morrison Hedwith, the man of which I've spoken."

Morrison bows slightly, on instinct. "Madam," he says, gravely. He realizes then the absurdity of the situation and turns back to Rhoades. "Perhaps you could remove her gag then, Lyman."

Later, in the doctor's private office, Lyman Rhoades tells the story of Elizabeth McDaniel, Alexander Potter's treachery, and an expurgated version of the fate of the medicine show. The full truth will come out eventually but, for now, he merely explains how Potter and his big blackamoor had staged a bloody coup, almost killing him, Lyman, in an attempt to steal a supply of the fixative Salt and make off on their own for parts unknown. He tells of crawling from his own grave, muddy and bloody and weak, of how he'd then discovered that the girl, Elizabeth McDaniel, who had been injured in Potter's uprising, is by all evidence the catalyst from Salt to Stone, found at last. *She is the one*, he says again and again, more excitedly each time.

The doctor, ensconced behind his wide cherrywood desk, merely nods calmly, hiding his thoughts behind an impassive face. *Could Lyman be right?* The girl is safely locked in one of the bathrooms, given a chance to soak the dirt of the road off herself in the large copper tub. Later, Morrison will examine her thoroughly, to see if what Lyman has said could be true. Rhoades is manic, his eyes glassy and empty; he still hasn't taken the time to clean himself up and remains coated with filth. He smells of piss and blood and earth and something very akin to rot. When Lyman speaks, he has to press a hand to the red, oozing wound across his neck, which he claims Potter had given him. Morrison has a hard time believing this: Potter is nothing but a weak, broken old man, had been since the war, if not before. The idea that he could attack and gravely wound a man of Lyman's talents is preposterous. Not for the first time since Rhoades had come into his office, Dr Hedwith wonders if Lyman has finally gone entirely mad.

Castle himself doesn't buy a word of Lyman's story. The broad strokes might be there, but Castle is too observant, too experienced, to accept the finer details. Rhoades has done something, has finally gone off the rails, finally succumbed to the baser elements of his nature. This wild story of an uprising is no doubt merely the man's way of covering his tracks with the doctor, as best he can. Castle wouldn't be surprised to discover that Rhoades has killed every man, woman, and child he'd traveled with, on some unfathomable whim. The wound on his neck is likely self-inflicted and the girl... well, the girl is something else entirely. Maybe she's the next Mercy. Castle is glad that the time is nearing when the presence of Lyman Rhoades will no longer be necessary. It's long overdue. He'll have to discuss the particulars with Dr Hedwith but, soon enough, Lyman Rhoades will be superfluous to requirements.

Lyman watches Castle as the doctor sits nodding over his story, wondering why the man is even here, in the doctor's private office, listening to what should have been the purview of his betters. He and Dr Hedwith don't require drinks or biscuits or their asses wiped, so the man is unneeded. He doesn't trust Joe Castle, hasn't from the first moment the man started to have ideas above his station. Obviously Castle has used Lyman's extended absence to somehow worm his way into the doctor's confidences. No matter: once Dr Hedwith uses the girl to extract and refine the Stone, Lyman will be healthy once more and will teach Castle his place.

He is a bit concerned, though, that the doctor isn't more animated upon hearing of their success. *She is the one.* The Stone is not fifty feet from them, in the body of that girl, and yet there Dr Hedwith sits, slowly, gravely nodding, as if Lyman is reporting on the weather, rather than the salvation that they've been working towards for decades. *She is the one.* The girl already should be strapped to the table, the experiments beginning. Lyman is so sore, so tired; the wound in his neck has further festered and he feels achy and feverish, half-dead still. He wants the pain to end. He *needs* it to end. He wants his body back. He wants to be healthy and beautiful again, Quick Lyman, fast and strong and lovely once more. *She is the one.*

Finally, after what seems an age of passively, placidly nodding from behind the big desk, Dr Hedwith shakily stands up from his chair. He looks old, Lyman thinks, half-dead himself; he needs the Stone as much as I need it. Castle steps forward from his place by the side wall, taking the doctor by an arm, supporting him physically as Lyman has supported him in all else during these long years. For a moment, the doctor wobbles until steadied by Castle's big hand, looking up at the man with an expression of pathetic gratitude that makes Lyman's own hand clench at his throat, as if willing that it was on Castle's.

"Well, Lyman," the doctor says. "Well, you have

certainly been busy, my friend. The Stone, eh?" He nods
yet again. "I suppose there's only one thing to do, then."

Lyman had stood out of respect when the doctor had
slowly gotten up. Now, looking across the big desk at
his employer, benefactor, his friend and colleague, he is
nodding too. The doctor understands him, understands
his need. *Their* need. There is only one thing to do.

She is the one.

5.

ELIZABETH STARTS CRYING when she lowers herself into the bath, unashamedly bawling as she feels the steaming water in the tub start to soak away the grime and ache. Her thighs and bottom are red and chafed, with open sores in spots that the water stings, but even that is welcome: it's a healing, cleansing pain after an eternity of suffering. She has no idea how long the dark, dull nightmare of the ride away from Baker City actually lasted, gagged and bound, bag on her head, sitting in her own urine. Days came and went, one the same as the next, periods of dark and shadow filled with the agony of her aching body, the smell of her rank breath filling the sack over her head, the feel of her dirty body and lank, greasy hair. She'd lost all track of time after a while and really had no idea how they'd even gotten here, to what she's been told is Portland, although she has no windows to look out of to verify this. At some point, the bag had come off her head and she'd realized they were indoors, in a brick building, as if they'd just materialized there. She vaguely wonders what has become of the horse.

Elizabeth stays in the tub until long after the water has gone cold, leaving a filthy ring around the edge when she finally climbs out. She dries herself and puts on the clean shift and dressing gown that have been left on a small table, not noticing that the sores on her skin are entirely gone now. Eventually, there's a gentle knock and a man with a crooked leg leads her down some stairs to a small room with a narrow bed in it. A pitcher of water and plate of food are on a table; she pours herself a glass and drinks gratefully, not even hearing the sound of the door locking behind her. She's only able to manage a few bites of food before her exhaustion catches up with her and she sinks down onto the clean white sheets.

When she wakes, a man is sitting on a stool, watching her. She isn't surprised or concerned; she feels logy and dull-minded, as if her head has been wrapped in cotton. Distantly, she suspects that she's been drugged. The man is smiling, though, so she smiles back.

"Hello, Miss McDaniel," he says. "Elizabeth. May I call you Elizabeth?"

"You may," she replies. The man seems pleasant. He's to the smaller side of middle in size, with grey hair and a lined face. He looks not unlike her grandfather, in a way, although this man seems sick and her grandfather had been as healthy as a horse until dropping dead in his barn one day.

"My name, again, is Dr Morrison Hedwith. It's a pleasure to re-make your acquaintance."

"Hello."

"Did you sleep well?"

"I did, yes. Thank you." He is a very nice man.

"We'll bring you something to eat shortly, Elizabeth. I imagine you're hungry."

"Yes, thank you." She *is* hungry, in a vague sort of way. She watches as the man lifts a small bag from the floor, placing it on his lap and pulling out a large syringe and a pad of clean white cloth.

"I understand you've been unwell, Elizabeth," the doctor says, removing a small bottle from the bag and dampening the cloth with it.

"Unwell? No." Elizabeth is confused, but that's all right. She remembers, then. "Oh, I got cut."

"Yes, you did, my dear. I heard about that. It is a wonder that you're still with us." He leans forward, gently taking one of her arms and rolling it over so her palm faces up. "This may be a little cold," he says, dabbing the crook of her arm with the cloth. He picks up the syringe, looking her in the eye. "I need to take a little blood, my dear. Just a small bit. Is that all right?"

"OK." She doesn't understand why he needs her blood, but it's hard to think. She's sure it will be fine.

"Just a small poke," the man says, sliding the needle into her arm. Fascinated, she watches as the blood rushes into the glass of the syringe when he pulls back on the plunger. The blood roils and bubbles, a shiny, dark red that fills up the large barrel in a remarkably short time. "There," the doctor says, pulling the syringe out and placing the cloth over the puncture. "Just hold that there for me, if you would, Elizabeth." He pokes the needle of the syringe through the cap of another small bottle, pushing down the plunger and transferring her blood into it. When done, he holds it up to the gaslight. "Beautiful," he says.

There's a quiet knock on the door and a very large man with a scarred face steps into the room, a tray in his big hands. There is another pitcher and glass on the tray, along with a bowl of something that steams. A single white lilac stands upright in a narrow crystal vase, flooding the room with its scent. That's nice, Elizabeth thinks. She loves the smell of lilacs.

"Ah, Mr Castle," the doctor says. "Right on time, sir."

He turns to look at Elizabeth, smiling his genial smile again. "Now, you've had a trying time, young lady, so eat heartily. You need to regain your strength, after all. We will leave you to your breakfast now and, later, Mr Castle here will return to check on you, bring you some more water for washing, that sort of thing. If you need anything before then, you need only to ring." He points at a small bell on the nightstand. Before he stands up, he reaches over and gently pats the bedcovers over her knee. "Don't worry, Elizabeth," he says, with another smile. "You'll be well in no time."

But I'm not sick, she thinks, distantly, as the door shuts behind the two men, the lock clicking afterward. Shrugging, she pulls the food closer to the bed and starts to eat.

When her eyes open, Elizabeth has no doubt that she'd been drugged: something in the food or water that had sent her to sleep again but, now, there's only pain, and she feels it with an instant, crystalline clarity. She struggles against what she realizes are straps holding her to a table, screaming against the hollow rubber gag in her mouth. Arching her neck forward, she looks down and sees that her right forearm has been flayed to the bone for several inches, stickpins holding the flesh open. She screams and screams, thrashing against the leather bonds, until the doctor comes into the room. He is followed by the large man, who again holds a tray in his hands. There's no lilac this time, only a collection of shiny, sharp-looking instruments. Dr Hedwith smiles at her, a sad smile this time. She notices that his gums are bleeding, coating his teeth in a thin slick of red. He raises another large syringe, leaning down. "Just a small poke," he says.

Her world shrinks down to a repeating cycle of sleep and suffering; she falls over and over into a logy, drugged stupor but every time she comes awake, she's clear-headed from the pain coursing through her body. At some point, her arm heals, far too quickly, like her belly had, and then they cut it again. The doctor and the other man enter her room, inject her and, when she next awakes, something else has been cut, burned, or severed. She loses two fingers; the next time it's a big toe. Fortunately she's always unconscious when they do their work, but the pain is there after waking. She always heals. Or she thinks she does; at some level she wonders if she's lost her mind and this is all some awful dream. If, in reality, she's still tied to the horse on the endless ride from Baker City with that dead man.

Once, before losing consciousness, she thinks she sees him in the doorway, standing there with his hand at his neck, smiling. She tries to pull herself away, back into the hazy unreality of that long ride, to lose herself, but every time she comes awake again the pain is closer.

6.

OLIVER FEELS MORE conspicuous than he's ever felt in his entire life, sitting here in this dingy basement saloon, wrapped in a heavy coat and trying to pretend that he's anything but a large black man at a table with a white boy. The ceiling of the place looms low overhead, so much so that he'd had to stoop when he, Sol, and Alexander had entered. The bar stinks of mildew, unwashed bodies, and old, soured beer. It has a dank heat that makes him sweat under the coat, which he refuses to take off, covering as it does the old pistol stuck in his belt.

The bar had been half-empty when they came in, and what conversation there was had stilled when he'd ducked under the low doorway. The small crowd was a rough mix of boatmen, the odd working girl, and assorted scum; they'd predictably taken exception to his presence, at least until he'd stood up to his full height, as much as the room would allow. Still, one drunk had called out, rising with two of his companions, "The fuck is he doing in here?" Oliver had subtly reached under his coat, but Alexander had stepped in front of him, saying, "Shut your fucking mouth, boy, he's with me." Which did little to calm the situation, until he'd added, "and this round is on us, hey?" The prospect of free alcohol had defused the situation, although the men still look over from time to time, glaring at Oliver and muttering darkly.

Alexander is now over at another table, deep in conversation with the man Oliver assumes is the crimp, Rick or Ricky or Red Rich or whatever he calls himself, the man that Alexander had been looking for. In the years that he's known Alexander, Oliver had had no idea that Dr Potter was such an accomplished actor. Perhaps it was all the time on the road with the medicine show, selling bullshit by the bottle, but the man has a real talent for deception. Gone is Captain Alexander Potter, MD, surgeon; in his place is Alexander Potter, scumbag and scheming criminal. Somehow, when he'd put on the shabby clothes they'd bought from a charity relief store, Dr Potter had shrugged into a complete, believable alternate personality. It's strange and disconcerting.

More worrying is the physical deterioration that Alexander has undergone just in these last few days since they reached town. He'd been bad on the train but now he looks terrible, far worse than he did before: coughing incessantly, burning with fever, bloody gummed and rheumy eyed. Even increasing the dose of what little Sagwa they had left doesn't seem to be helping.

"I don't fucking like this," Sol murmurs into his beer, taking a tiny sip and then laying his head on the scarred wooden table for a moment. "I don't like it."

"Shut up, boy," Oliver replies, rubbing his face, trying to convincingly sway in his seat. He and Sol are supposed to be drunk and drugged by now, hanging on the edge of consciousness. They've been pretending to drink for more than an hour, quaffing mug after mug of the beer that Alexander keeps sending over, which supposedly has been well-laced with laudanum. In reality, it's just beer and they let most of it spill, hiding the fact as best they can in the dimly lit, smoky room. If they don't get after it soon, he and Sol will be knee-deep in the stuff.

"I don't like this," Red Rich is saying, at the far table, pulling on his cigarette. "I don't usually deal in the darkies."

"Fuck off, Rich," Alexander replies. "Lookit the size of him." He coughs into his shoulder, trying to focus his watering eyes. "Worth two normal men." He rubs his lips with a stained handkerchief and takes another pull on his beer, squinting at the little man across the battered table. Red Rich is a thief, pimp, and general no account that Alexander had once met with Lyman, years before. From time to time Lyman had used the man for various unsavory tasks, things that required the local touch. He considers himself a gentleman, Rich, at least as such is measured in the criminal classes and, these days, holds himself to a higher, more managerial level of work. He's a facilitator, is what he is. He's moved past muggings and violence, personally. He has men for that now, men that accord him the respect due his station. One of these, a slab of a fellow whose nose is flattened almost completely sideways across his face, looms behind him, projecting the proper air of gutter gravitas.

Alexander, Oliver, and Sol have been in Portland for several days now, trying to lay low in a shabby hotel on the outskirts of town, as low as a nervous farm-boy, a huge Negro, and a dying old man can manage. Alexander has spent those days prowling the low areas of town, down near the river, gathering intelligence and looking for a man that will suit their purposes. It's hard work, sick as he is, and has taken far longer than desired because of his poor health, but it needed to be done and is something that Oliver and Sol just wouldn't have been able to manage on their own. So he's sat in bars, walked the streets, and watched, hoping that the right person would cross his path. Eventually, he'd seen Rich and bought him a drink, using Lyman's name as an introduction and dangling the prospect of easy cash before him, setting up this meeting. Mentioning Lyman is a risky prospect, in case he's already looking for them; Alexander had wagered that Portland was safe ground, though, at least for now, that Lyman would never suspect that they'd come to him.

"I deal in the skilled trades, you know," Rich continues. "For this sort of thing, I mean. Able seamen, carpenters and the like. Your boys there sailors? They have a trade?"

"Fuck off, Rich," Alexander says again, waving his mug towards the barmaid for a refill. "They're as fucking able as you want them to be. That boy there is huge, and the white kid ain't small neither. Well, he's broad, anyway. Meaty. Mate on a ship can always find work for a strong back, you know that." He already knows that Red Rich will take the deal; it's easy money, after all. This is just prefatory bargaining.

"I don't know," Rich says, doubtfully, eyeing the two at the table. The darkie *is* huge; Taggart will pay him over standard for that one. The white boy looks healthy enough; even with no sea skills the *Orphan*'s mate will take him on. Taggart isn't known to be choosy when there's money to be made. This sickly old fool here wants a fifty-fifty split on the up-front, but he'll get what he has coming to him, namely nothing; Arthur will see to that. But he has to go through the forms. "Yeah, I don't know, old man. This isn't my normal line of work, you realize. I *might* have someone who could take them, but it's risky and we'd have to do seventy-five my way."

Alexander holds in his smile, masking it in another cough. His head feels huge and hot with his now-constant fever. "Bullshit," he says. "I'll do fifty-five."

"Seventy-thirty."

"Fuck off. Sixty."

"Sixty-five."

"Done."

"All right, then. Done."

They shake hands; Rich pulls on his beer. "Now how much more is that big bastard going to drink before he goes out, old man?"

"That's it," Oliver mutters to Sol. "Deal's done."

Sol glances over at Dr Potter, trying to not to be conspicuous about it. "He's just coughing," he whispers back. "That ain't it."

"Damn it, boy, that's the signal. Get ready to go down. *Not right this second*, fool, give me a minute first." Oliver lets his head slip from the cup of his palm, coming to rest with his cheek in a puddle of spilled beer atop the table, watching Sol through squinted eyes. The boy is no actor like Alex, that's for sure. Instead of gradually falling into a reasonably convincing drunken stupor, he looks as if he is having the fits, weaving and bobbing his head around like a preacher in the grip of the Spirit. Eventually Sol slumps over in his chair and begins snoring. Oliver wants to roll his eyes but, instead, he concentrates on staying motionless. His belly is in a knot and what he truly wants to do is shit his pants. This plan of Alexander's is terrible. There's no way it's going to work.

After a time, Oliver feels himself being tugged upright and moved. Out of the corners of his half-lidded eyes he sees the bartender and another man walking to either side of him, holding him up with their shoulders under his arms. They grunt and huff as they steer him towards a set of stairs, and then walk him downwards. Ahead of them, the big man with the broken nose has Sol looped in a hefty arm. Alexander and Rich the crimp lead the little procession. None too gently, Oliver and Sol are dumped into a small basement room that has a thick, sturdy door propped open with a heavy prybar.

The bartender and the other man return upstairs, leaving Rich and busted-nosed Arthur to pay off Dr Potter.

"So, yeah, Potter, sixty-five is what we agreed, right? Or was it seventy-five? Either one seems a bit low to me now, though, come to think of it. I got expenses, you know." Rich pauses, lighting a cigarette with a stinking match, shaking it out and squinting through the smoke. "You seem like a sharp old fucker, though, so I think maybe you'll take a little less."

"The fuck is this, Rich?" Alexander says, nervously. "We had a fucking deal."

"Sorry, old man, it's just business." Rich says this last with a tight smile, shrugging. He glances up at Arthur and nods.

Arthur takes a step towards Alexander but, before he can get too close, Oliver stands up, grabbing the prybar from the door and laying about with it for a moment. Sol jumps to his feet and begins hopping around beside him, looking to add some shots of his own but, by that time, Arthur and Rich are already on the ground.

Oliver looks down at the two men. The big man, Arthur, is out cold, a goose-egg raised on his forehead where Oliver had cracked him with the bar. Red Rich is still awake, cursing them through the hands held to his bleeding face.

"You broke my fucking nose, you son of a bitch!"

"I can't believe that worked, Alex," Oliver mutters.

"My fucking nose!"

Alexander nods, coughing around a smile. "Should have taken sixty, Rich," he says, when he's able to catch his breath. He reaches down to pat the man's cheek condescendingly, stuffing a rag in the crimp's mouth. At the muffled burst of invective, the doctor looks over at Sol, who is still hopping about.

"Well, go ahead then, Sol," he says.

Red Rich, thief, pimp, and crimp, has one last thought before the handle of the boy's gun comes down between his eyes: *should have fucking taken sixty*. There's a flash of white, a flash of black, and then–

"OK, Sol, stop now, stop," Alexander says. "We don't want to kill him. I think he's out."

Sol is breathing hard and his hand stings. Knocking a man out with a pistol is harder than he'd expected. He'd hit the guy first with the bottom handle of his gun, which jarred his fingers something fierce. When he'd switched to hitting with the barrel, it felt better but didn't seem to have enough force. He'd then switched to *holding* the pistol by the barrel, and was ready to hit down with the handle like he was hammering a nail, when the doctor had stopped him. Good that he had, Sol realizes now: if the pistol had contrived to go off, he would have shot himself in the fucking belly. "Yeah, I reckon he's out," he says, trying to cover up his ineptitude with an air of casual nonchalance.

He looks around the low brick cellar they're in. According to Dr Potter, there's a whole network of tunnels running under this part of the city. They use them to ferry goods from the river landings to the storage areas underneath hotels, bars, businesses and whatnot, avoiding the street traffic. From time to time, though, enterprising criminals like Red Rich there move drugged, beaten, or otherwise incapacitated men from bars and catteries through the tunnels, to be forcibly signed on with merchant vessels working the Asian trade, the crimp and the boarding master sharing the man's first few months' sea wages. The doctor says that Hedwith's apothecary business is above some of these tunnels, his laboratory down in the cellars. If Elizabeth is anywhere, she'll be there. They can't very well just knock on the front door and ask for her so, instead, they'll find their way in via the underground route. Sol himself isn't sure that a more direct method wouldn't be the better plan, but has decided to defer to Dr Potter's wisdom. To be fair, the old man has gotten them this far.

"So what now?" Sol says.

Alexander is looking around, coughing again, consulting the crude map he'd made over the last days, trying to read his compass in the dim light of the lantern Oliver had found on a shelf and lit. He has little idea how exactly to translate surface direction into the twists of the tunnels but they'll have to figure out something, as he's low on ideas as it is. The damp air down here is wreaking havoc on his lungs and, for long seconds, he can only cough, deep racking hacks, spitting up a bloody spume when he's done. He can feel the fever coming on stronger again, building hot inside him. Just hang on a bit longer, he tells himself.

"What now?" he finally gasps out. "Now we go find that fucking Lyman."

This is not going well at all, Sol thinks, sometime later, and not for the first time. They've been stumbling along through these dirty, dank fucking tunnels for who knows how long, and he's yet again managed to find some way to crack his head on a low beam, even as short as he is. He doesn't know how Oliver is managing; judging from the repeated, muffled curses, not very well. This is a goddamn stupid idea. It's unmanly, too, is what it is. He'd trusted Dr Potter when the man had outlined the plan, but now he realizes that this has been a stupid, over-complicated idea all along.

"We should just turn around, get out of here, and go to the goddamn front door," he softly calls again over his shoulder, holding out the lantern and ducking under another low lintel. "We've got fucking guns, let's just go in shooting and be done with it. They won't be expecting us. Right? Because we're damn near lost down here."

"Shut up, Sol," Oliver mutters, helping Alexander along. Potter is struggling, barely able to stand upright from his constant coughing. He wheezes and there is a thin drift of bloody foam at the corner of his lips; from time to time he reaches an arm up and wipes it off, staring at his sleeve blankly. Even in the damp chill, Alexander is sweating and his eyes are fever-bright again. Oliver wonders if they *are* lost; more than once they've had to backtrack at a dead end and it feels like they've been working their way through these low brick cellars for hours now. As the crow flies, Dr Hedwith's apothecary shop wasn't more than a half mile away from where they'd started, at most. Even given Alexander's slow pace and the backtracking, they should have been there by now.

"I said, *we're damn near lost*, Doctor," Sol repeats, a bit more loudly, turning another corner. For a moment he's quiet and then says, "Well, shit."

Oliver comes around the corner to see yet another bricked-up dead-end. Sol is standing before the wall that blocks their path, holding the lantern up and cursing.

"You look like Diogenes, Sol," Dr Potter whispers, trailing off into another cough.

Sol turns around. "That you said? Listen, *I'm* not the one who got us lost, Dr Potter, so I'll thank you to keep the smart remarks to a fucking minimum, whatever the hell you meant." He pauses, pointing with his free hand, before continuing. "To the pressing matter at hand, *Doctor*: where the *hell* are we? This all part of your cunning plan, then, us wandering around these goddamn tunnels for a few weeks? Reckon they'll never suspect *that*. Element of fucking surprise, yeah? Jesus."

Oliver has never really taken to Sol Parker and is ready to step forward and give the boy something to think about, when Alexander's cough gets even more violent, requiring his assistance. He holds Potter up for a moment and then, thinking better of it, eases him to a seated position on the ground, back to the wall, which will hopefully give his lungs some relief. Alexander hunches over, hands to his ribs, eyes closed, as he hacks away. Even with the coughing, Oliver can see Potter's body shivering from the fever and, when Alexander opens his eyes, he sees that the white of his left one is now red with blood. Digging into his pocket, Oliver pulls out his last remaining bottles of the fixative; hunkering down in front of Alexander, he extends it forward. "Drink, old man," he says. "You need it."

Alexander weakly pushes the bottle away. "Save it," he whispers. "It's not working anyway. We're almost there. I can hang on a bit longer. Just need a minute. We're almost there."

"Almost there? What? We're fucking lost!" Sol yells as quietly as he can, pointing at the wall in front of them. "How many goddamn tunnels does this town have?"

"I said *shut up*, *Sol*," Oliver repeats, with some heat, rising and clenching his fist, stepping forward. He's had enough of this young fool's whining and bitching and griping. Oliver knows it's just nerves, but it irks him. Just now they need to trust Dr Potter. The boy needs to shut his mouth or Oliver will shut it for him. With an effort, he loosens his fist and, instead, presses one meaty index finger into Sol's chest, pushing him backward into the wall. "You shut up, boy," he says.

"What, you going to fucking hit me now, big man? Well, go ahead, by God, do it." Sol can't help but bluster; it's in his nature, stupid as even he knows it to be. "Go on, then," he hears himself say again, with some dismay, feeling his chest puff out, pushing back against Oliver's finger. *Shut up, Parker*, he tries to tell himself. "Pounding on me isn't going to make us less fucking lost now, is it? But go on, by God, get to it." *Shut up, Parker!*

Oliver may have actually hit Sol, if Alexander hadn't murmured from the ground then, "He's right, Oliver. He's right. We *are* fucking lost." He coughs again. "Should have been there by now. Should *be* there, according to this." He loosely rattles the rough map he'd made. The map is suspect at best, relying on what little information he'd been able to glean around the docks, some hazy recollection of conversations with Hedwith down in his cellar laboratory, back when they'd first come to Portland, years ago, and general observations while he'd walked the streets. It wasn't much, but it should have been enough to get them from the bar to Hedwith's, a reasonably short distance, after all. Maybe it *isn't* enough, though; maybe the boy is right, maybe they *should* just turn around. Alexander doesn't know how much longer he's going to be able to keep going. That's the simple fact of it.

Oliver takes a step back from Sol, slowly removing his extended finger and giving him a lingering look, one that says *don't push it*. They're all tense, and Oliver knows he is no Job from the Good Book: his patience has limits. If that boy doesn't back down soon, he isn't sure what he'll do. Taking his bottle of Sagwa, he takes the tiniest sip, just to take the edge off. He's doing better than Alexander is, of course, but the starvation rations of fixative they've been on are taking a toll: his guts feel hot and tight and there's a phantom ache in his right arm. He flexes his hand, sinking down to the ground next to Dr Potter, closing his eyes for a moment and then looking over.

"What are we going to do then, Alex?" he says softly. "We need to rethink this?" For once, Sol is mercifully silent.

"I don't know," Dr Potter says, shivering, eyes closed. "Need to think for a minute, though. Rest. Just a minute."

Sol sinks to his haunches, setting the lantern down and leaning back against the wall they've come up against. He watches Dr Potter and Oliver, wondering if he should just go his own way and find Elizabeth by himself. *Goddamn that Ag*, he thinks again. If Ag was here right now, useless as he is, Sol knows there would be no doubt in his mind what they would do: he and Ag would leave and find a way to finish this thing on their own. They wouldn't be stumbling around these cellars like fucking fools. He wills himself to just get up and go, then, to wish Dr Potter and Oliver the best of luck and then be on his way, but he can't seem to do it. It's just too hard. Sol has never been alone, not really. Not *alone* alone. Even when he'd left the ranch to start a new life, his brother had been there with him. He might have *wanted* to be alone, at times, but he just doesn't have the knack of it. Doing it now, leaving by himself, shuffling alone through these dark tunnels, thick with rats and spiders and vermin, is more than he has in him. Better, then, to stay partnered up with a dying old man and an angry giant, at least for now, as much as it galls him to admit it.

After a while, the quiet, broken only by the sounds of the rats in the walls and Dr Potter's wheezing and coughing, begins to prove oppressive. Sol has never been a man comfortable with silence. Particularly now, sitting here in the dim light, listening to the rats, waiting for Potter to do something, makes Sol's already agitated mind spin up to another level. He fidgets, cracking the knuckles of one hand, then the other, and then unloads and reloads his Colt for the hundredth time. Shifts his position then, again, rolling his shoulders to ease them up. He tries to whistle, but is only able to manage a breathy peep that still sounds overloud in the dead air. Yet again, he mentally composes the poignant fucking jeremiad he plans on delivering to faithless Agamemnon Rideout whenever he finally catches up to him, polishing the insults and accusations of perfidy to a brighter gloss. Finally, though, he can bear it no longer, and says, "You know, fellas, what about–"

"Shut up, Sol," Oliver says, opening his eyes the merest crack. For the last little while, he's been listening to the rats himself, the germ of a thought in his mind. There's something about the way they're moving, the rats, something about the sound. He closes his eyes again, trying to concentrate. The doctor isn't coughing for once, just wheezing low in his throat. Oliver can feel him shivering beside him.

"Come on, Oliver. I just mean–"

"*Shh.*" Yet again he wishes that boy would just shut

up. Oliver needs to focus, to follow what he thinks his ears are telling him. Is it that obvious? Well, maybe there's an easy way to find out. If he's wrong, they'll be no worse off than they are now. He opens his eyes, glancing over to Alexander, who's staring at the map, his eyes shiny and empty. A drip of blood is leaking from one nostril.

"Don't fucking shush me, Oliver! I got a right to speak. Now…" Sol knows, right then, that he's finally pushed the big man too far: Oliver stands up, pulling the prybar from the ground, his eyes narrowed. He crosses the space between them in one long stride, raising the heavy iron. Sol scrambles to the side, fumbling with his Colt, dropping it in his haste. "Don't!" he yells, just before the prybar comes down.

There's a hollow thud as the bar hits the brick wall above Sol's head. Crumbles of mortar and pieces of shattered brick patter down on Sol's hat as he pushes himself back with heels and hands, sliding on his ass away from the wall that Oliver is attacking. It only takes several heavy blows with the bar before a hole the size of a pumpkin has opened up in the bricks. Oliver puts the bar inside, moving it around in a circle to clear things out a bit. He looks down. "I told you to shut up, Sol," he says, mildly. "Now hand me that lantern, boy." Wordlessly, eyes wide, Sol passes it up.

Oliver holds the lantern to the hole, peering inside for a long moment. "I guess we're here," he says.

7.

AND HERE WE *are then, at last*, Joseph Castle thinks, smiling inwardly.

Lyman Rhoades is strapped to the table, screaming.

The sound is surprisingly loud for a gagged man with his throat cut, Castle notes. Looking down, interested, he sees that Rhoades is missing parts of his front teeth, having cracked them clean through from biting down too hard on the thick rubber tube in his mouth. Lyman's back is arched as much as the leather straps will allow, his wrists bouncing in the restraints. Castle idly wonders if the man is strong enough to break his own arms. He hopes so. With each scream, blood and snot blows out of Lyman's nostrils; his eyes have been tightly shut but, when they open, they fix on Castle with hatred.

"Sclera have burst," Dr Hedwith says calmly, pointing with his pen. "Subconjunctival hemorrhage, in the parlance. Likely from straining too hard." He looks at the level of fluid in the bottle hanging by the table, checking his pocketwatch and noting the time. "Does that line still look good, Mr Castle? He's moving around quite a bit, even in the restraints. Let's see if we can cinch them up."

Castle leans down, checking that the needle hasn't worked its way loose. "Seems all right, sir, but perhaps you should verify." He pushes down, none too gently, on Rhoades' heaving chest, managing one more notch in the belt that crosses it. The wrist restraints are as tight as they can get, but he double-checks their connection to the table, just in case. For a fat man, he knows that Lyman is incredibly strong.

Dr Hedwith inspects the intravenous line, satisfied that it hasn't pulled loose or ruptured the vein. "How are you holding up, Lyman?" he asks, repeating it more loudly when he gets no more response than another scream around the gag. There is blood leaking out of the eyes now, which he gently wipes off with a clean pad. "Can you hear me, Lyman?"

"He seems to be in some distress, sir," Castle says blandly, keeping the smile from his lips. It's no more than Lyman deserves and, after all, the man had asked for it, hadn't he? Begged, even, to try this new Salt variant, made from a sample of the girl's blood, which the doctor had recently completed. They'd already tested it on a rat and a stray cat; both creatures had been healed from considerable physical mortification. More mundane, but no less amazing to Castle, was another experiment: the doctor had soaked a small quantity of iron in the substance, heated it, and then let it cool after adding the tiniest flake of gold leaf. When the preparation had solidified, later that day, the retort contained pure gold.

Ever cautious, the doctor is reserving judgment on the substance until more tests can be performed. Rotting, stinking Lyman, though, he had been insistent that it *was* the Stone, was certain, had pleaded to try it before he got even sicker, before his decomposing body finished falling to pieces. *Please, doctor, I need it. Please.* Castle had seen the fear in Lyman's eyes: the fear of death, with life potentially so close. Life everlasting. So near, but he would die too soon to have it. *Please, let me try. Help me, doctor.*

Finally, the doctor had acquiesced and Castle had taken quiet pleasure in strapping Lyman down to the table. *I'll be coming for you, monkey,* Lyman had whispered. *When the Stone has restored me, I will come for you.* Castle hadn't responded, merely levered the straps down tighter, patting Lyman's chest. We'll see about that, fat man.

Rhoades had begun screaming soon after the first languid drips of the Salt entered his veins. He's continued screaming in the hours since.

It's an almost musical sound, Castle thinks now, with calm content. Relaxing, in its way. Here you are, then, Lyman. Enjoy this, as I am. It's in the name of science, after all.

"Quite a bit of distress," he says aloud.

"Indeed," the doctor replies, sensing the sarcasm in Castle's voice, slightly irked. A flippant attitude is unwelcome here. They are doing the great work, which demands sober respect. It is a pure and noble thing that they do here.

Lyman screams again, louder than before, blowing blood from between his cracked teeth. Morrison looks over at the level of fluid in the bottle again, tapping it with his fingernail. "About halfway," he murmurs, not knowing if the man can hear him.

Later, Castle sees that Lyman's forearm is bent at an unnatural angle. Apparently the fat man *is* strong enough to break his own bones. Castle can't help but be impressed. He glances over at the bottle of dark fluid that's still slowly dripping. It's almost empty. Rhoades will finally die, soon enough, it looks like; he's spent his last hours in constant agony, his body tearing itself apart from the inside out, by the sound of it. It is no more than he deserves, so good riddance. This world is a better place without you in it, Lyman.

Dr Hedwith checks his watch again, jotting down notes, holding back a sigh. It doesn't look good for Lyman, or the formula. Something is still missing. A human being is not a rat or a cat but, based on his calculations, on observations of the animal subjects, the Salt should have started working by now. At least to slow further deterioration if not actually start the healing process. Even given corrections for size and the differences in mammalian metabolisms, Lyman should, at the very least, have been rendered unconscious by now. Instead, his screams have gotten louder and more tortured, though they've been at it for several hours. It doesn't look good at all.

Something is missing.

He pats Lyman on the shoulder as the man shrieks around the bloodied rubber gag, and checks the time once again.

Much later, it is over. Castle, smiling, pulls the sheet over the bloody remains of what was once Lyman Rhoades, and he and Dr Hedwith leave the laboratory, abandoning Lyman to the dark. Good riddance, he thinks again, closing the door behind him.

Good riddance.

8.

"THE FUCK WAS that screaming?" Sol whispers again. "What were they *doing* in there?" They'd pushed their way through the hole Oliver had made, down another short tunnel and into this storeroom or whatever it is. On the other side of the door, a man had been shrieking in agony, for what felt like hours. "We should have stopped it, Oliver. We should have stopped it," Sol says.

"That's not on us, boy," Oliver murmurs, though he'd been equally unnerved by the sound. "We don't know that man. We got to focus on Elizabeth. Pay mind to what we came here to do. So we're not going anywhere. Not yet. We're going to wait, like Alexander said. Give it time. We go busting in there now, who knows what might be waiting for us?" He looks over at Alexander, who is shivering beside him. "Besides, the doctor needs a bit more time to get himself back together. He'll know what to do after that."

Alexander needs more than time, by the look of it. Dr Potter hasn't even been lucid for a while now. At some point, while Oliver had quietly been expanding the hole in the wall, Alexander had slipped into unconsciousness, still shivering and coughing. From time to time his eyes would open blankly and he'd mutter something but, wherever he was, it wasn't with them. Blood dripped from his nose nearly constantly, until Oliver tore off a little bit of his shirt, making two small twists and putting them in Alexander's nostrils to staunch the flow. Now, he puts the back of his hand to Potter's forehead, feeling the feverish heat there. Opening his bottle of Sagwa, he pours a little into Dr Potter's mouth, tilting his chin up and doing his best to get the man to swallow it. Instead, Alexander merely coughs it out.

"Jesus, he doesn't look good, Oliver," Sol whispers. They need Dr Potter; if there's a plan, now, he's the only one who has it. Oliver doesn't seem to know what they're going to do, and Sol himself can't think of a damn thing either. The fucking screaming from the other room hadn't helped him to relax any, either, come to that. What had they done to that guy in there? Sol tries not to think about what they might have already done to Elizabeth. They should have fucking gotten here quicker, he knows; they've wasted too much time already. That screaming has made him feel hot and jittery, but it's also brought his anger on. Maybe it's just easier to be angry than terrified, he reckons.

"What the fuck are we going to do, Oliver?"

"I told you, Sol. Wait. Alex will be feeling better in a while, after he's had some more rest, and we can finish this up. That man is cunning, don't you worry." Oliver hopes his voice sounds more confident than he feels. What *are* they going to do? Stupid gun-happy farm-boy and a big ol' dumb nigger, just busting in? They going to tear down the temple like Sampson? They have two old pistols, a prybar. Oliver doesn't even remember if he knows how to shoot a gun and Sol had made a mess of it the last time around. Alexander has strategies in him; he can figure this all out. On his own, Oliver doesn't know how to see it through.

"Then what?" Sol whispers, checking the rounds in his Colt yet again.

Oliver just stares at Dr Potter. *Come on, old man.* He pulls out his battered pocket watch, checking the time, trying to forget whatever has happened on the other side of that door.

They wait.

They huddle in the storeroom for a long time after the screaming had finally, mercifully stopped, after the muffle of muted conversation and the sounds of feet going up stairs had turned back into silence. There is no further sound, no light, only their own breathing and the occasional skitter of a rat.

They listen at the door until, eventually, Oliver decides that enough time has passed, near as he can tell, anyway. That what they need to do can't be put off any longer, and they stand up.

9.

LIFE IS A CIRCLE. Life is a wheel.

Yet again he falls into the blackness, the pain, looking up at the receding disk of light above him, gradually drawing away, leaving him in the dark.

Life is a well.

For a lifetime he lies at the bottom of the well, the light shrinking down to a pinprick at the far edge of his vision. There are sounds around him, but they are distant and muffled. The pain is enfolding and complete, though; it wraps him in a burning, shivery embrace, in the cold deepening dark.

He knows that when the light finally fades he will be done, gone, dead at last, left only with the dark and the pain, forever. Some tiny lucid corner of his mind is screaming.

But life is a circle. Life is a wheel. Yet again, he comes back, rising slowly up out of the blackness, out of the pain, crawling to the top of the well, gasping for air, born again.

Three times he has died. Three times he's been reborn. It is a holy number, perfect.

Lyman opens his eyes, taking a slow, steady breath. The

laboratory is dark, empty, but it is a comfortable dark, rich with life, a warm enclosure as of the womb. For long moments he lies there, breathing, feeling the rhythmic motion of the muscles in his chest, the pull of his lungs. He feels the remembered ache of pain, of fear, but that is all it is, a memory. He sits up on the table, crossing his arms in an X across his chest, lowering his head, listening.

It's night: Lyman can feel the pull of the queen, the moon, the incarnation of becoming, high in the sky. Biding her time before she can receive her king. The old mystics had been right; Lyman can feel the deep knowledge in his bones and his blood, the thrumming of the Stone inside him. Three times he's died. Three times life's wheel has circled him back.

He is a holy, perfect thing.

He is immortal.

He laughs quietly in the dark, around the distant itch in his mouth, of teeth regrowing.

10.

SLOWLY, OLIVER opens the door. He steps through, unable to see, supporting Alexander with one arm, fumbling for his matches with his free hand. He can feel Sol at his back, one hand pressed onto his shoulder. He scratches a match into life.

He has just enough time to twist into Lyman's knife before it hits Alexander's neck, taking it instead in his own broad shoulder. It doesn't hurt, not at first but, after he kicks out at Lyman, who backs away with that ridiculous speed of his, the wound starts to throb, low and hot and steady. Before he loses the initiative, Oliver lowers Dr Potter to the ground, propping him up against a wall again and stepping in front of him. Blood runs down Oliver's arm, dripping from his fingertips, threatening to quench the match that is already beginning to burn his hand. He doesn't want to be in the dark again, now that he knows Lyman is here. Alexander moans, muttering something unintelligible.

"Why, Oliver Wilson," Lyman says, smiling, stepping back and lighting a lantern with a match of his own. "Whatever brings you here, sir?" He holds up his knife, rubbing the blood off on the shoulder of his filthy coat. "And Dr Potter! What a lovely surprise, to see you both!"

He pauses, hunkering down and waving a hand where the doctor's eyes are sightlessly pointing. "I don't think he sees me, Mr Wilson. Doing poorly, is he? The man needs a bit of the Sagwa, is my guess." Lyman ducks, still smiling, as a pistol fires from somewhere behind Oliver's big frame.

Oliver steps across the door, blocking it with his body.

"Goddamn it, Oliver, move! Get the fuck out of the way!" Sol yells, trying to push past. He's so keyed up that he'd almost shot Oliver when the door had first opened. Now, he's wasted a shot from haste; that fucker Rhoades had simply dodged it. Oliver is in front of him now and Sol can't get his pistol into a clear position; the man is too goddamn big to get around. "*Move!*" What is Oliver doing? One shot, that's all he needed, and they'd be done with the fat bastard and could go find Elizabeth. Whoever this Hedwith was could take another fucking bullet and then they'd gather Elizabeth, Dr Potter, and be on their goddamn way. It was that simple, if only Oliver would *move.*

"Just hang on a minute, Sol. I need to talk to this man." Oliver holds one hand to his shoulder, trying to staunch the blood. He isn't cut bad, but it hurts and he's bleeding steadily. He needs to think. But seeing Lyman here, smiling like this, scares the hell out of him. Lyman looks good, healthy, not a wound to be seen on that neck of his. Maybe a little thinner, even. Certainly he's just as quick; it had mostly been luck that Oliver had gotten himself in front of Dr Potter.

"You're bleeding, nigger," Lyman says, pointing with the knife at the pats of blood hitting the cellar floor.

"Imagine I am," Oliver says, nodding, trying to buy time. For what, he isn't sure. "Thought we killed you, fat man."

Lyman's eyes harden for a moment. "I'd say you

didn't," he says. "But you're owed nonetheless."

"Well, come on then," Oliver says, nodding, wondering where the bravado is coming from. "Let's get to it." He knows that they are lost, had known it from the second Lyman stabbed him, their supposed element of surprise rendered nonexistent. Lyman will cut them apart, piece by piece, no matter how many guns they have. Remembering, Oliver swipes at his waistband, grabbing the pistol stuck there and raising it to shoot.

"Now, now," Lyman says, darting forward, his knife cutting across Oliver's knuckles, making the pistol drop to the ground. "Where's the sport in that?"

Oliver clenches his bleeding hand, wondering how long it will be until the end, how long Lyman will stretch it out. *Let's get to it.*

From the stairs, a man shouts Lyman's name.

At the sound, Sol sees Oliver and Lyman turn their heads, distracted for a moment. Figuring the two are done trading quips, he pushes Oliver's arm aside as best he can, taking a moment to steady his pistol this time, and then he squeezes the trigger. Lyman's head snaps back in a burst of red; he takes a half-step backward and then drops bonelessly to the floor.

As the echo of the shot fades, Oliver looks from Lyman's twitching body to Sol, dumbfounded.

Sol shrugs, oddly serene, holding up the smoking Colt. "What? Sometimes things don't have to be so fucking hard, Oliver," he says.

Oliver returns his attention to the stairwell, where scar-faced Joe Castle is descending, Dr Hedwith limping slowly along behind him. Seeing the calm look in Castle's eyes, Oliver looks back to Sol for a moment, sighing.

"Well, Sol, sometimes they do, too."

●●●

Castle slowly walks down the stairs, his eyes on Oliver Wilson, the Black Hercules. He looks for a moment at the boy with the gun, gauging his angles. Castle hates guns, reckons them the tools of cowards. The fact that the boy has one is no matter; it will be short work, in this enclosed space, to get it off him without real danger. Even with Mr Wilson to deal with, it will be short work.

After one quick, satisfied glance downward, he ignores Lyman's body, crumpled on the floor, healthy and whole but for the pool of blood spreading from his head. The irony of it all makes him want to laugh aloud: he and the doctor had left Lyman dead, hours ago, torn apart and broken by the Salt. Life had well and truly flown from the man – been torn from him, really – but, now, from the evidence of Rhoades' body, that substance they'd called Salt should more properly be called Stone. Dying, rotting, screaming Lyman had been right, after all.

I hope you enjoyed your brief immortality, *Mr Rhoades*, he thinks.

Oliver steps forward as Castle comes towards him. Castle is a big man, not quite as large as Oliver, a bit taller perhaps but not so broad. The man is certainly more dangerous; that's clear just by looking at him, regardless of what Oliver knows of his reputation for competent violence. Behind Castle, Oliver can see Dr Hedwith. He realizes, then, that there is only one way this is likely all going to play out. But he still has to try.

"Go find Elizabeth," Oliver says over his shoulder, moving aside to give Sol room. "Go find her."

Sol steps out from behind Oliver, raising his pistol. "What! I'm going to shoot that fucking guy, too. Jesus, Oliver, what the fuck is wrong with you?"

Oliver reaches back, pushing down the pistol, not entirely knowing why, just knowing that it needs to be done. Sometimes you just feel these things. Instinct, what have you. Sol might have a chance to make it out of here, maybe even get to the girl, but not if he points that Colt at Joe Castle. Castle is his own problem. "No, Sol, you save those bullets. Go find Elizabeth, now."

"Goddamn it, Oliver–"

"Go find her, Sol."

Something in Oliver's voice, then, tells Sol to listen. He tries to catch his eye, but Oliver's gaze is fixed on the large, tough-looking character who is now standing a few feet in front of them.

"Go find her, Sol."

Warily, Sol inches past Oliver, giving a wide leeway around the scar-faced man, who is rocking his head from side to side on his shoulders and cracking his knuckles. The man calmly nods at him before returning his attention to Oliver.

"I heard a commotion, Mr Wilson," Castle says. He glances towards Rhoades on the floor. "You know, it doesn't have to be this way." He seems almost sad.

"Afraid it does, Mr Castle," Oliver replies, rolling his injured shoulder, trying to work the stiffness out.

As he moves around the two men, Sol almost stumbles over Lyman Rhoades' body. Looking down, he can't help but admire his shot. Blood drips from Lyman's temple and his eyes are wide open. Sol pauses, bending down to spit in the man's face. "Fuck you, Rhoades," he mutters. "Who's a little shit now?"

From the floor, Alexander watches, eyes half closed. *Get up*, he tells himself. Oliver's pistol is only a few feet away. *Just stand up. You can do that much.* His thoughts feel loose in his head and his heart is pounding hard in his chest. *All you have to do is stand up.*

Here he is, once again, trying to will himself to action. It's as if his life keeps circling back to these same moments, over and over.

Get up.

He takes a deep breath, gathering himself.

When they come together, Oliver gets one punch in, and then another and, for a hot second, he thinks he'll see the end of this fight, but then Castle's fist hits him, knocking him back a step. Before he has a chance to recover, a foot crashes against his knee, making it buckle, sending him lurching to one side. Castle's fist hits the side of his head, then, again and again and again, *one two three* and, as he tries to shift himself out of the way, something pounds against his wounded shoulder, knocking him off-balance, onto his ass.

"It doesn't have to be this way," Castle repeats, looking down over Oliver.

"Afraid it does," Oliver mutters again, light-headed from the punching. He staggers to his feet and, feinting a shot one way, instead dives down towards Castle's knees, looking to take him to the ground where he can use his greater bulk. Castle merely steps out of the way, anticipating the move, bringing an elbow down on Oliver's crown, knocking him face-first to the floor. A boot hits Oliver's ribs; he feels a cracking and the wind is driven out of him.

"*It doesn't have to be this way,* Mr Wilson," Castle says once more, not even out of breath. "It's done. The girl will have to stay, of course, but the rest of you can go. Just get your people and leave. I have no quarrel with you. In fact, really I should thank you, for Lyman."

He nods towards the body on the floor, but Rhoades is gone.

Troubled, Castle pushes the thought of Lyman from his mind, forcing himself to concentrate on the task at hand. Lyman Rhoades will have to wait.

Oliver lurches to his hands and knees, trying to rein in his thoughts. Big as he is, he's never been much of a fighter. *What am I doing?* he wonders. I should get Alexander and Sol and get out of here, like the man says, before I get killed.

He hears gunfire and a girl screaming then and knows that, at the very least, he can buy Sol a little more time. He pushes himself the rest of the way upright.

"All right, then," Oliver mumbles, trying to straighten his vision.

Castle shrugs, with something akin to a sigh.

"All right." He steps forward.

It seems to take an age, but Alexander rises to a knee. He leans forward, one palm on the ground, mustering the energy to push himself the rest of the way up. The other hand is wrapped around Oliver's big pistol. Pats of blood drip from his nose to spat onto the floor in front of him, marking the passing seconds. It's hard to think.

Just get up.

Move. Just stand right the fuck up, Potter. He yells it inside his head, or perhaps aloud. *You've got this. Stand up, old man.*

His knuckles creak around the handle of the gun.

"Well, *goddamn it*!" Sol's pistol clicks empty. One moment, he was letting loose the last of Elizabeth's bonds and, the next, that fucking Lyman Rhoades was coming at him again, dodging and weaving around, entirely too quickly, making Sol shoot up his ammunition. He's no longer serene but, strangely, Sol isn't scared any more; he isn't even all that angry. He's just irritated, plain and simple, which he distantly understands is because he's had to take a little too much in, that his mind is just calling it quits on him and backing away from the over-excitement.

"Christ, *how many goddamn times* do we have to fucking kill you, Rhoades?" he asks, exasperated. "You're like a goddamn prairie dog, keep popping out your hole."

Lyman laughs. He has one hand pressed to his temple, where the bleeding has almost stopped. "A bit more to the right and you might have, boy. Yes. Even the Stone has its limits. Good thing you can't shoot." He looks at the blood on his hand, shaking his head ruefully. He smiles. "But I suppose you'll need to kill me at least one more time. Although I must say I'm surprised to see you here. Yes. Surprised you didn't just drop your gun again, too. After you shat your pants, I mean." He laughs again. "Hello, dear," he says, courteously, looking around Sol to Elizabeth, who is freeing herself from the last of the restraints. "Don't worry, Miss McDaniel, this will all be over soon."

He raises his knife, his expression hardening. "Although you may want to look the other way. I don't take kindly to spitting."

Sol feels his anger and stupid bluster returning from somewhere. "What the fuck are you going to do about it then, you piece of shit?" He spits on the ground. "There. Fuck you, Rhoades."

"Again? And is that it, boy? *Fuck you*? Surely you have some better last words, some noble, dramatic speech for your fair maiden here to cherish until the end of her days." Lyman smiles. "Yes, the end of her days, when I rape her to death."

"I reckon you'd need a functional cock for that, fat man. *Per se*," Sol adds, childishly proud of his last quip as he leaps forward, snatching a scalpel off the tray by the bed. He's amazed to feel his wild swing briefly connect with Lyman's face, drawing a thin line of blood from the man's doughy cheek.

"You cut me," Lyman says, stepping back for a moment, raising fingers to the side of his face. He sounds almost impressed, and then he slashes his own knife across Sol's forearm, laying it open. The scalpel clatters to the ground.

Sol backs up a few steps, holding his arm, imposing himself between Lyman and Elizabeth. "Well, shit," he mutters.

Lyman smiles, holding up the knife again. "Ready?"

"Now, goddamn it, just hang on a second," Sol says, hastily. He still isn't afraid, but his bluster has gone back to wherever it had been before. He glances back over his shoulder. "Miss McDaniel," he says, "I'm sorry this didn't work out better, because I sure would have liked to have made your acquaintance in finer circumstances."

Elizabeth is so angry her teeth hurt. She should have never left Baker City, never gone off after Josiah. But she did, because she'd had to, because he was family, and now it doesn't seem fair that things have turned out as they have. It's not fair at all. Elizabeth isn't used to being balked in her life, but she's had more of that these past days than she'd had her whole life, up to now, and she hates it and now look where it has gotten her. Just look. She doesn't quite fathom why Solomon Parker is even here, but he is, and that makes her angry too, though she doesn't understand why.

A lot has happened over these last days or weeks or however long it's been; she isn't sure how much time she'll have to assimilate it all, if any, and that makes her mad, too. She feels herself on the edge of tears, which makes her even angrier. In short, every little bit of emotional response she has is used up by that one fiery and furious emotion, which she knows is not a normal, healthy way for a woman to feel, even given the circumstances, but there it is.

This isn't fair at all.

"Mr Parker, you shouldn't have tackled me off my horse," she says, then, apropos of nothing, merely going with the first of her long list of grievances at the world that has sprung to mind. "You shouldn't have done that, sir."

Lyman laughs, not understanding, but enjoying the look on the boy's face. "You two have given me a day to remember, one of many, in what will be a long, long life. For which I should thank you, Miss McDaniel. Perhaps even you too, Mr Parker, if that's your name, for forcing the issue." He shakes his head, smiling. "There's one thing I want you to know, though, right here at the end. Perhaps it will make you feel better."

Lyman Rhoades spreads his hands apart, looking at Sol and Elizabeth, shaking his head in wonder. His eyes are wide and manic and there's the foamy glisten of spittle at the corners of his lips. "You couldn't have killed me. It wouldn't have happened, no matter what you'd done. No, you see, it couldn't. *Because I'm going to live forever,*" he says.

There's a loud click and, as Lyman starts to turn, a voice from the doorway says:

"No, I don't think you will."

•••

Oliver can't get to his feet. No matter how he tries, he just doesn't have the strength. One of his hands is broken, he can't bend his right knee, and the vision in his one open eye is swimming. At some point, he'd thrown up from a kick to the ribs or a punch in the belly, and the front of his shirt is damp and brackish with vomit and blood. His breath comes in shallow, painful gasps. He can't even *see* Castle any more; the man is just a shadowy blur that moves in at irregular intervals, never where Oliver expects, and hits him again. He wishes Castle would just end it; this is unnecessarily cruel.

He tries, once again, to rise.

"It doesn't have to be this way," Castle says for the third, maybe the hundredth time. He still isn't breathing hard; beating Oliver down has required no real exertion at all. "It's not too late for you to just go, Mr Wilson."

"Well?" another voice says.

"I think he's done, Doctor," Castle replies. "Or close enough not to matter."

"And?"

"And what, sir?"

"And… well, are you just going to leave him like that?"

Castle turns to look at Dr Hedwith, standing there behind him with a look of distaste on his face, as if he'd eaten something rotten. It's strange, as Castle has watched the man carve the girl apart, day after day, with no more emotion than cutting a steak. He's heard tell of the other things the man has done, from the doctor's own lips, the cruelties and horrors performed in the name of his research. Yet here, watching one man fight another, honestly, giving everything, Dr Hedwith looks disgusted.

"Like what, Doctor?" Castle asks, falsely ingenuous,

hiding his anger. *Say it*, he thinks. *Say what you want. Say that you want him dead because he's inconvenient, distressing, because the sight of him offends your sensibilities. Honesty, that's a condition of our arrangement, remember?*

"Well, *there*. Just lying there." Dr Hedwith waves a hand, vaguely. He wants to return to work. He needs to examine Lyman; where is the man? This outbreak has been unfortunate, and it needs to end. He looks around the cellar, seeing a crumpled form by the storeroom door. "Oh," he says. "Alexander." Ignoring Castle, stepping over the Negro orderly, whose name he never can remember, Dr Hedwith walks over and squats down beside Dr Potter.

"Alexander, can you hear me?" He lightly taps the man's cheek. Dr Potter's lips are caked with blood, his eyes red-veined and gluey. He looks almost as he had when they'd first met, back in the war. "Alexander!"

Dr Potter opens his eyes, focusing on the blurry shape in front on him. "Morrison," he whispers, finally. "Out of time. Kill you." He reaches up a hand that holds an old pistol, which Dr Hedwith gently lifts aside.

"I've done it, Alexander. *I've found the Stone*." He squeezes Dr Potter's palm. "Can you believe it?"

"Can't believe it, Morrison," Alexander mutters. "Where's Oliver?"

"I've done it, Alexander," Dr Hedwith repeats, smiling sadly down at his erstwhile colleague, who never understood the great work. Two lifetimes and more of effort, of struggle, of sin, but he, Morrison Hedwith, has found the Stone, at long last. He's done it. And there is a pleasing symmetry here, finding Dr Potter, at the end, much as he'd found him in the beginning. It's a sign, he supposes. For a moment, he thinks of poor Price, of Isaac, Taubenschus, the others, all dead now. But he lives, still, and will continue to live.

Forever.

"Goodbye, Alexander," Morrison says, surprised to find himself leaning down and tenderly kissing the old man's forehead.

He stands up, turning his back on Dr Potter, stepping over the Negro again. "Well?" he asks, pausing, looking up at Castle, exasperated. "We have work to do, my friend," he says, forcing a smile, mastering his irritation. "Are you ready? This is the first day of a new history, Mr Castle. Where *is* Lyman?"

Joseph Castle looks at Dr Hedwith, seeing long days stretching ahead. He sees himself watching this new history pass. It seems strange that he, Giuseppe Castello, just a poor gutter rat from Napoli, has been given this chance. He's lived this first part of his life taking his chances, though, doing things that other men would perhaps not have done, trying to wrest something better from the world than his birth and station would have otherwise allowed. This is his reward, he thinks, watching Oliver Wilson, prone on the floor, trying to get up once more. This is his reward and he has only to take it. It's regrettable, what he must do, but this is his reward.

"Are you ready, Joseph?" the doctor repeats.

After a long second, Castle nods. "I'm ready, sir."

"Well, make an end of this, then," Dr Hedwith says, waving at Watson or Wilbur or whatever the man's name had been, the man Alexander had convinced him to take on, years ago, for reasons that had always eluded him. But no matter.

Castle looks down, flexing his hand, twisting his shoulder in the socket. He sighs, and then drives his fist into Dr Hedwith's throat.

•••

Oliver, waiting for the final blow, feels something heavy land on him and then roll off, something that feels like a body. He hears a high, panicked gasping sound, and then Joe Castle's low voice.

"You have to *earn* immortal life, Doctor," Castle says, sadly. "Here, or anywhere else, I suppose. *You have to earn it*. Shh, just relax. Just relax. It will only take a moment." After a time, the gasping stops, and Oliver hears Castle sigh again and stand up. "Wait here, Mr Wilson," he says.

Oliver rolls onto his back, trying to catch his breath, drawing what energy he retains into himself. Turning his head, he sees the wide, sightless eyes of Dr Morrison Hedwith staring back at him, a terrified expression on his face, hands grasping his mottled and swollen throat. It's hard to think; Oliver doesn't quite understand what has happened, not even when Castle kneels over him, putting two small bottles in his hand, folding his fingers over them. "It's the last of the Stone, Mr Wilson. What Lyman was given, that which brought him back. It's all that's left of what the doctor had made so far." He shrugs. "Use it as you like."

Castle stands up, looking at the two young men standing close together in the doorway; one, tall and thin, holds a large, rusty shotgun, his clothes well-splattered with blood. They both put their bodies in front of the girl behind them. "Miss McDaniel," he says, looking around them, "I'm truly sorry for any hurt I caused you. You'll just have to believe that." He takes a deep breath, letting it out. He shrugs again, his mind just starting to catch up with his actions, with what he's done. He points at another doorway. "Stairs through there that go up to the back alley. If you head out that way, I doubt anyone will see you. Mr Wilson here could likely use some help. Now, I'll bid you good evening."

With that, Joseph Castle nods and walks out of the cellar, into the new history, fingering the small bottle in his pocket.

11.

"GODDAMN IT, AG, give me a hand! He's fucking heavy and I got this cut arm," Sol says, trying to get his shoulder under Oliver's armpit.

"I'm trying, Sol! Move out of the way!" Ag elbows his brother aside, looking to fit his lanky frame under Oliver's other arm and lever him up.

"Quit it, you two," Oliver mumbles, once they have him seated, back against a wall. "Just leave me alone."

"We got to get out of here, Oliver," Sol says.

"Law will be coming, what with the gunshots," Ag adds.

Oliver looks at Ag, trying to focus. "What are you even doing here, boy?" he says, muzzily. "Thought you left."

Ag shrugs, looking away, embarrassed. "Came back, I guess."

"You don't leave family," Sol says.

Oliver shakes his head. He looks at Elizabeth, who stands there, wild-eyed. "You all right, miss?"

Elizabeth just shakes her own head, and then nods, still angry, although the emotion is bleeding and swirling off inside her into some other volatile mix. It doesn't matter what she's been through; it's too much to think about; she's afraid that if she opens her mouth, she'll start yelling or crying or cursing or all three at once.

Oliver seems to understand. "You all need to get out of here. Law's coming, like Ag said. Go on, now."

The brothers look at each other. "What about you?" Sol says. "Just get up. You ain't hurt that bad." He nods in what he hopes is an encouraging manner.

"Come on, we got to go. We'll help you," Ag says.

Oliver shakes his head again. "Gonna take Alexander and go out the cellar way. We should split up, anyway."

Sol has a momentary flash of guilt, forgetting Dr Potter as he has. "He all right? Dr Potter?"

"He'll be fine," Oliver says. "Help me up, now." With a heave, the brothers lurch him to his feet, where he stands, swaying, for a moment. "All right then, go on."

"Where should we meet?" Ag asks.

Oliver thinks for a minute, trying to keep his face expressionless. He won't see Sol and Ag and Elizabeth again, not if he can help it. They deserve a chance of their own, whatever that might be. "You know that hotel we stayed at, after the train?" he asks Sol. "One with the good breakfast?" Sol nods. "We'll see you there tomorrow morning. If we're not there tomorrow, be the next day. Order me up some extra bacon." He sticks out his left hand, the one that isn't broken. "See you then. You be safe, hear?" He awkwardly shakes hands with Ag and Sol, surprised when Elizabeth gives him a quick, tight hug, kissing his cheek. *Thank you*, she whispers in his ear.

"Go on, then," he says, turning towards Dr Potter and limping over.

Elizabeth and Ag go through the door, heading up the stairs. Before he leaves, Sol turns, looking back. The last time he sees the Black Hercules, Oliver Wilson is awkwardly kneeling in front of Dr Potter, holding his hand.

•••

"We done it, old man," Oliver says, sinking to a seated position next to Alexander. He isn't sure if he's going to be able to get up again.

"You did it," Dr Potter murmurs, eyes closed. "I didn't do shit. I couldn't get up. I fucking tried, but I couldn't even stand up. Waited too long, Oliver. Nothing left in me."

Oliver laughs one soft bark of a laugh. "Bullshit, Alex. You got us here, didn't you? Plus you killed Lyman that one time."

"Man takes some killing." Dr Potter opens his eyes, as best he can, looking around. "Happened to him, Lyman?"

"Sol said Ag shot him in the face with a damn scattergun, coupla feet away. You believe that boy? Guess that 10-gauge didn't leave much left of ol' Lyman. Don't reckon we be seeing him again, this time."

Alexander gives what sounds like a laugh. "Huh. Thought Ag left. Man takes some killing, though, Lyman. Hell of a thing. Takes some killing…" he repeats, trailing off.

"Hell of a thing, old man." Oliver pauses, fishing around his pocket. "How you feel?"

"I'm done."

"Nah, you're not. Here." Oliver tries to hand him one of the small bottles that Castle had given him.

"Don't want it, Oliver," Dr Potter mumbles, closing his eyes.

"Not the Sagwa, old man. *It's the real thing*. They found it, they really did. Here." He tries again to push the bottle into Dr Potter's hands.

Alexander shakes his head. "I know what it is, Oliver. Don't want it."

Oliver stops, not entirely surprised, he realizes, although he can feel his eyes filling nonetheless. He puts the bottle back in his pocket. For a time they're quiet. "What should I do about all this?" he eventually says, gesturing with his good arm.

Dr Potter is silent for so long that Oliver is afraid he's already gone; he isn't coughing and his breath is still. Finally, Alexander murmurs something that Oliver has to lean close to hear: "Burn this fucking place to the ground, Oliver. *Burn it.*"

"Yeah, I'll do that, Alex," he replies in a thick voice, when he can. A minute or two later, swallowing, he asks again, "How you feel?"

He leans forward, putting his ear by Alexander's lips. After a long time, he hears Dr Potter whisper, "*I feel good.*"

Oliver doesn't quite know how long he sits but, eventually, rubbing his eyes, he stands up, slowly and painfully. Laid up as he is, it takes him a while to get the fire started but, once he has, the chemicals in the laboratory flare up quick and hot. Lifting Dr Potter's body in his arms, he steps through the storeroom door and back into the tunnels.

Sol, Ag, and Elizabeth stand a block or so away, watching Dr Hedwith's Apothecary Emporium burn to the ground. The three have never seen a fire of this magnitude and it has a strange kind of beauty, particularly when the various powders and chemicals in the shop start to burn, turning the flames multicolored like a Celestial's firework show. Fire crews are running around, getting hoses tangled, shouting and, in general, trying to seem more in charge than the others.

"Too many cooks in that kitchen," Ag says, pointing at two crews fighting to move a single pumper car. "Whole damn city will burn down before they figure this all out." He shakes his head. Close to the front of the building, as near as the flames will allow, two men with identical features are yelling at one another, pointing and cursing. A stacked display of Sagwa in the front window goes up with an explosion of glass and the twins tumble into each other, backing away hastily. Knowing brothers, Ag imagines that soon enough they'll come to blows.

"You reckon they got out, Oliver and Dr Potter?" Sol asks, worried. "Neither of them looked too good."

Ag shrugs. "I reckon so. Oliver seems a competent type of gentleman."

Sol gives his brother a strange, appraising look. "Yeah, I suppose." Sol looks over at Elizabeth. He wants to sidle a bit closer, say a few things, but something keeps him from doing it. Now that he's found her, all of his fine words have deserted him, burnt up in his brain like the fire they watch.

A tall, skinny, birdy-looking woman is running towards the blaze, screaming. The twins stop their bickering long enough to grab hold of her arms, keeping her from running into the building. Down the block, Ag can see a bent-leg man limping away, somehow furtively, a bag of something heavy in his hands. The birdy woman collapses to her knees between the twins, holding her head in her hands and weeping, which sets the men off yelling at each other again.

"Come on," Ag says, shaking his head again. "Let's get out of here." He turns and heads off down a side street.

Sol catches hold of Ag's arm, stopping him. He looks down at the ground and then back up, trying to summon the words.

"You don't leave family, Sol," Ag says, before his brother can open his mouth, already knowing what Sol wants to say. "You're right about that." He shrugs, condensing the longer story, all that he'd felt after leaving the train, the doubts and guilt and anger and fear, into those four bland words: *you don't leave family*. Because it's the truth, when it comes right down to it, regardless of whatever else he might want to add.

Sol nods, squeezing Ag's bicep. They look at each other uncomfortably for a moment. Finally, he smiles and shakes his head. "But how the *hell* did you just show up like that, right when we needed you, blazing away with that scattergun like a goddamn outlaw, brother? How did you even *find* us?"

Ag crumples his brow, extending one long arm, pointing at the large sign for Dr Hedwith's Apothecary Emporium that blazes on the roof of the burning building, raising and shaking the rusty shotgun with his other hand. "Hell, Sol, I just went in the damn front door, showed those boys in there this gun and asked where you all were."

He gives Sol an exasperated look. "Don't know why you always got to make everything so complicated, brother."

Ag shrugs his arm free and walks off, muttering to himself. Sol pauses for a moment, staring after his brother's lanky frame, and then motions Elizabeth to go before him. He's surprised when he feels the small pressure of her arm, looping through his. They walk east, the fire burning like a sun at their backs.

AFTER

[OREGON, PRESENT DAY]

"For the fore-runners of this Art, who have founde it out by their philosophie, do point out with their finger the direct & plain way, when they say: Nature, containeth nature: Nature overcommeth nature: & Nature meeting with her nature, exceedingly rejoyceth, and is changed into other natures."

A LARGE HILL, the remains of a volcanic cinder-cone, juts above the city of Portland, Oregon, east of the Willamette river. It has long been a park, this hill, home to a series of reservoirs; it is a place for families to picnic, couples to spoon, somewhere to watch the sunset and the lights of town. Originally the mountaintop was private land, the acres owned by the Reverend Hosford, who'd made his money during the Gold Rush, buying land here and there, opening schools and continuing to spread the word of God, as he saw it.

At the top of the hill is a statue, placed there in the 1930s to honor an esteemed newspaper editor and Freemason of the Scottish Rite.

Coincidentally, the statue at the top of the mountain resides over the exact spot where, about twenty years before construction on the reservoirs began, one Dr Alexander Ronald Parker, huckster, snake-oil salesman, and surgeon – the fastest man with a bonesaw in the Hospital Corps – was laid to rest, one evening, by parties unknown. This event occurred in the late spring of 1878, in what, later, was remembered as a particularly wet year.

For a few years, before it rotted away in the damp Oregon climate, a small wooden monument stood above the grave, seen by few. It read:

DR ALEXANDER POTTER
1815—1878
CAPT UNION ARMY, SURGEON
"A GOOD FRIEND"

Placed under the monument were two small bottles, unlabeled. It is unknown whether, at the time of their placement, they had been empty or full.

A NOTE ON ALCHEMICAL HISTORY

To most modern eyes, alchemy is known only as mystical nonsense, the product of a pre-scientific, ignorant age. I've played very loosely with the particulars of the art, for purposes of story, but, in truth, the classical alchemists should be considered more proto-scientists than sorcerers. To be sure, some alchemical experiments were essentially indistinguishable from magical or religious practice but, more and more, historians of science are recognizing in these hermetic arts many of the roots of what we now call chemistry. Modern scientists and historians have examined hermetic texts and begun to decode and decipher the layers of obfuscation and symbology with which the secrecy-obsessed alchemists would hide their work; in some cases they've managed to replicate what were essentially recipes for chemical formulae discovered hundreds of years ago. While the alchemists themselves worked under a framework that pre-dated Baconian (Francis, not Roger) empiricism, many of the great thinkers of Western science practiced, or built on, alchemical methods. Robert Boyle, one of the founders of modern chemistry, essentially plundered the work of the German alchemist Daniel Sennart, while Antoine Lavoisier used ideas already widespread in alchemy when he built his list of the elements we know today as oxygen, hydrogen, carbon, etc. One of the greatest minds in the history of science, Isaac Newton, wrote or transcribed around a million words about alchemy during his lifetime, and was obsessed with teasing out meaning from the proportions and mystical geometry of Solomon's vanished temple.

That said, the history of alchemy has any number of interesting characters to choose from. Taubenschus, James Price, and Johann Semler, briefly mentioned in *Dr Potter's Medicine Show*, were all historical figures, roughly contemporaneous with one another and active towards the tail-end of the eighteenth century; these men represented some of the last figures in classical alchemy, which was by then mostly subsumed into the new scientific thinking of the Enlightenment. James Price did indeed deliberately and fatally consume laurel water (aka hydrocyanic acid) in front of his peers, after becoming disheartened following failed attempts to replicate his apparent feat of converting so-called inferior metals to gold. Semler provided a hint of comedy to his own public disgrace when it was discovered that his devoted manservant had been secretly slipping tiny fragments of gold leaf into his employer's preparation of "the salt of life", the servant wanting nothing more than for Semler's experiments to appear successful.

Interestingly enough, the *Doctor Mirabilis* himself, philosopher, scholar, and that "thrice-famous and learned fryer, Roger Bachon" was actually imprisoned (or perhaps placed under house arrest) in 1292 for his excessive credulity in alchemy.

Moving forward in time, now.

In the age before government health regulations, the creation, promotion, and sale of medical remedies was open to anyone with the desire and wherewithal to produce them. Before the passage of the Pure Food and Drug Act in 1906, there were any number of products touted to cure all ills of the human condition, from cough to cancer, piles to plague. Whereas, now, patent medicines of these sorts are largely derided as "snake oil" – and many were in fact useless, fraudulent, or outright harmful concoctions – some of these products did actually provide symptomatic relief as advertised… the fact that many contained fair amounts of alcohol, opium, cocaine, and the like certainly having something to do with their efficacy.

Ironically, unlike "Rattlesnake King" Clark Stanley's bogus product – the name of which is now forever linked with the style of patent medicines of this era – the oil of the Erabu sea snake, an ingredient in traditional Chinese medicine for centuries, brought to America by Transcontinental Railroad laborers in the nineteenth century, contains large amounts of omega-3 fatty acids, which scientists have shown do in fact reduce inflammation and relieve joint pain, the purpose for which it was used by weary railroad workers.

Continuing with medicine, I must confess that I've implied a far quicker-acting and more virulent form of aconite than is likely possible. Aconite, which comes from the family of plants commonly known as monkshood, wolf's bane, and the like, is indeed an extremely deadly poison which can be absorbed through the skin. Its potency has been known since antiquity and has made regular appearances in literature over the years but, so far as I'm aware, a liquid of such would not take effect instantly, even if hurled into someone's eyes.

Finally, an apology to those familiar with Portland, Oregon's famous Shanghai Tunnels which, alas, are not nearly as large or maze-like as I have portrayed them in this book. The tunnels do in fact exist under the Old Town section of Portland (as well as in Seattle), near the Willamette river, and can still be toured today. While they have had a number of uses over the years, from their original purpose for moving freight from the river to businesses without clogging roads, to more nefarious and alcoholic endeavors during Prohibition, there remains some doubt as to whether they were every *truly* used for the practice of Shanghaiing sailors or, if so, exactly how often this occurred.

ACKNOWLEDGMENTS

This book was conceived and first written in an unnecessarily secretive and ridiculously paranoid manner, because I am a ninny. That said, there are several people who subsequently helped me drag *Dr Potter's Medicine Show* from the shadows. In no particular order, then, I'd like to thank:

My agent, the marvelous Jennie Goloboy, who plucked me from the query pile, graciously endured staggering amounts of my own naiveté and, with a keen eye, helped turn an adequate draft into a much better final product.

The splendid folks at Angry Robot: Marc Gascoigne, Phil Jourdan, Penny Reeve, Mike Underwood and Nick Tyler, for signing me on and being enormously supportive through all phases of the publication process.

Steven Meyer-Rassow, for fantastic cover art.

Lovely beta-readers Megan Fiero and Randi Mysse Ristau, and French translatrix Rebecca "Owens" Owens, for giving generously of their time.

My first two fellow-writer besties, Arianne "Tex" Thompson and Carrie Patel, for their invaluable advice and for squiring me around at writerly functions.

Photographic wizards Sol Neelman and Bob Cumming,

for somehow making me look dapper in the pictures.

Delia and the much-missed Betty, my canine support unit, for barking at me, cuddling, and generally making me happy.

And, most importantly, Tara "Tata" Fields, for a long, long, long list of things. This book would never have seen the light of day without you.

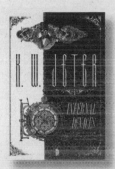

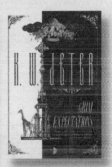

WHERE MAGIC HAPPENS

angryrobotbooks.com

twitter.com/angryrobotbooks